India Knight was born in 1965. She lives in North London with her three children, writes a weekly column for *The Sunday Times*, and a weblog about bringing up a child with special needs. She has also written two novels, *My Life on a Plate* and *Don't You Want Me?*

The Dirty Bits - for girls

Edited by

INDIA KNIGHT

virago

To Annabel Moorsom,
and the other naughties
— you know who you are

VIRAGO

First published in Great Britain in 2006 by Virago Press
This edition published in 2008

Introduction and collection copyright © India Knight 2006

Acknowledgements for all copyright material used are given on pages 264–266,
which constitute an extension of this copyright page.

The moral right of the authors has been asserted.

A CIP catalogue record for this book
is available from the British Library.

ISBN 978-1-84408-228-5

Papers used by Virago are natural, recyclable products made from
wood grown in sustainable forests and certified in accordance
with the rules of the Forest Stewardship Council.

Typeset in Spectrum by M Rules
Printed and bound in Great Britain by
Clays Ltd, St Ives plc
Paper supplied by Hellefoss AS, Norway

Virago Press
An imprint of
Little, Brown Book Group
100 Victoria Embankment
London EC4Y 0DY

An Hachette Livre UK Company

www.virago.co.uk

Contents

Introduction

I knew about the mechanics of sex — or 'sexual intercourse', as we solemnly called it at school, guffawing behind our hands — from a relatively early age, thanks to a gruesome, rather medical book that my mother, worn down by my incessant questioning, bought for me when I was seven or eight. The line drawings — blue for the man, pink for the woman — showed two featureless outlines, the blue one's, um, loins (furious blush) neatly inserted into the pink one's (cough, choke) front bottom. It took me nearly another decade to fathom out that coitus involved pelvic motion; I'd happily assumed the couple just lay there cosily for a little while, all still, clicked into each other like jigsaw pieces, and that this was called sex. It seemed overrated.

Five years or so after the line drawings, I went to an all-girls boarding school, and changed my mind. Aged thirteen and fourteen and perfectly virginal, we were suddenly tremendously, robustly, joyously interested in sex, rather in the way that Labrador puppies are interested in bouncing. We weren't interested in actually doing it, which seemed scary and gross, but our appetite for gathering information was vast. Everything about the subject fascinated us, not least the snort-making vocab, which we liked to keep formal. Take the aforementioned 'sexual intercourse': I still see many of my schoolfriends, and we're immediately transported back to teenagehood at the mere mention of the words. Aged forty, the following conversation can still render us more giggly than might be seemly, or sane:

'So how was your date?'
'Fine — we went for dinner, and then back to his for a nightcap.'

'Did you want to have sexual intercourse with him?'
'Yes.'
'Did you touch him on the member?'
'Yup.'
'And afterwards?'
'We mated.'

Which I do see is very lame. But to us, hilarious beyond belief, not merely because the exchange is so puerile, but because that particular language immediately summons up the comical, awkward sweetness of teenage afternoons twenty-five years ago. (I've kindly spared you the next sentence of the exchange, which involves keeling over with mirth over 'bodily fluids'.)

We also liked the words 'loins', 'groin', 'seed' and 'crotch', and were pleased, in music lessons, to come across the cutely midget-sounding 'crotchets'. We looked 'penis' up in the dictionary whenever we were bored. We never said 'member' without falling about (*plus ça change*; thank goodness none of us became a parliamentarian). We had a male art teacher, and whenever it was pottery and he talked about 'tools', we'd collapse en masse. We must have been exceedingly tiresome. 'Quim' struck us as being an especially hilarious word, which I suppose it is. (I don't think any of us knew the C-word – and we had no idea what a clitoris was, either, which explains why, when I first said it out loud, I pronounced it cli-TOR-is. We referred to our own pudenda as 'parts', like Matron. There's a poem by Henry Reed called 'Naming of Parts': imagine our delight at coming across it in *The Albatross Book of Verse*.)

I still remember the lone biology class devoted to human reproduction: as the allocated hour ended and our hysteria reached fever pitch, our Australian teacher suddenly went off-piste. She grinned, in a manner we subsequently agreed had been deeply depraved, half closed her eyes, and said: 'I can tell you how it works, girls, but I can't tell you how it *feels*.' We were profoundly shocked, and fell silent.

That was the thing, of course, the crux of it. The words were all very well, but we wanted to know how it *felt*. Some of us had come across porn mags before (I have perfect recall of a girl sneaking in a Dutch one, and of someone saying: 'Oh, it's too grim, I can see every drop of his seed'), but once you'd got over the initial shock of the curiously anatomical and luridly pink displays, they seemed somehow static and uninformative. Our greatest desire was to understand what it would be like to actually, you know, Do It. *Have sexual intercourse.*

Incredible as it may now seem, I don't think any of us knew about masturbation; if anyone did it, it was certainly never discussed, and it must have been performed with fantastic stealth (we slept in dorms). Nor — and every single man I've ever dated always asks about this, droolingly and with tiresome predictability — was there any sapphic action that I was aware of. There was one unfortunate girl who was known as the school lezzy, but I think this was based on the slightest of theories (she had mannish hair) rather than on any actual evidence. Back in the late seventies and early eighties, we were *spectacularly* naïve on the subject of sex. Compared to today's teenagers, with access to the Internet in all its hardcore glory, to pornographic 'lads' mags', and used to a degree of explicitness from television, from advertising and even from daily newspapers, we were unbelievably backward, what with our giant school-regulation knickers, our love of 'tuck', our puppy fat and our interest in ponies.

But we were eager to learn. And then one day someone came back from half-term with a book she'd either bought or found lurking somewhere: *Delta of Venus*, by Anaïs Nin.

Well. *Well.* To say we were agog would be an understatement. The book briskly did the rounds, getting tattier and tattier with each reading. Mouths dropped open in shock. Eyes popped with disbelief. Did people really . . . Did men really want to . . . What, *with her mouth?* Oh, yuck. Oh, surely not. Of course, the book was French, and everyone knew the French were *absolutely filthy* and obsessed with sex, but still. And the women! The women in the book seemed as keen on sexual intercourse as the men, even if they were often completely submissive (of which more later). It was extraordinary. It was mind-blowing. It was, well, kind of hot. And, in places, kind of gay, although we didn't say 'gay', we said 'homosexual'. You can imagine the quandary: you're thirteen or fourteen. You're reading Anaïs Nin. Some bits make you feel slightly bothered, or 'a bit tingly', in the argot of the day. Gosh! Golly! Might you be a homosexual yourself? Because, yikes! I also remember encountering the unlovely phrase 'his heavy sex' in *Delta of Venus*, and practically wanting to sick up with disgust (this happened again elsewhere, with 'thick-veined member'). But I wanted to turn the page more.

The second book to appear was called *Blue Skies, No Candy*. I recall very little about it, apart from its cover, which featured a close-up photograph of a man's zippered, denimed crotch (rather gayly, in retrospect). There was one particular passage that we all read, feverishly, but it can't have been that impressive, because I can't remember much about it, except that it featured the word 'pussy', encountered by me for the first time in a sexual context. This caused me to feel a sudden and overwhelming sense of embarrassment about our cat: I wanted to ring my parents right away to tell them to stop saying 'pussy cat', because it sounded *really dirty* and they didn't realise — innocent fools! — but I couldn't possibly, because there was no way I felt equipped to explain it to them, and besides, we were only allowed one phone call home a week.

So that was how it started: with a bang and a collective whimper. Soon 'sexy books' were everywhere. Once you started looking, there was no stopping. The majority of them were relatively explicit, but sometimes you'd be reading the most innocuous thing — a historical novel about Bess of Hardwick, say, or a short story by Maupassant — and a sentence would jump out at you and strike you as really unbearably sexy (and, it turns out, lodge itself in your head for all eternity). And you'd pass it on to your friend, in the spirit of sharing and of education. I do think this passing around of 'the dirty bits' is, or was, uniquely female. I don't know of any male equivalents: I've asked around, and although a large number of men recall finding a particular sex scene in Mario Puzo's *The Godfather* extremely erotic, that's pretty much the only book that came up — well, and *Jaws*. Statistically, women read more than men; it seems to be a habit that is started young. And of course, we share.

None of the men who remember *The Godfather* had been shown that particular passage by their friends; they'd stumbled upon it alone, and kept it to themselves. It is also true, I think, that girls tend to educate themselves through books, and boys through experience. Certainly, when it came to sex, all of my friends' and my carnal knowledge, such as it was, had been garnered from what we'd read. Boys', I think, had been garnered from what they'd seen (it's no coincidence that both the above books were also movies), or done.

Of course, the books I mention are specific to me, but the female experience of reading for kicks is universal. Every generation of women had its own library of 'dirty bits'. Many of them stand the test of time and make it through the decades, which is how my generation came across *Forever Amber*, which was written in the late 1940s and scandalised an entire generation of schoolgirls (and their mothers) in the mid-fifties. When I was at school, the hoo-ha surrounding *Lady Chatterley's Lover* seemed to have taken place in the distant mists of time, but that didn't stop us from making a beeline for it. Jacqueline Susann's *Valley of the Dolls* may have 'belonged' to another generation, but that didn't prevent it from being on our must-read list. And many wonderful historical novels, such as those by Georgette Heyer, may traditionally have been seen as belonging to genteel 'ladies', of the Oolong and petit point variety, but we fell upon them too. They may not have been anywhere near as explicit as the more contemporary material on offer during my own schooldays, but they certainly carried a gentle erotic charge all of their own. (Oddly enough, and unlike the majority of 'women's books' written several decades later, Heyer's novels largely feature unusually feisty heroines, who know their own minds, are not compliant, and have little regard for the social niceties of the day — or for the concept of women 'knowing their place'. This was, and remains, thrilling in itself.)

The books anthologised here are, as you are about to see, a mixture of the explicit and/or shocking, and the shockingly mild. Women's imagination — unlike men's, I would argue — does not always need the erotic equivalent of Semtex to ensure detonation. What we find arousing is not necessarily what is most explicit, which is why words, to us, can often do the job far more swiftly and pleasurably than images. We like to do our imagining for ourselves, far more than we like to be shown things in Technicolor detail. Which in itself is another way of saying that for women, the primary sexual organ is the brain.

Sometimes – though this is a bit later – something you'd be reading for English would cause you to blink and wonder: is it just me, or is this about sex? Keats's *The Eve of St Agnes* was the first sexy thing I ever read that was also beautiful; *Antony and Cleopatra* seemed to me so incredibly sexy ('his delights/Were dolphin-like; they show'd his back above/The element they liv'd in') that I didn't quite know where to look during class. Elizabeth and Darcy were hardly at it like rabbits, obviously, but he certainly struck a classroom of fifteen-year-olds studying *Pride and Prejudice* for O level as the absolute acme of brooding, saturnine male sexiness, and it occurred to us that it was possible for something to be erotic without being explicit, and without featuring pussies or – waah – the old veiny tools. And then there was the Wife of Bath (and, thrillingly, her use of the word 'cunt': 'Is it for ye wolde have my queynte allone?'), which made us all long to be gap-toothed, much-married and guiltlessly bawdy.

We devoured Jilly Cooper, who seemed to know so much about sex and to write about it in a way that didn't make it sound quite as terrifying as other books – in a way, in fact, that made it sound jolly and fun and, we thought, 'amaaaaazing'. All those single-name novels – *Emily*, *Octavia*, *Harriet* – did the rounds again and again: if I try, I can still remember each individual plot. Once we'd read *Lady Chatterley's Lover*, of course we started to check out the school gardeners with interest, in case they were all horny-handed and Mellorsy. Alas, they weren't, which is probably just as well: it was only when I was rereading *Lady Chatterley* for this anthology that I realised that at one point Mellors buggers Constance. The scene completely passed me by at the time, probably because, in those innocent days, buggery, or 'anal sex' – as I said, we only ever used the technical terms – was not understood by us to be a heterosexual practice (not until we encountered Pauline Réage's *Story of O* at any rate). Anyway: the trickle of books turned into a torrent. We couldn't stop reading.

I remember how astounded I was when I realised that home was fertile ground for my expeditions into smut. I'd grown up with my parents' bookshelves, obviously, and spent hours, over the years, staring at them absent-mindedly looking for things to read, only to turn away on the grounds that their library, with its Trollope and Dickens and Proust and Anthony Powell and blah blah, seemed profoundly boring. And then one day, overcome by more teenage ennui than usual, I pulled out a book on the basis that its title, *Couples*, sounded vaguely promising.

It delivered, in spades, not least because the idea of a pregnant woman feeling, and arousing, sexual desire seemed simply extraordinary. And it was a proper book, by someone called John Updike, a respectable-looking book that lived on my parents' bookshelf. A hardback! This discovery instilled a feeling of something very like pure panic: a) I'd been missing out on a rich seam of filth for years: this particular book had been sitting there since 1968, *when I was three*; b) hardback books by serious-looking writers were dirty too – who knew?; c) the book may have been 'dirty', but I registered that it was also literature – tremendous shock; and d) what on earth were my parents doing reading this kind of stuff, the pervs? Bad enough to know they had sexual intercourse. But a library full of dirty books? Too much to take in. And what was this, a few down from *Couples*? Something called *Fear of Flying*. Better take a look at that one too, just in case.

With all of this came the gradual realisation that sex was omnipresent. It didn't just live in 'dirty' books. It wasn't just about porn or, one ardently hoped, about heavy and/or veiny members. Proper writers were preoccupied with it – as much so, apparently, as giggly schoolgirls. Our parents weren't depraved sex fiends, as far as we knew, and yet their bookshelves contained plenty of good material. Maybe it wasn't something to be furtive and hysterical about. Maybe having sex was OK – not shameful, not weird, not hilarious, just sort of . . . normal. Maybe. It was a thought, at any rate.

Back at school, the era of the 1980s bonkbuster was well and truly upon us (it is a source of some amusement to me that one of the reasons the publishing house that commissioned the book you are holding was explicitly set up was to offer women a counterpoint to these so-called 'trashy' books). We were already familiar with its predecessors, such as Jacqueline Susann or Harold Robbins, both of whom seemed perhaps overly preoccupied with large breasts, but bonkbusters took things a stage further. They were unimaginably shocking: in *Scruples*, one of Judith Krantz's heroines, freshly widowed, fucks the pilot of the private plane which is bringing her back from her husband's funeral. A woman called Meggie has sex — really sexy sex — with Father Ralph, *who is a priest*, in *The Thorn Birds*. *And* she bears him a child. We were astounded all over again.

Revisiting the books that were such a significant part of my teenagehood and adolescence has been the most delicious treat. Some aren't very good, but that's not the point. For me, reading *Scruples* is to remember, with absolute and poignant clarity, sitting on the lawns of my boarding school on a hot summer afternoon, chewing a blade of grass, simply not believing what I was reading, and turning to a girlfriend saying, 'Read this. From halfway down that page. The dirty bit.'

A word about the selection I've made: it is, obviously, subjective, and in being subjective it reflects my age and experience, which is why the extracts end in the late eighties. There are some obvious things I've omitted: Georges Bataille's *Story of the Eye*, for instance, absolutely flabbergasted me when I read it, but that wasn't until I was at university, and I wanted, in these pages, to try and convey some sense of the big-eyed schoolgirl wonderment with which these passages were first encountered. Bataille's book, and Hubert Selby Jr's *Last Exit To Brooklyn*, another formative tome, came later, when I was still far from the woman of the world I pretended to be, but no longer quite as green as I'd been a few years previously. If I'd read them at school I'd have probably died of fright. Cleland's *Fanny Hill* is in here, but those anonymous Victorian sexual memoirs aren't (except for the explicit lesbian bit in *My Secret Life*); again, I read them much later, ditto the Marquis de Sade. *Flowers in the Attic* is another omission: too creepy, too trashy even for me, and those incest-loving Aryan children gave me the heebie-jeebies. So these books aren't included in my selection. Which is not entirely *my* selection, as it happens: the books extracted in the following pages are here because of a general consensus between me and fifty or so of my girlfriends (of varying ages). Some came up time and again and are thus included, even though they are not personal favourites and I failed to find them thrilling at the time – *Story of O* being a case in point.

This leads rather niftily to the question of women and submission. Unlike poor old O, who was apparently delighted with her branded buttocks and labial adornments, many of the fictional women whose exploits are detailed in the following pages come across as being submissive. There is, I am afraid, a great deal of 'her tiny fists beat against his manly chest', and a great deal about women being 'taught' or 'shown' very heterosexual ways of finding pleasure. This is most noticeable in the eighties bonkbusters, where ground-breaking, ball-breaking women, mistresses of the boardroom, suddenly want nothing more than a manly man to treat them like a pliable, little girly plaything.

But really, so what? This is fiction, and I don't think it's safe to patrol or police fantasy, or to try and impose random notions of political correctness upon it. Besides, if we accept that the men most likely to crave the services of a dominatrix are often captains of industry, we also have to accept that powerful women – or women *tout court* – may, in their fantasy life, like the idea of relinquishing control. (The most cursory glance at the 'erotica' imprints which exist nowadays will confirm this: wall-to-wall tales of 'restraint'.) Women like manly men who do manly things, in bed and out of it. Women don't, by and large, like the idea of sensitive wusses with flowers in their hair, lisping sweet nothings and making camomile tea. There are no such men in these pages, and there are an awful lot of women 'submitting' to their exact opposites. If that idea bothers you, you should maybe stop reading.

But yes, I do think that a lot of it is quite sexy, although I don't find much of it as sexy as I did when I was a teenager (for what it's worth, my favourite piece in this book is the extract from *Forever Amber*, which I find both truly sexy and emotionally devastating. One word of warning: if you haven't read this marvellous book, please go out and buy it. Reading the extract first will seriously ruin the plot). Sexiness wasn't the only criterion for inclusion, though: I wanted to try and paint a picture, really, of my generation's literary sexual awakening, and by extension of other generations' experience. Some things we found funny, some outré, some strange, some erotic, some grotesque, some disturbing, some thought-provoking, some inane. And sometimes we found all these at the same time, and still got a 'funny feeling' in the pit of our stomachs. The purpose of this book, then, isn't to anthologise my favourite erotica, or to try and compile a selection of massively sexy writing to be dipped into whenever you've got the horn. It is to try and capture a sense of what it was like being aged thirteen to seventeen, *virgo intacta* and ravenously curious about sex, reading by torchlight after lights out, amazed, with all our adult life ahead of us.

And the point of all this? Well, the point is that women are formed by what they read to a greater and more emotional extent than men, and that what thrilled or titillated us in adolescence is bound to have left its mark in many different ways. I can't be alone in being able to quote from the formative books of my youth, or to remember the precise plot points of second-rate sexy novels. That's because we didn't just lie about reading these books and giggling, or gawping, or both: we were awakened by them to an entire world of sexual and emotional possibilities – and, not least, to the notion of female solidarity, of sharing, talking, wondering, laughing together: a good lesson to learn, and one which we have carried into our adult lives. Those books also bridged the path between childhood and adulthood and lodged themselves, in the way that pop lyrics sometimes do, in our collective consciousnesses, so that when adulthood finally came (not a moment too soon, as far as we were concerned), we felt equipped. We knew what to do, and what to expect, and we could even guess at how we might feel about it afterwards. The dirty bits weren't just dirty bits; they were textbook manual and social anthropology. They were an education. They grew us up.

India Knight
London, May 2006

The Rake

I'm easing you in gently (as it were). There is nothing remotely explicit about the following extracts – though there *is* an exposed ankle, which in Regency terms was pretty damned saucy – and yet it's totally sexy, knowing, and full of wit and charm. And there is an extremely spirited heroine – a Heyer speciality – who seemed worthy of a minor crush. Most to the point, here for your delectation is Julian St John Audley, 5th Earl of Worth, as arrogant, caustic and devastating a creature as you could hope to meet. Phwoar, basically.

*H*e was the epitome of a man of fashion. His beaver hat was set over black locks carefully brushed into a semblance of disorder; his cravat of starched muslin supported his chin in a series of beautiful folds; his driving-coat of drab cloth bore no less than fifteen capes, and a double row of silver buttons. Miss Taverner had to own him a very handsome creature, but found no difficulty in detesting the whole cast of his countenance. He had a look of self-consequence; his eyes, ironically surveying her from under weary lids, were the hardest she had ever seen, and betrayed no emotion but boredom. His nose was too straight for her taste. His mouth was very well-formed, firm but thin-lipped. She thought it sneered.

Worse than all was his languor. He was uninterested, both in having dexterously averted an accident, and in the gig's plight. His driving had been magnificent; there must be unsuspected strength in those elegantly gloved hands holding the reins in such seeming carelessness, but in the name of God why must he put on an air of dandified affectation?

As the tiger jumped nimbly down on to the road Miss Taverner's annoyance found expression in abrupt speech: 'We don't need your assistance! Be pleased to drive on, sir!'

The cold eyes swept over her. Their expression made her aware of the shabbiness of the gig, of her own country-made dress, of the appearance she and Peregrine must present. 'I should be very pleased to drive on, my good girl,' said the gentleman in the curricle, 'but that apparently unmanageable steed of yours is – you may have noticed – making my progress impossible.'

Miss Taverner was not used to such a form of address, and it did not improve her temper. The farmer's horse, in its frightened attempts to drag the gig out of the ditch, was certainly plunging rather wildly across the narrow road, but if only Peregrine would go to its head instead of jobbing at it, all would be well. The tiger, a sharp-faced scrap of uncertain age, dressed in a smart blue and yellow livery, was preparing to take the guidance of matters into his own hands. Miss Taverner, unable to bear the indignity of it, said fiercely: 'Sir, I have already informed you that we don't need your help! Get down, Perry! Give the reins to me!'

'I have not the slightest intention of offering you my help,' said the exquisite gentleman, rather haughtily raising his brows. 'You will find that Henry is quite able to clear the road for me.'

And, indeed, by this time the tiger had grasped the horse's rein above the bit, and was engaged in soothing the poor creature. This was very soon done, and in another minute the gig was clear of the ditch, and drawn up at the very edge of the road.

'You see, it was quite easy,' said that maddening voice.

Peregrine, who had till now been too much occupied in trying to control his horse to take part in the discussion, said angrily: 'I'm aware the fault was mine, sir! Well aware of it!'

'We are all well aware of it,' replied the stranger amicably. 'Only a fool would have attempted to turn his carriage at this precise point. Do you mean to keep me waiting very much longer, Henry?'

'I've said I admit the fault,' said Peregrine, colouring hotly, 'and

I'm sorry for it! But I shall take leave to tell you, sir, that you were driving at a shocking pace!'

He was interrupted somewhat unexpected!y by the tiger, who lifted a face grown suddenly fierce, and said in shrill Cockney accents: 'You shut your bone-box, imperence! He's the very best whip in the country, ah, and I ain't forgetting Sir John Lade neither! There ain't none to beat him, and them's blood-chestnuts we've got in hand, and if them wheelers ain't sprained a tendon apiece it ain't nowise your fault!'

The gentleman in the curricle laughed. 'Very true, Henry, but you will have observed that I am still waiting.'

'Well, lord love yer, guv'nor, ain't I coming?' protested the tiger, scrambling back on to his perch.

Peregrine, recovering from his astonishment at the tiger's outburst, said through his teeth: 'We shall meet again, sir, I promise you!'

'Do you think so?' said the gentleman in the curricle. 'I hope you may be found to be wrong.'

The team seemed to leap forward; in another minute the curricle was gone.

'Insufferable!' Judith said passionately. '*Insufferable!*'

*

Judith doesn't at this point realise that the Earl of Worth is her legal guardian. Here she is meeting him for a second time.

Miss Taverner spent a pleasant morning exploring the town. There was scarcely anyone about, and that circumstance, coupled with the fineness of the weather, tempted her to take another stroll after her luncheon of cakes and wine. There was nothing to do at the George beyond sit at her bedroom window and wait for Peregrine's return, and this prospect did not commend itself to her. Walking about the town had not tired her, and she understood from the chambermaid that Great Ponton church, only three miles from Grantham, was generally held to be worth a visit. Miss Taverner decided to walk there, and set out a little before midday, declining the escort of her maid.

The walk was a pretty one, and a steep climb up the highroad into the tiny village of Great Ponton quite rewarded Miss Taverner for her energy. A fine burst of country met her eyes, and a few steps down a by-road brought her to the church, a very handsome example of later perpendicular work, with a battlemented tower, and a curious weathervane in the form of a fiddle upon one of its pinnacles. There was no one of whom she could inquire the history of this odd vane, so after exploring the church, and resting a little while on a bench outside, she set out to walk back to Grantham.

At the bottom of the hill leading out of the village a pebble became lodged in her right sandal and after a very little way began to make walking an uncomfortable business. Miss Taverner wriggled her toes in an effort to shift the stone, but it would not answer. Unless she wished to limp all the way to Grantham she must take off her shoe and shake the pebble out. She hesitated, for she was upon the highroad and had no wish to be discovered in her stockings by any chance wayfarer. One or two carriages had passed her already: she supposed them to be returning from Thistleton Gap: but at the moment there was nothing in sight. She sat down on the bank at the side of the road, and pulled up her frilled skirt an inch or two to come at the strings of her sandal. As ill-luck would have it these had worked themselves into a knot which took her some minutes to untie. She had just succeeded in doing this, and was shaking out the pebble, when a curricle-and-four came into sight, travelling at a brisk pace towards Grantham.

Miss Taverner thrust the sandal behind her and hurriedly let own her skirts, but not, she felt uneasily, before the owner of the curricle must have caught a glimpse of her shapely ankle. She picked up her parasol, which she had allowed to fall at the foot of the bank, and pretended to be interested in the contemplation of the opposite side of the road.

The curricle drew alongside, and checked. Miss Taverner cast a fleeting glance upwards at it, and stiffened. The curricle stopped 'Beauty in distress again?' inquired a familiar voice.

Miss Taverner would have given all she possessed in the world to have been able to rise up and walk away in the opposite direction. It was not in her power, however. She could only tuck her foot out of sight and affect to be quite deaf.

The curricle drew right in to the side of the road, and at a sign from its driver the tiger perched up behind jumped down and ran to the wheel-horses' heads. Miss Taverner raged inwardly, and turned her head away.

The curricle's owner descended in a leisurely fashion, and came up to her. 'Why so diffident?' he asked. 'You had plenty to say when I met you yesterday?'

Miss Taverner turned to look at him. Her cheeks had reddened, but she replied without the least sign of shyness: 'Be pleased to drive on, sir. I have nothing to say to you, and my affairs are not your concern.'

'That – or something very like it – is what you said to me before,' he remarked. 'Tell me, are you even prettier when you smile? I've no complaint to make, none at all: the whole effect is charming – and found at Grantham too, of all unlikely places! – but I should like to see you without the scowl.'

Miss Taverner's eyes flashed.

'Magnificent!' said the gentleman. 'Of course, blondes are not precisely the fashion, but you are something quite out of the way, you know.'

'You are insolent, sir!' said Miss Taverner.

He laughed. 'On the contrary, I am being excessively polite.'

She looked him full in the eyes. 'If my brother had been with me you would not have accosted me in this fashion,' she said.

'Certainly not,' he agreed, quite imperturbably. 'He would have been very much in the way. What is your name?'

'Again, sir, that is no concern of yours.'

'A mystery,' he said. 'I shall have to call you Clorinda. May I put on your shoe for you?'

She gave a start; her cheeks flamed. 'No!' she said chokingly. 'You may do nothing for me except drive on!'

'Why, that is easily done!' he replied, and bent, and before she had time to realize his purpose, lifted her up in his arms, and walked off with her to his curricle.

Miss Taverner ought to have screamed, or fainted. She was too much surprised to do either; but as soon as she had recovered from her astonishment at being picked up in that easy way (as though she had been a featherweight, which she knew she was not) she dealt her captor one resounding slap, with the full force of her arm behind it.

He winced a little, but his arms did not slacken their hold; rather they tightened slightly. 'Never hit with an open palm, Clorinda,' he told her. 'I will show you how in a minute. Up with you!'

Miss Taverner was tossed up into the curricle, and collapsed on to the seat in some disorder. The gentleman in the caped greatcoat picked up her parasol and gave it to her, took the sandal from her resistless grasp, and calmly held it ready to fit on to her foot.

To struggle for possession of it would be an undignified business; to climb down from the curricle was impossible. Miss Taverner, quivering with temper, put out her stockinged foot.

He slipped the sandal on, and tied the string.

'Thank you!' said Miss Taverner with awful civility. 'Now if you will give me your hand out of your carriage I may resume my walk.'

'But I am not going to give you my hand,' he said. 'I am going to drive you back to Grantham.'

His tone provoked her to reply disdainfully: 'You may think that a great honour, sir, but—'

'It is a great honour,' he said. 'I never drive females.'

'No,' said his tiger suddenly. 'Else I wouldn't be here. Not a minute I wouldn't.'

'Henry, you see, is a misogynist,' explained the gentleman apparently not in the least annoyed by this unceremonious interruption.

'I am not interested in you or in your servant!' snapped Miss Taverner.

'That is what I like in you,' he agreed, and sprang lightly up into the curricle, and stepped across her to the box-seat. 'Now let me show you how to hit me.'

Miss Taverner resisted, but he possessed himself of her gloved hand and doubled it into a fist. 'Keep your thumb down so, and hit like that. Not at my chin, I think. Aim for the eye, or the nose, if you prefer.'

Miss Taverner sat rigid.

'I won't retaliate,' he promised. Then, as she still made no move-ment, he said: 'I see I shall have to offer you provocation,' and swiftly kissed her.

Miss Taverner's hands clenched into two admirable fists, but she controlled an unladylike impulse, and kept them in her lap. She was both shaken and enraged by the kiss, and hardly knew where to look. No other man than her father or Peregrine had ever dared to kiss her. At a guess she supposed the gentleman to have written her down as some country tradesman's daughter from a Queen's Square boarding school. Her old-fashioned dress was to blame, and no doubt that abominable gig. She wished she did not blush so hotly, and said with as much scorn as she could throw into her voice: 'Even a dandy might remember the civility due to a gentle-woman. I shall not hit you.'

'I am disappointed,' he said. 'There is nothing for it but to go in search of your brother. Stand away, Henry.'

The tiger sprang back, and ran to scramble up on to his perch again. The curricle moved forward, and in another minute was bowling rapidly along the road towards Grantham.

'You may set me down at the George, sir,' said Miss Taverner coldly. 'No doubt if my brother is come back from the fight he will oblige you in the way, I, alas, am not able to do.'

He laughed. 'Hit me, do you mean? All things are possible, Clorinda, though some are – unlikely, let us say.'

She folded her lips, and for a while did not speak. Her compan-ion maintained a flow of languid conversation until she interrupted him, impelled by curiosity to ask him the question in her mind. 'Why did you wish to drive me into Grantham?'

He glanced down at her rather mockingly. 'Just to annoy you, Clorinda. The impulse was irresistible, believe me.'

She took refuge in silence again, for she could find no adequate words with which to answer him. She had never been spoken to so in her life; she was more than a little inclined to think him mad.

From *Regency Buck* by Georgette Heyer, 1935

The Brothel

In which bored and frustratedly naïve public schoolgirls decide to sell their charms to the nearby boys' school, for experience and pocket money – a notion which seemed almost unimaginably naughty, and quite dizzying, especially if you were a bored and frustratedly naïve public schoolgirl yourself. Note the pitch-perfect dialogue. Yes, people really did speak like that.

I was very nearly fifteen when I read Virginia's book about prostitution. So I was quite old enough not to be influenced by it. In any case, we all discussed it a good deal (at night, of course, but also on walks, and drinking packaged soup we made, and during rehearsals for the Play), and I find that discussing things makes them lose their influence. I find the same with Shelley and Dylan Thomas and the Georgians.

> *Taken by light in her arms at long and dear last*
> > *I may without fail*
> *Suffer the first vision that set fire to the stars.*

That seems to me enough to influence anybody. I was quite clear, after I read it a few times and learned it, that as soon as I was in love I would take him in my arms *by light*. But we discussed it (Mary-Rose and Melissa and Janet and Virginia and I) and I saw that, of course, the whole thing might turn out to be different. For all sorts of reasons: it would be night, probably, and if *he* said 'Shall I put the light out?' what would he think if I said 'No?' Virginia pointed this out; and then Melissa and Mary-Rose had an argument about whether men liked girls they thought were tarty, regardless of whether the girls actually were tarty or not. Melissa said they liked girls that *were* actually tarty, but the men didn't realize it.

'Not in my experience,' said Mary-Rose.

'Ha ha, *your* experience.'

'At a party last holidays.'

'Well, tell us.'

'I'm not certain I want to.'

'*Sacred*, Mary-Rose?'

'Important to me.'

'Of course, we wouldn't,' said Janet expectantly, 'want to intrude on anything you hold precious.'

'Oh, all right,' said Mary-Rose. 'Well, I was wearing my blue with those thin straps. We did one of those reels, and I was dancing with this *much* older boy—'

'How much older?'

'Sixteen and a half at least. Or *more*.'

'Bass.'

'Shave?'

'Every other day at least.'

'Spots?'

'A few, but only on the back of his neck.'

'All right, you were dancing this reel. *And then?*'

'One of the straps kept slipping down over my shoulder.'

'Just by itself?'

'The thing is, if I lean forward when the straps are *up*, it's all right. But if one of them's down, I think you can see my bosom.'

'Your *bosom*, Mary-Rose?'

'My left, in this case.'

'But you haven't got a bosom.'

'I most certainly have.'

'Not compared to Sarah,' said Janet.

'Leave me out of his,' I said. But it is true. I have got a bosom.

'Or even compared to me,' said Melissa.

'I most emphatically have more bosom than you,' said Mary-Rose.

'Pneumatically,' I said.

'Bet?' said Melissa.

'Sixpence.'

'Done.'

They took off their sweaters and vests (we were out on walk, so this was a bit chilly and risky) and we measured them. Janet had a tape-measure. Janet has everything, except, *I* think, sex-appeal. Mary-Rose won: it was thirty-three to thirty-two and a half.

'I think you both have beautiful breasts,' said Virginia.

'Can't you tell the difference between politeness and lesbianism?'

'Yes, I can. What worries me is, can you?'

Presently they were dressed again and Janet said, '*So*, Mary-Rose? He saw your breast and *then* what?'

'After supper he took me outside. It was very warm and almost dark and the stars were beginning to show—'

'That's enough *Woman's Own*, thanks. What did he say in his great bass voice?'

'Nothing. He kissed me quite silently.'

'On the mouth?'

'Just beside. Actually, I think he missed.'

'Open or shut?' I said.

'What do you mean, Sarah?'

'If you don't know yet,' I said, 'I wouldn't want the responsibility of telling you.'

'Go on, Mary-Rose,' said Janet. I had a feeling Janet's sex-life would always be lived vicariously.

'Well, he put his hand on my front.'

'Outside your dress?'

'First of all.'

'*So then?*'

He had wanted to kiss it, Mary-Rose claimed, but she refused to say whether she had let him or not. I personally did not believe this story, although I pretended to. But it was dreadful to think that it *might have been true*. I am far more advanced, physically and emotionally, than Mary-Rose, and nothing like that had ever happened to me. Nothing remotely like that.

Anyway, the influence of 'Taken by light in her arms' got totally eroded by all this. As always – it was exactly the same with *Lolita*. Virginia brought a copy back at the beginning of the winter term, and we all read it before we discussed it. We agreed that the situation was feasible, but it was irrelevant to our own lives. Lolita was younger (though physically precocious) and much more naïve. All those sweets and comics – we got over most sweets and things like *Girl* the term before last. The real difference is being European. I personally am extremely European. Even Virginia, who is Jewish and rather cosmopolitan, is no more utterly European than I am.

(On some things I take a totally mature view. If anyone said to me: 'Do you like Jews?' I should reply: 'Do you like people with red hair?' This is, I think, mature. But no one has ever asked me this question, or any of the others I have got good answers ready for.)

One *Lolita* discussion we had was in a yellowish place called the History Library. We belonged to Form 5B, to which I personally felt no sense of loyalty. Form 5B was allowed in the History Library. It had books and a table, and quite comfortable chairs, and half a huge window. (The other half lit the Senior Day-Room; the two rooms had been one when the house was a house, and painted in pretty colours, and there were flowers in the rooms and no notice-boards, or fear, or lavatories with incomplete doors like loose-boxes.) The best thing in the History Library was an electric fire which you could turn on its back. On this we made soup from packets. Many of my best remarks were first uttered there. Other members of 5B sometimes tried to get into the History Library when we were talking there. We dealt with them depending. A girl called Lydia Radcliffe we beat up. Johnson-Johnson we froze. Anne-Louise Campion we shocked. Fat slob Jennifer Bostwicke we did something exceptional to, which Janet thought up. (Janet has rather a dirty mind.) They all went back to the Senior Day-Room, where they belonged. We were very unpopular and anti-social and domineering, and this got us by.

'For instance,' said Mary-Rose, drinking her Mixed Vegetable a bit greedily, 'she took utterly the whole entire initiative that first time.'

'Cheapening,' said Janet.

'One has a certain pride.'

'No man I know,' said Melissa, 'would think the same of me.'

'When you say *know*, Melissa——?'

'My measurements may be less bloated than some, but I too have shoulder-straps.'

'Why?'

'What we all need,' said Virginia, with very European tact, 'is a situation where we don't have to take the initiative, and yet——'

'And yet be certain——'

'Be certain they're thinking along the same lines——'

'There ought to be a specialized kind of Universal Aunts,' said Melissa.

'Universal Procureuses,' said Virginia. I must admit she can pronounce the French 'R' very well. I can too, as it happens, but I always feel shy about it. If I were in France, with nobody English listening, my R's would gurgle sexily, practically from my diaphragm.

'Yes,' said Mary-Rose thoughtfully, 'what one wants is to be somewhere comfortable——'

'Darkish——'

'Warmish——'

'And you both know——'

'Without having to say so——'

'Somebody should set up an organization.'

'It would be a service.'

'I'd almost pay.'

'They'd pay, I'm sure.'

'Boys? God, yes. Any amount.'

'In advance,' I murmured.

And at that moment, I think, I had the Idea.

*

SECRET AND UTTERLY CONFIDENTIAL

THE SYNDICATE

Chairman:	Miss Sarah Callender
Members of the Inner Council:	Miss Virginia Goldsmith
	The Lady Janet Wigtoun
	Miss Mary-Rose Byng-Bentall
	The Hon. Melissa Bristow
Members of the Outer Division:	To be appointed

OBJECTS OF THE SYNDICATE

Whereas the female approaching maturity is denied male companionship by the modern upper-class educational system, thus being exposed to the dangers of perversion, introversion, and frustration;

And whereas, during our periodic opportunities for contact with the male sex, outworn and restrictive social conventions make it difficult if not impossible for true and fruitful relations to develop;

And whereas adolescent members of both sexes are conditioned by training and upbringing to a sterile and unnatural caution and reserve;

And whereas we know jolly well exactly the same applies to boys;

And whereas we can't go on like this.

It is hereby resolved that Selected Representatives of each sex shall meet in places appointed by The Syndicate, the meetings to be guaranteed free from interruption by whomsoever, for Purposes of mutual research and education.

Scale of charges: To be determined.

'The Syndicate Will Meet Your Needs.'

I pulled the paper efficiently out of the typewriter and read the document through to myself.

'Finished your sociology?' said my father.

'Hardly begun,' I said.

'May I see?'

'It is only some preliminary notes.'

'Perhaps I can help.'

'Well, I think it will be more valuable if we do it all by ourselves, you see. It will be more instructive.'

'Perhaps you're right. But if you want a hand let me know. I'm really quite well-informed, though you may not find that easy to believe.'

'I *know*, Daddy.' I tucked my document away in the pocket of my trousers. 'Really I ought to go and pack now.'

'All right, Professor.'

After I had gone out I heard them laughing again. Ho, I thought, little do you know.

'It's beautiful,' said Melissa a week later in the History Library.

'Your names are in no particular order,' I said. 'It's just the way I happened to type it.'

'What is the Outer Division?'

'Demand may exceed supply if it's only us,' I said.

'We can supply a good bit.'

'Yes, but my research indicates—'

'What research?'

'My preliminary market research. I carried out a pilot survey.'

'Goodness. Hark at the Chairman.'

'Somebody,' I said quickly, 'must be Chairman.'

'All right, we're not complaining.'

'I don't like "adolescent" much,' said Mary-Rose. 'It sounds baby-ish.'

'What about "sub-adult"?' said Virginia.

'Sub-normal, sub-human.'

'Oh, all right. Near-adult?'

'I think that's a fair description of us.'

'"Near-adult",' I said, clinching it. 'I'll make that change as the Inner Council directs.'

'The "whereas" bits are divine, Sarah,' said Mary-Rose, 'but—'

'Especially the last but one,' said Virginia.

'Especially the last,' said Janet.

'But,' went on Mary-Rose, 'the *it-is-hereby-resolved* bit sounds utterly vague to me.'

'I couldn't spell it out,' I said.

'Yes you could,' said Melissa. She gurgled a bit. 'All those words are frightfully easy to spell.'

'I mean,' I said patiently, 'in a formal document of this kind, one naturally automatically chooses suitable language.'

'I suppose French would be the most suitable language.'

'D'accord,' said Virginia.

'What I mean,' said Mary-Rose, 'is, when you say "mutual research and education", what exactly is involved?'

'I imagine we all know what is involved,' I said stiffly.

'Don't get violent.'

'I am completely calm.'

'Ah well,' said Mary-Rose, 'all right. If you mean what it sounds as though you mean, that's all right. I just don't want to find myself being told things.'

'What is required is action, not words,' said Virginia.

'They speak louder,' said Melissa.

'Much louder.'

'Why not add that as a sort of additional slogan, Sarah? "Actions speak louder than words."'

'Yes, do, Sarah.'

'Is that the wish of the Inner Council?'

'*Nem. con.*'

'It is so resolved.'

'And when you put "selected representatives of each sex" in the same bit,' said Janet, 'how *many* representatives?'

'One of each, naturally,' I said.

'Ah, good.'

'We don't want Roman orgies, do we? Or do you?'

'No,' said Melissa. 'We want English orgies.'

'You shall have them,' I promised.

'Yum.'

'"*The Syndicate will meet your needs.*"'

'Hurray. Actions speak louder than words.'

'Yum.'

'Shall we propose a vote of thanks to the Chairman?' said Virginia.

'Agreed, agreed.'

'Thank you,' I said, bowing.

'More soup, Sarah?'

'A drop.'

'So now what?'

'Now that we are agreed on the general policy of The Syndicate,' I said, 'we must negotiate with Longcombe.'

'Ah, Longcombe,' said Melissa.

'What else? Do you pine for a bus driver?'

'No, Longcombe will do nicely. The whore of Longcombe.'

'Less smelly than bus drivers,' said Mary-Rose.

'Better spoken.'

'Richer.'

'No,' I said, 'not so rich. But more respectful.'

'Agreed, agreed.'

'I have got my contacts alerted,' I said. 'Do I have the Inner Council's authority to proceed?'

'I think we should give the Chairman authority to proceed.'

'Do you want a secretary or anything, Sarah?' said Janet. 'An *assistant* Chairman?'

'Not at this stage.'

'But might you?'

'We shall see.'

'Can it be me?'

'We shall see.'

The bell went for classes and we all stood up.

'Bloody maths.'

'Attend to your maths,' I said. 'We shall need maths.'

'For what?'

'For money.'

'Money too. Yum,' said Melissa. 'I feel like Christmas all over again.'

'I feel like spring.'

'I feel like throbbing, teeming summer.'

'Hurry,' I said. 'Maths.'

That evening I wrote a business letter to Colin.

Dear Colin,

Further to our conversation on New Year's Eve. If you and the other Longcombes are still as frustrated as you said, The Syndicate is prepared to be of service to selected clients.

It is clearly understood that all payment will be Cash in Advance.

Please reply at your earliest convenience, and we will arrange a meeting place suitable to both, to discuss matters.

Half-way between would be best.

Awaiting the favour of your esteemed reply.

Love from,

SARAH (CALLENDER)

'The Syndicate Will Meet Your Needs.'
'Actions Speak Louder Than Words.'

I posted it on Tuesday afternoon, and nothing happened for days. The others kept saying 'Well?' Then on the following Monday morning, at breakfast, a ridiculous prefect gave me a blue envelope with a shield on the back and a tiny Latin motto.

'Well!' said Melissa, who sat next to me.

'My contact, I think.'

Colin's letter said:

Dear Sarah,

Thank you for your letter. I should say we are frustrated. And the term has hardly begun. What is the syndicate? Are you one of it?

We would pay in advance if you like, but not much, except for a few people who get colossal allowances.

Half-way between or a bit further towards you would be fine. I could bike.

Looking forward to seeing you,
Many thanks again,
Yours,

COLIN (SANDERSON)

I gave it to Melissa and she read it with a frown.

'He's got hopelessly unformed writing.'

'Yes, he is nothing special.'

'And he doesn't sound very keen.'

I remembered his hand in the little office place at the Myrtles'. 'He's keen all right. He's just cowardly.'

'Sounds divine, I don't think.'

'He'd be perfectly all right if he felt absolutely safe.'

'Does one ever?'

'But Melissa,' I pointed out softly, 'that is what The Syndicate is for.'

'Ah, yes. Gumdrops. When will you meet him?'

'Let's see — when can I? I shall want a whole afternoon.'

'No such thing in this joint.'

'It'll have to be at night, then.'

'Golly. Will he?'

'I don't know. Yes, of course he will. I'll have to write again. God, what a lot of time it wastes.'

Dear Colin,

Yours to hand. Do you know a Transport Café on the main Lingbourne road about two miles beyond the Horse and Hound? I mean two miles your side of it. Can you meet me there? They are discreet.

The best time would be about half past ten any night. Ring up here (tel. no. as above) and say you are my Uncle from Shropshire. Ring up between 7 and 8. Then we will fix the night. This meeting will be purely a business discussion.

Yours,

SARAH

'The Syndicate Will Meet Your Needs.'
'Actions Speak Louder Than Words.'

I showed this to the others before I sent it, and they were decently impressed with my planning.

'How will you get there?' asked Janet.

'Your bicycle.'

'OK.'

'Will you go alone?'

'No, I think one other person.'

'Why?'

'Security. Witness.'

'God. Who? Me?'

'Or shall we draw lots?'

'I trust you all equally,' I said. 'I suggest you draw lots.'

They drew lots with pencils, and it was Mary-Rose.

'Oh Mummy,' she said. 'How petrifying.'

'Be brave.'

'I'll try.'

'Sarah will be there.'

'Yes, that's comforting.'

Colin rang up three nights later.

'Hullo?'

'Hullo? Uncle Colin?'

'Aunt Sarah?'

'You're not alone?'

'No, are you?'

'No,' I said. I was in the little room off the Staff Common-Room, where we were allowed to take telephone calls. I had to be careful because I knew they could hear perfectly through the door and there were several odious mistresses sitting in the staff room correcting things.

'I got your letter,' said Colin.

'Yes? Is it all right?'

'Can't you manage an afternoon?'

'No.'

'It's a bit awkward. I've got to . . . make all kinds of arrangements, then.'

'Well, so have I.'

'Yes, I suppose so. All right. When? Tonight?'

'Yes,' I said eagerly. 'No,' I added, feeling it was bad for business to sound too compliant.

'Tomorrow?'

'Yes.'

'Fine, then. Shall I come alone?'

'If you like, or bring one other. I shall bring one other.'

'I will too, then. Ellis, I expect.'

'See you there.'

'Goodbye. See you there.'

I emerged from the telephone room, and an old bag called Ex-Lax looked up from a lot of verbs.

'Sarah.'

'Yes, Miss Laxton?'

'Was that your uncle you were talking to?'

I felt a terrible blush go simmering up my face. 'Yes, Miss Laxton.'

She stared at me beadily through her little steel spectacles. I stood there palpitating, wondering if everything was going to be kiboshed before we even started.

'You did not speak to him very respectfully.'

'Oh.' I felt a wave of relief like a Cornish roller. 'He's a very young uncle. Really a cousin. Only about — well about — only about twenty-five.'

'Nevertheless, you should be polite. Especially on the telephone.'

'Why especially on the telephone, Miss Laxton?'

'Don't be impertinent, Sarah. Run back to your prep.'

I beamed at her maternally, poor old bag, and undulated out of the Staff Common-Room.

So the next night we set out, and it was horrid.

We bundled up our clothes before we went to bed, and crept out together at ten. Getting out was childishly easy, and we would have done it often if there had been anything to do once out.

Now there would be, I thought.

We dressed in the bicycle-shed, and then sped away towards our rendezvous.

'This is utterly loathsome,' said Mary-Rose.

'You didn't have to come.'

'I didn't mean that. Everyone accepts you as Chairman.'

'Anyway it's not raining.'

'Yet.'

We pedalled and pedalled, and got there ten minutes early.

'Got any dough?' I said.

'Yes, masses. Shall we scoff something while we wait?'

'Or do you suppose they'll wait outside and not dare come in?'

'If they're like that,' said Mary-Rose, 'we'd better find somebody else anyway.'

This was sensible of her. Mary-Rose may be quite useful, I thought.

So we went in and had greasy coffee and some ham-rolls. They were excellent after our revolting high tea. One or two lorry drivers were sitting quite still and silent over empty teacups. It was a dismal place, made of cardboard and tin-cans.

'So what is this Ellis?' said Mary-Rose.

'I don't know. Another witness.'

'He and I are seconds.'

'We're not *duelling*.'

'Almost. Bargaining.'

'Here they are.'

Colin was peering in through the dirty glass door. He saw us and pushed in. He was wearing about six sweaters and huge gloves and a great scarf; he looked overcome with heat prostration.

'We came like stink,' he said. 'Hullo, Sarah. I didn't know you wore glasses.'

'I wear them for bicycling at night,' I said. I took them off and put them on the table. 'This is Mary-Rose Byng-Bentall. Colin Sanderson.'

'How do you do? This is Ellis.'

'Harold Ellis,' said Ellis, coming up behind Colin. I could not see him properly because of not having my glasses, but he seemed dark and stocky and about thirty.

'How do you do?' I said. 'Are you a *master*?'

Ellis laughed. 'I ought to be. What are you drinking? Coffee? Any beer in this dive, do you suppose?'

But they had coffee and ham-rolls too, and we all sat down and looked at each other.

'What now?' said Colin.

'I don't know,' I admitted.

'Good lord, you made us come all this way against a ghastly head-wind—'

'I mean, we discuss arrangements,' I said firmly.

'Are *you* the syndicate?' said Ellis suddenly, looking at us both in an appraising way.

'Yes,' said Mary-Rose, looking at Colin in an appraising way.

'We are here purely as spokesmen,' I said.

'The syndicate will meet your needs,' said Ellis. 'Is that right?'

'That is our slogan.'

'If it meets my needs it must be quite something.'

'What are your needs?' I said distantly.

'The usual, but more and oftener.'

'Ellis doesn't play games because of his asthma,' said Colin 'So he hasn't got anything to work it all off on.'

'Goodness,' said Mary-Rose.

'The thing is,' said Ellis, 'do we have to come all the way your school? Every time? And *back*?'

'It's only twelve miles.'

'Twenty-four.'

'We will try to make it worth your while.'

'Yes, but, *and pay*?'

'It is normal, I believe.'

'How much?'

'Yes,' said Colin, 'how much?'

We had discussed this at enormous length. Janet at one end of the scale had said two pounds; Melissa at the other end had said ten bob. (It was funny, having them on opposite sides in an argument.) We fixed on a pound.

'Thirty shillings,' I said.

'Good lord. Count me out.'

'Or near offer.'

'Fifteen bob,' said Ellis.

'A pound.'

'Seventeen-and-six.'

'No, a pound. It's very cheap, actually.'

'All right. I don't know where we shall raise the wind.'

'Shall we have some more coffee?' I said.

'And ham-rolls?' said Mary-Rose.

'That's right,' said Ellis. 'Feed up for the sacrifice.'

One of the lorry drivers stumped out, and his mammoth lorry ground away. Colin went over to the counter to get another load of everything, and I went to help him.

He ordered, and then when the man went of to fiddle with the urn, turned to me. 'I say, Sarah—'

'Yes, Colin?'

'It is nice to see you again.'

'Thank you.'

'Really nice.'

Far from being the coward and wet I had briefly thought, I realized that he was actually very sweet, and respectful, and only needed confidence. Also he was very good-looking, especially now that he was not so overcome by his bicycling.

'It's nice to see you again, too,' I said.

'I don't expect you mean that.'

'Yes, I do,' I said truthfully.

'Look here,' he said. 'Listen—'

'Yes?'

'I don't like the idea of you being mixed up in this.'

'You're mixed up in it,' I pointed out.

'You know what I mean,' he insisted. 'People like Ellis, and so on . . . I should hate it,' he said, nervously but earnestly, 'if you *cheapened* yourself. I mean it would be horrible. I mean I don't mind about the others, in fact I'm glad, as you know, but not *you*.'

'That's all right,' I said. 'I'm just arranging things.'

'Oh good!'

'Of course, *I* wouldn't do anything like this.'

'Oh good,' said Colin. 'I am glad.'

As a matter of fact, I was not being altogether truthful: because I fully intended to cheapen myself terribly, and be dreadfully mixed up, and participate utterly. But one must be diplomatic with men. They do not understand. Colin might one day be adult enough to know the truth, but not yet.

Then our food and coffee came, and we carried it over to the others.

'At last,' said Ellis. 'Now listen — I take it you don't want ten-year-olds. You obviously want a guarantee of adequate, er—'

'Adequate maturity,' I suggested.

'Hey, here,' said Colin.

'Think of Squeaks Manson,' said Ellis. 'Waste of the syndicate's time.' He turned to us again. 'And you, on your side, of course too—'

'We are in business,' I said coldly.

'So are we. Where do we start?'

We agreed that an unnamed client would arrive at the main gate of Bryant House on Friday evening at eleven. He would be met, and would pay a pound in advance. Then he would be guided to the assignation. We fixed a password.

'That seems to settle it,' said Ellis.

'You've got to guarantee this business of no possible interruption,' said Colin.

'We so guarantee.'

'And not just a bit of flowerbed,' said Ellis.

'What?'

'I mean, where will it be?'

'Adequate comforts are part of the syndicate service,' I said.

'One part,' said Mary-Rose.

Ellis laughed, and then paid for all our coffee and ham-rolls.

'Thank you very much. Who will come on Friday?'

'Someone with a quid.'

'He will be met.'

We went out and got our bicycles. It was pitch black and freezing and there was a howling wind.

'Goodbye,' said Mary-Rose, 'thank you for the coffee and stuff.'

'See you soon.'

'Ooh.'

They got on and whizzed away very fast. We wobbled out of the pull-in and rode away more slowly. We had the head-wind all the way back, and there was a bit of rain. We finally got to the dormitory and back into bed very late indeed.

'I hope I don't get Ellis,' whispered Mary-Rose.

'This is business,' I whispered back sternly. 'The Syndicate will meet your needs.'

She giggled. 'Actions speak louder than words. Happy dreams.'

Bryant House is a large Georgian edifice standing in secluded parkland in quite nice country in a healthy part of Southern England. Its former owners went broke, and it started being a school in about 1930. There can only have been six girls then, but now there are ninety, all paying rather high fees. They range from eleven to seventeen – mostly, of course, in the middle bracket of this range. The academic standard is unusually high, and the moral tone of the school is supposed to be high, too. The social tone is extremely high. All the girls and most of the mistresses live in the one vast building, which therefore has under its enormous leaded roof a prodigious quantity of repressed female emotion.

I thought about all this emotion as we crossed the stable yard from the labs at the beginning of break, the morning after our business meeting. We had been doing Biology. It must be awful for a spinster to teach Biology. Perhaps some of the younger mistresses could be included in the Outer Division one day. Perhaps they would entertain bachelor masters from Longcombe. But that was for the future.

'Time to draw lots,' said Melissa.

'History Library?'

'Come on.'

It was very solemn. We sat in the History Library and sipped cups of Chicken Noodle, and it felt almost sacramental, which I suppose is rather awful. We felt a more ritual form of drawing lots than usual would suit this historic occasion. Normally we drew pencils – the one that wasn't bust was it. After an argument we did it with books: five identical green ones called *England In The Middle Ages: An Introduction For Junior Forms*. We put a bit of paper in one, well hidden in the middle, which said 'You!' Then we shuffled them around like playing-cards, on top of the History Library table.

'Junior Forms,' said Virginia. 'Is that what we've got? Junior Forms?'

Mary-Rose inhaled her breath and stuck out her bosom. 'I think some of us have got very nice senior forms.'

'Meet your needs,' murmured Melissa.

Janet giggled in a high, whiny way. I felt excited and frightened.

Finally we decided that the books were shuffled and we each took one.

I picked mine up very carefully, as though it were full of static electricity. I opened it. There didn't seem to be a bit of paper. I rifled through it quickly, and then held it upside down and shook it. No bit of paper. I felt numb. It was partly disappointment and partly relief, and a very dead, flat feeling.

The others all held their books upside-down and shook them. Nothing happened for ages.

'It must be one of us,' murmured Virginia.

'None of us,' said Mary-Rose.

Then a white thing fluttered out of Melissa's book and lay on the table saying 'You!'

'Ooh . . .'

'Melissa!'

'Congratulations!'

'Are you pleased?'

'Yes, I think so,' said Melissa in a choky voice.

'You were very keen,' said Mary-Rose.

'I am, only—'

'Backing out?'

'No, of course not.'

'Of course she's not,' said Janet.

'Good,' I said coolly. But I still felt shaky and peculiar. 'We must work out a lot of details.'

'Free Walk this afternoon.'

'Yes, we'll decide everything then.'

'I don't know if I'm thankful or disappointed,' said Virginia, voicing exactly my own thoughts.

'I do,' said Mary-Rose.

'Which?'

'Both at once.'

'Don't worry,' I said. 'Your turn will come.'

'Yes, of course.'

The bell went, and we put the fateful little green books away on the shelf. The piece of paper saying 'You!' stayed where it was, face up on the table. But just before Melissa went out, she picked it up and tucked it carefully away.

'Souvenir?' said Mary-Rose.

'Oh, shut up.'

'Windy?'

'Not in the slightest, thank you very much.'

'Come on,' I said. 'Scripture calleth.'

'Here come the women of Babylon,' said Virginia. 'After you, Delilah.'

'Oh, shut up,' said Melissa.

She was a bit silent for the rest of the day.

On the Free Walk we went to a place off by itself near a dripping wood where three sad haystacks stood in a field. There was a large, a medium-sized, and a small haystack, and we called them the Three Bears. We always sat under Mother Bear, which may have been a bit psychological.

'This will be a wonderful place in the summer,' said Virginia.

'What for?'

'Us. Them.'

'The Syndicate?'

'Meeting needs.'

'These haystacks?'

'Our dear Bears.'

'Prickly.'

'We'll have rugs and things. Hay is very sexy stuff.'

'Not for poor Ellis,' said Mary-Rose, 'with his asthma.'

'I wonder who will appear tomorrow night,' said Janet. 'You must be wondering, Melissa.'

'Yes,' said Melissa shortly.

'He will have bicycled a long way. Will he be exhausted?'

'Oh God,' said Melissa.

'What will you wear?'

'It doesn't matter, does it?'

'But it does. You must wear something slinky and provocative.'

'Rot.'

'Well,' said Virginia, 'remember what it said in *Prostitution – A Sociological Analysis*. They always wear sexy clothes. It's half the battle.'

'That's a comfort,' said Melissa. 'Battle.'

'It's only an expression, dear.'

'That's another thing,' said Janet. 'Will he call you dear? Or what?'

'Darling?' suggested Mary-Rose.

'Tootums-Wootums?' said Virginia.

'Oh for God's sake,' said Melissa.

'Please all be quiet,' I said. 'We've got a lot of business to discuss.'

'Sorry, Boss.'

'It's all very well for all of you,' said Melissa. 'I'm the bloody guinea-pig.'

'I think it must be very alarming, being first,' I said gently. A true leader is always deeply concerned with the morale of subordinates.

'Not *alarming*,' said Melissa crossly. 'I'm not *alarmed*, good heavens, why should I be? You just all jabber about it so much.'

'We won't now,' I said. 'We'll discuss business details.'

So very efficiently we fixed times and places and duties, and splashed back to tea in a January drizzle.

The next afternoon was the afternoon of The Night. Janet and I slunk into the gym and piled a mass of old costumes and drapes and things in the best tunnel under the stage. When we had formed all we could find and drag into a huge double bed Janet flopped down on to it.

'Nice?' I said.

'Very comfortable.'

'Does it make you feel amorous?'

'Ye-es. It's a bit dusty.'

'They can't expect four-posters for a pound.'

'What are they going to do for light?'

'Torches.'

'What a waste of the batteries.'

'I expect they'll switch them off after a bit.'

'I suppose so. Sarah—'

'Yes?'

'Do you wish it was you and not Melissa?'

'I'm not sure. If it was me I should feel wildly excited, but—'

'But?'

'But I'd have rather a fear-of-the-unknown thing.'

'I wouldn't.'

'Are you sure, Janet?'

'Yes,' said Janet positively. 'I wish it was me. I'm dying for it to be me.'

'I didn't realize.'

'Neither did I.'

*

Yet again everything went perfectly smoothly on The Night.

(The discipline at school was not so much lax as unenforced. They thought they were strict, but they were bad at making sure. It was an extremely expensive school.)

Virginia was in the tunnel, in a quilted dressing-gown belonging to a girl called Anne Mostyn. Underneath that she had on pyjamas and under them (she insisted, and wouldn't be budged) woolly knickers. The sexy soap we had used to make Melissa provocative had obviously done nothing for her, so we used a bit of the first pound to buy some scent from a horrid, bald old woman in a horrid little shop. (Another furtive expedition.) The scent was called 'Jungle Venom' and smelt common but penetratingly sexy. Better than soap. And it gave Virginia confidence. The dim mysterious amorous non-embarrassing light was easy, of course: we put some red Cellophane over the yellow Cellophane over the glass of the torch, and shone the torch against the wall of the tunnel instead of outwards over the bed. To me it all looked almost frighteningly right. One imagined orgies.

I was again at the gate, to take the money. But this time I was braver. The violent arrival of the new Client's bicycle hardly discomposed me, and I said 'Good evening, sir.'

'Q5,' he replied, panting, but thank God he didn't clear his throat.

'Password?'

'"I love my love with a W——"'

'"Because she is Willing." Right. One pound, please.'

'Here.'

It was all small silver.

'I shall have to check this,' I said.

'It's quite correct, unless I've dropped some.'

'One must be businesslike. Very well, follow me.'

Melissa challenged us by the door of the gym and Janet by the entrance to the tunnel. We lifted the matting.

'Mademoiselle Chantal is waiting,' I said.

The Client went 'Hmm!' and dashed in.

Janet and I checked the money by the light of my torch. It was exactly a pound. Then the others joined us, and we settled down to wait in the enormous whispering blackness of the gym.

The Client emerged distraught. He stared about him wildly, blinking in the beam of our torch. He was panting.

'There you are, then,' I said awkwardly, as something had to be said. I must have sounded like a nanny.

He cleared his throat, which was a thing I had hoped this one didn't do. (But of course it was January, and he may have had a slight cold.) 'I'm not sure—' he said. 'I didn't realize . . . I don't think it's what I meant . . .'

'Complaint?' I said coldly. 'Mademoiselle Chantal did not please you?'

'No no,' he said hoarsely, 'no, no, no. I mean she did. I . . . Will you tell her I'm sorry?'

'Did you hurt her? What? Or what?'

'What is all this?' said Janet.

'Oh no, no, no.' The Client gasped. He was gingery and curly and quite nearly going into the army, one would have supposed. 'Well, goodnight.'

He hurried off, and once again we all looked at one another. Then Virginia emerged.

'Your Client seemed in a state,' said Janet.

'Upset about something,' said Melissa.

'Surely not Melissa's trouble?' said Mary-Rose.

'Or was it?' said Melissa, obviously hoping it was.

'A bit different,' said Virginia slowly. She looked cool, but as though she had been uncool.

'Well?'

'Shall I tell you it all now? Or as we go back? Or tomorrow?'

'Now.'

'It's not very homey here in the dark.'

'Yes it is.'

'If you prefer, we'll go into your chambre d'amour,' said Mary-Rose.

'No thanks. It's a very nice chambre, but I don't want any more of it just now.'

'Then here.'

'All right. So. The light was right, because we could see what we were doing, but we couldn't see each other's faces properly. So it wasn't embarrassing in *that* way.'

'Good,' I said.

'Yes. And the scent was right, I think.'

'Three cheers for Jungle Venom,' said Mary-Rose.

'And the Yvette-Q5 business was right. So we didn't have a start-ing point for an ordinary conversation. So we didn't have any ordinary conversation. In fact we hardly talked at all.'

'Oh the bliss,' said Melissa.

'Though actually his voice was quite nice. So was his curly hair,' said Virginia.

'The Professional,' said Janet, 'never gets emotionally involved.'

'I am not emotionally involved, thank you very much. I am merely stating a fact.'

'All right, all right.'

'His hair happens, as a point of pure objective actual fact, to be curly. I happen to mention this. Any objections?'

'No. Go on.'

'Thank you very much. Anyway, the rightest thing of all was the dressing-gown. The dressing-gown was terrifically right.'

'Good,' I said unemotionally, noting the point in my mind.

'Well.' Virginia paused, rather teasingly. 'Do you want to know what happened?'

'Yes, *dear*.'

'He crawled in.'

'We guessed he did,' said Janet sarcastically.

'And he crawled up and said "Q5."'

Virginia paused again. We were sitting in a row along the front of the stage, dangling our legs over the edge. I had switched off my torch to save the battery (one must think of overheads in running any business) so it was pitch dark. Virginia was in the middle, her drawly voice coming quietly out of the blackness.

'So he started kissing me.'

'Passionately?'

'Laboured breathing and stuff, yes. Then he started sort of gently jabbing at my front.'

'Outside?'

'Yes. Then he started sort of gently prodding inside. Then he found the dressing-gown cord and undid that. Then he jabbed and prodded and fiddled a bit more.'

'Pyjamas?'

'Outside them. Then he undid one button. Then he didn't know whether to go on. Then he did go on. So he undid all my pyjama coat buttons. So then he was inside.'

'Oh Virginia,' whispered Janet, 'oh Virginia, was it divine?'

'Yes, actually it was,' said Virginia in a matter of fact way.

'Exciting?'

'Riveting.'

'But actually,' I said, 'nice? I mean pleasant? A nice feeling? I mean actually a *pleasant feeling*?'

'Well, of course, it's quite impossible to describe it to *you*, you see.'

'Try,' said Janet.

'Well, tingly. Starting just there and going all over.'

'Goodness . . .'

'A sort of tingly twitchy, a sort of shivery—'

'Like electricity?'

'Like radioactivity. Everything felt much *bigger*.'

'You mean his hands felt bigger?'

'They felt vast. But I meant, my bosoms.'

'Goodness . . .'

'Did you take them *off*, or just have them *undone*?' said Melissa.

'My pyjamas? Well, he sort of hauled the dressing-gown off. And the pyjama top sort of slid off.'

'Cold?'

'*God* no.'

'And the pyjama bottoms?'

'Yes, them, well. He was sort of tickling my tummy—'

'Nice?'

'Absolutely marvellous. And then he found the pyjama bottoms' button.'

'You mean string?'

'No, this button. He tried to undo it, but he couldn't quite get the hang of it. So I did.'

'Quite right,' I said approvingly.

'Well, I quite wanted to.'

'Of course,' sighed Janet.

'So then it was my pants, under that.'

'Pants! We *said* you shouldn't have the pants.'

'Perhaps you were right. They surprised him, I think. But he was brave. He—'

'He—'

'His hand sort of wriggled down inside—'

'To—?'

'My tummy still. My *lower* tummy. And then it whizzed round to my behind.'

'Why?'

'I don't know. But he prodded it a bit.'

'Nice?'

'Absolutely heavenly. And then, at that point, I dimly remembered a bit in that book of my papa's.'

'*Prostitution — A Sociological Analysis?*'

'About what they do. They excite The Client. They even undress The Client—'

'Virginia!'

'Well. So I tugged at his shirt buttons. And his hand jumped away from my behind and disappeared. So I thought that meant the next bit was up to me. So I tugged at his trouser buttons. Then he began to shiver a bit, which I thought was passion, and then . . .'

'Oh Virginia,' breathed Mary-Rose.

'You didn't undo them?' whispered Janet.

'I tried to. Perhaps it was a zip. So I tried to explore down a bit . . .'

'Was that nice?'

'I was excited. Yes, I *was* excited. I didn't know quite what I'd find—'

'Yes you did.'

'Yes, of course I did, in theory. But then and there—'

'Yes,' I murmured, 'I see.'

'So then?' demanded Janet.

'That's all.'

'Oh no.'

'He shot away to the edge of the tunnel and wrapped himself up frantically in all his scarves and whizzed off and disappeared.'

'Oh, no.'

'I think I see,' said Mary-Rose very sensibly. 'He hadn't bargained for that. I mean he *literally* hadn't bargained for it. He hadn't paid for it.'

'I believe you're right,' said Virginia slowly. 'He was getting his money's worth just by—'

'Prodding?'

'And rubbing and – tickling and – so on. So I felt silly.'

'Of course. Poor Virginia.'

'Not a wash-out, though,' said Mary-Rose.

'God no.'

'But a lesson,' I said. 'Mary-Rose hit it. Well done, Mary-Rose.'

'Ce n'est rien, cherie.'

'You mean,' said Melissa, 'Q – whatever-he-was – thought he was paying for—'

'Prodding,' said Janet.

'All right,' I said. 'Law of supply and demand.'

'I don't get it,' said Melissa.

'Prodding is a pound.'

'Ah,' said Virginia. 'And, say, just *looking*—'

'Ten bob.'

'And only looking at the top half?'

'Well, and so on. We'll make out a price list.'

'I won't do a thing,' said Melissa, 'for half-a-crown.'

'As for what *we do*,' I said, 'that begins to come expensive.'

'You're a marvel, Boss,' said Mary-Rose handsomely.

'Thank you,' I said. 'Inner Council business discussion tomorrow.'

'Break.'

'History Library.'

'We've got some Cream of Mushroom.'

'Price list.'

'Scale of charges.'

'Yum.'

*

Once again, now very brave, and with a sense of cleverness, I waited at the main gates. It was raining a bit, and extremely dark and beastly, but not too cold. (This was lucky, because goose-flesh all over Janet and Mary-Rose would have been unarousing, as well as horrid for them.)

Presently a lot of murmurs and rustles and gravelly crunchings told me that the Clients had arrived, and I challenged them.

'Who goes there?'

'Us . . .'

'Well?'

'I mean, for The Syndicate, you know—'

'Password?'

'Oh yes. Er, I love my love with a D—'

'Because she is dangerous. Right.'

There is, it became clear to me, a lot of sameness in business. Or in men. Or, in the case of a specialized business like mine, in the one *because* of in the other.

'Follow me, please,' I said. 'Quietly, please.'

'Is it far?' piped a treble voice nervously.

'Buck up, Squeaks,' said a bass voice. 'You'll soon be a man.'

I led them cautiously to the gym, where Melissa challenged us in a dutiful whisper.

'D1 and Clients,' I said.

'Pass, D1 and Clients.'

We got into the gym, and a tall boy with purple spots counted out the money for the Category One: Above Waist Only party. I appraised the four of them: they looked Above Waist Only types – timorous, and rather poor. But probably Janet was right, and they would be aroused, and go on to higher (or lower) and anyway more expensive and delicious things.

Then a squat fair boy, with little beady eyes behind little beady glasses, paid out the huge sum of two pounds two shillings and six-pence for the Category One: Entire Operative party. I counted it, and it was all correct, and it jingled, and weighed my corduroy trousers heavily and marvellously down.

'If the Above Waist Only party will proceed to the front of the hall,' I said grandly, 'Princess Puma is waiting in the wings.'

'Just the job,' said a curly-headed boy in a rather common way.

'What about us?' said one of the Entire Operative five.

'I must ask you to wait outside the theatre until Princess Puma has finished.'

'Hey, in the rain?'

'I know. But it's only fifteen minutes. And you can't see her unless you pay. Perhaps,' I said hopefully, 'you'd like to pay to see her *too*?'

'That rain's ghastly—'

'How much for all of us?'

'Er – under the special circumstances, we can do you a special rate of a pound.'

'*A pound!*'

'That's only four shillings each.'

'I'll stay for four bob,' said a boy who looked like a pastry-cook (I mean *clean*, but doughy).

None of the others could, not having four bob.

'Credit?' they said hopefully.

'Terms strictly cash in advance,' I said with regretful sympathy, but firmly. 'And if it's only one, of course, then it's five bob.'

'You said four.'

'That's the special party rate.'

'But I'm joining that other party.'

'Oh, yes. Oh, all right.'

He handed over four shillings, mostly in halfpennies, and shuffled up to near the stage where the others were. I shoo'd the rest outside, and Melissa stood guard over them.

(Virginia, of course, was guarding the other door, and missing all the fun. They had drawn lots, between them, for which door.)

I personally had promised Mary-Rose and Janet that I would stay outside and not watch their performances, except to lean in without looking, to call the time (Time Limit 15 Minutes). But I decided that the smooth operation of the Passion-Flower Hotel

And Novelty Theatre demanded that I stay inside and supervise the comfort and decorum of our Clients. So I did.

I looked at my watch (actually Janet's – luminous hands). It was twenty-five past eleven. Then I went to the edge of the stage and called up, 'Princess Puma?'

'Pronto,' growled Mary-Rose, hidden behind a wooden bluff, in a strange strip-teaser's voice.

I crept back to about the middle of the gym, and leant on a big vaulting-horse where it would be nice and dark, and I would be nice and invisible, and waited.

We had arranged things rather well. The gym was copiously equipped with thick, prickly coconut mats (you landed on them, as gracefully as possible, after bounding like a bird over the vaulting-horse) which were rolled up and left about when nobody was bounding like birds over vaulting-horses. We dragged two of them to the front of the stage (I mean, of course, near it, and below) and they made quite a comfortable seat. And there, in a sad little row, the Above Waist Only Clients now sat in the darkness.

The stage itself was a bit bare. We had drawn each of the great, dusty, green curtains (one pulled them by huge ropes) about a third of the way across, leaving about a third of the stage visible in the middle. And we put three torches on the stage, propped on bits of wood to make them point upwards, to be footlights. But of course we left these switched off, till The Time, because of the batteries, and overheads, and the profitability of the operation.

So we waited in the darkness.

Then I heard a hoarse little bleat from the stage. 'D1!'

'Someone's calling,' said one of the Clients, turning back towards me.

'Princess Pumice-stone,' said another, and they all laughed in a coarse, nervous way.

'Lights!' said Mary-Rose's funny new voice.

'Check,' I said, and hurried forward and switched on the three torches. They made a nice sort of multiple pool of light for beauty to be displayed in.

'Right, Princess Puma,' I said.

I faded back into the darkness, and there was another longish pause. The Clients coughed and the coconut-matting front-stalls rustled under them. The rain was dripping on to a bit of tin somewhere miles above in the roof.

The whole atmosphere was deeply and depressingly unsexy, but somehow in an odd way that made it sexier.

Then Mary-Rose came on.

She was wearing a long skirt, in a kind of off-beige, made of a kind of flannelly material, which we had purloined from a girl called Sandra Laverton. (We took the view that no one, not even Sandra Laverton, could possibly ever want to wear it for *normal* purposes.) This utterly obscured her lower half right to the ground. On top she wore a cotton shirt, rather Italian and divine and almost-Pucci, taken from another girl so utterly contemptible that we all pretended not to know what she was called. And she was interestingly masked with a sort of bat-winged Venetian mask, made of black thinnish cardboard cut out with nail-scissors and fastened round the back with a bit of black ribbon, which covered nearly the whole of her face and stuck out at the sides.

She really looked very nice in the provocative light of the three unblinking torches.

She sidled on, and stood with her hands on her hips in the middle of the stage, between the two half-drawn curtains, full in the multiple torch-beams.

One of the Clients cleared his throat in a shrill, excited way, and several of them shifted about so that the sausage-roll front-stalls creaked under their eager curiosity.

Then Mary-Rose undid the bottom button of her shirt, and they all seemed to freeze. Then she undid the next, and the next.

There were five buttons in all and even I (who had after all seen Mary-Rose with nothing on dozens of times, and who wouldn't anyway be *interested*) even I was agog.

Then she undid the next to top, and then the top. Then she seemed to stop, and I wasn't sure if this was deliberate or just bashful, but it was very effective.

And then she slowly took the shirt off.

Of course, it was just bosom. One bosom, to me, is much like another, though I have to admit that Mary-Rose's is nicely formed. It looked terribly white, and a bit pathetic, but not wobbly, even when she began to walk very slowly to and fro.

The five black heads of the Clients, silhouetted against the torch-beams, were absolutely motionless.

Mary-Rose stood still again, bang in the middle of the stage, in the cream-coloured dusty beams of the footlights. The rain was still dripping on to the bit of tin far above me.

Then she turned very slowly round a few times, and slowly raised her arms above her head. It was terribly quiet, and I made a mental note: soft evocative music next time.

And some sort of compère or announcer. Possibly me, or perhaps Virginia, unless she herself was actually performing.

Very, very slowly the minutes ticked by, and Mary-Rose seemed to have run out of Princess Puma gestures. It is difficult to stand on a stage, I suppose, and do nothing in particular, and just be looked at, even if you haven't got anything on Above Waist Only. So I made another mental note: for next time work out a Routine. We would rehearse, and fit to the soft, evocative music. It would be easier for Princess Puma, and better, and more of an arouser.

Meanwhile Mary-Rose was standing rather helplessly, and I thought it must be fifteen minutes. But it was only *four*. We would give her another two, and then she could sidle off again.

So for two more eternally utterly endless minutes she stood about, and turned round once or twice, and raised her arms up, and stood about, and then I called 'Time!'

She sort of jumped, and then whizzed off into the wings.

I walked briskly forward and said, 'Thank you, gentlemen.'

'Thank you,' one of them said in a choky voice.

'But that' — said the doughy-looking one who had paid the extra four bob — 'that wasn't fifteen minutes.'

'So?' I asked coldly.

'It said on your programme. Time limit fifteen minutes.'

'Outer limit,' I said, thinking quickly.

'I paid for fifteen minutes.'

'You are very fortunate to have seen Princess Puma at all,' I said.

'But I paid *four shillings*—'

'Goodness, you've *seen* her,' I said. 'You won't see any more of her if she hangs about up there for another ninety-nine hours.'

'Yes,' said one of the others impatiently, 'come on, Cradders.'

'Anyway, you've got another go,' said another boy.

'I want my money's worth of this go. Or a refund.'

'Quite impossible,' I said.

'Come *on*, Cradders. We don't want to sit here all night.'

Mary-Rose's shirt was still lying on the stage where she had dropped it. I picked it up and threw it into the wings, and a pale figure in the shadows swooped on it and scooped it up and put it on. Then I switched off the torches.

'Princess Puma is tired,' I said diplomatically.

'Oh, all right,' said the beastly one they called Cradders, which I suppose meant his name was Craddock. 'I'll sit tight then, and you poor suckers go out and huddle in the rain.'

'Oh Christmas, to be rich like Cradders,' said the little treble voice.

I led the Above Waist Only party, minus Cradders, to the door of the gym, and they shuffled out.

'Well?' said excited voices, clustering round from the dripping blackness.

'What was it like?'

'Are you a *man* now, Squeaky?'

'Our turn!'

'Come on, men!'

'Follow me quietly, please,' I said.

I got them arranged in the stalls, and switched on the footlights, and looked at my watch – eleven-thirty-four, only nine minutes after Princess Puma had *started*.

'Miss de la Gallantine!' I called softly.

'Ici,' whispered Janet, waiting right at the edge of the half-drawn curtain, and startling me.

I turned to the audience. 'Announcing with pride – Miss Gaby de la Gallantine!'

I faded back again, as was fitting, to my station by the vaulting-horse, and put my glasses on.

And then, almost at once, Miss Gaby de la Gallantine undulated amazingly on.

And twenty minutes later *she was still there*.

We had, in Miss Gaby de la Gallantine — and who would have thought it in a trillion years — a Natural. A Star Is Born — the star of the Passion-Flower Hotel And Novelty Theatre, or anyway the Novelty Theatre.

She had ransacked the entire school for her wardrobe, which, as she wore it, was indeed a bit special. She came on in a big white macintosh with the collar turned up, and she held an umbrella open as though it was raining (as it was of course — though not, naturally, in the Passion-Flower Hotel And Novelty Theatre). Then the rest you could see was rather dark nylon stockings, French looking, and black high heels which fitted her, luckily, though actually until that evening they belonged to somebody unimportant. And of course a mask, though not nearly as much of one as Princess Puma — just a domino. Rather sexy.

She walked on very slowly, pushing her hips about under the big white mac, right to the end of the stage in front of the curtain, and right back again to the other end, and stood still. Then with a terrific din, she suddenly shut the umbrella, and everybody jumped. And she put the umbrella down. And that was the beginning. Then, without the umbrella, she walked about some more, tremendously hippily, and utterly and completely unrecognizable, and wholly not Janet but some strange stranger called Miss Gaby de la Gallantine.

After a bit she unbuckled the belt of the macintosh, which took about two minutes. The rustle and click of the buckle and belt sounded fearfully loud, in spite of the continual whisper of rain and the drip-drip-drip on the bit of tin in the roof.

In the next twenty minutes, which seemed about two lifetimes, Miss Gaby de la Gallantine removed all her clothes, except just the mask. And then she padded about for a bit, and even did a sort of semi-dance which was incredible, and far beyond the call of duty.

And finally she undulated off, leaving bits of clothing and things dotted about all over the stage, as though hit by a Kansas tornado.

The audience, when I ushered them courteously out, also looked like remnants of a tornado in Kansas: broken men. (Broken boys, of course, really.) It was clear that they had been through a great experience, which they would remember all their lives. Even Cradders was silent and abstracted.

I glowed with pride at the Service The Syndicate was offering these luckless celibates in their artificial and monastic predicament; and I gave them all, as they clustered dumbly round the door of the gym, our leaflet.

THE PASSION-FLOWER HOTEL AND NOVELTY THEATRE

To Our Patrons

The Management hopes you have enjoyed your evening. If so, please recommend our service to your friends. And if you have any suggestions or criticisms, please let us know. Our aim is to serve you.

Full price-list on application.

Special party rates. Individual requirements catered for.

> *The Syndicate Will Meet Your Needs.*
> *Actions Speak Louder Than Words.*
> *Save Today The Syndicate Way.*

I congratulated Janet later.

'Did you *watch*?' she said.

'You didn't watch me, did you?' asked Mary-Rose furiously.

'No, of course not, after I *promised*.' (One must use a good deal of diplomacy with staff.) 'I just leaned in at the end, for the time thing.'

'Ah.'

'But you didn't time my end,' said Janet.

'Well, I met them coming out.'

'What did they say?'

'Nothing,' said Melissa with grudging admiration. 'They couldn't.'

'Ooh,' said Virginia.

'I suppose Janet's aroused them all,' said Mary-Rose crossly.

'I'm sure you did your own more limited performance brilliantly,' I said kindly.

'Well, it was the first time.'

'Mine too,' said Janet, seeming to remember happily.

'I suppose it's your natural bent.'

'Yes, I suppose it is,' agreed Janet placidly.

———

From *The Passion-Flower Hotel* by Rosalind Erskine, 1962

The Help

What can I say? John Thomas, Lady Jane. Yorkshire dialect. The c-word. Bummage. Blimey.

*W*hen Connie went up to her bedroom she did what she had not done for a long time: took off all her clothes and looked at herself naked in the huge mirror. She did not know what she was looking for, or at, very definitely. Yet she moved the lamp till it shone full on her.

And she thought as she had thought so often: what a frail, easily-hurt, rather pathetic thing a naked human body is: somehow a little unfinished, incomplete!

She was supposed to have a good figure, but now she was out of fashion: a little too female, not enough like an adolescent boy. She was not very tall – a bit Scottish and short: but she had a certain fluent, down-slipping grace that might have been beauty. Her skin was faintly tawny, her limbs had a certain stillness, her body should have had a full, downward-slipping richness. But it lacked something.

Instead of ripening its firm, down-running curves, her body was flattening and going a little harsh. It was as if it had not had enough sun and warmth. It was a little greyish and sapless. Disappointed of its real womanhood, it had not succeeded in becoming boyish and unsubstantial and transparent. Instead, it had gone opaque.

Her breasts were rather small, and dropping pear-shaped. But they were unripe, a little bitter, without meaning hanging there.

And her belly had lost the fresh round gleam it had had when she was young, in the days of her German boy, who loved her really physically. Then it was young and expectant, with a real look of its own. Now it was going slack and a little flat, thinner – but with a slack thinness. Her thighs, too, that used to look so quick and glimpsey, in their odd female roundness, somehow they too were going flat, slack, meaningless.

Her body was going meaningless, going dull and opaque, so much insignificant substance. It made her feel immensely depressed, and hopeless. What hope was there? She was old, old at twenty-seven, with no gleam and sparkle in the flesh. Old through neglect and denial: yes, denial. Fashionable women kept their bodies bright, like delicate porcelain, by external attention. There was nothing inside the porcelain. – But she was not even as bright as that. The mental life! Suddenly she hated it with a rushing fury, the swindle!

She looked in the other mirror's reflection at her back, her waist, her loins. She was getting thinner, but to her it was not becoming. The crumple of her waist at the back, as she bent back to look, was a little weary: and it used to be so gay-looking. And the longish slope of her haunches and her buttocks had lost its gleam and its sense of richness. Gone! Only the German boy had loved it, and he was ten years dead, very nearly. How time went by! And she was only twenty-seven. Ten years dead, that healthy boy with his fresh, clumsy sensuality that she had then been so scornful of! Where would she find it now? It was gone out of men. They had their pathetic, two-seconds spasms, like Michaelis. But no healthy, human sensuality that warms the blood and freshens the whole being.

Still she thought the most beautiful part of her was the long-sloping fall of the haunches, from the socket of the back, and the slumberous round stillness of the buttocks. Like hillocks of sand, the Arabs say, soft and downward-slipping with a long slope. Here the life still lingered, hoping. – But here too she was thinner, and going unripe, astringent.

But the front of her body made her miserable. It was already beginning to slacken with a slack sort of thinness, almost withered, going old before it had ever really lived. She thought of the child she might somehow bear. Was she fit, anyhow?

She slipped into her nightdress and went to bed, where she sobbed bitterly. And in her bitterness burned a cold indignation against Clifford and his writings and his talk: against all the men of his sort, who defrauded a woman even out of her own body. Unjust! Unjust! The sense of deep physical injustice burned through her very soul.

*

She was watching a brown spaniel that had run out of a side-path, and was looking towards them with lifted nose, making a soft, fluffy bark. A man with a gun strode swiftly, softly out after the dog, facing their way, as if about to attack them; then stopped instead, saluted, and was turning downhill. It was only the new gamekeeper, but he had frightened Connie, he seemed to emerge with such a swift menace. That was how she had seen him, like a sudden rush of a threat out of nowhere.

He was a man in dark green velveteens and gaiters – the old style – with a red face and red moustache, and distant eyes. He was going quickly downhill.

'Mellors!' said Clifford.

The man faced lightly round, and saluted with a swift little gesture: a soldier!

'Will you turn the chair round and get it started. That makes it easier,' said Clifford.

The man at once slung his gun over his shoulder, and came forward, with the same curious swift, yet soft movements, as if keeping invisible. He was moderately tall, and lean; and silent. He did not look at Connie, only at the chair.

'Connie, this is the new gamekeeper Mellors. You haven't spoken to her ladyship yet, Mellors?'

'No Sir!' came the ready, neutral words.

The man lifted his hat as he stood, showing his thick, almost fair hair. He was almost handsome without a hat. He stared straight into Connie's eyes with a perfectly fearless, impersonal look, as if he wanted to see what she was like. He made her feel shy. She bent her head to him shyly, and he changed his hat to his left hand, and made her a slight bow, like a gentleman; but he said nothing at all. He remained for a moment still with his hat in his hand.

'But you've been here some time, haven't you?' Connie said to him.

'Eight months, Madam – your ladyship!' he corrected himself calmly.

'And do you like it?'

She looked him in the eyes. His eyes narrowed a little, with irony, perhaps with impudence.

'Why yes, thank you, your ladyship! I was reared here—'

He gave another slight bow, turned, put his hat on, and strode to take hold of the chair. His voice, on the last words, had fallen into the heavy broad drag of the dialect – perhaps also in mockery, because there had been no trace of dialect before. He might almost be a gentleman. Anyhow he was a curious, quick, separate fellow, alone but sure of himself.

Clifford started the little engine, the man carefully turned the chair and set it nose-forwards to the incline that curved gently to the dark hazel thicket.

'Is that all then, Sir Clifford?' said the man.

'No! You'd better come along, for fear she sticks. The engine isn't really strong enough for the uphill work.'

The man glanced round for his dog – a quick, thoughtful glance. The spaniel looked at him and faintly moved her tail. A little smile, mocking or teasing her, yet gentle, came into his eyes for a moment, then faded away and his face was expressionless. They went fairly quickly down the slope, the man with his hand on the rail of the chair, steadying it. He looked like a free soldier rather than a servant. And something about him reminded Connie of Tommy Dukes.

When they came to the hazel grove Connie suddenly ran forward and opened the gate into the park. As she stood holding it, the two men looked at her in passing, Clifford critically, the other man with a curious cool wonder: impersonally wanting to see what she looked like. And she saw in his blue, impersonal eyes a look of suffering and detachment, yet a certain warmth. But why was he so aloof, apart?

Clifford stopped the chair, once through the gate, and the man came quickly, courteously, to close it.

'Why did you run to open?' said Clifford, in his quiet calm voice that showed he was displeased. 'Mellors would have done it.'

'I thought you could go straight ahead,' said Connie.

'And leave you to run after us?' said Clifford.

'Oh well, I like to run sometimes!'

Mellors took the chair again, looking perfectly unheeding. Yet Connie felt he noted everything. As he pushed the chair up the steepish rise of the knoll in the park, he breathed rather quickly through parted lips. He was rather frail, really. Curiously full of vitality, but a little frail, and quenched. Her woman's instinct sensed it.

Connie fell back, let the chair go on. The day had greyed over: the small blue sky that had poised low on its circular rims of haze was closed in again, the lid was down, there was a raw coldness. It was going to snow. All grey, all grey! The world looked worn out.

The chair waited at the top of the pink path. Clifford looked round for Connie.

'Not tired, are you?' he asked.

'Oh no!' she said.

But she was. A strange, weary yearning, a dissatisfaction had started in her. Clifford did not notice: those were not things he was aware of. But the stranger knew. To Connie, everything in her world and life seemed worn out, and her dissatisfaction was older than the hills.

They came to the house, and round to the back where there were no steps. Clifford managed to swing himself over on to a low, wheeled house-chair: he was very strong and agile with his arms. Then Connie lifted his burden of dead legs after him.

The keeper, waiting at attention to be dismissed, watched everything narrowly, missing nothing. He went pale with a sort of fear, when he saw Connie lifting the inert legs of the man in her arms, into the other chair, Clifford pivoting round as she did so. He was frightened.

'Thanks then for the help, Mellors,' said Clifford casually, as he began to wheel down the passage through the servants' quarters.

'Nothing else, Sir?' came the neutral voice, like one in a dream.

'Nothing. Good morning.'

'Good morning, Sir.'

'Good morning! It was kind of you to push the chair up that hill — I hope it wasn't heavy for you,' said Connie, looking back at the keeper outside the door.

His eyes came to hers in an instant, as if he wakened up. He was aware of her

'Oh no, not heavy!' he said quickly. Then his voice dropped again into the broad sound of the vernacular: 'Good mornin' to your ladyship!'

'Who is your gamekeeper?' Connie asked at lunch.

'Mellors! You saw him,' said Clifford.

'Yes! But where did he come from?'

'Nowhere! He was a Tevershall boy — son of a collier, I believe.'

'And was he a collier himself?'

'Blacksmith on the pit-bank, I believe: overhead smith. But he was keeper here for two years before the war — before he joined up. My father always had a good opinion of him, so when he came back and went to the pit for a blacksmith's job, I just took him back here as keeper. I was really very glad to get him — it's almost impossible to find a good man round here, for a gamekeeper — and it needs a man who knows the people.'

'And isn't he married?'

'He was! But the wife went off with various men — but finally with a collier at Stacks Gate, and I believe she's living there still.'

'So this man is alone?'

'More or less! He has a mother in the village — and a child, I believe.'

Clifford looked at Connie with his pale, slightly prominent blue eyes, in which a certain vagueness was coming. He seemed alert in the foreground, but the background was like the Midlands atmosphere, haze, smoky mist. And the haze seemed to be creeping forward. So when he stared at Connie in his peculiar way, giving her his peculiarly precise information, she felt all the background of his mind filling up with mist, with nothingness. And it frightened her. It made him seem impersonal almost to idiocy.

*

'Do you know what I thought?' she said suddenly. 'It suddenly came to me. You are the "Knight of the Burning Pestle".'

'Ay! And you? Are you the Lady of the Red-hot Mortar?'

'Yes!' she said. 'Yes! You're Sir Pestle and I'm Lady Mortar.'

'All right – then I'm knighted. John Thomas is Sir John, to your Lady Jane.'

'Yes! John Thomas is knighted! I'm my-lady-maidenhair, and you must have flowers too. Yes!'

She threaded two pink campions in the bush of red-gold hair above his penis.

'There!' she said. 'Charming. Charming! Sir John!'

And she pushed a bit of forget-me-not in the dark hair of his breast.

'And you won't forget me *there*, will you?' She kissed him on the breast, and made two bits of forget-me-not lodge one over each nipple, kissing him again.

'Make a calendar of me!' he said. He laughed, and the flowers shook from his breast.

'Wait a bit!' he said.

He rose, and opened the door of the hut. Flossie, lying on the porch, got up and looked at him.

'Ay, it's me!' he said.

The rain had ceased. There was a wet, heavy, perfumed stillness. Evening was approaching.

He went out and down the little path in the opposite direction from the riding. Connie watched his thin, white figure, and it looked to her like a ghost, an apparition moving away from her. When she could see it no more, her heart sank. She stood in the door of the hut, with a blanket round her, looking into the drenched, motionless silence.

But he was coming back, trotting strangely, and carrying flowers. She was a little afraid of him, as if he were not quite human. And when he came near, his eyes looked into hers, but she could not understand the meaning.

He had brought columbines and campions, and new-mown-hay, and oak-tufts and honeysuckle in small bud. He fastened fluffy young oak-sprays round her head, and honeysuckle withes round her breasts, sticking in tufts of bluebells and campion: and in her navel he poised a pink campion flower, and in her maidenhair were forget-me-nots and wood-ruff.

'That's you in all your glory!' he said. 'Lady Jane, at her wedding with John Thomas.'

And he stuck flowers in the hair of his own body, and wound a bit of creeping-jenny round his penis, and stuck a single bell of a hyacinth in his navel. She watched him with amusement, his odd intentness. And she pushed a campion flower in his moustache, where it stuck, dangling under his nose.

'This is John Thomas marryin' Lady Jane,' he said. 'An' we mun let Constance an' Oliver go their ways. Maybe—' He spread out his hand with a gesture, and then he sneezed, sneezing away the flowers from his nose and his navel. He sneezed again.

'Maybe what?' she said, waiting for him to go on.

He looked at her a little bewildered.

'Eh?' he said.

'Maybe what? Go on with what you were going to say,' she insisted.

Ay, what *was* I going to say?—'

He had forgotten. And it was one of the disappointments of her life, that he never finished.

*

It was a night of sensual passion, in which she was a little startled, and almost unwilling: yet pierced again with piercing thrills of sensuality, different, sharper, more terrible than the thrills of tenderness, but, at the moment, more desirable. Though a little frightened, she let him have his way, and the reckless, shameless sensuality shook her to her foundations, stripped her to the very last, and made a different woman of her. It was not really love. It was not voluptuousness. It was sensuality sharp and searing as fire, burning the soul to tinder.

Burning out the shames, the deepest, oldest shames, in the most secret places. It cost her an effort to let him have his way and his will of her. She had to be a passive, consenting thing, like a slave, a physical slave. Yet the passion licked round her, consuming, and when the sensual flame of it passed through her bowels and breast, she really thought she was dying: yet a poignant, marvellous death.

She had often wondered what Abélard meant, when he said that in their year of love he and Heloïse had passed through all the stages and refinements of passion. The same thing, a thousand years ago: ten thousand years ago! The same on the Greek vases — everywhere! The refinements of passion, the extravagances of sensuality! And necessary, forever necessary, to burn out false shames and smelt out the heaviest ore of the body into purity. With the fire of sheer sensuality.

In this short summer night she learnt so much. She would have thought a woman would have died of shame. Instead of which, the shame died. Shame, which is fear: the deep organic shame, the old, old physical fear which crouches in the bodily roots of us, and can only be chased away by the sensual fire, at last it was roused up and routed by the phallic hunt of the man, and she came to the very heart of the jungle of herself. She felt, now, she had come to the real bed-rock of her nature, and was essentially shameless. She was her sensual self, naked and unashamed. She felt a triumph, almost a vainglory. So! That was how it was! That was life! That was how oneself really was! There was nothing left to disguise or be ashamed of. She shared her ultimate nakedness with a man, another being.

And what a reckless devil the man was! really like a devil! One had to be strong to bear him. But it took some getting at, the core of the physical jungle, the last and deepest recess of organic shame. The phallos alone could explore it. And how he had pressed in on her! And how, in fear, she had hated it! But how she had really wanted it! She knew now. At the bottom of her soul, fundamentally, she had needed this phallic hunting out, she had secretly wanted it, and she had believed she would never get it. Now suddenly there it was, and a man was sharing her last and final nakedness, she was shameless.

What liars poets and everybody were! They made one think one wanted sentiment. When what one supremely wanted was this piercing, consuming, rather awful sensuality. To find a man who dared do it, without shame or sin or final misgiving! If he had been ashamed afterwards, and made one feel ashamed, how awful! What a pity that fine, sensual men are so rare! What a pity most men are so doggy, a bit shameful. Like Clifford! Like Michaelis even! Both sensually a bit doggy and humiliating. — The supreme pleasure of the mind! And what is that to a woman? What is it, really, to the man either! He becomes merely messy and doggy, even in his mind. It needs sheer sensuality even to purify and quicken the mind. Sheer fiery sensuality, not messiness.

Ah God, how rare a thing a man is! They are all dogs that trot and sniff and copulate. To have found a man who was not afraid and not ashamed! She looked at him now, sleeping so like a wild animal asleep, gone, gone in the remoteness of it. She nestled down, not to be away from him.

Till his rousing waked her completely. He was sitting up in bed, looking down at her. She saw her own nakedness in his eyes, immediate knowledge of her. And the fluid, male knowledge of herself seemed to flow to her from his eyes and wrap her voluptuously. Oh, how voluptuous and lovely it was to have limbs and body half-asleep, heavy and suffused with passion!

'Is it time to wake up?' she said.

'Half past six.'

She had to be at the lane-end at eight. Always, always, always this compulsion on one!

'But we needn't get up yet,' she said.

'I might make the breakfast and bring it up here — should I?'

'Oh yes!'

Flossie whimpered gently below. He got up and threw off his pyjamas, and rubbed himself with a towel. When the human being is courageous and full of life, how beautiful it is! So she thought, as she watched him in silence.

'Draw the curtain, will you?'

The sun was shining already on the tender green leaves of morning, and the wood stood bluey-fresh, in the nearness. She sat up in bed, looking dreamily out through the dormer window, her naked arms pushing her naked breasts together. He was dressing himself. She was half-dreaming of life, a life together with him: just a life.

He was going, fleeing from her dangerous, crouching nakedness.

'Have I lost my nightie altogether?' she said.

He pushed his hand down in the bed, and pulled out the bit of flimsy silk.

'I knowed I felt silk at my ankles,' he said.

But the nightdress was slit almost in two.

'Never mind!' she said. 'It belongs here, really. I'll leave it.'

'Ay, leave it – I can put it atween my legs at night, for company. There's no name nor mark on it, is there?'

'No! It's just a plain old one.'

She slipped on the torn thing, and sat dreamily looking out of the window. The window was open, the air of morning drifted in, and the sound of birds. Birds flew continually past. Then she saw Flossie roaming out. It was morning.

––––––––––

From *Lady Chatterley's Lover* by D.H. Lawrence, 1928

A Poem!

Beauty, sexiness and eroticism in the classroom. Whatever next? All this, and the odd iambic hexameter chucked in for good measure: quite a lot to take in during Double English.

XXX
And still she slept an azure-lidded sleep,
In blanched linen, smooth, and lavender'd,
While he from forth the closet brought a heap
Of candied apple, quince, and plum, and gourd;
With jellies soother than the creamy curd,
And lucent syrops, tinct with cinnamon;
Manna and dates, in argosy transferr'd
From Fez; and spiced dainties, every one,
From silken Samarcand to cedar'd Lebanon.

XXXI
These delicates he heap'd with glowing hand
On golden dishes and in baskets bright
Of wreathed silver: sumptuous they stand
In the retired quiet of the night,
Filling the chilly room with perfume light. —
'And now, my love, my seraph fair, awake!
'Thou art my heaven, and I thine eremite:
'Open thine eyes, for meek St Agnes' sake,
'Or I shall drowse beside thee, so my soul doth ache.'

XXXII

Thus whispering, his warm, unnerved arm
Sank in her pillow. Shaded was her dream
By the dusk curtains: — 'twas a midnight charm
Impossible to melt as iced stream:
The lustrous salvers in the moonlight gleam;
Broad golden fringe upon the carpet lies:
It seem'd he never, never could redeem
From such a stedfast spell his lady's eyes;
So mus'd awhile, entoil'd in woofed phantasies.

XXXIII

Awakening up, he took her hollow lute, —'
Tumultuous, — and, in chords that tenderest be,
He play'd an ancient ditty, long since mute,
In Provence call'd, 'La belle dame sans mercy:'
Close to her ear touching the melody; —
Wherewith disturb'd, she utter'd a soft moan:
He ceased — she panted quick — and suddenly
Her blue affrayed eyes wide open shone:
Upon his knees he sank, pale as smooth-sculptured stone.

XXXIV

Her eyes were open, but she still beheld,
Now wide awake, the vision of her sleep:
There was a painful change, that nigh expell'd
The blisses of her dream so pure and deep
At which fair Madeline began to weep,
And moan forth witless words with many a sigh;
While still her gaze on Porphyro would keep;
Who knelt, with joined hands and piteous eye,
Fearing to move or speak, she look'd so dreamingly.

XXXV

'Ah, Porphyro!' said she, 'but even now
'Thy voice was at sweet tremble in mine ear,

'Made tuneable with every sweetest vow;
'And those sad eyes were spiritual and clear:
'How chang'd thou art! how pallid, chill, and drear!
'Give me that voice again, my Porphyro,
'Those looks immortal, those complainings dear!
'Oh leave me not in this eternal woe,
'For if thou diest, my Love, I know not where to go.'

XXXVI
Beyond a mortal man impassion'd far
At these voluptuous accents, he arose,
Ethereal, flush'd, and like a throbbing star
Seen mid the sapphire heaven's deep repose;
Into her dream he melted, as the rose
Blendeth its odour with the violet, –
Solution sweet: meantime the frost-wind blows
Like Love's alarum pattering the sharp sleet
Against the window-panes; St Agnes' moon hath set.

———————

From *The Eve of St Agnes* by John Keats, 1820

The Pilot

Unbelievably shocking, not least because shagging someone on the way back from your husband's funeral seemed so crazily immoral. Arguably the bonkiest of the eighties bonk-busters – and the one, along with *Lace*, that everybody remembers. With good reason. Fasten your seatbelts . . .

*U*ntil Ellis Ikehorn died, at seventy-one, Billy Ikehorn had not realized the extraordinary difference between being the wife of an enormously rich man and being an enormously rich young woman without a husband. For the last five years of their twelve-year marriage Ellis had been in a wheelchair, partly paralysed and unable to speak as the result of a stroke. Although, from the day Billy had married him, she had thrown in her lot with the rich and powerful of this world, she had never really established a position in that stronghold from which to organize her widowhood. During the years of her husband's last illness, she had lived, in many ways, as a recluse in their Bel Air fortress, enduring, as far as her peers knew, the restricted life of the wife of a serious invalid.

Now, suddenly, she was thirty-two, without responsibilities to a family, and the mistress of an income that was virtually unlimited. Billy realized with amazement that it scared the shit out of her, all this endless money. Yet was that not what she had craved during the long years of her childhood as a poor relation? But now her fortune was so great that it was deeply disquieting. The potentials of vast sums of money seemed to flatten out, to shadow, to turn into prospects and perspectives so blurred at the edges that they led nowhere.

On that last morning when one of Ellis's three male nurses had come to tell Billy that he had had a final stroke in his sleep, she felt relief mingled with sadness for that part of the past that had been so good. But she had grieved over the past five years; she had had too long to prepare herself for his death to feel a fierce personal loss. Yet, even less than half alive, Ellis had protected her. During his lifetime she had never bothered to think about money. A corps of lawyers and accountants handled all that. Of course she was aware that after their marriage he had given her ten million dollars' worth of tax-free municipal bonds, on which he had paid the gift tax, and that he had repeated the same practice on each of her seven birthdays until his first stroke in 1970. Even before she became his sole heir, inheriting all of his stock in Ikehorn Enterprises, her own fortune had swelled to eighty million dollars from which she derived an income of four million tax-free dollars a year. Now a platoon of IRS auditors spent weeks working on the Ikehorn-estate tax return, but do what they would, Billy was still left with roughly one hundred twenty million additional dollars. This new money confused and frightened her. In theory she understood that she could go anywhere, do anything. It was only by reflecting that she certainly could not pay for a moon shot that Billy was able to bring herself back to a sense of reality. Her magnifying mirror reassured her as she looked into it to put on her mascara. All the familiar tasks remained. Bathing, brushing her teeth, weighing herself as she had done every morning and every evening since she was eighteen, dressing — it all restored the grain and texture of life. She would make one move at a time she told her image in the mirror, which showed none of the panic she felt. To a stranger who might have seen her for the first time at that moment, and assessed her height, her proud walk, her strong throat, her imperious head, she would have looked as autocratic and as strong as a young Amazon queen.

The immediate need was to decide about the funeral. Billy almost welcomed it because it gave her such a precise and limited set of decisions to make.

Ellis Ikehorn had never been a religious man, nor was he sentimental except on matters that touched on Billy. His will contained no instructions about a funeral, and he had certainly never expressed any preference about the matter of his burial. That form of anticipatory intimation of morality held as little appeal to him as it did to most men, rich or poor.

Cremation, obviously, thought Billy. Yes, cremation followed by a memorial service in the Episcopal Church in Beverly Hills. Whatever his religion might have been, and he had always refused to discuss it, she had been brought up as a Boston Episcopalian and that would have to serve. Fortunately, there were enough local employees of his corporation and men he had done business with in the past to fill the church. If Billy had had to depend on her own personal friends to make up a respectable crowd, she could, she estimated, hold the service in the back room at La Scala's and still have space left over for a large choir and a three-piece combo.

She telephoned her lawyer, Josh Hillman, to ask him to make the necessary arrangements, and then directed her attention towards the next thing, a dress suitable for the funeral. Mourning. But she had lived in California too long, even for a woman who had spent years on the Best-Dressed List. There was nothing in her wardrobe, enormous as it was, that resembled a short, thin black dress appropriate for daytime wear in September 1975 with temperatures in the nineties accentuated by hot, dry Santa Ana winds. If only Scruples were finished she could go there, she thought longingly, but it was still under construction.

As she picked out several black silk linens from Galanos at Amelia Gray's, her gaze again went to the mirror. She was plagued by so much *unused* loveliness. Billy was not modest about her beauty. She had been desperately unattractive throughout her first eighteen years, and now that she was beautiful she gloried in it. She never wore a bra. Her breasts were high and almost lush. Any hint of support, which always provided uplift, would have made her too bosomy for chic. She thanked heaven that her ass was flat for a wide handspan below her waist, not becoming full until safely past the point where it would have destroyed the line of her clothes.

Naked, she was unexpectedly rich in flesh. Flesh, Billy thought, with a dry, brittle heaviness of frustration, that had not felt the touch of a man's hand in many, many months. Since Christmas, when Ellis's decline had become more terrible day by day, she had, whether out of pity or a sense of taboo, deliberately deprived herself of the secret sexual life she had established almost four years before.

As she put her own clothes back on and waited for the new dresses to be packed, she turned her thoughts away from herself and attacked the next problem: the question of the ashes. She only knew that she had to do something with them. Ellis, when she had first met him, would probably have wanted to be dusted lightly into the speaking end of as many telephones as possible, she thought with a small smile of memory. He had been not quite sixty then, a vigorous emperor in the world of international wealth, who had made his first million of what he called 'keeping money' a good thirty years before. Perhaps he would have preferred to have his ashes rubbed, a pinch at a time, into the linings of the brief-cases of his battalion of executives. He had always enjoyed keeping them off-balance. The saleslady looked at her oddly, and Billy suddenly realized that she had made a small sound of mirth. She mustn't start that. It would be all over town by lunchtime that Billy Ikehorn was laughing on the morning her husband died. But hadn't there been something, besides their life together, that Ellis had been sentimental about before he got sick? He used to say that a glass of good wine and the new issues of *Fortune* and *Forbes* magazine was his favourite way to spend a quiet evening – of course – the vineyard, Silverado. Perhaps she was in more of a state than she realized, after all. Normally she would have thought of it immediately.

They couldn't use the Learjet. Hank Sanders, the head pilot, explained it to her. For the purpose she had described to him they needed a plane that could fly slowly, with a window open. The young pilot had been on the Ikehorn payroll for a little more than five years. It was he who had flown them all out from New York City to California after Ellis's first stroke, he who had occupied the left-hand seat on the many trips the sick old man and his remote young wife had made to their vineyard in St Helena or to Palm Springs or to San Diego. Occasionally Hank had left the controls to the co-pilot and walked back to the main cabin to report on weather conditions to Mr Ikehorn, sitting by the window in his wheelchair; a formality, since he either paid no attention to them or seemed not to. But Mrs Ikehorn had always thanked him gravely, pausing in whatever book or magazine she was reading to ask him a few questions about how he liked his new life in California, to tell him how many days they would be in the Napa Valley, even to suggest that he try a bottle from a particular vintage while he was there. He admired her dignity enormously and felt flattered when she looked him in the eye during their brief exchanges. He also thought she was a flaming, fabulous piece of ass, but he tried not to dwell on that.

But now, with Mrs Ikehorn sitting inches away from him in the rented Beechcraft Bonanza as they took off from Van Nuys Airport four days after the cremation, he sat rather nervously at the controls. His uneasiness did not stem from any unfamiliarity with a small plane. Actually, Hank Sanders owned a second-hand Beech Sierra for weekend trips to Tahoe and Reno. There was nothing, he had discovered, like flying a girl away for a weekend to insure as much pussy as you could eat. No, it was sitting next to Mrs Ikehorn, so serious, so preoccupied, and so unreasonably sexy – too close for comfort considering the circumstances. He carefully avoided looking at her. If only she had some relatives there with her, sisters or something.

He had filed a round-trip flight plan for St Helena, some six hundred and fifty air miles in all, a trip that the Bonanza could make in no more than four and a half hours, maybe less, depending on the winds. As they approached Napa, Billy finally broke her silence.

'Hank, we're not going to land there on the strip. I want you to follow Route 29 straight up, losing altitude all the way until you get to St Helena. Then bank to the right. Please enter slow flight by the time you've reached our boundaries at Silverado. Then level off as low as you possibly can – five hundred feet is legal, right? – and then circle the vineyards.'

The Napa Valley is not wide, but it is exceedingly lovely, especially as the September sunlight showered down on the densely planted, miraculous acres of valley floor and the steep wooded hills that shelter it on all sides. The finest wines in the United States, considered by many experts to rival and often surpass the greatest wines of France, come from these mere twenty-three thousand aces, where wineries jostle each other almost as closely as they do on the hillsides of Bordeaux, although they are each many times as large as the French holdings.

In 1945, Ellis Ikehorn, who detested the French on principle, which principles he did not choose to divulge, bought the old Hersent and de Moustiers property near St Helena. That fine winery had fallen on ruinous days and had been badly neglected as Prohibition and the Depression and World War II dealt successive blows to American wine making. Its three thousand acres included a vast, elaborately shingled, twin-turreted, stone manor house, unmistakably Victorian in style, which Ikehorn restored to glory and renamed Château Silverado after the old road, once a coaching trail, which followed the length of the valley. From Germany he lured Hans Weber, the celebrated cellar master, and gave him free rein. The purchase of the winery and the interest Ellis Ikehorn took in consuming the great Pinot Chardonnay and the equally splendid Cabernet Sauvignon, which were eventually produced, some seven years and nine million dollars later, was the closest he ever came to having a hobby

As they circled the vineyards, speckled with workers in the last days before the harvest, Billy opened the window on her right. In her hands she held a massive Georgian presentation box of solid gold, about six inches square, bearing the London hallmark for 1816–17 and the maker's mark, that of the great craftsman Benjamin Smith. Inside the box were engraved these words:

> *Presented to Arthur Wellesley,*
> *Duke of Wellington*
> *On the occasion of the first anniversary of*
> *The Battle of Waterloo*

By the Respectful Company of Merchants
and Bankers
Of the City of London
'The Iron Duke will dwell eternally
in our hearts.'

Billy carefully put her right hand through the small window, tensing her wrist against the rush of air. As the Bonanza circled low over the Silverado vines at eighty-five miles an hour, Billy barely released the catch on the lid of the box and, little by little, allowed Ellis Ikehorn's ashes to drift down on the rows of heavy bunches of grapes hidden beneath the deep green leaves. Her task completed, she returned the empty box to her handbag. 'They say this will be a vintage year,' she murmured to the speechless pilot.

During the flight back, Billy sat wrapped in a strange, quivering silence, which seemed in Hank Sanders' tense imaginings to expect something of him. However, they landed at Van Nuys uneventfully, and as he pushed the Bonanza back on its blocks on the tarmac and went inside the Beech Aero Club to return the keys to the plane, he felt that the strangeness of the episode must have been due solely to the reason for the trip. But when he came out to the parking lot, he found Billy waiting for him, sitting in the driver's seat of the enormous, dark green Bentley Ellis had favoured and which she had never sold.

'I thought we'd take a little drive, Hank. It's still early.' Her dark eyebrows were raised in amusement as she looked into his confused face. This was an invitation for which he was totally unprepared.

'A drive! Why? I mean, yeah, sure, Mrs Ikehorn, whatever you say,' he answered, struggling between politeness and embarrassment. Billy laughed at him gently, thinking how like a strong, young farm boy he looked with his fresh, blunt, freckled features, his straw-blond hair, and his absolute lack of interest, as far as she had been able to tell over the years, in anything besides aeroplanes.

'Then get in. You don't mind if I drive, do you? I'm the wizard of the right-hand drive. Isn't it fun in this old thing? I feel as if we're about ten feet off the road.' She was as natural and gay as someone going off to the beach.

Billy drove expertly, seeming to know where she was going, gaily humming a bit to herself, while Hank Sanders tried to relax, as if going for an outing with Mrs Ikehorn was something he did frequently. He was desperately uncomfortable, so preoccupied with the etiquette of the situation that he hardly noticed as Billy left the freeway, took Lankershim for a few miles, and then turned off the broad street into a narrow road. She made an abrupt right turn and pulled into the driveway of a small motel. She stopped the Bentley in one of the carports, which were built next to each room.

'I'll be right back, Hank — it's time for a drink I think, so don't go away. She disappeared into the motel's office for a minute and came back, casually flourishing a key and holding a plastic container full of ice cubes. Still humming, she handed him the ice, opened the trunk of the car, and took out a large leather case. She opened the door of the motel and laughingly waved him in.

Hank Sanders looked around the room with apprehension mixed with wonder, while Billy busily opened the portable bar case, made to order in London ten years before for race meetings and country-house shooting parties, a relic of an era in her life that seemed as archaic as the silver-topped decanters she set in a row on the carpet for lack of a table. The floor of the air-conditioned room was covered from one wall to another in thick, soft raspberry carpet, which also covered three of its walls as all the way up to the ceiling, which, like the fourth wall, was entirely mirrored. Hank nervously walked about, noting that there were no windows in the room, no chairs, nothing but a small chest in one corner. Light came from three poles, which reached from floor to ceiling, to which were attached spotlights fitted with pink bulbs, which could be pointed in any direction. A large, low bed took up almost half the space. It was covered in rosy-pink satin sheets and piled with pillows. He was pointlessly investigating the spotless bathroom when Billy called to him.

'Hank, what are you drinking?'

He walked back into the bedroom. 'Mrs Ikehorn, are you all right?'

'Perfectly. Please don't worry. Now, what can I offer you?'

'Scotch, please, on the rocks.'

Billy was sitting on the floor, leaning against the bed. She handed him a glass as naturally as if they were at a cocktail party. He sat down on the carpet – it was either that or the bed he thought wildly – and took a long pull on his drink, which she had poured into a sterling-silver cup. In her white, handkerchief-linen blouse and her French-blue cotton wrap-around skirt, with her long, brown legs sprawled on the carpet, she looked as if she were at a picnic. Billy drank too, playfully clinking her cup against his.

'To the Essex Motel, garden spot of the San Fernando Valley – and to Ellis Ikehorn, who would approve,' she toasted.

'What!' he said, deeply shocked.

'Hank, you don't have to understand it, just believe me.' She moved closer to him, and with the same casual, yet precise, gesture she might have used to shake hands, she deliberately reached out and laid her elegant hand directly over the tight V of his jeans. Her fingers expertly searched out the outline of his penis.

'Jesus!' In an electric reaction, he tried to sit up straight but only succeeded in spilling his drink.

'I think you'd enjoy this more if you just sat still,' Billy murmured, as she unzipped his jeans. His cock was completely limp with shock, curled on a broad mat of blond hair. Billy took a long breath of delight. She loved it like this, all soft and small. This way she could get every bit of it into her mouth with ease, and hold it there, not even tonguing it yet, just feeling it grow and grow in the wet warmth, experiencing her power without moving a muscle. Even the hair on those pouchy globes squeezed together between his legs was straw-coloured. Gently she nuzzled them, inhaling deeply the secret smell. Until a woman has smelled a man precisely there, she thought, driftingly, she can't know him. She heard the pilot moan protestingly above her questing head but paid no attention. He was recovering from his surprise, his cock beginning to twitch and grow. She cupped his balls with her free hand, her middle finger stealthily sliding and pressing upwards along the taut skin of his scrotum. Now her lips and tongue were working together around the almost erect penis, which, though fairly short, was thick, as sturdily built as the rest of him. He lay back against the edge of the bed, abandoning himself entirely to the novelty of the passive role, feeling his cock jerking and leaping with a pulsating movement as more and more blood filled it. As he grew thick and then thicker still, she shifted her mouth slightly and worked only on the swelling tip, treating it with a strong, unfaltering suction while the fingers of both her hands now slid up and down his wet, straining shaft. With a groan, unwilling to come too soon, he raised her dark head up from his lap and buried his face in her hair, kissing her beautiful neck, thinking that she was only a girl, only a girl. He lifted her on to the bed and flung his jeans to the carpet. Soon he had unbuttoned her blouse – her bare breasts were bigger than he had ever imagined them, the nipples dark and silky.

'Can you imagine how wet I've been for the last hour?' she muttered against his mouth. 'No, I don't think you can – you'll have to see for yourself – I'll just have to show you.' Billy undid her skirt in one movement; under it she was naked. She sat up and pushed him down on the bed, holding his shoulders on the sheet with the heels of her hands. She threw one knee over him and moved higher, straddling him, so that her cunt was directly over his mouth. His tongue reached out to capture it, but she kept undulating back and forth above him so that he was only able to lap at her from second to second. Finally maddened, unable to stand her teasing, he clutched her ass and pulled her down, firmly planting his mouth between the tumid, plump lips, sucking and licking and pulling and tugging blindly. She tensed, her back arched, and with a muffled scream she came, almost immediately. His cock was so hard he was afraid he might spurt into the air. Frantically he took her by the waist, pulled her down on top of it and plunged up into her savagely while she still shuddered with her own spasms.

The hours that followed never happened again, but Hank Sanders would have remembered them for the rest of his life even without the Georgian presentation box, once the property of the

Duke of Wellington, which Billy gave him late that night as she said good-bye to him back at the mansion on the hill in Bel Air.

As she walked up the wide staircase, the house seemed empty even though it was full of a dozen sleeping servants. Ellis was really and truly gone now, she thought, remembering the lusty man she had married twelve years before. When she had told Hank Sanders that Ellis would have approved of them that night, he hadn't understood, but she had been speaking the truth. If it had been she who had died, an old woman, and Ellis who had survived, a young man, he would probably have fucked the first woman he could lay hands on in private celebration of the past, a past in which they had loved each other so thoroughly. It might not be everybody's idea of a sentimental way to salute a memory, but it suited both of them perfectly. His ashes clinging to the ripe grapes, the smell of cock in her hair, the welcome soreness she felt between her legs – Ellis would have not only approved, he would have applauded.

*

A week later when Alan Wilton suggested that Valentine return to his place for a drink after dinner, she felt a sharp snap of relief. She'd seen enough movies to know that it was the classic seduction ploy. Now that he'd finally made his move, she was enchanted with herself for having waited without betraying her impatience.

When they had left his apartment earlier in the evening, he had turned off almost all the lights, and now he made no move to light them again. With endearing nervousness he poured them each a large brandy, and silently, trembling slightly, he guided Valentine's elbow with his warm hand, leading her to his bedroom. He disappeared into his bathroom and Valentine gulped the brandy quickly, kicked off her shoes, and went to stand by the window, looking out at the dark garden. Her mind refused to work. She just stared outside as if she might see something vitally important if she kept on looking long enough. Suddenly she realized that Alan was standing closely behind her, entirely naked, kissing the back of her neck, unbuttoning the tiny buttons that ran down the back of her dress. 'Lovely, lovely,' he murmured, slipping off her dress, undoing her bra, pushing down her half-slip. She tried to turn to face him, but he held her firmly with her back to him as he slid off her wisp of underpants. His fingers slowly traced the line of her backbone and her rib cage, his hands came around to clasp her breasts briefly and then returned to their delicate, deliberate celebration of her back, gradually reaching her small, firm bottom. There he lingered a long while, cupping her buttocks in his hands with hot, eager fingers, squeezing them together and then, alternately, flirting with the line that separated one from another until gradually he had worked a finger in between them for an inch or two. Valentine felt his penis rise and grow stiff against her back, but still he had said only 'lovely', repeated over and over.

Now he knelt on the floor and gently widened her stance so that her legs were parted. She felt his hot tongue tracing her ass and the sensation was so maddeningly good that she pushed against him and found herself rotating her pelvis without conscious design. Just as she felt that she couldn't stand still one minute longer without turning around, he lifted her in his arms and carried her over to the open bed. There was no light except a small bedside spot, which he turned off before he laid her down on the sheets and finally kissed her repeatedly on her open, waiting mouth.

As Valentine felt herself getting wetter she tried to clasp him close to her, exploring with her hands the well-muscled, hairy body she couldn't see. She didn't dare to touch his penis. She had never felt one in her life and she realized that she didn't know what to do – how to touch it. But his kisses were so hard, so devouring that she let herself stop worrying about whether she was responding properly. Suddenly, unmistakably, she felt him trying to turn her over on her stomach. She felt a clutch of dismay – she wanted more kisses on the mouth, her nipples ached for his lips, but she turned over obediently. He began kissing her softly down the back, but very soon he was licking and sucking her bottom, almost bruising her with the ferocity of his demanding lips, bared teeth, and strong hands, kneading her ass in an eruption of passion. She was disoriented in the dark; she wasn't sure exactly where on the bed he was, but now she realized that he was kneeling over her, his legs were holding her thighs wide apart and his hands were clasping the cheeks of her rump so that she was spread wide open. She felt the firm head of his cock thrust into the entrance of her vagina. It went in easily for an instant and then stopped as she gave a gasp of pain. He pushed again, and again she gasped. He pulled out and turned her over abruptly.

'You're not a virgin?' he whispered, horrified.

'Yes, of course.' Her virginity was so much on her mind that it had never occurred to Valentine that he wouldn't know.

'Oh, shit – no!'

'Please, please, Alan – keep on – go on – don't worry if it hurts a little – I want it,' she said urgently, as she tried to find his cock in the dark with her hands to show him that she meant her words. She heard him grinding his teeth, and suddenly, as she lay sprawled on her back in a jumble of sexual quickening, pain, and the beginnings of a huge embarrassment, she felt him shoving roughly into her with two of his fingers, like a battering ram. She bit her lip but forced herself not to cry out. When Wilton had assured himself that the passage was open all the way he turned her over on her stomach again and, with a cock that felt less firm than it had a few minutes earlier, slid into her. As he rooted and grunted inside, Valentine felt him growing stiffer, bigger, until, much too soon, with a cry of triumph that sounded like agony, he came.

Afterwards they lay silently, Valentine filled with unspoken words. She was totally confused, almost in tears. Was this how it was? Why had he not been more tender? How could he not know that she was aroused and unsatisfied? But in a minute he put his arms around her and pulled her over so that they were lying face to face.

'Darling Valentine – I know it wasn't good, but I couldn't believe – I was so surprised – forgive me – let me—' and with his fingers he played so expertly with her clitoris that she too finally came in a burst of pleasure that made her forget her questions. Of course, she thought hazily, when she came back to her sense of logic, he didn't expect a virgin – that explained everything.

The next few weeks were among the most puzzling of Valentine's life. She and Alan Wilton had dinner every second or third night and, invariably, afterwards they went back to his house and made love. Since that first time he had been much more determined to arouse her before he entered her, driving her to a pitch of sexual rapture with his lips and his fingers, but he insisted on doing everything silently and in the dark, which she found terribly frustrating. She wanted to see his naked body and she wanted him to see her. With innocent vanity Valentine knew that her very white, perfect skin and her fragile body with the dainty, uptilted breasts and the lusciously tight, firm bottom would please any man. But even worse was his evident reluctance to enter her from the front as she had always imagined a man would do. Now when he pushed his prick into her as she lay on the big bed, he raised her ass in the air with several pillows so that he could use his expert fingers to caress her clitoris in the front while he fucked her from behind, but rarely did he want to try the ordinary position that she longed for. He explained that she wouldn't feel as much that way, that it was manual stimulation that brought her to orgasm, not mere penetration, which wouldn't, in any case, stimulate her clitoris directly. But something in her demanded face-to-face confrontation, which seemed, in a symbolic way, to be a meeting of equals in the game of love.

And love it must be, she told herself, as she found herself unable to think about anything besides her rapidly growing feelings for Alan Wilton. She was not just in love; she was obsessed by him because he continued to mystify her. He treated her as one would a beloved, he showed her extraordinary consideration and admiration, he shouted her name out loud now when he came, but she didn't feel that anything between them was – settled? No, that wasn't the right word. It was some sort of deep understanding that was lacking – a *compréhension*. With all the dining and talking, all the lovemaking, she still waited to divine the true man she knew she had not yet seen in him.

As the new line of clothes neared completion, Valentine was forced to work late several nights during the last two weeks. Normally Wilton left the office at six, leaving Valentine, Sergio, and their technical helpers to continue without him when his own day was finished. One Monday, rather late, as Valentine passed his office door on her way home, she saw, with surprise, that it was slightly open and that voices, Alan's and Sergio's, were coming from it. She started to hurry by when she heard her own name. Was Sergio complaining about her, she wondered, stopping to listen. She would put nothing past him.

'. . . your dirty piece of French gash.'

'Sergio, I forbid you to talk like that!'

'You make me puke! You *forbid* me? Mr Straight forbids me! If there is anything as pathetic as a fag trying to convince himself that he can make it with a woman—'

'Listen, Sergio, just because—'

'Because what? Because you can get it up for her? Sure you can — that's no surprise. You got it up for Cindy for almost ten years, didn't you? You got it up often enough to have two kids, didn't you? But why did Cindy divorce you, Alan, you sickening hypocrite? Wasn't it because you couldn't get it up for her any more after you found out what you really wanted? Do you think that just because you do it to me instead of my doing it to you that you are any less of a fag?'

'Sergio, shut up! I admit all that shit, but it's in the past – ancient history. Valentine is different, fresh, young—'

'Christ! Will you listen to the world's biggest lying cock-sucker. Until she came along you couldn't get enough of me, could you? And just where were you last night? I seem to remember you sticking that big thing of yours up my ass until I thought I'd burst – and afterwards, who was that sucking me off and moaning and groaning – Santa Claus? It was you, you shithead – and you loved every second of it!'

'It was a lapse. It's not going to happen again – that's over.'

'Over! Sure it's over. Just look at me, Alan, look at my prick. Don't you want to put it in your mouth? Nice and juicy? Look at my ass, Alan – I'm going to bend over this chair and spread it apart, nice and open, just the way you like it. Can you tell me you aren't hard already? Can you?

'You're dying for it — it's the only thing you really want — stop kidding yourself. I'm going to lock this door and you are going to give it to me in the ass right here on the floor — every way, Alan, every way you want. Oh, the *things* you're going to do to me. Aren't you, Alan? *Aren't you?*'

Valentine only heard him gasping 'Yes, yes!' in a voice of abject, joyful surrender before she was able to break out of her trance and flee down the hall.

*

Spider suddenly scooped her up out of the chair and gently laid her on his bed. 'My love, my little love, let me be your slave — only what you want, darling, only what you want.' He was actually shaking in the shamelessness of his passion. Melanie, taken by surprise, realized that it wouldn't be easy to slip away from Spider when he was this wild. He knew she was taking the first plane tomorrow morning. It seemed simpler to let him have his way.

She lay back, offering herself docilely, while he undressed her and then hastily stripped himself naked, his graceful athlete's body a shadowy bulk against the faint light of the room. She wouldn't do a thing, she thought, not a single thing, just lie there and let him have his fun.

Spider bent tenderly over her, all his weight on his knees and his elbows, staring at her composed wide-eyed face. His heavy cock was already so hard that it was horizontal, almost flat up against his belly as he knelt. She didn't look at it. Slowly, never touching her except with his lips, he kissed her marvellous mouth, outlining her lips with the tip of his tongue as carefully as if he were creating them. When she didn't open her lips to him, he thought that she was asking him, without words, to suck her nipples. He settled back on his heels, leaned forward, and cupped a small breast softly in each hand. He paid homage to each breast in turn, rimming the nipple with his tongue until it stood up, then sucking it with his mouth for long intent minutes — the silence unbroken except for his suckling sounds. Once he whispered, 'Good? Is it good?' and she breathed quietly, 'Hmm.' After a long while Spider gently pushed Melanie's breasts together with both his hands so that the nipples were only inches apart. Holding them firmly, he darted his tongue from one to the other, now sucking, now nuzzling, now nipping her delicately with his teeth, now opening his mouth as wide as possible to take in as much of her breast as he could, the suction coming from his cheeks and throat as well as from his lips. Her breasts were wet and pink and suddenly they seemed bigger, fuller, than he'd ever felt them before. Spider hadn't felt the touch of her hands anywhere on his body; her arms were still lying at her sides. Playing virgin, he thought tenderly. But she must be ready. He slid down the bed to enter her.

'No,' she hissed. 'You said you'd be my slave. You may not put it in me – I forbid you. Absolutely. You may not!'

'Then you know what a good slave would have to do, don't you,' he said deeply in his throat, on fire at the prohibition. 'That thing you've never let me do to you – that's what you have a slave for.'

'I don't know what you mean,' she said tonelessly, giving him tacit permission.

He cupped his hands under her buttocks. She hastily laced her hands together over her pubic hair but made no protest. After searching with his tongue, Spider found a tiny space between her fingers and pushed his strong, impatient tongue through it until he reached the silky hair and the warm skin. Still she said nothing. Victoriously, he spread her knees apart, firmly grasped her wrists and pinned her hands at her sides. He slid down further on the big bed and lay flat on his pulsating penis, his head held just above her pussy. The feathers of fine hair barely covered her deliciously white and childish-looking outer lips. He covered her pubic hair with long lappings of his tongue, so that the hair grew wet. Then, using only the tip of his tongue, he traced and retraced the indentation deep between the outer lips and the pinker inner lips, folded secretly inside. Finally his tongue found the furrow between those soft inner lips and pushed upwards into her vagina. He curled and pointed his long tongue so that it was as firm as possible and plunged it in deeply.

'No! Stop. Remember your promise – no further,' she panted, beginning to wriggle away from him in earnest. Still holding her down with his hands he pulled his tongue back and sought the nub of her clitoris with his lips. It was tiny, almost hidden, but he sucked persistently on it once he had found it, stopping only to slowly rub his tongue back and forth across it several times before he resumed sucking. As he sucked he found that rhythmically, unconsciously, he was rubbing his hugely engorged penis on the sheets that covered the bed. Suddenly the silent girl started to make lunging movements towards his mouth as if she wanted him to take her whole pussy in his mouth at once. She pushed it in his face with total abandon, grunting, 'Don't put your cock in — whatever you do — keep your promise, slave.' As he sucked and licked frantically, increasing the pace, he heard her moaning and muted ferocity, as if she could hardly keep from screaming out loud. He forgot his own self so completely that it seemed as if all the world contained was this wide-open cunt, which he was not allowed to enter, only to pleasure. Suddenly she went very still, all her muscles rigid. Finally she was shaken by contractions and she shouted. As he felt this climax, Spider's cock had been excited beyond endurance from the friction of the sheets as he worked on her. He felt himself shooting sperm convulsively, over the bed, unable to hold back another second.

They fell apart, exhausted, as their orgasms subsided. After a minute Spider, still lying face down on the bed, felt her stir. 'Don't move — I'm just going to the bathroom.' She slipped away as he lay there, too happy and too drained to look after her. She's finally made it, he thought, finally, finally. So that's what she'd wanted all along. What a shy, repressed silly darling, afraid to do the thing that delighted her beyond all else — next time I'll know what she really wants — and I'll give it to her, and give it— His thoughts trailed off into a short sleep.

When he woke up she was gone.

From *Scruples* by Judith Krantz, 1978

How the French Do It

Really dirty, and really French. Quite scary, frankly, at the time. Suddenly, the longed-for French exchange over the summer holidays felt a bit alarming. Were they all like that, the whole nation? (I think the answer to that one is quite possibly 'yes'.)

*W*henever I left the sculptor's studio, I would always stop in a coffee shop nearby and ponder all that Millard had told me. I wondered whether anything like this were happening around me, here in Greenwich Village, for instance. I began to love posing, for the adventurous aspect of it. I decided to attend a party one Saturday evening that a painter named Brown had invited me to. I was hungry and curious about everything.

I rented an evening dress from the costume department of the Art Model Club, with an evening cape and shoes. Two of the models came with me, a red-haired girl, Mollie, and a statuesque one, Ethel, who was the favorite of the sculptors.

What was passing through my head all the time were the stories of Montparnasse life told to me by the sculptor, and now I felt that I was entering this realm. My first disappointment was seeing that the studio was quite poor and bare, the two couches without pillows, the lighting crude, with none of the trappings I had imagined necessary for a party.

Bottles were on the floor, along with glasses and chipped cups. A ladder led to a balcony where Brown kept his paintings. A thin curtain concealed the washstand and a little gas stove. At the front of the room was an erotic painting of a woman being possessed by two men. She was in a state of convulsion, her body arched, her eyes showing the whites. The men were covering her, one with his penis inside of her and the other with his penis in her mouth. It was a life-size painting and very bestial. Everyone was looking at it, admiring it. I was fascinated. It was the first picture of the sort I had seen, and it gave me a tremendous shock of mixed feelings.

Next to it stood another which was even more striking. It showed a poorly furnished room, filled by a big iron bed. Sitting on this bed was a man of about forty or so, in old clothes, with an unshaved face, a slobbering mouth, loose eyelids, loose jaws, a completely degenerate expression. He had taken his pants down halfway, and on his bare knees sat a little girl with very short skirts, to whom he was feeding a bar of candy. Her little bare legs rested on his bare hairy ones.

What I felt after seeing these two paintings was what one feels when drinking, a sudden dizziness of the head, a warmth through the body, a confusion of the senses. Something awakens in the body, foggy and dim, a new sensation, a new kind of hunger and restlessness.

I looked at the other people in the room. But they had seen so much of this that it did not affect them. They laughed and commented.

One model was talking about her experiences at an underwear shop:

'I had answered an advertisement for a model to pose in underwear for sketches. I had done this many times before and was paid the normal price of a dollar an hour. Usually several artists sketched me at the same time, and there were many people around – secretaries, stereographers, errand boys. This time the place was empty. It was just an office with a desk, files and drawing materials. A man sat waiting for me in front of his drawing board. I was given a pile of underwear and found a screen placed where I could change. I began by wearing a slip. I posed for fifteen minutes at a time while he made sketches.

'We worked quietly. When he gave the signal, I went behind the screen and changed. They were satin underthings of lovely designs, with lace tops and fine embroidery. I wore a brassière and panties. The man smoked and sketched. At the bottom of the pile were panties and a brassière made entirely of black lace. I had posed in the nude often and did not mind wearing these. They were quite beautiful.

'I looked out of the window most of the time, not at the man sketching. After a while I did not hear the pencil working any longer and I turned slightly towards him, not wanting to lose the pose. He was sitting there behind his drawing board staring at me. Then I realized that he had his penis out and that he was in a kind of trance.

'Thinking this would mean trouble for me since we were alone in the office, I started to go behind the screen and dress.

'He said, "Don't go. I won't touch you. I just love to see women in lovely underwear. I won't move from here. And if you want me to pay you more, all you have to do is wear my favorite piece of underwear and pose for fifteen minutes. I will give you five dollars more. You can reach for it yourself. It is right above your head on the shelf there."

'Well, I did reach for the package. It was the loveliest piece of underwear you ever saw – the finest black lace, like a spider web really, and the panties were slit back and front, slit and edged with fine lace. The brassière was cut in such a way as to expose the nipples through triangles. I hesitated because I was wondering if this would not excite the man too much, if he would attack me.

'He said, "Don't worry. I don't really like women. I never touch them. I like only underwear. I just like to see women in lovely underwear. If I tried to touch you I would immediately become impotent. I won't move from here."

'He put aside the drawing board and sat there with his penis out. Now and then it shook. But he did not move from his chair.

'I decided to put on the underwear. The five dollars tempted me. He was not very strong and I felt that I could defend myself. So I stood there in the slit panties, turning around for him to see me on all sides.

'Then he said, "That's enough." He seemed unsettled and his face was congested. He told me to dress quickly and leave. He handed me the money in a great hurry, and I left. I had a feeling that he was only waiting for me to leave to masturbate.

'I have known men like this, who steal a shoe from someone, from an attractive woman, so they can hold it and masturbate while looking at it.'

Everyone was laughing at her story. 'I think,' said Brown, 'that when we are children we are much more inclined to be fetishists of one kind or another. I remember hiding inside my mother's closet and feeling ecstasy at smelling her clothes and feeling them. Even today I cannot resist a woman who is wearing a veil or tulle or feathers, because it awakens the strange feelings I had in that closet.'

As he said this I remembered how I hid in the closet of a young man when I was only thirteen, for the same reason. He was twenty-five and he treated me like a little girl. I was in love with him. Sitting next to him in a car in which he took all of us for long rides, I was ecstatic just feeling his leg alongside mine. At night I would get into bed and, after turning out the light, take out a can of condensed milk in which I had punctured a little hole. I would sit in the dark sucking at the sweet milk with a voluptuous feeling all over my body that I could not explain. I thought then that being in love and sucking at the sweet milk were related. Much later I remembered this when I tasted sperm for the first time.

Mollie remembered that at the same age she liked to eat ginger while she smelled camphor balls. The ginger made her body feel warm and languid and the camphor balls made her a little dizzy. She would get herself in a sort of drugged state this way, lying there for hours.

Ethel turned to me and said, 'I hope you never marry a man you don't love sexually. That is what I have done. I love everything about him, the way he behaves, his face, his body, the way he works, treats me, his thoughts, his way of smiling, talking, everything except the sexual man in him. I thought I did, before we married. There is absolutely nothing wrong with him. He is a perfect lover.

He is emotional and romantic, he shows great feeling and great enjoyment. He is sensitive and adoring. Last night while I was asleep he came into my bed. I was half-asleep so I could not control myself, as I usually do, because I do not want to hurt his feelings. He got in beside me and began to take me very slowly and lingeringly. Usually it is all over quickly, which makes it possible to bear. I do not even let him kiss me if I can help it. I hate his mouth on mine. I usually turn my face away, which is what I did last night. Well, there he was, and what do you think I did? I suddenly began to strike him with my closed fists, on the shoulder, while he was enjoying himself, to dig my nails into him, and he took it as a sign that I was enjoying it, growing rather wild with pleasure, and he went on. Then I whispered as low as I could, "I hate you." And then I asked myself if he had heard me. What would he think? Was he hurt? As he was himself partly asleep, he merely kissed me good night when it was over and went back to his bed. The next morning I was waiting for what he would say. I still thought perhaps he had heard me say, "I hate you." But no, I must have formed the words without saying them. And all he said was, "You got quite wild last night, you know," and smiled, as if it pleased him.'

Brown started the phonograph and we began to dance. The little alcohol I had taken had gone to my head. I felt a dilation of the whole universe. Everything seemed very smooth and simple. Everything, in fact, ran downward like a snowy hill on which I could slide without effort. I felt a great friendliness, as if I knew all these people intimately. But I chose the most timid of the painters to dance with. I felt that he was pretending somewhat, as I was, to be very familiar with all of this. I felt that deep down he was a little uneasy. The other painters were caressing Ethel and Mollie as they danced. This one did not dare. I was laughing to myself at having discovered him. Brown saw that my painter was not making any advances, and he cut in for a dance. He was making sly remarks about virgins. I wondered whether he was alluding to me. How could he know? He pressed against me, and I drew away from him. I went back to the timid young painter. A woman illustrator was flirting with him, teasing him. He was equally glad that I came back

to him. So we danced together, retreating into our own timidity.
All around us people were kissing now, embracing.

The woman illustrator had thrown off her blouse and was dancing in her slip. The timid painter said, 'If we stay here we will soon
have to lie on the floor and make love. Do you want to leave?'

'Yes, I want to leave,' I said.

We went out. Instead of making love, he was talking, talking. I
was listening to him in a daze. He had a plan for a picture of me. He
wanted to paint me as an undersea woman, nebulous, transparent,
green, watery except for the very red mouth and the very red
flower I was wearing in my hair. Would I pose for him? I did not
respond very quickly because of the effects of the liquor, and he said
apologetically, 'Are you sorry that I was not brutal?'

'No, I'm not sorry. I chose you myself because I knew you would
not be.'

'It's my first party,' he said humbly, 'and you're not the kind of
woman one can treat – that way. How did you ever become a
model? What did you do before this? A model does not have to be a
prostitute, I know, but she has to bear a lot of handling and
attempts.'

'I manage quite well,' I said, not enjoying this conversation at all.

'I will be worrying about you. I know some artists are objective
while they work, I know all that. I feel that way myself. But there is
always a moment before and after, when the model is undressing
and dressing, that does disturb me. It's the first surprise of seeing the
body. What did you feel the first time?'

'Nothing at all. I felt as if I were a painting already. Or a statue. I
looked down at my own body like some object, some impersonal
object.'

I was growing sad, sad with restlessness and hunger. I felt that nothing would happen to me. I felt desperate with desire to be a woman,
to plunge into living. Why was I enslaved by this need of being in
love first? Where would my life begin? I would enter each studio
expecting a miracle which did not take place. It seemed to me that
a great current was passing all around me and that I was left out. I

would have to find someone who felt as I did. But where? Where?

The sculptor was watched by his wife, I could see that. She came into the studio so often, unexpectedly. And he was frightened. I did not know what frightened him. They invited me to spend two weeks at their country house where I would continue to pose – or rather, she invited me. She said that her husband did not like to stop work during vacations. But as soon as she left he turned to me and said, 'You must find an excuse not to go. She will make you miserable. She is not well – she has obsessions. She thinks that every woman who poses for me is my mistress.'

There were hectic days of running from studio to studio with very little time for lunch, posing for magazine covers, illustrations for magazine stories, and advertisements. I could see my face everywhere, even in the subway. I wondered if people recognized me.

The sculptor had become my best friend. I was anxiously watching his statuette coming to a finish. Then one morning when I arrived I saw that he had ruined it. He said that he had tried to work on it without me. But he did not seem unhappy or worried. I was quite sad, and to me it looked very much like sabotage, because it seemed spoiled with such awkwardness. I saw that he was happy to be beginning it all over again.

It was at the theater that I met John and discovered the power of a voice. It rolled over me like the tones of a pipe organ, making me vibrate. When he repeated my name and mispronounced it, it sounded to me like a caress. It was the deepest, richest voice I had ever heard. I could scarcely look at him. I knew that his eyes were big, of an intense, magnetic blue, that he was large, rather restless. His foot moved nervously like that of a racehorse. I felt his presence blurring everything else – the theater, the friend sitting at my right. And he behaved as if I had enchanted him, hypnotized him. He talked on, looking at me, but I was not listening. In one moment I was no longer a young girl. Every time he spoke, I felt myself falling into some dizzy spiral, falling into the meshes of a beautiful voice. It was truly a drug. When he had finally 'stolen' me, as he said, he hailed a taxi.

We did not say another word until we reached his apartment. He had not touched me. He did not need to. His presence had affected me in such a way that I felt as if he had caressed me for a long time.

He merely said my name twice, as if he thought it sufficiently beautiful to repeat. He was tall, glowing. His eyes were so intensely blue that when they blinked, for a second it was like some tiny flash of lightning, giving one a sense of fear, a fear of a storm that would completely engulf one.

Then he kissed me. His tongue went around mine, around and around, and then it stopped to touch the tip only. As he kissed me he slowly lifted my skirt. He unrolled my garters, my stockings. Then he lifted me up and carried me to the bed. I was so dissolved that I felt he had already penetrated me. It seemed to me that his voice had opened me, opened my whole body to him. He sensed this, and so he was amazed by the resistance to his penis that he felt.

He stopped to look at my face. He saw the great emotional receptiveness, and then he pressed harder. I felt the tear and the pain, but the warmth melted everything, the warmth of his voice in my ear saying, 'Do you want me as I want you?'

Then his pleasure made him groan. His whole weight upon me, pressing against my body, the shaft of pain vanished. I felt the joy of being opened. I lay there in a semidream.

John said, 'I hurt you. You did not enjoy it.' I could not say, 'I want it again.' My hand touched his penis. I caressed it. It sprung up, so hard. He kissed me until I felt a new wave of desire, a desire to respond completely. But he said, 'It will hurt now. Wait a little while. Can you stay with me, all night? Will you stay?'

I saw that there was blood on my leg. I went to wash it off. I felt that I had not been taken yet, that this was only a small part of the breaking through. I wanted to be possessed and know blinding joys. I walked unsteadily and fell on the bed again.

John was asleep, his big body still curved as when he was lying against me, his arm thrown out where my head had been resting. I slipped in at his side and fell half-asleep. I wanted to touch his penis again. I did so gently, not wanting to wake him. Then I slept and was awakened by his kisses. We were floating in a dark world of flesh, feeling only the soft flesh vibrating, and every touch was a joy. He gripped my hips tautly against him. He was afraid to wound me. I parted my legs. When he inserted his penis it hurt, but the pleasure was greater. There was a little outer rim of pain and, deeper in, a pleasure at the presence of his penis moving there. I pressed forwards, to meet it.

This time he was passive. He said, 'You move, you enjoy it now.' So as not to feel the pain, I moved gently around his penis. I put my closed fists under my backside to raise myself toward him. He placed my legs on his shoulders. Then the pain grew greater and he withdrew.

I left him in the morning, dazed, but with a new joy of feeling that I was growing nearer to passion. I went home and slept until he telephoned.

'When are you coming?' he said. 'I must see you again. Soon. Are you posing today?'

'Yes, I must. I'll come after the pose.'

'Please don't pose,' he said, 'please don't pose. It makes me desperate to think of it. Come and see me first. I want to talk to you. Please come and see me first.'

I went to him. 'Oh,' he said, burning my face with the breath of his desire. 'I can't bear to think of you posing now, exposing yourself. You can't do that anymore. You must let me take care of you. I cannot marry you because I have a wife and children. Let me take care of you until we know how we can escape. Let me get a little place where I can come and see you. You should not be posing. You belong to me.'

So I entered a secret life, and when I was supposed to be posing for everyone else in the world, I was really waiting in a beautiful room for John. Each time he came, he brought a gift, a book, colored stationery for me to write on. I was restless, waiting.

The only one who was taken into the secret was the sculptor because he sensed what was happening. He would not let me stop posing, and he questioned me. He had predicted how my life would be.

The first time I felt an orgasm with John, I wept because it was so strong and so marvelous that I did not believe it could happen over and over again. The only painful moments were the ones spent waiting. I would bathe myself, spread polish on my nails, perfume myself, rouge my nipples, brush my hair, put on a negligée, and all the preparations would turn my imagination to the scenes to come.

I wanted him to find me in the bath. He would say he was on his way. But he would not arrive. He was often detained. By the time he arrived I would be cold, resentful. The waiting wore out my feelings. I would rebel. Once I would not answer when he rang the doorbell. Then he knocked gently, humbly, and that touched me, so I opened the door. But I was angry and wanted to hurt him. I did not respond to his kiss. He was hurt until his hand slipped under my negligée and he found that I was wet, in spite of the fact that I kept my legs tightly closed. He was joyous again and he forced his way.

Then I punished him by not responding sexually and he was hurt again, for he enjoyed my pleasure. He knew by the violent heartbeats, by the changes in the voice, by the contraction of my legs, how I had enjoyed him. And this time I lay like a whore. That really hurt him.

We could never go out together. He was too well known, as was his wife. He was a producer. His wife was a playwright.

When John discovered how angry it would make me to wait for him, he did not try to remedy it. He came later and later. He would say that he was arriving at ten o'clock and then come at midnight. So one day he found that I was not there when he came. This put him in a frenzy. He thought I would not come back. I felt that he was doing this deliberately, that he liked my being angry. After two days he pleaded with me and I returned. We were both very keyed up and angry.

He said, 'You've gone back to pose. You like it. You like to show yourself.'

'Why do you make me wait so long? You know that it kills my desire for you. I feel cold when you come late.'

'Not so very cold,' he said.

I closed my legs tightly against him, he could not even touch me. But then he slipped in quickly from behind and caressed me. 'Not so cold,' he said.

On the bed he pushed his knee between my legs and forced them open. 'When you are angry,' he said, 'I feel that I am raping you. I feel then that you love me so much you cannot resist me, I see that you are wet, and I like your resistance and your defeat too.'

'John, you will make me so angry that I will leave you.'

Then he was frightened. He kissed me. He promised not to repeat this.

What I could not understand was that, despite our quarrels, being made love to by John made me only more sensitive. He had awakened my body. Now I had even a greater desire to abandon myself to all whims. He must have known this because the more he caressed me, awakened me, the more he feared that I would return to posing. Slowly, I did return. I had too much time to myself, I was too much alone with my thoughts of John.

Millard particularly was happy to see me. He must have spoiled the statuette again, purposely I knew now, so he could keep me in the pose he liked.

The night before, he had smoked marijuana with friends. He said, 'Did you know that very often it gives people the feeling that they are transformed into animals? Last night there was a woman who was completely taken by this transformation. She fell on her hands and knees and walked around like a dog. We took her clothes off. She wanted to give milk. She wanted us to act like puppies, sprawl on the floor and suckle at her breasts. She kept on her hands and knees and offered her breasts to all of us. She wanted us to walk like dogs – after her. She insisted on our taking her in this position, from behind, and I did, but then I was terribly tempted to bite her as I crouched over her. I bit into her shoulder harder than I have ever bitten anyone. The woman did not get frightened. I did. It sobered me. I stood up and then saw that a friend of mine was fol- lowing her on his hands and knees, not caressing her or taking her, but merely smelling exactly as a dog would do, and this reminded me so much of my first sexual impression that it gave me a painful hard-on.

'As children we had a big servant girl in the country who came from Martinique. She wore voluminous skirts and a colored kerchief on her head. She was a rather pale mulatto, very beautiful. She would make us play hide-and-seek. When it was my turn to hide she would hide me under her skirt, sitting down. And there I was, half-suffocated, hiding between her legs. I remember the sexual odor that came from her and that stirred me even as a boy. Once I tried to touch her but she slapped my hand.'

I was posing quietly and he came over to measure me with an instrument. Then I felt his hand on my thighs, caressing me so lightly. I smiled at him. I stood on the model's stand, and he was caressing my legs now, as if he were modeling me out of clay. He kissed my feet, he ran his hands up my legs again and again, and around my ass. He leaned against my legs and kissed me. He lifted me up and brought me down to the floor. He held me tightly against him, caressing my back and shoulders and neck. I shivered a little. His hands were smooth and supple. He touched me as he touched the statuette, so caressingly, all over.

Then we walked towards the couch. He lay me there on my stomach. He took his clothes off and fell on me. I felt his penis against my ass. He slipped his hands around my waist and lifted me up slightly so that he could penetrate me. He lifted me up toward him rhythmically. I closed my eyes to feel him better and to listen to the sound of the penis sliding in and out of the moisture. He pushed so violently that it made tiny clicks, which delighted me.

His fingers dug into my flesh. His nails were sharp and hurt. He aroused me so much with his vigorous thrusts that my mouth opened and I was biting into the couch cover. Then at the same time we both heard a sound. Millard rose swiftly, picked up his clothes and ran up the ladder to the balcony where he kept his sculpture. I slipped behind the screen.

There came a second knock on the studio door, and his wife came in. I was trembling, not with fear, but the shock of having stopped in the middle of our enjoyment. Millard's wife saw the studio empty and left. Millard came out dressed. I said, 'Wait for me a minute,' and began to dress too. The moment was destroyed. I was still wet and shivering. When I slipped on my panties the silk touch affected me like a hand. I could not bear the tension and desire any longer. I put my two hands over my sex as Millard had done and pressed against it, closing my eyes and imagining Millard was caressing me. And I came, shaking from head to foot.

Millard wanted to be with me again, but not in his studio where we might be surprised by his wife, so I let him find another place. It belonged to a friend. The bed was set in a deep alcove and there were mirrors above the bed and small dim lamps. Millard wanted all the lights out, he said he wanted to be in the dark with me.

'I have seen your body and I know it so well, now I want to feel it, with my eyes closed, just to feel the skin and the softness of the flesh. Your legs are so firm and strong, but so soft to the touch. I love your feet with the toes free and set apart like the fingers of a hand, not cramped – and the toenails so beautifully lacquered and the down on your legs.' He passed his hand all over my body, slowly, pressing into the flesh, feeling every curve. 'If my hand stays here between the legs,' he said, 'do you feel it, do you like it, do you want it nearer?'

'Nearer, nearer,' I said.

'I want to teach you something,' said Millard. 'Do you want to let me do it?'

He inserted his finger inside my sex. 'Now, I want you to contract around my finger. There is a muscle there that can be made to contract and expand around the penis. Try.'

I tried. His finger there was tantalizing. Since he was not moving it, I tried to move inside of my womb, and I felt the muscle that he mentioned, weakly at first, opening and closing around the finger.

Millard said, 'Yes, like that. Do it stronger, stronger.'

So I did, opening, closing, opening, closing. It was like a little mouth inside, tightening around the finger. I wanted to take it in, suckle at it, so I continued to try.

Then Millard said that he would insert his penis and not move and that I should continue to move inside. I tried with more and more strength to clutch at him. The motion was exciting me, and I felt that at any moment I would reach the orgasm, but after I had clutched at him several times, sucking his penis in, he suddenly groaned with pleasure and began to push quickly, as he himself could not hold back the orgasm. I merely continued the inner motion and I felt the orgasm, too, in the most marvelous deep way, deep inside of the womb.

He said, 'Did John ever show you this?'

'No.'

'What has he shown you?'

'This,' I said. 'You kneel over me and push.'

Millard obeyed. His penis did not have much strength, for it was too soon after the first orgasm, but he slipped it in, pushing it with his hand. Then I reached out with my two hands and caressed the balls and put two fingers at the base of the penis and rubbed as he moved. Millard was instantly aroused, his penis hardened, and he began to move in and out again. Then he stopped himself.

'I must not be so demanding,' he said in a strange tone. 'You will be tired out for John.'

We lay back and rested, smoking. I was wondering if Millard had felt more than sensual desire, whether my love for John weighed on him. But although there was always a hurt sound to his words, he continued to ask me questions.

'Did John have you today? Did he take you more than once? How did he take you?'

In the weeks to come, Millard taught me many things I had not done with John, and as soon as I learned them I tried them with John. Finally he became suspicious of where I was learning new positions. He knew I had not made love before I met him. The first time I tightened my muscles to clutch at the penis, he was amazed.

The two secret relationships became difficult for me, but I enjoyed the danger and the intensity.

From *Delta of Venus* by Anaïs Nin, 1969

In the Classroom

Hot. Just hot. Unexpectedly enough.

ACT I
SCENE I. Alexandria. A room in CLEOPATRA's palace.

Enter DEMETRIUS *and* PHILO

PHILO
Nay, but this dotage of our general's
O'erflows the measure: those his goodly eyes,
That o'er the files and musters of the war
Have glow'd like plated Mars, now bend, now turn,
The office and devotion of their view
Upon a tawny front: his captain's heart,
Which in the scuffles of great fights hath burst
The buckles on his breast, reneagues all temper,
And is become the bellows, and the fan,
To cool a gipsy's lust. Look, where they come.

Flourish. Enter ANTONY *and* CLEOPATRA *with their Trains; Eunuchs fanning her.*

Take but good note, and you shall see in him
The triple pillar of the world transform'd
Into a strumpet's fool: behold and see.

CLEOPATRA
If it be love indeed, tell me how much.

MARK ANTONY
There's beggary in the love that can be reckon'd.

CLEOPATRA
I'll set a bourn how far to be beloved.

MARK ANTONY
Then must thou needs find out new heaven, new earth.

Enter an Attendant

ATTENDANT
News, my good lord, from Rome.

MARK ANTONY
Grates me: the sum.

CLEOPATRA
Nay, hear them, Antony:
Fulvia, perchance, is angry; or, who knows
If the scarce-bearded Caesar have not sent
His powerful mandate to you, 'Do this, or this;
Take in that kingdom, and enfranchise that;
Perform 't, or else we damn thee.'

MARK ANTONY
How, my love!

CLEOPATRA
Perchance! nay, and most like,
You must not stay here longer, your dismission
Is come from Caesar; therefore hear it, Antony.
Where's Fulvia's process? Caesar's, I would say? both?

Call in the messengers. As I am Egypt's queen,
Thou blushest, Antony; and that blood of thine
Is Caesar's homager; else so thy cheek pays shame,
When shrill-tongu'd Fulvia scolds. The messengers!

MARK ANTONY
Let Rome in, Tiber melt, and the wide arch
Of the rang'd empire fall! Here is my space.
Kingdoms are clay; our dungy earth alike
Feeds beast as man: the nobleness of life
Is, to do thus; when such a mutual pair

Embracing

And such a twain can do't, in which I bind,
On pain of punishment, the world to weet,
We stand up peerless.

CLEOPATRA
Excellent falsehood!
Why did he marry Fulvia, and not love her?
I'll seem the fool I am not; Antony
Will be himself.

MARK ANTONY
But stirr'd by Cleopatra.
Now, for the love of Love and her soft hours,
Let's not confound the time with conference harsh:
There's not a minute of our lives should stretch
Without some pleasure now. What sport to-night?

CLEOPATRA
Hear the ambassadors.

MARK ANTONY
Fie, wrangling queen!
Whom everything becomes, to chide, to laugh,

To weep; whose every passion fully strives
To make itself, in thee, fair and admir'd.
No messenger; but thine, and all alone,
To-night we'll wander through the streets, and note
The qualities of people. Come, my queen;
Last night you did desire it. Speak not to us.

Exeunt ANTONY *and* CLEOPATRA *with their Train.*

––––––––––

From *Antony and Cleopatra* by William Shakespeare, 1623

The Zipless Fuck

An interesting one, because even though you were flicking through the book in a hurry, the narrative voice was so captivating and interesting that you'd find yourself veering willingly from the quest for smut, able, for a moment or two, to actually digest the words and think about what she was saying. And what she was saying was quite thought-provoking: cue embryonic feminist stirrings, as well as the usual ones.

*W*hat *was* it about marriage anyway? Even if you loved your husband, there came that inevitable year when fucking him turned as bland as Velveeta cheese: filling, fattening even, but no thrill to the taste buds, no bittersweet edge, no danger. And you longed for an overripe Camembert, a rare goat cheese: luscious, creamy, cloven-hoofed.

I was not against marriage. I believed in it in fact. It was necessary to have one best friend in a hostile world, one person you'd be loyal to no matter what, one person who'd always be loyal to you. But what about all those other longings which after a while marriage did nothing much to appease? The restlessness, the hunger, the thump in the gut, the thump in the cunt, the longing to be filled up, to be fucked through every hole, the yearning for dry champagne and wet kisses, for the smell of peonies in a penthouse on a June night, for the light at the end of the pier in *Gatsby* . . . Not those *things* really — because you knew that the very rich were duller than you and me – but what those things *evoked*. The sardonic, bittersweet vocabulary of Cole Porter love songs, the sad sentimental Rodgers and Hart lyrics, all the romantic nonsense you yearned for with half your heart and mocked bitterly with the other half.

Growing up female in America. What a liability! You grew up with your ears full of cosmetic ads, love songs, advice columns, whoreoscopes, Hollywood gossip, and moral dilemmas on the level of TV soap operas. What litanies the advertisers of the good life chanted at you! What curious catechisms!

'Be kind to your behind.' 'Blush like you mean it.' 'Love your hair.' 'Want a better body? We'll rearrange the one you've got.' 'That shine on your face should come from him, not from your skin.' 'You've come a long way, baby.' 'How to score with every male in the zodiac.' 'The stars and sensual you.' 'To a man they say Cutty Sark.' 'A diamond is forever.' 'If you're concerned about douching . . .' 'Length and coolness come together.' 'How I solved my intimate odor problem.' 'Lady be cool.' 'Every woman alive loves Chanel No. 5.' 'What makes a shy girl get intimate?' '*Femme*, we named it after you.'

What all the ads and all the whoreoscopes seemed to imply was that if only you were narcissistic *enough*, if only you took proper care of your smells, your hair, your boobs, your eyelashes, your armpits, your crotch, your stars, your scars, and your choice of Scotch in bars – you would meet a beautiful, powerful, potent, and rich man who would satisfy every longing, fill every hole, make your heart skip a beat (or stand still), make you misty, and fly you to the moon (preferably on gossamer wings), where you would live totally satisfied forever.

And the crazy part of it was that even if you were *clever*, even if you spent your adolescence reading John Donne and Shaw, even if you studied history or zoology or physics and hoped to spend your life pursuing some difficult and challenging career – you *still* had a mind full of all the soupy longings that every high-school girl was awash in. It didn't matter, you see, whether you had an IQ of 170 or an IQ of 70, you were brainwashed all the same. Only the surface trappings were different. Only the *talk* was a little more sophisticated.

Underneath it all, you longed to be annihilated by love, to be swept off your feet, to be filled up by a giant prick spouting sperm, soap-suds, silks and satins, and of course, money. Nobody bothered to tell you what marriage was really about. You weren't even provided, like European girls, with a philosophy of cynicism and practicality. You expected *not* to desire any other men after marriage. And you expected your husband not to desire any other women. Then the desires came and you were thrown into a panic of self-hatred. What an evil woman you were! How could you keep being infatuated with strange men? How could you study their bulging trousers like that? How could you sit at a meeting imagining how every man in the room would screw? How could you sit on a train fucking total strangers with your eyes? How could you *do* that to your husband? Did anyone ever tell you that maybe it had nothing whatever to do with your husband?

And what about those other longings which marriage stifled? Those longings to hit the open road from time to time, to discover whether you could still live alone inside your own head, to dis-cover whether you could manage to survive in a cabin in the woods without going mad; to discover, in short, whether you were still whole after so many years of being half of something (like the back two legs of a horse outfit on the vaudeville stage).

Five years of marriage had made me itchy for all those things: itchy for men, and itchy for solitude. Itchy for sex and itchy for the life of a recluse. I knew my itches were contradictory – and that made things even worse. I knew my itches were un-American – and that made things *still* worse. It is heresy in America to embrace any way of life except as half of a couple. Solitude is un-American. It may be condoned in a man – especially if he is a 'glamorous bache-lor' who 'dates starlets' during a brief interval between marriages. But a woman is always presumed to be alone as a result of aban-donment, not choice. And she is treated that way: as a pariah. There is simply no dignified way for a woman to live alone. Oh, she can get along financially perhaps (though not nearly as well as a man), but emotionally she is never left in peace. Her friends, her family, her fellow workers never let her forget that her husbandlessness, her childlessness — her *selfishness*, in short — is a reproach to the American way of life.

Even more to the point: the woman (unhappy though she knows her married friends to be) can never let *herself* alone. She lives as if she were constantly on the brink of some great fulfillment. As if she were waiting for Prince Charming to take her away 'from all this.' All what? The solitude of living inside her own soul? The certainty of being herself instead of half of something else?

My response to all this was not (not yet) to have an affair and not (not yet) to hit the open road, but to evolve my fantasy of the Zipless Fuck. The zipless fuck was more than a fuck. It was a platonic ideal. Zipless because when you came together zippers fell away like rose petals, underwear blew off in one breath like dandelion fluff. Tongues intertwined and turned liquid. Your whole soul flowed out through your tongue and into the mouth of your lover.

For the true, ultimate zipless A-1 fuck, it was necessary that you never get to know the man very well. I had noticed, for example, how all my infatuations dissolved as soon as I really became friends with a man, became sympathetic to his problems, listened to him *kvetch* about his wife, or ex-wives, his mother, his children. After that I would like him, perhaps even love him — but without passion. And it was passion that I wanted. I had also learned that a sure way to exorcise an infatuation was to write about someone, to observe his tics and twitches, to anatomize his personality in type. After that he was an insect on a pin, a newspaper clipping laminated in plastic. I might enjoy his company, even admire him at moments, but he no longer had the power to make me wake up trembling in the middle of the night. I no longer dreamed about him. He had a face.

So another condition for the zipless fuck was brevity. And anonymity made it even better.

During the time I lived in Heidelberg I commuted to Frankfurt four times a week to see my analyst. The ride took an hour each way and trains became an important part of my fantasy life. I kept meeting beautiful men on the train, men who scarcely spoke English, men whose clichés and banalities were hidden by my ignorance of

French, or Italian, or even German. Much as I hate to admit it, there are *some* beautiful men in Germany.

One scenario of the zipless fuck was perhaps inspired by an Italian movie I saw years ago. As time went by, I embellished it to suit my head. It used to play over and over again as I shuttled back and forth from Heidelberg to Frankfurt, from Frankfurt to Heidelberg:

A grimy European train compartment (Second Class). The seats are leatherette and hard. There is a sliding door to the corridor outside. Olive trees rush by the window. Two Sicilian peasant women sit together on one side with a child between them. They appear to be mother and grandmother and granddaughter. Both women vie with each other to stuff the little girl's mouth with food. Across the way (in the window seat) is a pretty young widow in a heavy black veil and tight black dress which reveals her voluptuous figure. She is sweating profusely and her eyes are puffy. The middle seat is empty. The corridor seat is occupied by an enormously fat woman with a moustache. Her huge haunches cause her to occupy almost half of the vacant center seat. She is reading a pulp romance in which the characters are photographed models and the dialogue appears in little puffs of smoke above their heads.

This fivesome bounces along for a while, the widow and the fat woman keeping silent, the mother and grandmother talking to the child and each other about the food. And then the train screeches to a halt in a town called (perhaps) CORLEONE. A tall languid-looking soldier, unshaven, but with a beautiful mop of hair, a cleft chin, and somewhat devilish, lazy eyes, enters the compartment, looks insolently around, sees the empty half-seat between the fat woman and the widow, and with many flirtatious apologies, sits down. He is sweaty and disheveled but basically a gorgeous hunk of flesh, only slightly rancid from the heat. The train screeches out of the station.

Then we become aware only of the bouncing of the train and the rhythmic way the soldier's thighs are rubbing against the thighs of the widow. Of course, he is also rubbing against the haunches of the fat lady — and she is trying to move away from him — which is quite unnecessary because he is unaware of her haunches. He is watching the large gold cross between the widow's breasts swing back and forth in her deep cleavage. Bump. Pause. Bump. It hits one moist breast and then the other. It seems to hesitate in between as if paralyzed between two repelling magnets. The pit and the pendulum. He is hypnotized. She stares out the window, looking at each olive tree as if she had never seen olive trees before. He rises awkwardly, half-bows to the ladies, and struggles to open the window. When he sits down again his arm accidentally grazes the widow's belly. She appears not to notice. He rests his left hand on the seat between his thigh and hers and begins to wind rubber fingers around and under the soft flesh of her thigh. She continues staring at each olive tree as if she were God and had just made them and were wondering what to call them.

Meanwhile the enormously fat lady is packing away her pulp romance in an iridescent green plastic string bag full of smelly cheeses and blackening bananas. And the grandmother is rolling ends of salami in greasy newspaper. The mother is putting on the little girl's sweater and wiping her face with a handkerchief, lovingly moistened with maternal spittle. The train screeches to a stop in a town called (perhaps) PRIZZI, and the fat lady, the mother, the grandmother, and the little girl leave the compartment. Then the train begins to move again. The gold cross begins to bump, pause, bump between the widow's moist breasts, the fingers begin to curl under the widow's thighs, the widow continues to stare at the olive trees. Then the fingers are sliding between her thighs and they are parting her thighs, and they are moving upward into the fleshy gap between her heavy black stockings and her garters, and they are sliding up under her garters into the damp unpantied place between her legs.

The train enters a *galleria*, or tunnel, and in the semidarkness the symbolism is consummated. There is the soldier's boot in the air and the dark walls of the tunnel and the hypnotic rocking of the train and the long high whistle as it finally emerges.

Wordlessly, she gets off at a town called, perhaps, BIVONA. She crosses the tracks, stepping carefully over them in her narrow black shoes and heavy black stockings. He stares after her as if he were Adam wondering what to name her. Then he jumps up and dashes out of the train in pursuit of her. At that very moment a long freight train pulls through the parallel track obscuring his view and blocking his way. Twenty-five freight cars later, she has vanished forever.

One scenario of the zipless fuck.

Zipless, you see, *not* because European men have button-flies rather than zipper-flies, and not because the participants are so devastatingly attractive, but because the incident has all the swift compression of a dream and is seemingly free of all remorse and guilt; because there is no talk of her late husband or of his fiancée; because there is no rationalizing; because there is no talk at *all*. The zipless fuck is absolutely pure. It is free of ulterior motives. There is no power game. The man is not 'taking' and the woman is not 'giving.' No one is attempting to cuckold a husband or humiliate a wife. No one is trying to prove anything or get anything out of anyone. The zipless fuck is the purest thing there is. And it is rarer than the unicorn. And I have never had one. Whenever it seemed I was close, I discovered a horse with a papier-mâché horn, or two clowns in a unicorn suit. Alessandro, my Florentine friend, came close. But he was, after all, one clown in a unicorn suit.

Consider this tapestry, my life.

From *Fear of Flying* by Erica Jong, 1974

In the Shower

Hot lezzy action, or swinging both ways, as we quaintly used to call it (also, AC/DC). This book was also extremely enlightening about 'blue balls', or being such a 'tease' that the boy you were snogging got testicle-ache. Fancy!

*S*he stopped reading. I heard some movements to one side. Then she asked matter-of-factly, 'Ginny, could you please put some of this baby oil on my back? I was out yesterday, and I'm getting burned.'

Wonder of wonders, I tossed off my quilt, sat up obediently, took the lotion from her, and began rubbing it into her smooth reddish brown back.

Then I lay back down on my stomach and wrapped up in the quilt and resumed my shivering.

'Shall I put some on you? You're looking pink, too.'

When I didn't answer, she crawled over and removed the quilt and started anointing my back. She covered my arms and shoulders and hips and legs with the oil as well. It was as though she were rubbing life back into me. Where her hands had been, my flesh glowed with warmth. She pushed me, and I rolled over co-operatively. She rubbed the baby oil into my chest and breasts and abdomen and legs. My shivering subsided. The lump in my stomach began breaking up under her hands like a frozen pond in the spring. She crawled down to my feet and massaged them. Then she crawled up to my shoulder level and patted oil on my cheeks and forehead and across my upper lip. Then she lay down next to me and cradled me in her arms, my head on her chest right over her heart.

I don't know how long we'd been lying like that, me listening to her pounding heart and timing my breathing to it. It might have been minutes or hours. In any case, at some point, we heard a rapid flapping sound. And soon our bodies were being swept by great swirling eddies of air.

Above us hovered a helicopter from the nearby air force base. A shaven male head leaned out and shouted through cupped hands at the top of his voice, 'You goddam Worthley dykes!' Then a hand reached out with a can of some sort, and soon Eddie and I were splattered with showers of Coca-Cola.

Eddie leapt up in all her nude magnificence and raised both arms high above her head and shook her middle fingers. 'Pigs!' she screamed. 'Goddam fucking fascist pigs!'

The copter swept off on its other missions of national defense. The rehearsal in the courtyard was a shambles as the May Court stood staring skyward at Eddie's gorgeous body, poised on the roof five floors above them. 'Don't jump!' someone screamed, and the courtyard erupted in a flurry of activity, people racing for the doors to take the elevator to the roof to restrain Eddie.

'Well!' Eddie said with a grin, 'shall we be licking the Coke off each other when they arrive?'

We crawled rapidly to her window and scrambled through it. As we raced, hand in sticky hand, to the bathroom, we heard the whir of ascending elevators.

I hesitated at the bathroom door. 'It's been cleaned up,' Eddie assured me grimly. I walked in with all the enthusiasm of a plane crash survivor boarding a new plane. I sniffed and thought I could smell sour vomit. I began shivering as I looked in the tub enclosure.

Eddie pulled me into the shower stall. She lathered me with soap. Then I lathered her. Then we held each other and kissed in the spray. We stayed there until we'd used up all the hot water in the dorm; the pipes began clanking furiously.

We spent that night in Eddie's narrow lumpy institutional bed, sleeping in each other's arms until after lunch. I woke up delighted finally to know who put what where in physical love between women.

From *Kinflicks* by Lisa Alther, 1976

How the Georgians Did It

No dirty words, but wall-to-wall dirty bits. This book made me think it might be really interesting to be a prostitute. What can I tell you? I was fifteen.

The first that stood up, to open the ball, were a cornet of horse, and that sweetest of olive-beauties, the soft and amorous Louisa. He led her to the couch 'nothing loath', on which he gave her the fall, and extended her at her length with an air of roughness and vigour, relishing high of amorous eagerness and impatience. The girl, spreading herself to the best advantage, with her head upon the pillow, was so concentered in what she was about, that our presence seemed the least of her care and concern. Her petticoats, thrown up with her shift, discovered to the company the finest turn'd legs and thighs that could be imagined, and in broad display, that gave us a full view of that delicious cleft of flesh, into which the pleasing hairgrown mount over it, parted and presented a most inviting entrance, between two closehedges, delicately soft and pouting. Her gallant was now ready, having disencumber'd himself from his clothes, overloaded with lace, and presently, his shirt removed, shew'd us his forces in high plight, bandied and ready for action. But giving us no time to consider the dimensions, he threw himself instantly over his charming antagonist who receiv'd him as he pushed at once dead at mark, like a heroine, without flinching; for surely never was girl constitutionally truer to the taste of joy, or sincerer in the expressions of its sensations, than she was: we could observe pleasure lighten in her eyes, as he introduc'd his plenipo-tentiary instrument into her; till, at length, having indulg'd her to its utmost reach, its irritations grew so violent, and gave her the spurs so furiously, that collected within herself, and lost to every-thing but the enjoyment of her favourite feelings, she returned his thrusts with a just concert of springy heaves, keeping time so exactly with the most pathetic sighs, that one might have number'd the strokes in agitation by their distinct murmurs, whilst her active limbs kept wreathing and intertwisting with his, in convulsive folds: then the turtlebilling kisses, and the poignant painless love-bites, which they both exchang'd, in a rage of delight, all conspiring towards the melting period. It soon came on, when Louisa, in the ravings of her pleasure-frenzy, impotent of all restraint, cried out: 'Oh, Sir! . . . Good Sir! . . . pray do not spare me! ah! ah! . . .' All her accents now faltering into heartfetched sighs, she clos'd her eyes in the sweet death, in the instant of which she was embalmd by an injection, of which we could easily see the signs in the quiet, dying, languid posture of her late so furious driver, who was stopp'd of a sudden, breathing short, panting, and, for that time, giving up the spirit of pleasure. As soon as he was dismounted, Louisa sprung up, shook her petticoats, and running up to me, gave me a kiss, and drew me to the side-board, to which she was herself handed by her gallant, where they made me pledge them in a glass of wine, and toast a droll health of Louisa's proposal in high frolic.

By this time the second couple was ready to enter the lists: which were a young baronet, and that delicatest of charmers the winning, tender Harriet. My gentle esquire came to acquaint me with it, and brought me back to the scene of action.

And, surely, never did one of her profession accompany her dis-positions for the bare-faced part she was engaged to play with such a peculiar grace of sweetness, modesty, and yielding coyness, as she did. All her air and motions breath'd only unreserv'd, unlimited complaisance without the least mixture of impudence or prostitu-tion. But what was yet more surprising, her spark-elect, in the midst of the dissolution of a public open enjoyment, doted on her to distraction, and had, by dint of love and sentiments, touched her heart, tho' for a while the restraint of their engagement to the house laid him under a kind of necessity of complying with an institution which himself had had the greatest share in establishing.

Harriet was then led to the vacant couch by her gallant, blushing as she look'd at me, and with eyes made to justify anything, tenderly bespeaking of me the most favourable construction of the step she was thus irresistibly drawn into.

Her lover, for such he was, sat her down at the foot of the couch, and passing his arm round her neck, preluded with a kiss fervently applied to her lips, that visibly gave her life and spirit to go thro' with the scene; and as he kiss'd, he gently inclined her head, till it fell back on a pillow disposed to receive it, and leaning himself down all the way with her, at once countenanc'd and endear'd her fall to her. There, as if he had guess'd our wishes, or meant to gratify at once his pleasure and his pride, in being the master, by the title of present possession, of beauties delicate beyond imagination, he discovered her breasts to his own touch, and our common view; but oh! what delicious manuals of love devotion! how inimitably fine moulded! small, round, firm, and excellently white: the grain of their skin, so soothing, so flattering to the touch! and their nipples, that crown'd them, the sweetest buds of beauty. When he had feasted his eyes with the touch and perusal, feasted his lips with kisses of the highest relish, imprinted on those all-delicious twin orbs, he proceeded downwards.

Her legs still kept the ground; and now, with the tenderest attention not to shock or alarm her too suddenly, he, by degrees, rather stole than rolled up her petticoats; at which, as if a signal had been given, Louisa and Emily took hold of her legs, in pure wantonness, and, in ease to her, kept them stretched wide abroad. Then lay exposed, or, to speak more properly, display'd the greatest parade in nature of female charms. The whole company, who, except myself, had often seen them, seemed as much dazzled, surpriz'd, and delighted, as anyone could be who had now beheld them for the first time. Beauties so excessive could not but enjoy the privileges of eternal novelty. Her thighs were so exquisitely fashioned, that either more in, or more out of flesh than they were, they would have declined from that point of perfection they presented. But what infinitely enrich'd and adorn'd them was the sweet intersection formed, where they met, at the bottom of the smoothest, roundest, whitest belly, by that central furrow which nature had sunk there, between the soft relieve of two pouting ridges, and which, in this girl, was in perfect symmetry of delicacy and miniature with the rest of her frame. No! nothing in nature could be of a beautifuller cut; then, the dark umbrage of the downy springmoss that overarched it, bestowed, on the luxury of the landscape, a touching warmth, a tender finishing, beyond the expression of words, or even the pain of thought.

The truly enamour'd gallant, who had stood absorbed and engrossed by the pleasure of the sight long enough to afford us time to feast ours (no fear of glutting!) addressed himself at length to the materials of enjoyment, and lifting the linen veil that hung between us and his master member of the revels, exhibited one whose eminent size proclaimed the owner a true woman's hero. He was, besides, in every other respect an accomplish'd gentleman, and in the bloom and vigour of youth. Standing then between Harriet's legs, which were supported by her two companions at their widest extension, with one hand he gently disclosed the lips of that luscious mouth of nature, whilst with the other, he stooped his mighty machine to its lure, from the height of his stiff stand-up towards his belly; the lips, kept open by his fingers, received its broad shelving head of coral hue: and when he had nestled it in, he hovered there a little, and the girls then deliver'd over to his hips the agreeable office of supporting her thighs; and now, as if meant to spin out his pleasure, and give it the more play for its life, he passed up his instrument so slow that we lost sight of it inch by inch, till at length it was wholly taken into the soft laboratory of love, and the mossy mounts of each fairly met together. In the mean time, we could plainly mark the prodigious effect the progressions of this delightful energy wrought in this delicious girl, gradually heightening her beauty as they heightened her pleasure. Her countenance and whole frame grew more animated; the faint blush of her cheeks, gaining ground on the white, deepened into a florid vivid vermillion glow, her naturally brilliant eyes now sparkled with ten-fold lustre; her languor was vanish'd, and she appeared quick spirited and alive all over. He had now fixed, nailed, this tender creature, with his home-driven wedge, so that she lay passive by force, and unable to stir, till beginning to play a strain of arms against this vein of delicacy, as he urged the to-and-fro friction, he awaken'd rous'd, and touch'd her so to the heart, that, unable to contain herself, she could not but reply to his motions, as briskly as her nicety of frame would admit of, till the raging stings of the pleasure rising towards the point made her wild with the intolerable sensations of it, and she now threw her legs and arms about at random, as she lay lost in the sweet transport; which on his side declared itself by quicker, eager thrusts, convulsive grasps, burning sighs, swift laborious breathings, eyes darting humid fires: all faithful tokens of the imminent approaches of the last gasp of joy. It came on at length: the baronet led the ecstasy, she sympathetically joined in, as she felt the melting symptoms from him, in the nick of which glewing more ardently than ever his lips to hers, he shewed all the signs of that agony of bliss being strong upon him, in which he gave her the finishing titillation; inly thrill'd with which, we saw plainly that she answered it down with all effusion of spirit and matter she was mistress of, whilst a general soft shudder ran through all her limbs, which she gave a stretchout of, and lay motionless, breathless, dying with dear delight; and in the height of its expression, showing, through the nearly closed lids of her eyes, just the edges of their black, the rest being rolled strongly upwards in their ecstasy; then her sweet mouth appear'd languishingly open, with the tip of her tongue leaning negligently towards the lower range of her white teeth, whilst the natural ruby colour of her lips glowed with heightened life. Was not this a subject to dwell upon? And accordingly her lover still kept on her, with an abiding delectation, till compressed, squeezed, and distilled to the last drop, he took leave with one fervent kiss, expressing satisfy'd desires, but unextinguish'd love.

As soon as he was off, I ran to her, and sitting down on the couch by her, rais'd her head, which she declin'd gently, and hung on my bosom, to hide her blushes and confusion at what had pass'd, till by degrees she recomposed herself, and accepted of a restorative glass of wine from my spark, who had left me to fetch it her, whilst her own was readjusting his affairs and buttoning up; after which he led her, leaning languishingly upon him, to our stand of view round the couch.

And now Emily's partner had taken her out for her share in the dance, when this transcendently fair and sweet tempered creature readily stood up; and if a complexion to put the rose and lily out of countenance, extreme pretty features, and that florid health and bloom for which the country-girls are so lovely might pass her for a beauty, this she certainly was, and one of the most striking of the fair ones.

Her gallant began first, as she stood, to disengage her breasts, and restore them to the liberty of nature, from the easy confinement of no more than a pair of jumps; but on their coming out to view, we thought a new light was added to the room, so superiorly shining was their whiteness; then they rose in so happy a swell as to compose her a well-formed fullness of bosom that had such an effect on the eye as to seem flesh hardening into marble, of which it emulated the polished gloss, and far surpassed even the whitest, in the life and lustre of its colours, white veined with blue. Refrain who could from such provoking enticements to it in reach? He touched her breasts, first lightly, when the glossy smoothness of the skin eluded his hand, and made it slip along the surface; he press'd them, and the springy flesh that filled them, thus pitted by force, rose again reboundingly with his hand, and on the instant effac'd the pressure: and alike indeed was the consistence of all those parts of her body throughout, where the fulness of flesh compacts and constitutes all that fine firmness which the touch is so highly attach'd to. When he had thus largely pleased himself with this branch of dalliance and delight, he truss'd up her petticoat and shift, in a wisp to her waist, where being tuck'd in, she stood fairly naked on every side; a blush at this overspread her lovely face, and her eyes downcast to the ground, seemed to be for quarter, when she had so great a right to triumph in all the treasures of youth and beauty that she now so victoriously display'd. Her legs were perfectly well shaped and her thighs, which she kept pretty close, shewed so white, so round, so substantial and abounding in firm flesh, that nothing could offer a stronger recommendation to the luxury of the touch, which he accordingly did not fail to indulge himself in. Then gently removing her hand, which in the first emotion of natural modesty, she had carried thither, he gave us rather a glimpse than a view of that soft narrow chink running its little length downwards and hiding the remains of it between her thighs; but plain was to be seen the fringe of light-brown curls, in beauteous growth over it, that with their silky gloss created a pleasing variety from the surrounding white skin, whose lustre too, their gentle embrowning shade, considerably raised. Her spark then endeavoured, as she stood, by disclosing her thighs, to gain us a completer sight of that central charm of attraction, but not obtaining it so conveniently in that attitude, he led her to the foot of the couch, and bringing to it one of the pillows, gently inclin'd her head down, so that as she leaned with it over her crossed hands, straddling with her thighs wide spread, and jutting her body out, she presented a full back view of her person, naked to her waist. Her posteriors, plump, smooth, and prominent, form'd luxuriant tracts of animated snow, that splendidly filled the eye, till it was commanded down the parting or separation of those exquisitely white cliffs, by their narrow vale, and was there stopt, and attracted by the embowered bottom-cavity that terminated this delightful vista and stood moderately gaping from the influence of her bended posture, so that the agreeable interior red of the sides of the orifice came into view, and with respect to the white that dazzled round it, gave somewhat the idea of a pink slash in the glossiest white satin. Her gallant, who was a gentleman about thirty, somewhat inclin'd to a fatness that was in no sort displeasing, improving the hint thus tendered him of this mode of enjoyment, after settling her well in this posture, and encouraging her with kisses and caresses to stand him through, drew out his affair ready erected, and whose extreme length, rather disproportion'd to its breadth, was the more surprising, as that excess is not often the case with those of his corpulent habit; making then the right and direct application, he drove it up to the guard, whilst the round bulge of those Turkish beauties of hers tallying with the hollow made with the bent of his belly and thighs, as they curved inwards, brought all those parts, surely not undelightfully, into warm touch, and close conjunction; his hands he kept passing round her body, and employed in toying with her enchanting breasts. As soon too as she felt him at home as he could reach, she lifted her head a little from the pillow, and turning her neck, without much straining, but her cheeks glowing with the deepest scarlet, and a smile of the tenderest satisfaction, met the kiss he press'd forward to give her as they were thus close joined together: when leaving him to pursue his delights, she hid again her face and blushes with her hands and pillow, and thus stood passively and as favourably too as she could, whilst he kept laying at her with repeated thrusts and making the meeting flesh on both sides resound again with the violence of them; then ever as he backen'd from her, we could see between them part of his long white staff foamingly in motion, till, as he went on again and closed with her, the interposing hillocks took it out of sight. Sometimes he took his hands from the semi-globes of her bosom, and transferred the pressure of them to those larger ones, the present subjects of his soft blockade, which he squeez'd, grasp'd, and play'd with, till at length a pursuit of driving, so hotly urged, brought on the height of the fit with such overpowering pleasure that his fair partner became now necessary to support him, panting, fainting, and dying as he discharged; which she no sooner felt the killing sweetness of than, unable to keep her legs, and yielding to the mighty intoxication, she reeled, and falling forward on the couch, made it a necessity for him, if he would preserve the warm pleasure-hold, to fall upon her, where they perfected, in a continued conjunction of body and ecstatic flow, their scheme of joys for that time.

As soon as he had disengag'd, the charming Emily got up, and we crowded round her with congratulations and other officious little services; for it is to be noted, that though all modesty and reserve were banished from the transaction of these pleasures, good manners and politeness were inviolably observ'd: here was no gross ribaldry, no offensive or rude behaviour, or ungenerous reproaches to the girls for their compliance with the humours and desires of the men; on the contrary, nothing was wanting to soothe, encourage, and soften the sense of their condition to them. Men know not in general how much they destroy of their own pleasure, when they break through the respect and tenderness due to our sex, and even to those of it who live only by pleasing them. And this was a maxim perfectly well understood by these polite voluptuaries, these profound adepts in the great art and science of pleasure, who never shew'd these votaries of theirs a more tender respect than at the time of those exercises of their complaisance, when they unlock'd their treasures of concealed beauty, and showed out in the pride of their native charms, evermore touching surely than when they parade it in the artificial ones of dress and ornament.

The frolick was now come round to me, and it being my turn of subscription to the will and pleasure of my particular elect, as well as to that of the company, he came to me, and saluting me very tenderly, with a flattering eagerness, put me in mind of the compliances my presence there authoriz'd the hopes of, and at the same time repeated to me that if all this force of example had not surmounted any repugnance I might have to concur with the humours and desires of the company, that though the play was bespoke for my benefit, and great as his own private disappointment might be, he would suffer anything, sooner than be the instrument of imposing a disagreeable task on me.

To this I answered, without the least hesitation, or mincing grimace, that had I not even contracted a kind of engagement to be at his disposal without the least reserve, the example of such agreeable companions would alone determine me and that I was in no pain about any thing but my appearing to so great a disadvantage after such superior beauties. And take notice, that I thought as I spoke. The frankness of the answer pleas'd them all; my particular was complimented on his acquisition, and, by way of indirect flattery to me, openly envied.

Mrs Cole, by the way, could not have given me a greater mark of her regard than in managing for me the choice of this young

gentleman for my master of the ceremonies: for, independent of his
noble birth and the great fortune he was heir to, his person was
even uncommonly pleasing, well shaped and tall; his face mark'd
with the smallpox, but no more than what added a grace of more
manliness to features rather turned to softness and delicacy, was
marvellously enliven'd by eyes which were of the clearest sparkling
black; in short, he was one whom any woman would, in the familiar style, readily call a very pretty fellow.

I was now handed by him to the cockpit of our match, where, as
I was dressed in nothing but a white morning gown, he vouchsafed
to play the male-Abigail on this occasion, and spared me the confusion that would have attended the forwardness of undressing
myself: my gown then was loosen'd in a trice, and I divested of it;
my stay next offered an obstacle which readily gave way, Louisa
very readily furnishing a pair of scissors to cut the lace; off went that
shell and dropping my uppercoat, I was reduced to my under one
and my shift, the open bosom of which gave the hands and eyes all
the liberty they could wish. Here I imagin'd the stripping was to
stop, but I reckoned short: my spark, at the desire of the rest, tenderly begged that I would not suffer the small remains of a covering
to rob them of a full view of my whole person, and for me, who was
too flexibly obsequious to dispute any point with them, and who
considered the little more that remain'd as very immaterial, I readily assented to whatever he pleased. In an instant, then, my under
petticoat was untied and at my feet, and my shift drawn over my
head, so that my cap, slightly fasten'd, came off with it, and brought
all my hair down (of which, be it again remembered without vanity,
that I had a very fine head) in loose disorderly ringlets, over my
neck and shoulders, to the not unfavourable set-off of my skin.

I now stood before my judges in all the truth of nature, to whom
I could not appear a very disagreeable figure, if you please to recol-
lect what I have before said of my person, which time, that at
certain periods of life robs us every instant of our charms, had, at
that of mine, then greatly improved into full and open bloom, for
I wanted some months of eighteen. My breasts, which in the state of
nudity are ever capital points, now in no more than in graceful

plenitude, maintained a firmness and steady independence of any stay of support, that dared and invited the test of the touch. Then I was as tall, as slim-shaped as could be consistent with all that juicy plumpness of flesh, ever the most grateful to the senses of sight and touch, which I owed to the health and youth of my constitution. I had not, however, so thoroughly renounc'd all innate shame, as not to suffer great confusion at the state I saw myself in; but the whole troop round me, men and women, relieved me with every mark of applause and satisfaction, every flattering attention to raise and inspire me with even sentiments of pride on the figure I made, which my friend gallantly protested, infinitely out-shone all other *birthday* finery whatever; so that had I leave to set down, for sincere, all the compliments these connoisseurs overwhelmed me with upon this occasion, I might flatter myself with having pass'd my examination with the approbation of the learned.

My friend however, who for this time had alone the disposal of me, humoured their curiosity, and perhaps his own, so far, that he placed me in all the variety of postures and lights imaginable, pointing out every beauty under every aspect of it, not without such parentheses of kisses, such inflammatory liberties of his roving hands, as made all shame fly before them, and a blushing glow give place to a warmer one of desire, which led me even to find some relish in the present scene.

But in this general survey, you may be sure, the most material spot of me was not excus'd the strictest visitation! nor was it but agreed, that I had not the least reason to be diffident of passing even for a maid, on occasion: so inconsiderable a flaw had my preceding adventures created there, and so soon had the blemish of an over-stretch been repaired and worn out at my age, and in my naturally small make in that part.

Now, whether my partner had exhausted all the modes of regaling the touch or sight, or whether he was now ungovernably wound up to strike, I know not; but briskly throwing off his clothes, the prodigious heat bred by a close room, a great fire, numerous candles, and even the inflammatory warmth of these scenes, induced him to lay aside his shirt too, when his breeches, before loosen'd, now gave up their contents to view, and shew'd in front the enemy I had to engage with, stiffly bearing up the port of its head unhooded, and glowing red. Then I plainly saw what I had to trust to: it was one of those just true-siz'd instruments, of which the masters have a better command than the more unwieldy, inordinate siz'd ones are generally under. Straining me then close to his bosom, as he stood up fore-right against me and applying to the obvious niche its peculiar idol, he aimed at inserting it, which, as I forwardly favoured, he effected at once, by canting up my thighs over his naked hips, and made me receive every inch, and close home; so that stuck upon the pleasure-pivot, and clinging round his neck, in which and in his hair I hid my face, burningly flushing with my present feelings as much as with shame, my bosom glew'd to his; he carried me once round the couch, on which he then, without quitting the middle-fastness, or dischannelling, laid me down, and began the pleasure-grist. But so provokingly predisposed and primed as we were, by all the moving sights of the night, our imagination was too much heated not to melt us of the soonest: and accordingly, I no sooner felt the warm spray darted up my inwards from him, but I was punctually on flow, to share the momentary ecstasy; but I had yet greater reason to boast of our harmony: for finding that all the flames of desire were not yet quench'd within me, but that rather, like wetted coals, I glowed the fiercer for this sprinkling, my hot-mettled spark, sympathizing with me, and loaded for a double fire, recontinu'd the sweet battery with undying vigour; greatly pleas'd at which, I gratefully endeavoured to accommodate all my motions to his best advantage and delight, kisses, squeezes, tender murmurs, all came into play, till our joys growing more turbulent and riotous, threw us into a fond disorder, and as they raged to a point, bore us far from ourselves into an ocean of boundless pleasures, into which we both plunged together in a transport of lust. Now all the impressions of burning desire, from the lively scenes I had been spectatress of, ripened by the heat of this exercise, and collecting to a head, throbb'd and agitated me with insupportable irritations: I perfectly fevered and madden'd with their excess. I did not now enjoy a calm of reason enough to perceive, but I ecstatically, indeed, *felt* the power of such rare and exquisite provocatives, as the examples of the night had proved towards thus exalting our pleasures: which, with great joy, I sensibly found my gallant shared in, by his nervous and home expressions of it: his eyes flashing eloquent flames, his action infuriated with the stings of it, all conspiring to rise my delight, by assuring me of his. Lifted then to the utmost pitch of joy that human life can bear, undestroyed by excess, I touch'd that sweetly critical point, whence scarce prevented by the injection from my partner, I dissolved, and breaking out into a deep drawn sigh, sent my whole sensitive soul down to that passage where escape was denied it, by its being so deliciously plugged and chok'd up. Thus we lay a few blissful instants, overpowered, still, and languid; till, as the sense of pleasure stagnated, we recover'd from our trance, and he slipt out of me, not however before he had protested his extreme satisfaction by the tenderest kiss and embrace, as well as by the most cordial expressions.

The company, who had stood round us in a profound silence, when all was over, help'd me to hurry on my clothes in an instant, and complimented me on the sincere homage they could not escape observing had been done (as they termed it) to the sovercignty of my charms, in my receiving a double payment of tribute at one juncture. But my partner, now dress'd again, signaliz'd, above all, a fondness unbated by the circumstance of recent enjoyment; the girls too kiss'd and embraced me, assuring me that for that time, or indeed any other, unless I pleased, I was to go thro' no farther public trials, and that I was now consummatedly initiated, and one of them.

From *Fanny Hill* by John Cleland, 1749

How the English Do It

I love Jilly Cooper. Loved her then, love her now. This is another extract in which not very much happens, but there was something very sexy about the hunky man having the bratty girl's number all along, and in the way (detached, aloof) he wanted to help her to be good. Also, he spanks her. It's only a sentence, but I've never forgotten it.

'Aren't they complete originals!' said Gussie, as she and I changed later. She was wandering around in the nude trying to look at her back. Between her fiery red legs and shoulders, her skin was as white as lard.

'I'm not peeling, am I?' she asked anxiously. 'It itches like mad.'

'Looks a bit angry,' I said, pleased to see that a few tiny white blisters had formed between her shoulders. It'd be coming off her in strips tomorrow.

'Isn't that girl Lorna quite devastating?' she went on. 'You could see Gareth wanted to absolutely gobble her up.'

'She's not that marvellous,' I said, starting to pour water over my hair.

'Oh but she is – quite lovely and so natural. Think of being seventeen again, all the things one was going to do, the books one was going to write, the places one was going to visit. I must say when a girl is beautiful at seventeen she gets a glow about her that old hags like you and I in our twenties can never hope to achieve.'

'Speak for yourself,' I muttered into the wash-basin.

I knew when I finally finished doing my face that I'd never looked better. My eyes glittered brilliantly blue in my suntanned face; my hair, newly washed and straight, was almost white from the sun. Gussie, I'm glad to say, looked terrible. She was leaning out of the window when there was a crunch of wheels on the gravel outside.

'Oh look, someone's arriving. It's the vicar.'

'We're obviously in for a wild evening,' I said.

'We'd better go down. Shall I wait?'

'No. I'll be ready in a minute. You go on.'

I was glad when she'd gone. I thought she might kick up a fuss at the dress I was going to wear. It was a short tunic in silver chain mail – the holes as big as half-crowns. High-necked at the front, it swooped to positive indecency at the back. Two very inadequate circles of silver sequins covered my breasts. I didn't wear anything underneath except a pair of flesh-coloured pants, which gave the impression I wasn't wearing anything at all.

Slowly I put it on, thinking all the time of the effect it would have on Jeremy when I walked into the sedate country living room. I gave a final brush to my hair and turned to look in the mirror. It was the first time I'd worn it with all my party warpaint, and the impact made even me catch my breath. Oh my, said I to myself, you're going to set them by their country ears tonight. I was determined to make an entrance, so I fiddled with my hair until I could hear that more people had arrived.

There was a hush as I walked into the drawing-room. Everyone gazed at me. Men's hands fluttered up to straighten their ties and smooth their hair, the women stared at me with ill-concealed envy and disapproval.

'Christ!' I heard Jeremy say, in appalled wonder.

But I was looking at Gareth. For the first time I saw a blaze of disapproval in his eyes. I've got under his guard at last, I thought in triumph.

There seemed to be no common denominator among the guests. They consisted of old blimps and tabby cats, several dons from the University, and their ill-dressed wives, a handful of people of Lorna's age, the girls very debbie, the boys very wet, and a crowd of tough hunting types with braying voices and brick red faces. It was as though the Hamiltons had asked everyone they knew and liked, with a total disregard as to whether they'd mix.

I wandered towards Jeremy, Gussie and Gareth.

'I see you've thrown yourself open to the public,' said Gareth, but he didn't smile. 'I suppose I'd better go and hand round some drinks.'

'You shouldn't have worn that dress, Octavia,' said Gussie in a shocked voice. 'This isn't London, you know.'

'That's only too obvious,' I said, looking round.

Bridget Hamilton came over and took my arm. 'How enchanting you look, Octavia. Do come and devastate our local MFH. He's dying to meet you.'

He wasn't the only one. Once those hunting types had had a few drinks, they all closed in on me, vying for my attention. Over and over again I let my glass be filled up. Never had my wit been more malicious or more sparkling. I kept them all in fits of braying laughter.

Like an experienced comedian, although I was keeping my audience happy, I was very conscious of what was going on in the wings — Jeremy, looking like a thundercloud because I was flirting so outrageously with other men, Gareth behaving like the Hamiltons' future son-in-law, whether he was coping with drinks or smiling into Lorna's eyes. Every so often, however, his eyes flickered in my direction, and his face hardened.

About ten o'clock, Bridget Hamilton wandered in, very red in the face, and carrying two saucepans, and plonked them down on a long polished table beside a pile of plates and forks.

'There's risotto here,' she said vaguely, 'if anyone's hungry.'

People surged forward to eat. I stayed put, the men around me stayed put as well. The din we were making increased until Gareth pushed his way through the crowd.

'You ought to eat something, Octavia,' he said.

I shook my head and smiled up at him insolently.

'Aren't you hungry?' drawled the MFH who was lounging beside me.

I turned to him, smiling sweetly. 'Only for you.'

A nearby group of women stopped filling their faces with risotto and talking about nappies, and looked at me in horror. The MFH's wife was among them. She had a face like a well-bred cod.

'The young gels of today are not the same as they were twenty years ago,' she said loudly.

'Of course they're not,' I shouted across at her. 'Twenty years ago I was only six. You must expect some change in my appearance and behaviour.'

She turned puce with anger at the roar of laughter that greeted this. Gareth didn't laugh. He took hold of my arm.

'I think you'd better come and eat,' he said in even tones.

'I've told you once,' I snapped, 'I don't want to eat. I want to dance. Why doesn't someone put on the record player?'

The MFH looked down at the circles of silver sequins.

'What happens to those when you dance?'

I giggled. 'Now you see me, now you don't. They've been known to shift off centre.'

There was another roar of laughter.

'Well, what are we waiting for?' said the MFH. 'Let's put a record on and dance.'

'All right,' I said, looking up at him under my lashes. 'But I must go to the loo first.'

Upstairs in the bathroom, I hardly recognized myself. I looked like some Maenad, my hair tousled, my eyes glittering, my cheeks flushed. God, the dress was so beautiful.

'And you're so beautiful too,' I added and, leaning forward, lightly kissed my reflection in the mirror.

Even in my alcoholic state, I was slightly abashed when I turned round and saw Gareth standing watching me from the doorway.

'Don't you know it's rude to stare?' I said.

He didn't move.

'I'd like to come past – if you don't mind,' I went on.

'Oh no you don't,' he said, grabbing my wrist.

'Oh yes I do,' I screamed, trying to tug myself away.

'Will you stop behaving like a whore!' He swore at me and,

pulling me into the nearest bedroom, threw me on the bed and locked the door.

'Now I suppose you're going to treat me like a whore,' I spat at him. 'What will your precious Lorna say if she catches us here together?'

Suddenly I was frightened. There was murder in his eyes.

'It's about time someone taught you a lesson,' he said, coming towards me. 'And I'm afraid it's going to be me.'

Before I realized it, Gareth had me across his knee. I've never known what living daylights were before, but he was certainly beating them out of me now. I started to scream and kick.

'Shut up,' he said viciously. 'No one can hear you.' The record player was still booming downstairs. I struggled and tried to bite him but he was far too strong for me. It was not the pain so much as the ghastly indignity. It seemed to go on for ever and ever. Finally he tipped me on to the floor. I lay there trembling with fear.

'Get up,' he said brusquely, 'and get your things together. I'm taking you back to the boat.'

The moon hung over the river, whitening the mist that floated transparent above the sleeping fields. Stars were crowding the blue-black sky, the air was heavy with the scent of meadowsweet.

Aching in every bone, biting my lip to stop myself crying, I let Gareth lead me across the fields. Every few moments I stumbled, held up only by his vice-like grip on my arm. I think he felt at any moment I might bolt back to the party.

Once we were on deck I said, 'Now you can go back to your darling teenager.'

'Not until you're safe in bed.'

I lay down on my bunk still in my dress. But when I shut my eyes the world was going round and round. I quickly opened them. Gareth stood watching me through cigar smoke.

I shut my eyes again. A great wave of nausea rolled over me.

'Oh God,' I said, trying to get out of bed.

'Stay where you are,' he snapped.

'I ought to be allowed to get out of my own bed,' I said

petulantly. 'I agree in your Mary Whitehouse role you're quite entitled to stop me getting into other people's beds but a person should be free to get out of her own bed if she wants to.'

'Stop fooling around,' said Gareth.

'I can't,' I said in desperation. 'I'm going to be sick.'

He only just got me to the edge of the boat in time, and I was sicker than I've ever been in my life. I couldn't stop this terrible retching, and then, because Gareth was holding my head, I couldn't stop crying from humiliation.

'Leave me alone,' I sobbed in misery. 'Leave me alone to die. Gussie and Jeremy'll be back in a minute. Please go and keep them away for a bit longer.'

'They won't be back for hours,' said Gareth, looking at his watch.

'Can I have a drink of water?'

'Not yet, it'll only make you throw up again. You'll just have to grin and bear it.'

I looked up at the huge white moon and gave a hollow laugh. 'It couldn't be a more romantic night, could it?'

In the passage my knees gave way and Gareth picked me up, carried me into the cabin and put me to bed as deftly as if I'd been a child. He gave me a couple of pills.

'They'll put you to sleep.'

'I wasn't actually planning to meet Jeremy on deck tonight.'

I was shivering like a puppy.

'I'm sorry,' I said, rolling my head back and forth on the pillow. 'I'm so terribly sorry.'

'Lie still,' he said. 'The pills'll work soon.'

'Don't go,' I whispered, as he stood up and went to the door.

His face was expressionless as he looked at me, no scorn, no mockery, not even a trace of pity.

'I'm going to get you some more blankets,' he said. 'I don't want you catching cold.'

That sudden kindness, the first he'd ever shown me, brought tears to my eyes. I was beginning to feel drowsy by the time he came back with two rugs. They smelt musty and, as I watched his hands tucking them in – powerful hands with black hairs on the back — I suddenly wanted to feel his arms around me and to feel those hands soothing me and petting me as though I were a child again. In a flash I saw him as the father, strict, yet loving and caring, that all my life I'd missed; someone to say stop when I went too far, someone to mind if I behaved badly, to be proud if I behaved well.

'Getting sleepy?' he asked.

I nodded.

'Good girl. You'll be all right in the morning.'

'I'm sorry I wrecked your party.'

'Doesn't matter. They're nice though, the Hamiltons. You should mix with more people like them; they've got the right values.'

'How did you meet them?'

He began to tell me, but I started getting confused and the soft Welsh voice became mingled with the water lapping against the boat; then I drifted into unconsciousness.

*

Nothing — not even the truth — prepared me for the horror of the photographic session with Andreas. I felt as though I was hurtling on a fast train towards Dante's Ninth Circle, the one where the treacherous are sealed in ice and eternally ripped apart by Satan's teeth. But I'd betrayed Jakey, so I deserved to be ripped apart.

I sat in a little side room in front of a mirror lined with lit bulbs, wearing only an old make-up-stained dressing gown. The wireless claimed it was the hottest day of the year. It was impossibly stuffy in the huge Wimbledon studio Cy Markovitz had hired for the afternoon, but I still couldn't stop shivering. I knew I looked terrible. I had covered my yellowing suntan with dark-brown make-up, but it didn't stop my ribs sticking out like a Belsen victim. I had poured half a bottle of blue drops into my eyes but they were still red-veined and totally without sparkle.

In one corner of the studio, an amazing faggot called Gabriel with very blue eyes and streaked strawberry blond hair, clad only in faded kneelength denim trousers and a snake bracelet, was whisking about supervising two sulky, sweating minions into building a set for me. It consisted of a huge bed with a cane bedhead, silver satin sheets, and a white antique birdcage. One minion kept staggering in with huge potted plants, the other was pinning dark brown patterned Habitat wallpaper to a huge rolled-down screen. Gabriel was arranging a Christopher Wray lamp, a silver teapot and glass paperweights on a bedside table.

'Andreas asked for something really classy to set you off, darling. I've never known him to take so much interest.'

In another corner of the studio to an accompaniment of popping flashbulbs and Ella Fitzgerald on the gramophone, Cy Markovitz was photographing a spectacular looking black girl with 44-20-44 measurements. She was wearing red lace open crotch pants, heels with nine inch spikes, and was writhing against a huge fur rug which was pinned against the wall.

'It's to make her black boobs fall better,' explained Gabriel with a shudder. 'In the pix, it'll look as though she's lying on a bed.'

I turned back to the mirror, sweat already breaking through my newly applied make-up. Then I heard the noise of men laughing; my mouth went dry, my shivering became more violent. Next moment the curtain was pushed aside and Andreas came in reeking of brandy and aftershave, a big cigar sticking out of his mouth. Even heat and drink hadn't brought any flush of pink to his man-tanned cheeks. He was carrying a bottle of Charles Heidsieck and two glasses which he put on the dressing table. I clutched the white dressing gown tighter round me. For a long time he stood behind me looking into the mirror, his eyes as triumphant as they were predatory. Then he said in his oily, sibilant voice,

'You look a bit rough, baby. Been up against it, have you?'

'I've been working hard.'

Andreas laughed.

'You're not cut out for a career, I always warned you. And Gareth Llewellyn's ditched you; I knew he would. You must listen to Uncle Andreas in future.'

He seemed to revel in my utter desperation.

'Never mind,' he went on soothingly. 'I'll see you right. A few weeks of cushy living and you'll soon get the ripe peachy look you had at Grayston.'

He ran his hands over me, lingeringly and feelingly, like a child trying to gauge the contents of a wrapped Christmas present. I gritted my teeth, trying to suppress the shudder of revulsion. He let go of me, and started to take the gold paper off the top of the champagne bottle. I watched his soft white hands in horror. God knows what they wouldn't be doing to me later this evening.

I took a deep breath. 'Can I have the cash now?'

Andreas shook his head. 'Uh-uh. You get the cash when you deliver the goods, and they'd better be good.'

The top shot off the bottle into the rafters. Andreas filled a glass and handed it to me.

'That should relax you,' he said. 'Make you feel nice and sexy.'

I took a belt of champagne, wondering if I was going to throw up.

'Come in, boys,' shouted Andreas over the curtain, and we were joined by a couple of Andreas' hood friends, flashing jewellery, sweating in waisted suits. They were the sort of guys who'd give even the Mafia nightmares.

'Meet Mannie and Vic,' said Andreas.

He must have brought them along to show me off. They were obviously disappointed I wasn't as fantastic as Andreas had promised but were too wary of him to show it.

'You wait till she's been with me for a bit,' purred Andreas, pinching my cheek. 'You won't recognize her.'

'Fattening her up for Christmas, are you?' said Mannie, and they all laughed.

Cy Markovitz, having finished with the black girl, wandered over and said he was almost ready. He was a tall, exhausted and melancholy man in his late forties, wearing army trousers, sneakers, and a khaki shirt drenched with sweat.

'Come and meet Octavia,' said Andreas, re-filling my glass. 'She's a bit nervous, first time she's done anything like this, so treat her with care. Lovely, isn't she?' he added, smoothing my hair back from my forehead.

Cy Markovitz nodded – he was, after all, being paid vast sums by Andreas – and said the camera would go up in smoke when it saw me.

'You needn't worry about the pix,' he went on. 'We'll shoot

through a soft-focus lens with the emphasis on the face and the direct gaze, very subdued and elegant.'

Oh God, what would Gareth say if he ever saw the results? I imagined him suddenly stumbling across them as he flicked through magazines on some foreign news-stand, his face hardening with disapproval, then shrugging his shoulders because he'd always known I was a bad lot. Was it really worth going through with it to help Xander? Was blood really thicker than water?

'Ready when you are, darlings,' said Gabriel, popping his golden head round the curtain.

Andreas gave me a big smile. 'Come on, baby, you'll enjoy it once we get started.'

I sat on the silver satin sheets, gazing in misery on the forest of potted plants. The studio seemed to be very full of people, all watching me with bored appraising eyes. I huddled even deeper into my dressing gown.

Cy Markovitz came over to me.

'You're not going to need that,' he said gently.

As I took it off, even Markovitz caught his breath. Andreas' thug friends were trying to preserve their poker faces, but their eyes were falling out.

'I told you she was the nearest thing to a Vargas girl you were ever likely to see,' said Andreas smugly.

Cy was gazing into the viewfinder. His assistant took some Polaroid pictures, peeling them off like a wet bikini. Andreas and Cy pored over them.

'We'll need the cold blower to stiffen her nipples,' said Cy.

Andreas was determined to get his 112 lbs of flesh. Two agonizing hours later, I had been photographed in every conceivable position and garment, including a white fox fur with a string of pearls hanging over one breast, a soaking wet cheesecloth shirt, black stockings and a suspender belt, and nothing but an ostrich feather.

Gabriel, who was fast losing his cool, had been sent out to hire a Persian cat for me to cuddle, but after 30 seconds of popping flash bulbs the poor creature, having lacerated my stomach with its claws, wriggled out of my clutches and took refuge in the rafters.

Now I was stretched out on the satin sheets, wearing a sort of rucked up camisole top. Cy Markovitz clicked away, keeping up a running commentary.

'Lovely, darling, just pull it down over your right shoulder, look straight into the camera. A bit more wind machine, Gabriel, please. Come on, Octavia, baby, relax, and let me have it, shut your eyes, lick your lips and caress yourself.'

'No,' I whispered. 'I won't do that.'

Markovitz sighed, extracted the roll of film from the camera, licked the flap, sealed it up and, taking another roll from the assistant, replaced it.

'Turn over,' he said. 'Bury your face in the sheets, stick your ass in the air, and freeze in that position.'

'I can't freeze when I'm absolutely baking,' I snapped.

'Hold it,' said Markovitz, 'hold it. That's fan-bloody-tastic. Come over and have a look, Andreas.'

Andreas joined him. They conferred in low voices, then Andreas came and sat down on the bed beside me, filling up my glass.

'You're too uptight, baby,' he said. 'You're not coming across.'

'How can I when you're all here gawping at me?'

It was like the times when I was a child and my mother insisted on being present when the doctor examined me.

'You'll have to try.' And once again I realized how much he was enjoying my utter humiliation, paying me back for all the times I'd put him down in the past. I lay back on the bed.

'Open your legs a bit further, open wide, that's lovely,' said Cy, clicking away. Any moment he'd ask me to say 'ah'. After this was all over, I supposed I could go out and throw myself over Westminster Bridge.

Gabriel was still whisking about, adjusting plants, his bronzed, hairless pectorals gleaming in the lights.

'Why don't we dress her up as a nun and let Angelica seduce her?' he said. 'Then it wouldn't matter her looking so uptight.'

'That's an interesting thought,' said Andreas.

There was a knock on the door. One of the assistants unlocked it, and let in a girl in a red dress with long black hair, and a pale, witchy, heavily made-up face. She looked furious and vaguely familiar. Perhaps miraculously she was going to take over from me.

'Hi, Angelica,' said Markovitz. 'Go and get your clothes off. We'll take a break for ten minutes.'

'She was on the gatefold of *Penetration* this month,' said one of Gabriel's minions. 'The blurb said Daddy was a regular soldier and that Angelica was reading philosophy at university, and spent the vacation pottering round ruins.'

'You could hardly call Andreas a ruin,' said Gabriel.

Andreas opened another bottle of champagne.

'I've booked a table at Skindles tonight,' he said, caressing my shoulder with a moist hand. 'I thought in this heat it'd be nice to get out of London.'

He took a powder puff from one of Cy's assistants, and carefully took the shine off my nose. Tears of utter despair stung my eyelids.

'If you could find a horse,' said the other of Gabriel's minions, 'she'd make a stunning Godiva.'

'Shut up,' hissed Gabriel. 'There's a riding school round the corner. I've had enough hassle getting that bloody cat.'

A few minutes later Angelica emerged from behind the curtain, wearing only a red feather boa and a corn plaster. She walked sulkily up to the bed, looking at Andreas with the mixture of terror and loathing such as a lion might regard a sadistic ringmaster.

'You've already met Angelica Burton-Brown, haven't you, Octavia?' said Andreas. He seemed to be laughing at some private joke.

'I don't think so,' I began, then realized that she was one of the tarts Andreas had brought down to Grayston. She was now glaring in my direction. Clytemnestra could hardly have looked more blackly on Agamemnon.

'Come and lie down, Angelica,' said Andreas, patting the bed.

She stretched out beside me, her black-lined eyes not quite closed. Underneath each false eyelash was a millimetre of dark venomous light raying straight in my direction. Trust Andreas to set up a scene that tortured both past and intended mistress.

'How's that?' he said to Cy. 'They make a good contrast, don't they? Profane and not-so-Sacred Love.'

I got to my feet and reached under the bed for the dressing gown. 'You've finished with me then?'

Andreas put a heavy hand on my shoulder, pressing me down again.

'On the contrary,' he said, 'we're only just beginning. Put the Nun's headdress on Angelica,' he said to Gabriel.

She looked so utterly ridiculous – talk about sour Angelica – that I was hard put not to giggle with hysterical laughter. But not for long; the next moment Andreas had hung a cross round my neck.

'Kneel beside her, Angelica,' he went on. 'That's right, as close as you can.'

I felt as though great toads were crawling all over me. I gazed down at the cross hanging between my breasts. Perhaps if I held it up to Andreas, he would suddenly age hundreds of years and shrivel into dust like Count Dracula.

'Now put your hand on Octavia's shoulder,' he said. I jumped away as I felt her fingers.

'No!' I screamed. 'No! I won't do it, I won't!'

'Cut it out,' said Andreas. 'Do you want two grand or not?'

I looked at him mutinously; then I remembered Xander and nodded.

Angelica looked about as cheerful as a cat with toothache. She'd obviously never had bread like that from him.

Andreas ruffled the sheets round us, and gazed into the viewfinder.

'Very nice,' he said softly. 'A bit more amiable, both of you.' Cy took over again.

'Put your hand on Octavia's throat, Angelica,' he said.

I steeled myself, feeling the tense hatred in her fingers. The sweat was glistening on her black moustache.

'Lovely,' said Cy. 'Now slide your hand down a bit, Angelica, and down a bit further.'

I couldn't bear it, even for Xander, I couldn't take any more. I shot a despairing supplicating glance at Andreas and was appalled by the expression of suppressed excitement on his face. I felt the tears coursing down my cheeks.

Then suddenly there was a tremendous crash outside. Everyone jumped, as someone started pummelling on the door.

'It's the fuzz,' squeaked Gabriel in excitement, patting his curls.

'You can't go in there,' screamed a female voice. 'The studio's booked.'

'Oh yes I bloody can,' shouted a voice.

There was another tremendous crash, the door seemed to tremble, then suddenly caved in. I gave a gasp, half of relief and half of horror, for in the doorway, fierce as ten furies, terrible as hell, stood Gareth. Slowly he looked round the room, taking in first Cy, then Andreas and his hood cronies, then finally me on the bed with Angelica. With a whimper I pulled one of the satin sheets round me.

'What the bloody hell's going on?' he howled, walking across the studio towards me. 'You whore, you bloody cheap whore! I might have known you'd end up like this. Get your clothes on.'

Andreas moved towards him.

'Take it easy, big boy,' he said softly. 'Don't get so excited.'

Gareth turned on him.

'You lousy creep,' he hissed. 'I know how long you've been scheming to get your dirty hands on her. I'll get you for this. Go on,' he added, out of the corner of his mouth, to me. 'For Christ's sake, get dressed.'

I stood up, still too frightened to move.

'How on earth did you know she was here?' asked Gabriel, looking at him with admiration.

'Andreas shouldn't go round boasting in restaurants,' said Gareth. 'These things get overheard.'

'Look, wise guy.' Andreas was talking slowly and patiently now, as though he was dictating to an inexperienced secretary. 'You're gatecrashing a very important party. Cy's booked for the day, and so's Octavia, and neither of them for peanuts. She needs the money, don't you, Octavia?'

Gareth glanced in my direction. I nodded miserably.

'So you can't come barging in here making a nuisance of yourself,' said Andreas.

'Oh, can't I?' said Gareth with ominous quiet.

There was a long pause; then, suddenly, he went berserk. Turning, he kicked Cy's camera across the room, then he smashed his fist into Cy's face, sending him flying after the camera. The next moment he'd laid out Cy's assistant with a punishing upper cut. Then Vic the hood picked up a rubber plant and hurled it at Gareth, who ducked just in time and, gathering up another plant, hurled it back.

Screaming like a stuck pig, still in the Nun's headdress, Angelica dived under the bed, followed immediately by the two minions and Gabriel.

'Oh dear,' sighed Gabriel as two more plants sailed through the air. 'Burnham Wood came to Dunsinane, now it's going back again.'

Ducking to avoid more flying vegetation, I shook off the silk sheets, ran across the room, dived behind the curtain and started to pull on my clothes. By the sound of it Gareth was still laying about him like a maddened bull. As I looked out he was having a punch-up with Mannie who wrong-footed him and sent him crashing to the ground. The next moment Gareth had got to his feet and thrown Mannie into the middle of the remaining potted plants.

'Oh my poor jardinière,' wailed Gabriel's voice from under the bed. 'What *will* the plant shop say?'

As I crept out from behind the curtain, a silver teapot and two glass paperweights flew across the room, none of them fortunately hitting their target.

Gareth paused; he was breathing heavily. Cy was still nursing his jaw in the corner. Mannie was peering out of the plants like a spy in *L'Attaque*. Vic was shaking his head and picking himself up. Cy's assistant got to his feet. As he started edging nervously towards the door, Gareth grabbed him by the collar.

'No you don't,' he said. 'Where are those rolls of film? Come on or I'll beat you to a pulp.' His fingers closed round the boy's neck.

'Over there on the trolley,' choked the boy in terror.

Gareth pocketed the rolls. As I sidled round the wall towards him, he glanced in my direction and jerked his head towards the door. He was just backing towards it himself when Vic moved in, catching him off guard with a blow to the right eye. Gareth slugged him back, sending him hurtling across the room, then, trying to right himself, tripped over one of the light wires and cannoned heavily into a pile of tripods. It was getting more like Tom and Jerry every minute.

Next minute, Andreas, who'd been watching the whole proceedings without lifting a finger, picked up the champagne bottle and, cracking it on the underneath of the bed, moved with incredible speed across the room towards Gareth. Cornered, Gareth scrambled out of the tripods, shaking his head. His right eye was beginning to close up. His forehead, just above his eyebrow, was bleeding where Vic's gold ring had gashed it.

He backed away from Andreas until he reached the wall.

'Now then, big boy,' murmured Andreas, his voice almost a caress. 'I'll teach you to get tough with me.' He brandished the jagged edge of the bottle in Gareth's face. 'Give me back that film.'

Gareth stared at him, not a muscle moving in his face.

'You lousy cheap punk,' he said.

Then I froze with horror as I saw that Mannie had extracted himself from the potted plants and, armed with a flick knife, was moving relentlessly in from the right. Without thinking, I picked up the Christopher Wray lamp and hurled it at him, slap on target. Just for a second Andreas' concentration flickered, giving Gareth the chance to leap on him, knocking him to the floor. Over and over they rolled like Tommy Brook and Mr Tod, yelling abuse at each other. Then finally Gareth was on top smashing his fists into Andreas' head. For a minute I thought he was going to kill him; then he got up, picked Andreas up and threw him through the Habitat wallpaper like a clown through a hoop.

There was another long pause. Gareth looked slowly round the room. Everyone flattened themselves against the wall or the floor. Then suddenly there was the sound of clapping, and Angelica emerged from under the bed, her Nun's headdress askew.

'I've been waiting three years for someone to do that,' she said.

Blood was pouring from Gareth's arm. He must have jagged it on Andreas' bottle.

'You'll bleed to death,' I moaned, gathering up a peach silk petticoat that was lying on the floor.

'Well, bags I give him the kiss of life,' said a little voice from under the bed. Gareth grabbed my wrist. 'Come on, let's get out of here.'

From *Octavia* by Jilly Cooper, 1977

Hot Lezzy Action

Sexual politics more or less passed us by, unfortunately, but given the grotty boys that we'd occasionally encounter at school dances, we might have done better batting for our own team. The following extract is certainly persuasive.

*F*rench women were much more free spoken than the English, who mostly said they disliked to touch another woman's cunt, which I believed was a lie. One or two only, said they'd had a flat fuck with a friend, and what harm was there? One night a woman threw herself upon another before me, and with a sham wriggle said, 'That's how we do it.'

Nelly one evening in November got me another English woman, and she mounted her and jogged as if fucking, their cunts were close together, but they laughed, – I told her that she shammed, and should go elsewhere where I would see two women really and truly flat fucking. She thought she might lose me and so got serious. The other woman then said, 'Nelly does it with Rosa B.' – The only time I think I ever saw Nell thoroughly angry was then. She threatened to stick the other for saying so. – The woman who was a little in liquor said, 'You do, Rosa flat cocked with me the other night, and told me she did it with *you*, *she* likes it, and *I* like it, I don't care a damn who knows it. Go to the bloody hell and suck her cunt. she says she sucks yours – there.' – Nell threw a glass at her head which missed her, and with trouble I pacified them. Another night, Nell confessed that she did flat fuck occasionally with Rosa B. She said, 'She came from my village, is fond of me, and likes it, so I let her do it.' – I have often found two harlots close friends whey they came from the same village or place.

*

I was impatient to see their flat fucking, and said so. Rising Rosa B gave Nell a kiss, and felt her cunt – Nell had only then her chemise on. – It makes me lewed to see a woman feel another's cunt. Then Rosa B. stripped to her chemise which was nice and clean. I pulled it off, and saw a very thin creature but straight and well formed, with a youthful looking cunt, darkish haired, and shewing as she stood with legs closed, a clitoris projecting well from it. I examined her notch which was little enough, but the clitoris and nymphae full sized. I then stripped Nell and looked at hers. Then we talked about flat fucking, cunt rubbing, clitoris', large and small – cock sucking, and fucking in general whilst we sat by the fire, we two drinking sherry, Rosa brandy and water, till to my astonishment I found her screwed and she'd emptied more than half the brandy bottle. Nell put the bottle out of her way. – 'You've had enough, I don't want you tight again,' said she.

Nelly was friskier with tipple than usual. I made myself naked, we all felt each other, then I set them to work. They laid on the bed feeling each other's cunts. Rosa was randiest, yet for a moment seemed hesitating. 'Never mind him, – he knows, – do it properly,' said Nell. – Rosa mounted her, her thin thighs fitted in between Nell's fat ones, Nell raised her feet over the other's buttocks and they rubbed cunts together. I put my hand between Rosa's thighs, my thumb up her cunt, two fingers up Nell's, and felt the two cunts joined together. I could even see and feel that they were rubbing against each other. They moved at first quietly with gentle fucking motions, then their arses wriggled, Nell seemed agitated, the other at first noisy, then they breathed short, murmured, and with sighs of pleasure their limbs straightened out and they lay still. Both spent in a few minutes. Encouraged by me, they soon recommenced.

<hr>

From *My Secret Life* by 'Walter', first published
in eleven volumes 1888–1894

In Suburbia

Published in 1956, and the second-ever American blockbuster after *Gone With the Wind*. Blew the lid off white-picket-fence suburban life, with an eye-popping mixture of repression, loneliness, illegitimacy, sexual and emotional abuse, abortion, unbridled lust and murder. Its author, Grace Metalious, equated the emotional well-being and happiness of her female characters with their finding sexual fulfilment – a bold move at the time, and one which was rewarded by fifty-nine weeks on the bestseller list.

'I guess I've just sort of outgrown Selena,' she told her mother.

But it had been bad, at first, losing Selena. Allison had thought that she would die of loneliness, and she spent many a long Saturday afternoon weeping in her room, rather than go poking about in the shops by herself. Then she had become friendly with Kathy Ellsworth, a new girl in town, and she no longer missed Selena. Kathy loved to read and walk and she painted pictures. It was this last which had prompted Allison to tell Kathy about the stories she had tried to write.

'I'm sure you'll understand, Kathy,' said Allison. 'I mean, one artist to another.'

Kathy Ellsworth was small and quiet. Allison often had the feeling that if anyone were to strike Kathy, that Kathy's bones would crumble and disintegrate, and she was often so still that Allison could forget that she was there at all.

'Do you like boys?' Allison asked her new friend.

'Yes,' said Kathy, and Allison was shocked.

'I mean, do you *really* like them?'

'Yes, I do,' said Kathy. 'When I grow up, I'm going to get married, and buy a house, and have a dozen children.'

'Well, I'm not!' said Allison. 'I am going to be a brilliant authoress. Absolutely brilliant. And I shall never marry. I just hate boys!'

Boys were another question that disturbed Allison that winter. Oftentimes, she lay awake in her bed at night and had the most peculiar sensations. She wanted to rub her hands over her body, but when she did, she always remembered her thirteenth birthday and the way Rodney Harrington had kissed her. Then she would either go hot and prickly all over, or else she would feel cold enough to shiver. She tried to imagine other boys kissing her, but the face that swam beneath her closed lids was always that of Rodney, and she almost wished that she could feel his lips again. She pressed her hands flat against her abdomen, then let them slide up to her small breasts. She rubbed her finger tips over her nipples until they were hard, and this caused an odd tightening somewhere between her legs that puzzled her but was, somehow, very pleasant. One night she began to wonder how it would feel if it were Rodney's hands on her breasts, and her face burned.

'I just hate boys,' she told her friend Kathy, but she began to practice sultry looks in her mirror, and all day long, at school, she was aware of Rodney in the seat next to hers.

'Did a boy ever kiss you?' she asked Kathy.

'Oh, yes,' replied Kathy calmly. 'Several of them. I liked it.'

'You didn't!' cried Allison.

'Yes, I did,' said Kathy, who, Allison had discovered, would not lie, or even be tactful if it occasioned a slight coloring of the truth. 'Yes,' repeated Kathy, 'I liked it very much. A boy even screwed me once.'

'Oh, my goodness!' said Allison. 'How did he do that?'

'Oh, you know. Put his tongue in my mouth when he kissed me.'

'Oh,' said Allison.

Kathy and Allison changed their reading habits radically that winter. They began to haunt the library in search of books reputed to be 'sexy,' and they read them aloud to one another.

'I wish I had breasts like marble,' said Kathy sadly, closing a book. 'Mine have blue veins in them that show through the skin. I think I'll draw a picture of a girl with marble breasts.'

*

Rodney Harrington, wearing a white jacket and with his curly black hair well slicked down with water, sat on the edge of a chair in the MacKenzie living room. Constance had left him there while she went upstairs to see if Allison was ready, and now Rodney sat and stared morosely at the braided rug on the floor.

What, he asked himself, ever prompted him to ask Allison MacKenzie to the biggest dance of the year? Especially to this dance, the very first that he was being allowed to attend. There was Betty Anderson, all eager and hot after him, just waiting for him to ask her to the dance, and he had gone and asked Allison MacKenzie. Ask a nice girl, his father had ordered, and look where Rodney had wound up. On the edge of a chair in the MacKenzie living room, waiting for skinny Allison. He could have had a good time with Betty, damn it all.

Rodney felt himself reddening and looked surreptitiously around the empty room. He did not like to think of the afternoon that he had spent in the woods at Road's End with Betty Anderson, unless he was sure that he was by himself. When he was alone, he could not keep from thinking of it.

That Betty! thought Rodney, letting memory take him. Boy, she was really something. Nothing kiddish about her or what she had shown him that afternoon. She didn't talk like a kid, either, or look like one. By God, she was something, whether her father was a mill hand or not, she was still something!

Rodney closed his eyes and felt his breath coming fast with the memory of Betty Anderson.

No, he shook himself, not here. I'll wait until tonight when I get home.

He looked around the MacKenzie living room and once again his thoughts began to lacerate him.

He could have had a swell time at the dance with Betty, and

here he was, waiting for Allison. And if that wasn't bad enough, Betty was mad at him for not asking her. You couldn't blame Betty for that, after all, when a girl shared a secret with you, she had a right to expect you to ask her to the biggest dance of the year. He just hoped she'd be at the dance. Maybe he'd get a chance to talk to her and find out if she was still mad. Damn it, he could have talked his father out of putting his foot down about Betty if he had really tried. And there was skinny Allison, always making cow eyes at him, and his father had said to ask a nice girl.

Fool! said Rodney Harrington to himself. Damn fool!

He could hear a stirring on the stairs in the hall, now, so he supposed that Allison was finally coming down. He just hoped she looked decent and wouldn't make those cow eyes at him at the dance, where some of the boys might see. He couldn't afford to have Betty overhear anyone teasing him about Allison or any other girl.

'Here's Allison, Rodney,' said Constance.

Rodney stood up. 'Hi, Allison.'

'Hi.'

'Well, my father's outside in the car.'

'All right.'

'You got a coat or something?'

'I have this. It's an evening coat.'

'Well, let's go.'

'I'm ready.'

'Good night, Mrs MacKenzie.'

'Good night, Mother.'

'Good night—' Constance caught herself just in time. She had almost said 'Children.' 'Good night, Allison,' she said. 'Good night, Rodney. Have a nice time.'

As soon as they were out the door, Constance sank wearily into a chair. It had been a difficult week, with Allison alternating between moments of unbearable impatience and hours of demoralizing panic. When she awakened on the day of the dance with an angry red pimple on her chin, she wept and demanded that Constance telephone Rodney immediately to tell him that Allison was ill and would not be able to go out that evening. Constance lit a cigarette and looked at the framed photograph on the mantelpiece.

'Well, Allison,' she said aloud, 'here we are. Alone at last.'

Your bastard daughter is all bathed, curled, perfumed, manicured and dressed, and here we are, Allison, you and I alone, waiting for her to return from her first formal engagement.

It frightened Constance when she thought in that fashion, with bitterness and self-pity, and it shocked her to realize that lately her bitterness was not only for the position in which Allison MacKenzie had placed her fourteen years before. In recent weeks she had been actively resenting the idea of being left alone to cope with a growing girl, and in her angry reasoning the blame for this fell entirely on the shoulders of her dead lover. Allison's crime, and in Constance's eyes it was a crime, was that he had claimed to love her. That being the case, his first thoughts should have been for her protection, coming ahead of his desire to lead her to bed but, as Constance put it to herself, he had not thought of protection until too late, and Constance had ended up by allowing Allison MacKenzie to become a habit with her. She knew that she had not loved him, for if she had, the relationship between them could never have been what it was. Love, to Constance, was synonymous with marriage, and marriage was something based on a community of tastes and interests, together with a similarity of background and viewpoint. All these were blended together by an emotion called 'love,' and sex did not enter into it at all. Therefore, reasoned Constance, she had certainly not loved Allison MacKenzie. Constance's eyes went again to the photograph on the mantelpiece, and she wondered where, eventually, she would find the words to explain the way of things to the daughter of Allison MacKenzie. The ringing of the doorbell cut across her mind, breaking sharply into her thoughts. Constance sighed again, more deeply than before, and rubbed the back of her neck where it ached. Allison, she supposed, had forgotten a handkerchief in her excitement.

Constance opened her front door and saw Tomas Makris

standing on the steps. For a moment she was unable to move or speak, overcome not so much by surprise, as by a feeling of unreality.

'Good evening,' said Tom into the silence. 'Since you always manage to avoid me on the street and even in your store, I thought I'd come to call formally.'

When Constance did not answer but continued to stand with one hand on the inside doorknob and the other leaning against the jamb, Tom went on in the same conversational tone.

'I realize,' he said, 'that it is not the conventional thing to do. I should have waited to call until after you had called on me, but I was afraid that you would never get around to performing your neighborly duty. Mrs MacKenzie,' he went on, pushing gently at the outside of the door, 'I have been standing on the street corner for over half an hour waiting for your daughter to be off with her date, and my feet are damned tired. May I come in?'

'Oh, yes. Please do,' said Constance at last, and her voice sounded breathy to her own ears. 'Yes, do. Please come in.'

She stood with her back against the panels of the closed door while Tom walked past her and into the hall.

'Let me take your coat, Mr Makris,' she said.

Tom took off his coat and folded it over his arm, then he walked to where Constance was standing. He stood close enough to her so that she had to raise her head to look up at him, and when she had done so, he smiled down at her gently.

'Don't be afraid,' he said. 'I'm not going to hurt you. I'm going to be around for a long time. There's no hurry.'

*

The gymnasium of the Peyton Place High School was decorated with pink and green crepe paper. The paper hung in twisted festoons from the ceiling and walls. It was wrapped carefully around the basketball hoops and backboards in a hopeful effort at disguise. Some imaginative senior, discouraged with the limp look of the basketball nets, had cleverly stuffed them with multicolored spring blossoms and someone else had fastened a balloon to every spot that provided a place to tie a string. On the wall, behind where the orchestra sat, huge letters cut of aluminum foil had been pasted.

PEYTON PLACE HIGH SCHOOL WELCOMES YOU
TO ITS ANNUAL SPRING HOP

The seniors who had been on the decorating committee drew sighs of relief and looked at their work with well-earned satisfaction. The gym, they assured one another, had never looked better for a spring dance than it did this year. The annual spring dance, which had become a custom in Peyton Place since the building of the new high school, was an affair given by the graduating seniors as a premature welcome to the grade school children who would be entering high school in the fall, and it had come to represent a number of things to different people. To most eighth grade girls it meant the time of their first formal and their first real date with a boy, while to most boys it meant the official lifting of the nine o'clock curfew which their parents had imposed on them. To Elsie Thornton, dressed in black silk and acting as a chaperon, it seemed to be a time of new awareness in the youngsters whom she had taught that year. She could discern in them the first stirrings of interest toward one another and knew that this interest was the forerunner of the searching and finding that would come later.

Not, thought Miss Thornton, that a few of them hadn't done their searching and finding already.

She watched Selena Cross and Ted Carter circling the floor slowly, their heads close together, and although she was not a believer in the myth of childhood sweethearts who grew up, married and lived happily ever after, she found herself hoping that it could be so in the case of Selena and Ted. Her feelings when she watched Allison MacKenzie and Rodney Harrington were very different. It had been like a blow to her heart to see Allison come in with Rodney. Miss Thornton had put up an involuntary hand, and lowered it quickly, hoping that no one had noticed.

Oh, be careful, my dear, she had thought. You must be very careful, or you'll get hurt.

Miss Thornton saw Betty Anderson, dressed in a red dress that was much too old for her, watching Allison and Rodney. Betty had come to the dance with a boy who was a senior in the high school and who already had a reputation as a fast driver and a hard drinker. But Betty had not taken her eyes off Rodney all evening. It was ten o'clock before Rodney got up the courage to approach Betty. He walked over to her the moment that Allison left him to go to the rest room, and when Allison returned to the gymnasium he was dancing with Betty. Allison went over to the line of straight chairs where the chaperons were sitting and sat down next to Elsie Thornton, but her eyes were fixed on Rodney and Betty.

Don't you care, darling, Miss Thornton wanted to say. Don't pin your dreams on that boy, for he will only shatter them and you.

'You look lovely, Allison,' she said.

'Thank you, Miss Thornton,' replied Allison, wondering if it would be proper to say, So do you, Miss Thornton. It would be a lie if she said it, because Miss Thornton had never looked uglier. Black was definitely not her color. And why was Rodney staying so long with Betty?

Allison kept her head up and her smile on, even when one set of dances ended and another began, and Rodney did not come to claim her. She smiled and waved at Selena, and at Kathy Ellsworth who had come with a boy who was in high school and kissed with his mouth open. She felt a small pang of compassion for little Norman Page who stood leaning against the wall, alone, and stared down at his feet. Norman, Allison knew, had been brought to the dance by his mother, who was going to leave him there until eleven o'clock while she attended a meeting of the Ladies' Aid at the Congregational church. Allison smiled at Norman when he raised his head, and wiggled her fingers at him, but her stomach had begun to churn and she did not know how much longer she could keep from being sick. Betty's finger tips rested on the back of Rodney's neck, and he was looking down at her with his eyes half closed.

Why is he doing this to me? she wondered sickly. I look nicer than Betty. She looks cheap in that sleazy red dress, and she's wearing gunk on her eyelashes. She's got awfully big breasts for a girl her age, and Kathy said they were real. I don't believe it. I wish Miss Thornton would stop fidgeting in her chair – and there's only one more dance left in this set and I'd better get ready to stand up because Rodney will be coming for me in a few minutes. I'll bet that dress belonged to Betty's big sister, the one who got in Dutch with that man from White River. Selena looks beautiful in that white dress. She looks so old. She looks twenty at least, and Ted does, too. They're in love, you can tell by looking at them. Everybody's looking at me. I'm the only girl sitting down. Rodney's gone!

Allison's heart began to beat in hot, heavy thuds as her eyes circled the dance floor wildly. She glanced at the door just in time to see a flash of red, and she knew then that Rodney had left her here alone while he went somewhere with Betty.

What if he doesn't come back? she thought. What if I have to go home alone? Everyone knows I came with him. EVERYONE IS LAUGHING AT ME!

Miss Thornton's hand was cold and hurtful on her elbow.

'My goodness, Allison,' laughed Miss Thornton. 'You *are* off in a dream world. Norman's asked you to dance with him twice, and you haven't even answered him.'

Allison's eyes were so full of tears that she could not see Norman, and her face hurt. It was only when she stood up to dance with him that she realized that she was still smiling. Norman held her awkwardly while the orchestra imported from White River for the occasion played a waltz.

If he says one thing – thought Allison desperately. If he says one word I shall be sick right here in front of everyone.

'I saw Rodney go outside with Betty,' said Norman, 'so I thought I'd ask you to dance. You were sitting next to Miss Thornton for an awfully long time.'

Allison was not sick in front of everyone. 'Thank you, Norman,' she said. 'It was nice of you to ask me.'

'I don't know what's the matter with Rodney,' continued

Norman. 'You're much prettier than that fat old Betty Anderson.'

Oh, God, prayed Allison, make him shut up.

'Betty came with John Pillsbury.' Norman pronounced it Pillsbree. 'He drinks and takes girls riding in his car. He got stopped by the state police once, for speeding and drunken driving, and the police told his father. Do you like Rodney?'

I love him! screamed Allison silently. I love him and he is breaking my heart!

'No,' she said, 'not particularly. He was just someone to come with.'

Norman whirled her around inexpertly. 'Just the same,' he said, 'it's a dirty trick for him to leave you sitting with Miss Thornton and go off with Betty like that.'

Please, God. Please, God, thought Allison.

But the orchestra continued to play, and Norman's hand was sticky in hers, and Allison thought of the girl in the fairy tale about the red shoes, and the electric lights glared down at her until her temples began to pound.

Outside, Betty Anderson was leading Rodney by the hand across the dark field that served as a parking lot for the high school. John Pillsbury's car was parked a short distance away from the others, under a tree, and when Betty and Rodney reached it, she opened the back door and got in.

'Hurry up,' she whispered, and Rodney climbed in behind her.

Swiftly, she pressed down the buttons on the four doors that locked them, and then she collapsed into the back seat, laughing.

'Here we are,' she said. 'Snug as peas in a pod.'

'Come on, Betty,' whispered Rodney. 'Come on.'

'No,' she said petulantly, 'I won't. I'm mad at you.'

'Aw, come on, Betty. Don't be like that. Kiss me.'

'No,' said Betty, tossing her head. 'Go get skinny Allison MacKenzie to kiss you. She's the one you brought to the dance.'

'Don't be mad, Betty,' pleaded Rodney. 'I couldn't help it. I didn't want to. My father made me do it.'

'Would you rather be with me?' asked Betty in a slightly mollified tone.

'*Would* I?' breathed Rodney, and it was not a question.

Betty leaned her head against his shoulder and ran one finger up and down on his coat lapel.

'Just the same,' she said, 'I think it was mean of you to ask Allison to the dance.'

'Aw, come on, Betty. Don't be like that. Kiss me a little.'

Betty lifted her head and Rodney quickly covered her mouth with his. She could kiss, thought Rodney, like no one else in the world. She didn't kiss with just her lips, but with her teeth and her tongue, and all the while she made noises deep in her throat, and her fingernails dug into his shoulders.

'Oh, honey, honey,' whispered Rodney, and that was all he could say before Betty's tongue went between his teeth again.

Her whole body twisted and moved when he kissed her, and when his hands found their way to her breasts, she moaned as if she were hurt. She writhed on the seat until she was lying down, with only her legs and feet not touching him, and Rodney fitted his body to her without taking his mouth from hers.

'Is it up, Rod?' she panted, undulating her body under his. 'Is it up good and hard?'

'Oh, yes,' he whispered, almost unable to speak. 'Oh, yes.'

Without another word, Betty jacknifed her knees, pushed Rodney away from her, clicked the lock on the door and was outside of the car.

'Now go shove it into Allison MacKenzie,' she screamed at him. 'Go get the girl you brought to the dance and get rid of it with her!'

Before Rodney could catch his breath to utter one word, she had whirled and was on her way back to the gymnasium. He tried to get out of the car to run after her, but his legs were like sawdust under him, and he could only cling to the open door and curse under his breath.

'Bitch,' he said hoarsely, using one of his father's favorite words. 'Goddamned bitch!'

He hung onto the open car door and retched helplessly, and the sweat poured down his face.

'Bitch!' he said, but it did not help.

At last, he straightened up and wiped his face with his handker-chief, and fumbled in his pockets for a comb. He still had to go back into the gymnasium to get that goddamned Allison MacKenzie. His father would drive up at eleven-thirty and expect to find him waiting with her.

'Oh, you rotten bitch,' he said under his breath to the absent Betty. 'Oh, you stinking, rotten, goddamned bitchy sonofabitch!'

He racked his brain to think of new swear words to direct at her, but he could think of nothing. He began to comb his hair, almost in tears.

Over Norman's shoulder, Allison saw Betty Anderson come back into the gymnasium, alone.

Dear God, she thought, maybe he's gone home alone! What shall I do?

'There's Betty,' said Norman. 'I wonder what happened to Rodney?'

'He's probably in the Men's,' said Allison who could not seem to keep her voice steady. 'Please, Norman. Couldn't we sit down. My feet hurt.'

And my head, she thought. And my stomach. And my arms, and hands, and legs, and the back of my neck.

It was eleven-fifteen when she saw Rodney walk through the door. She was so overwhelmed with relief that she could not be angry. He had saved her face by returning to her and not leaving her to go home alone. He looked sick. His face was red and swollen looking.

'You almost ready to go?' he asked Allison.

'Any time you are,' she said nonchalantly.

'My father's outside, so we might as well go.'

'We might just as well.'

'I'll get your coat.'

'All right.'

'Do you want to dance one more first?'

'No. No, thank you. I've been dancing so much all evening that my feet are ready to fall off.'

'Well, I'll get your coat.'

And that, thought Miss Elsie Thornton, is that. Valiant is the word for Allison.

'Good night, Miss Thornton. I had a lovely time.'

'Good night, dear,' said Miss Thornton.

———————

From *Peyton Place* by Grace Metalious, 1956

A Levels

Raunchy, bawdy, funny, knowing: made deciphering Middle
English a surprising pleasure.

Whan myn housbonde is fro the world ygon,
Som Cristen man shal wedde me anon,
For thanne, th' apostle seith that I am free
To wedde, a Goddes half, where it liketh me.
He seith that to be wedded is no sinne;
Bet is to be wedded than to brinne
What rekketh me, thogh folk seye vileynie
Of shrewed Lameth and his bigamie?
I woot wel Abraham was an hooly man,
And Jacob eek, as ferforth as I kan;
And ech of hem hadde wyves mo than two,
And many another holy man also.
Wher can ye seye, in any manere age,
That hye God defended mariage
By expres word? I pray yow, telleth me.
Or where comanded he virginitee?
I woot as wel as ye, it is no drede,
Th'apostel, whan he speketh of maydenhede,
He seyde that precept therof hadde he noon.
Men may conseille a womman to been oon,
But conseilling is no comandement.
He putte it in oure owene juggement;

Modern English Translation

No sooner than one husband's dead and gone
Some other Christian man shall take me on,
For then, so says the Apostle, I am free
To wed, o' God's name where it pleases me.
Wedding's no sin, so far as I can learn.
Better it is to marry than to burn.

'What do I care if people choose to see
Scandal in Lamech for his bigamy?
I know that Abraham was a holy man
And Jacob too — I speak as best I can —
Yet each of them, we know, had several brides,
Like many another holy man besides.
Show me a time or text where God disparages
Or sets a prohibition upon marriages
Expressly, let me have it! Show it me!
And where did He command virginity?
I know as well as you do, never doubt it,
All the Apostle Paul has said about it;
He said that as for precepts he had none.
One may advise a woman to be one;
Advice is no commandment in my view.
He left it in our judgement what to do.

For hadde God comanded maydenhede,
Thanne hadde he dampned wedding with the dede.
And certes, if ther were no seed ysowe,
Virginitee, thanne wherof sholde it growe?
Poul dorste nat comanden, atte leeste,
A thing of which his maister yaf noon heeste.
The dart is set up for virginitee:
Cacche whoso may, who renneth best lat see.

But this word is nat taken of every wight,
But ther as God lust give it of his might.
I woot wel that th'apostel was a maide;
But nathelees, thogh that he wroot and saide
He wolde that every wight were swich as he,
Al nis but conseil to virginitee.
And for to been a wyf he yaf me leve
Of indulgence; so nis it no repreve
To wedde me, if that my make die,
Withouten excepcion of bigamie.
Al were it good no womman for to touche,—
He mente as in his bed or in his couche;
For peril is bothe fyr and tow t' assemble:
Ye knowe what this ensample may resemble.
This is al and som, he heeld virginitee
Moore parfit than wedding in freletee.
Freletee clepe I, but if that he and she
Wolde leden al hir lyf in chastitee.

I graunte it wel, I have noon envie,
Thogh maidenhede preferre bigamie.
It liketh hem to be clene, body and goost;
Of myn estaat I nil nat make no boost.
For wel ye knowe, a lord in his houshold,
He nath nat every vessel al of gold;
Somme been of tree, and doon hir lord servise.
God clepeth folk to hym in sondry wise,

'Had God commanded maidenhood to all
Marriage would be condemned beyond recall,
And certainly if seed were never sown,
How ever could virginity be grown?
Paul did not dare pronounce, let matters rest,
His Master having given him no behest.
There's a prize offered for virginity;
Catch as catch can! Who's in for it? Let's see!

'It is not everyone who hears the call;
On whom God wills He lets His power fall.
The Apostle was a virgin, well I know;
Nevertheless, though all his writings show
He wished that everyone were such as he,
It's all mere counsel to virginity.
And as for being married, he lets me do it
Out of indulgence, so there's nothing to it
In marrying me, suppose my husband dead;
There's nothing bigamous in such a bed.
Though it were good a man should never touch
A woman (meaning here in bed and such)
And dangerous to assemble fire and tow
– What this allusion means you all must know –
He only says virginity is fresh,
More perfect than the frailty of the flesh
In married life – except when he and she
Prefer to live in married chastity.

'I grant it you. I'll never say a word
Decrying maidenhood although preferred
To frequent marriage; there are those who mean
To live in their virginity, as clean
In body as in soul, and never mate.
I'll make no boast about my own estate.
As in a noble household, we are told,
Not every dish and vessel's made of gold,
Some are of wood, yet earn their master's praise,
God calls His folk to Him in many ways.

And everich hath of God a propre yifte,
Som this, som that, as him liketh shifte.
    Virginitee is greet perfeccion,
And continence eek with devocion,
But Crist, that of perfeccion is welle,
Bad nat every wight he sholde go selle
Al that he hadde, and give it to the poore
And in swich wise folwe hym and his foore.
He spak to hem that wolde live parfitly;
And lordinges, by youre leve, that am nat I.
I wol bistowe the flour of al myn age
In the actes and in fruit of mariage.
    Telle me also, to what conclusion
Were membres maad of generacion,
And of so parfit wys a wight ywroght?
Trusteth right wel, they were nat maad for noght.
Glose whoso wole, and seye bothe up and doun,
That they were maked for purgacioun
Of urine, and oure bothe thinges smale
Were eek to knowe a femele from a male,
And for noon oother cause, — say ye no?
The experience woot wel it is noght so.
So that the clerkes be nat with me wrothe,
I sey this, that they maked ben for bothe,
This is to seye, for office, and for ese
Of engendrure, ther we nat God displese.
Why sholde men elles in hir bookes sette
That man shal yelde to his wyf hire dette?
Now wherwith sholde he make his paiement,
If he ne used his sely instrument?
Thanne were they maad upon a creature
To purge urine, and eek for engendrure.
    But I seye noght that every wight is holde,
That hath swich harneys as I to yow tolde,
To goon and usen hem in engendrure.
Thanne sholde men take of chastitee no cure.

To each of them God gave His proper gift,
Some this, some that, and left them to make shift.
Virginity is indeed a great perfection,
And married continence, for God's dilection,
But Christ, who of perfection is the well,
Bade not that everyone should go and sell
All that he had and give it to the poor
To follow in His footsteps, that is sure.
He spoke to those that would live perfectly,
And by your leave, my lords, that's not for me.
I will bestow the flower of life, the honey,
Upon the acts and fruit of matrimony.

    'Tell me to what conclusion or in aid
Of what were generative organs made?
And for what profit were those creatures wrought?
Trust me, they cannot have been made for naught.
Gloze as you will and plead the explanation
That they were only made for the purgation
Of urine, little things of no avail
Except to know a female from a male,
And nothing else. Did somebody say no?
Experience knows well it isn't so.
The learned may rebuke me, or be loth
To think it so, but they were made for both,
That is to say both use and pleasure in
Engendering, except in case of sin.
Why else the proverb written down and set
In books: 'A man must yield his wife her debt'?
What means of paying her can he invent
Unless he use his silly instrument?
It follows they were fashioned at creation
Both to purge urine and for propagation.

    'But I'm not saying everyone is bound
Who has such harness as you heard me expound
To go and use it breeding; that would be
To show too little care for chastity.

Crist was a maide, and shapen as a man,
And many a seint, sith that the world bigan;
Yet lived they evere in parfit chastitee.
I nyl envye no virginitee.
Lat hem be breed of pured whete-seed,
And lat us wyves hoten barly-breed;
And yet with barly-breed, mark telle kan,
Oure Lord Jhesu refresshed many a man.
In swich estaat as God hath cleped us
I wol persevere; I nam nat precius.
In wyfhod I wol use myn instrument
As frely as my Makere hath it sent.
If I be daungerous, God yeve me sorwe!
Myn housbonde shal it have bothe eve and morwe

———

From *The Wife of Bath's Prologue* by Geoffrey Chaucer, *c.* 1380

Christ was a virgin, fashioned as a man,
And many of his saints since time began
Were ever perfect in their chastity.
I'll have no quarrel with virginity.
Let them be pure wheat loaves of maidenhead
And let us wives be known for barley-bread;
Yet Mark can tell that barley-bread sufficed
To freshen many at the hand of Christ.
In that estate to which God summoned me
I'll persevere; I'm not pernickety.
In wifehood I will use my instrument
As freely as my Maker me it sent.
If I turn difficult, God give me sorrow!
My husband, he shall have it eve and morrow

———

From *The Wife of Bath's Prologue* by Geoffrey Chaucer.
Verse translation by Nevill Coghill, 1951

Story of Ow

I found the first chapter, extracted here, very sexy, but I was too freaked out by the rest to find it remotely erotic (though I suspect I'm in the minority). Of all the books I've reread for the purposes of this anthology, this is the only one to elicit exactly the same reaction I had when I was fourteen or fifteen: for me, it very quickly becomes too much. There's also something intensely disturbing about the pared-down, dehumanised, detached prose, and, well – branding irons: no thanks.

*H*er lover one day takes O for a walk, but this time in a part of the city – the Parc Montsouris, the Parc Monceau – where they've never been together before. After they've strolled awhile along the paths, after they've sat down side by side on a bench near the grass, and got up again, and moved on towards the edge of the park, there, where two streets meet, where there never used to be any taxi-stand, they see a car, at that corner. It looks like a taxi, for it does have a meter. 'Get in,' he says; she gets in. It's late in the afternoon, it's autumn. She is wearing what she always wears: high heels, a suit with a pleated skirt, a silk blouse, no hat. But she has on long gloves reaching up to the sleeves of her jacket, in her leather handbag she's got her papers, and her compact and lipstick. The taxi eases off, very slowly; nor has the man next to her said a word to the driver. But on the right, on the left, he draws down the little window-shades, and the one behind too; thinking that he is about to kiss her, or so as to caress him, she has slipped

off her gloves. Instead, he says: 'I'll take your bag, it's in your way.'
She gives it to him, he puts it beyond her reach; then adds: 'You've
too much clothing on. Unhitch your stockings, roll them down to
just above your knees. Go ahead,' and he gives her some elastics to
hold the stockings in place. It isn't easy, not in the car, which is
going faster now, and she doesn't want to have the driver turn
around. But she manages anyhow, at last; it's a queer, uncomfortable feeling, the contact of silk of her slip upon her naked and free
legs, and the unattached garters are sliding loosely back and forth
across her skin. 'Undo your garter-belt,' he says, 'take off your
panties.' There's nothing to that, all she has to do is get at the
hook behind and raise up a little. He takes the garter-belt from her
hand, he takes the panties, opens her bag, puts them away inside it;
then he says: 'You're not to sit on your slip or on your skirt, pull
them up and sit on the seat without anything in between.' The
seat-covering is a sort of leather, slick and chilly; it's a very strange
sensation, the way it sticks and clings to her thighs. Then he says:
'Now put your gloves back on.' The taxi goes right along and she
doesn't dare ask why René is so quiet, so still, or what all this
means to him: she so motionless and so silent; so denuded and so
offered, though so thoroughly gloved, in a black car going she
hasn't the least idea where. He hasn't told her to do anything or
not to do it, but she doesn't dare either cross her legs or sit with
them held together. One on this side, one on that side, she rests
her gloved hands on the seat, pushing down.

'Here we are,' he says all of a sudden. Here we are: the taxi
comes to a stop on a fine avenue, under a tree – those are plane
trees – in front of a small mansion, you could just see it, nestled
away between courtyard and garden, the way the Faubourg Saint-
Germain mansions are. There's no streetlight nearby, it is dark
inside the cab, and outside rain is falling. 'Don't move,' says René.
'Don't move a muscle.' He extends his hand towards the neck of
her blouse, unties the ribbon at the throat, then unbuttons the
buttons. She leans forward ever so little, and believes he is about to
caress her breasts. But no; he's got a small penknife out, he's only
groping for the shoulder-straps of her brassiere, he cuts the straps,

removes the brassiere. He has closed her blouse again and now, underneath, her breasts are free and nude, like her belly and thighs are nude and free, like all of her is, from waist to knee.

'Listen,' he says. 'You're ready. Here's where I leave you. You're going to get out and go to the door and ring the bell. Someone will open the door, whoever it is you'll do as he says. You'll do it right away and willingly of your own accord, else they'll make you, if you don't obey at once, they'll make you obey. What? No, you don't need your bag any more. You don't need anything, you're just the whore, I'm the pimp who's furnishing you. Yes, certainly, I'll be there, sure. Now go.'

Another version of the same beginning was simpler, more direct: similarly dressed, the young woman was taken off in a car by her lover and by a second man, an unknown friend of his. The stranger drove, the lover was seated beside the young woman; and the one who did the talking, the friend, the unknown stranger in front, explained to the young woman that her lover's task was to prepare her, that he was now going to tie her hands behind her back, unfasten her stockings and roll them down, remove her garter-belt, her panties, her brassiere, and blindfold her; that afterwards she would be taken to the château where she would receive instructions in due course, as events required. And so indeed it had been: once undressed and bound in this manner, and after about a thirty minutes' drive, she was helped out of the car and marched a few steps. Still blindfolded, she passed one or two doors and then found herself alone, the blindfold gone, standing in a darkened room where she was left for half an hour, for an hour, for two – I don't know, but it seemed as though it were an age. When the door finally opened and the light was turned on, you could see that she'd been waiting in a room, just a room, comfortable, yet odd. There was a thick carpet on the floor, but not a stick of furniture in that room. The walls were lined with cupboards. Two girls opened the door – two pretty young women costumed like eighteenth-century chambermaids, with long, light, puffy skirts that came to the floor, tight bodices that made the bust rise and swell and that were laced or hooked in back, gauze ker-chiefs at the neck, wearing elbow-length gauze gloves to match. Their eyes and mouths were painted. Each wore a collar around her neck and bracelets on her wrists.

And then I know that they released O's hands, until that point still tied behind her back, and told her to undress. They were going to bathe her and make her up. But they made her stand still; they did everything for her, they stripped her and laid her clothes neatly away in one of the cupboards. They did not let her do her own bathing, they washed her themselves and set her hair just as hairdressers would have, making her sit in one of those big chairs that tilt backwards when your hair is being washed and then come up again when the drier is applied. That took at least an hour. She was seated nude in the chair and they prohibited her from either crossing her legs or pressing them together. As, on the opposite wall, there was a mirror running from floor to ceiling and straight ahead of her, in plain view, every time she glanced up she caught sight of herself, of her open body.

When she was made up, her eyelids lightly shadowed, her mouth very red, the point and halo of her nipples rouged, the sides of the lips of her sex reddened, a lingering scent applied to the fur of her armpits and her pubis, to the crease between her but-tocks, to beneath her breasts and the palms of her hands, she was led into a room where a three-sided mirror and, facing it, a fourth mirror on the opposite wall enabled, indeed obliged, her to see her own image reflected. She was told to sit on a hassock placed between the mirrors, and to wait. The hassock was upholstered with prickly black fur; the rug was black, the walls red. She wore red slippers. Set in one of the little boudoir's walls was a casement window giving out upon a magnificent but sombre, formal garden. The rain had stopped and the trees were swaying in the wind while the moon raced high among the clouds. I don't know just how long she remained in the red boudoir, nor if she really was alone, as she thought she was, for someone may perhaps have been watching her through a peephole disguised somewhere in the wall. What I do know is that when the two chambermaids returned, one was carrying a tape-measure and the other had a basket over her arm. With them came a man wearing a trailing violet robe with sleeves cut wide at the shoulder and gathered in at the wrist; as he walked, the robe showed to be open at the waist. You could make out that he was in some kind of tights which covered his legs and thighs but left his sex free. It was the sex that O saw first, then the whip made of strands of leather, the whip was stuck in his belt, then she noticed that the man was masked in a black hood completed by a section of black gauze hiding his eyes — and finally she noticed the fine black kid-gloves he was wearing. He ordered her not to move, he told the women to hurry. The one with the tape took the measure of O's neck and wrists. Although somewhat small, her sizes were in no way out of the ordinary, and they had no trouble selecting a suitable collar and bracelets from the assortment contained in the basket. Both collar and bracelets were fashioned of many layers of thin leather, the whole being no thicker than a finger, fitted with a catch that worked automatically, like a padlock, and which needed a key to be opened. Next to the catch, and imbedded in the leather, was a metal ring. They fitted snugly, but not so tightly as to chafe or break the skin. After they had been set in place, the man told her to rise. He himself sat on the fur-covered hassock and made her approach until she stood against his knees. He passed his gloved hand between her thighs and over her breast and explained to her that she would be presented that same evening after she had dined. Still nude, she took her meal alone in a kind of small cabin; an unseen hand passed the plates to her through a little window. When she had finished eating, the two maids came for her again. In the boudoir, they had her put her hands behind her back and secured them there by means of the rings of her wristbands; they draped a long red cape over her shoulders, and it was fastened to the ring set in her collar. The cape covered her completely, but with her hands behind her back that way she couldn't prevent it from opening when she walked. One woman preceded her, and opened the doors; the second followed, and shut them again. They filed through a vestibule, through two drawing-rooms, and entered the library where four men were at coffee. They wore the same flowing robes as the first she had seen, but were not masked. Nevertheless, O did not have me to observe their faces or recognize whether her lover was there (he was), for one of the men trained a spotlight upon her face, dazzling her. Everyone stood in silence, the women on either side, the men in front, watching her. Then the light was switched off and the women went away, but a blindfold had been placed over O's eyes. Stumbling a bit, she was made to advance and could sense that she was standing before the fire around which the four men had been grouped. In the quiet, she could hear the soft crackling of the logs and feel the heat; she was facing the fire. Two hands lifted away her cape, two others checked the clasp on her wristbands and descended inspectingly down over her buttocks. These hands were not gloved, and one of them simultaneously penetrated her in two places – so brusquely that she let out a cry. Some voice laughed. Another said: 'Turn her around so we can see her breasts and belly.' She was turned about, and now it was on her buttocks that she felt the glow of the fire. A hand moulded itself round one of her breasts, squeezed, a mouth closed upon the nipple of her other breast. Suddenly, she lost her balance and tottered backwards into unknown arms. At the same instant, her legs were spread apart and her lips gently worked open – hair grazed the inner surfaces of her thighs. She heard a voice declare that she ought to be made to kneel, and she was. It was painful to be on her knees, seated on her heels in the position nuns take when they pray.

'You've never imposed physical restraints, for example tied her up?'

'No, never.'

'Or whipped her?'

'Never. Though, the fact is——' It was her lover who was answering.

'The fact is,' said the other voice, 'that if you do tie her up, if you use a whip on her, and if she likes that – then no, you understand. Pleasure, we've got to move beyond that stage. We must make the tears flow.'

She was then drawn to her feet, and they were probably about to detach her hands so as to tie her to some post or other or to the wall, when someone interrupted, saying that before anything else he wanted her — immediately. She was forced down upon her knees again, but this time a hassock was placed as a support under her chest; her hands were still fixed behind her back, her haunches were higher than her torso. One of the men gripped her buttocks and sank himself into her womb. When he was done, he ceded his place to a second. The third wanted to drive his way into the narrower passage and, pushing hard, violently, wrung a scream from her lips. When at last he let go of her, moaning and tears streaming down under her blindfold, she slipped sidewise to the floor only to discover by the pressure of two knees against her face that her mouth was not to be spared either. Finally, finished with her, they moved off, leaving her, a captive in her finery, huddled, collapsed on the carpet before the fire. She heard drink being poured, glasses tinkling, chairs stirring; logs were added to the fire. Then her blindfold was suddenly snatched away. It was a large room. Bookcases lined the walls, dimly lit by a bracketed lamp and the flicker of the fire. Two of the men were standing; they were smoking. Another was seated, a riding-crop across his knees, and there was still another leaning over her, caressing her breasts; that one was her lover. All four had taken her and she had not been able to distinguish him from amongst the rest.

It was explained to her that as long as she was in this château it would always be this way: she would see the faces of those who violated and bullied her, but never at night, and in this way she would never know which ones were responsible for the worst of her sufferings. When she was whipped the same would hold true, except when it was desired that she see herself being whipped, as happened to be the case this first time: no blindfold, but the men in masks in order to be unidentifiable. Her lover had picked her up and set her, in her red cape, on the arm of a large chair in the corner by the chimney, so that she might listen to what they had to tell her and see what they wished to exhibit to her. Her hands were still pinioned behind her back. She was shown the riding-crop, black, long and slender, made of fine bamboo sheathed in leather, an article such as one finds in the display-windows of expensive saddlemakers' shops; the leather whip – the one she'd seen tucked in the first man's belt – was long, with six lashes each ending in a knot; there was a third whip whose numerous light cords were several times knotted and stiff, quite as if soaked in water, and they actually had been soaked in water, as O was able to verify when they stroked her belly with those cords and, opening her thighs, exposing her hidden parts, let the damp, cold ends trail against the tender membranes. On the console there yet remained the collection of keys and the steel chains. Midway up one of the library's walls ran a balcony supported by two pillars. In one of these, as high up as a man standing on tip-toe could reach, was sunk a hook. O, whose lover had taken her in his arms, one hand under her shoulder, the other in her womb which was burning her almost unbearably, O was informed that when, as soon they would, they unfastened her hands, it would only be to attach them to this whipping-post by means of those bracelets on her wrists and this steel chain. With the exception of her hands, which would be immobilized a little above her head, she would be able to move, to turn, to face around and see the strokes coming, they told her; by and large, they'd confine the whipping to her buttocks and thighs, to the space, that is to say, between her waist and her knees, precisely that part of her which had been prepared in the car when she had been made to sit naked on the seat; it was likely, however, that some one of the four men would want to score her with the crop, for it caused fine, long, deep welts which lasted quite some time. They'd go about it gradually, giving her ample opportunity to scream and fight and cry to her heart's content. They'd pause to let her catch her breath, but after she'd recovered it, they'd start in again, judging the results not by her screams or her tears but by the more or less livid and durable marks traced in her flesh by the whips. It was called to her attention that these criteria for estimating the effectiveness of the whip, apart from their just impartiality and from the fact they rendered unnecessary any attempts victims might make to elicit pity by exaggerating their moans, did not by any means bar open-air whipping – there would indeed be a good deal of that in the park outside the château – or for that matter, whipping in any ordinary apartment or hotel room provided a tight gag were employed (they showed her a gag), which, while giving free rein to tears, stifles any scream and even makes moaning difficult.

They did not, however, intend to use the gag that night. To the contrary, they were eager to hear O howl, the sooner the better. Proud, she steeled herself to resist, she gritted her teeth; but not for long. They soon heard her beg to be let loose, beg them to stop, stop for a second, for just one second. So frantically did she twist and wheel to dodge the biting lashes that she almost spun in circles. The chain, although unyielding, for, after all, it was a chain, was nevertheless slack enough to allow her leeway. Owing to her excessive writhing, her belly and the front of her thighs received almost as heavy a share as her rear. They left off for a moment, deeming it better to tie her flat up against the post by means of a rope passed around her waist; the rope being cinched tight, her head necessarily angled to one side of the post and her flanks jutted to the other, thereby placing her rump in a prominent position. From then on, every deliberately aimed blow dealt her struck home. In view of the manner in which her lover had exposed her to this, O might well have supposed that an appeal to his pity would have been the surest way to increase his cruelty, so great was his pleasure in wresting or in having the others wrest these from her decisive proofs of his power over her. And it was in fact he who was the first to observe that the leather whip, with which they'd begun, marked her the least (for the moistened lash had obtained strong results almost instantly, and the crop with the first blow struck), and hence, by employing no other, they could prolong the ordeal and, after brief pauses, start in again just about immediately or according to their fancy. He asked that they use only that first whip. Meanwhile, the man who liked women only for what they had in common with men, seduced by the sight of that proffered behind straining out from under the taut rope and made all the more tempting by its wrigglings to escape, requested an intermission in order to take advantage of it; he spread apart the two burning halves and penetrated, but not without difficulty, which brought him to remark that they'd have to contrive to make this thoroughfare easier of access. The thing could be done, they agreed, and decided that the proper measures would be taken.

From *Story of O* by Pauline Réage, 1954

Swingers

Wife-swapping, husband-swapping, everybody doing it with everybody else, even when they're pregnant. And nursing. Another pick from the parental shelf. Another eye-opener.

*F*oxy was above him. With a stealth meant to wake her slowly, Piet moved through the unfinished rooms, testing joints with his pocket knife, opening and shutting cabinet doors that closed with a delicate magnetic suck. Above him, a footstep heavier than a cat's sounded. Furiously Piet focused on the details of the copper plumbing installed beneath the old sink, suspended in mid-connexion, where the plumbers had left it, open like a cry. She was beside him, wearing a loosely tied bathrobe over a slip, her face blurred by sleep, her blond hair moist on the pillowed side of her head. *They said they'd be back.*

I was trying to figure out why they had quit.

The explained it to me. Something about a male threader and a coupling.

Plumbers are the banes of this business. Plumbers and masons.

They're a vanishing breed?

Even vanishing they do slowly. You and Ken must be tired to death of living in the middle of a mess.

Oh, Ken's never here in the day and it's fun for me, to have men bringing me presents all day long. Adams and Comeau and I sit around the coffee table talking about the good old days in Tarbox.

What good old days?

Apparently it's always been a salty town. Look, would you like something to drink? I've woken up with a terrible thirst, I could make lemonade. That only needs cold water.

I ought to get back to the office and give the plumbers a blast.

They promised they'd be back so I'd have hot water. Do you mind if it's pink?

Pink lemonade? I prefer it. My mother used to make it. With strawberries.

In the good old days, Adams and Comeau tell me, the trolley car ran along Divinity Street and all the drinks would pile out because this was the only un-dry town between Boston and Plymouth. Even in the middle of a blizzard this would happen.

Funny about the trolley cars. How they came and went.

The used to make me sick. That awful smell, and the motorman's cigars.

Speaking of messes, what about where your porch was? Do you see that as lawn, or a patio, or what?

I'd love a grape arbour. Why is that funny?

You'd lose all the light you've gained. You'd lose your view from those windows.

The view bores me. The view is Ken's thing. He's always looking outward. Let me tell you about grape arbours.

Tell me.

When I was growing up one summer, the summer before Pearl Harbor, my parents wanted to get out of Bethesda and for a month we rented a brick house in Virginia with an enormous grape arbour over bricks where the ants made little hills. I must have been, what? '41, seven. Forgive me, I'm not usually so talkative.

I know.

I remember the little offshoots of the vines had letters in them, formed letters, you know. She made an A with her fingers. I tried to make a complete collection. From A to Z.

How far did you get?

I think to D. I never could find a perfect E. You'd think in all those vines there would have been one.

You should have skipped to F.

I was superstitious and I thought I couldn't. I inhibited myself all the time.

Piet grimaced and considered. The lemonade needed sugar. *It seems to be going out. Inhibition. In a way, I miss it.*

What a sad thing to say. Why? I don't miss it at all. Ever since I got pregnant I've become a real slob. Look at me, in a bathrobe. I love it. Her lips, in her clear pink complexion, looked whitish, as if rubbed with a chapstick. *Shall I tell you a secret?*

Better not. Tell me, what shade of white do you want your living-room woodwork? Flat white, glossy, ivory, or eggshell?

My secret is really so innocent. For years I wanted to be pregnant, but also I was afraid of it. Not just losing my figure, which was too skinny to care about anyway, but my body being somehow an embarrassment to other people. For months I didn't tell anybody except Bea Guerin.

Who told everybody else.

Yes, and I'm glad. Because it turns out not to matter. People just don't care. I was so conceited to think that people would care. In fact they like you a little better if you look beat-up. If you look used.

You don't look very used to me.

Or you to me.

Do men get used? They just use.

Oh, you're so wrong. We use you all the time. It's all we know how to do. But your saying that fits with your missing inhibition. You're very Puritan. You're quite hard on yourself. At first I thought you fell down stairs and did acrobatics to show off. But really you do it to hurt yourself. In the hope that you will. Now why are you laughing?

Because you're so clever.

I'm not. Tell me about your childhood. Mine was dreary. My parents finally got a divorce. I was amazed.

We had a greenhouse. My parents had Dutch accents I've worked quite hard not to inherit. They were both killed years ago in an automobile accident.

Yes, of course. Freddy Thorne calls you our orphan.

How much do you see of Freddy Thorne?

No more than I must. He comes up to me at parties.

He comes up to everybody at parties.

I know that. You don't have to tell me.

Sorry. I don't mean to tell you anything. I'm sure you know quite enough. I just want to get this job done for you so you and your baby can be comfortable this winter.

Her lips, stunned a moment, froze, bloodless, measuring a space of air like calipers. She said, *It's not even July.*

Time flies, he said. It was not even July, and he had never touched her, except in the conventions of greeting and while dancing. In dancing, though at least his height, she had proved submissive to his lead, her arm weightless on his back, her hard belly softly bumping. He felt her now expectant, sitting composed in a careless bathrobe on a kitchen chair, aggressive even, unattractive, so full of the gassy waitingness and pallor of pregnancy.

He said casually, *Good lemonade,* in the same moment as she asked, *Why do you go to church?*

Well, why do you?

I asked first.

The usual reasons. I'm a coward. I'm a conservative. Republican, religious. My parents' ghosts are there, and my older girl sings in the choir. She's so brave.

I'm sorry you're a Republican. My parents worshipped Roosevelt.

Mine were offended because he was Dutch, they didn't think the Dutch had any business trying to run the country. I think they thought power was sin. I don't have any serious opinions. No, I do have one. I think America now is like an unloved child smothered in candy. Like a middle-aged wife whose husband brings home a present after every trip because he's been unfaithful to her. When they were newly married he never had to give presents.

Who is this husband?

God. Obviously. God doesn't love us any more. He loves Russia. He loves Uganda. We're fat and full of pimples and always whining for more candy. We've fallen from grace.

You think a lot about love, don't you?

More than other people?

I think so.

Actually, I never think about love. I've left that to your friend Freddy Thorne.

Would you like to kiss me?

Very much, yes.

Why don't you?

It doesn't seem right. I don't have the nerve. You're carrying another man's child.

Foxy impatiently stood, exclaiming, *Ken's frightened of my baby. I frighten him. I frighten you.* Piet had risen from his chair and she stood beside him, asking in a voice as small as the distance between them, *Aren't we in our house? Aren't you building this house for me?*

Before kissing her, yet after all alternatives had been closed to him, Piet saw her face to be perfectly steady and clean of feeling, like a candleflame motionless in a dying of wind, or a road straight without strategies, like the roads of his native state, or the canals of

Holland, and his hands on her body beneath the loose robe found this same quality, a texture almost wooden yet alive and already his; so quickly familiar did her body feel that there was no question, no necessity, of his taking her that afternoon – as a husband and wife, embracing in the kitchen, will back off because they will soon have an entire night, when the children are asleep, and no mailman can knock.

Outdoors again, amid the tracked clay, the splinters, the stacked bundles of raw shingles, the lilac stumps, Piet remembered how her hair, made more golden by the Tarbox sun, had been matted, a few damp strands, to her temple. She had averted her blushing face from his kiss as if to breathe, exhaling a sigh and gazing past his shoulder at a far corner of the unfinished room. Her lips, visually thin, had felt wide and warm and slippery; the memory, outdoors, as if chemically transformed by contact with oxygen, drugged Piet with a penetrating dullness.

*

Piet turned in pain from the window and it seemed that the couples were gliding on the polished top of Kennedy's casket. An island of light in a mourning nation. 'Close Your Eyes.' 'Cuh-lozzz ur eyeszz': the velvet voice from Hollywood whispered an inch inside Piet's ear. The olive egg in his martini had been abandoned by its mother high and dry. His cankers hurt, especially the one his tongue had to stretch to reach, low and left on the front gum, at the root of his lip. A maze of membranes, never could have evolved from algae unassisted. God gave us a boost. He felt he shouldn't have another drink. No supper, empty stomach. Marcia's slithering had stirred him. Half-mast, subsided, lumpy. His kidneys signalled: the sweetness pealing of a silent bell: relieve me. The Thornes' bathroom. There Georgene would wash herself before and after. Said his jizz ran down her leg, too much of it, should screw Angela more. Hexagonal little floor tiles, robin's-egg toilet paper, posh purple towels. *Welcome to the post-pill* . . . Sashaying from the shower nude, her pussy of a ferny freshness. The grateful lumpiness following love. Well done, thou good and faithful. Turning up the familiar stairs, his black foot firm on the swaying treads, he glanced into the dark side room, where a few obscure heads were watching a weary flickering re-run of the casket's removal from the belly of the aeroplane. Ben was there, bent forward, his profile silvered as in Sunday-school oleographs, facing Sinai. Roger and Carol, sharing a hassock. Frank sucked a cigar whose smoke was charged with the dartings of light as casket became widow, widow became Johnson, Johnson became commentator. Ghouls. Foxy must be in the kitchen. The panelled bathroom door was closed. Tactfully he tapped. Her musical voice called, 'Just a min-ute.'

Piet said, 'It's me,' and pushed. The door gave. She was sitting on the toilet in her uplifted silver gown, startled, a patch of blue paper like a wisp of sky in her hand. The pressure of the oval seat widened her garter-rigged and pallid thighs; she was perched forward; her toes but not her heels touched the hexagonal tiles of the floor. 'I love you' was pulled from him like a tooth. The mirror above the basin threw him back at himself. His flat taut face looked flushed and astonished, his mouth agape, his black tie askew.

Foxy said in a whisper reverberant in the bright tiled space, 'You're mad to be in here.' Then with incongruous deliberation she patted herself, let the paper drop into the oval of water below, and, half-turning on the seat, depressed the silver handle. Sluggishly the toilet flushed: Georgene used to complain about the low water pressure on the hill. Foxy rose from the vortex and smoothed her gown downward. Facing him, she seemed tall, faintly challenging and hostile, her closed lips strangely bleached by pale pink lipstick, newly chic. He made sure the door behind them was shut, and moved past her to urinate standing. With a pang, initially reluctant, his golden arc occurred. 'God,' he said, 'it's a relief to see you alone. When the hell can we meet?'

She spoke hurriedly, above his splashing. 'I wasn't sure you wanted to. You've been very distant.'

'Ever since you've had the baby I've been frightened to death of you. I assumed it was the end of us.'

'That's not true. Unless you want it to be true.'

'The fact is, all fall I've been frightened of everything. Death, my work, Gallagher, my children, the stars. It's been hideous.' A concluding spurt, somewhat rhetorical, and a dismissive drying shake. He tucked himself in. 'My whole life seems just a long falling.'

'But it's *not*. You have a good life. Your lovely family, your nice square house, me if you want me. We can't talk here. Call me Monday. I'm alone again.'

He flushed, but the water closet had not filled. 'Wait. Please. Let me see your breasts.'

'They're all milky.'

'I know. Just for a moment. Please. I do need it.'

They listened for steps on the stairs; there were none. Music below, and the television monologue. Her mouth opened and her tongue, red as sturgeon, touched her upper lip as she reached behind her to undo snaps. Her gown and bra peeled down in a piece. Fruit.

'Oh. God.'

She blushed in answer. 'I feel so gross.'

'So veiny and full. So hard at the tops, here.'

'Don't get them started. I must go home in an hour.'

'And nurse.'

'Yes. What funny sad lines you're getting here, and here. Don't frown, Piet. And grey hairs. They're new.'

'Nurse me.'

'Oh darling. No.'

'Nurse me.'

She covered one breast, alarmed, but he had knelt, and his broad mouth fastened on the other. The thick slow flow was at first suck sickeningly sweet. The bright bathroom light burned on his eyelids and seemed to dye his insides a deep flowing rose, down to the pained points of his knees on the icy tile. Foxy's hand lightly cupped the curve of the back of his skull and now guided him closer into the flood of her, now warned by touching his ear that he was giving her pain. He opened his eyes; the nipple of her other breast jutted cherry-red between ivory fingers curled in protection; he closed his eyes. Pulses of stolen food scoured his tongue, his gums; she toyed with his hair, he caressed her clothed buttocks. She was near drowning him in rose.

Knocks struck rocklike at the unlocked door inches behind them. Harsh light flooded him. He saw Foxy's free hand, ringed, grope and cup the sympathetic lactation of the breast jutting unmouthed. She called out, as musically as before, 'One moment, please.'

Angela's lucid polite voice answered, 'Oops, sorry, Foxy. Take your time.'

'All ri-ight,' Foxy sang back, giving Piet a frantic look of interrogation. Her bare breasts giant circles. A Christian slave stripped to be tortured.

His body thundered with fear. His hands were jerking like puppets on strings but his brain took perspective from the well-lit room in which he was trapped. There was no other door. The shower curtain was translucent glass, two sliding panels; his shape would show. There was a little window. Its sill came up to his chest. Realizing the raising of the sash would make noise, he motioned Foxy to flush the toilet. As she bent to touch the silver handle the shape of her breasts changed, hanging forward, long-tipped udders dripping cloudy drops. He undid the brass catch and shoved up the sash as the water closet again, feebly, drained. Setting one black dancing slipper on the lip of the tub, he hoisted himself into the black square of air headfirst. Trees on this side of the house, elms, but none near enough to grasp. His hands could touch only vertical wood and freezing air pricked by stars. Too late he knew he should have gone feet first; he must drop. This the shady rural side of the house. Soft grass. The toilet had quieted and left no noise to cover the sounds of his scrambling as he changed position. Foxy thought to turn both faucets on full. By logic she must next open the door to Angela. Piet backed out of the widow. Foxy was standing by the roaring faucets staring at him and mopping herself with a purple washcloth and resecuring the bodice of her silver gown. He imagined she smiled. No time to think about it. He stood on the slick tub lip and got a leg through the little window and doing a kind of handstand on the radiator cover manoeuvred the other leg through also. Button. Caught. Ah. There. He slid out on his chest and dangled his weight by his hands along Thorne's undulate shingles. Loose nails, might catch on a nostril, tear his face like a fish being reamed. Air dangled under his shoes. Ten feet. Eleven, twelve. Old houses, high ceilings. Something feathery brushed his fingers gripping the sill inside the bathroom. Foxy begging him not to dare it? Angela saying it was all right, she knew? Too late. Fall. No apologies. Pushing off lightly from the wall with his slippers and trying to coil himself loosely against the shock, he let go. Falling was first a hum, then concussion: a harpstring in reverse. His heels hit the frost-baked turf; he took a somersault backwards and worried about grass stains on his tuxedo before he thought to praise God for breaking no bones. Above him, a pink face vanished and a golden window whispered shut. They were safe. He was sitting on the brittle grass, his feet in their papery slippers stinging.

From *Couples* by John Updike, 1968

The Priest

Meggie sleeps with Father Ralph and bears him a child. Fantastically depraved-seeming at the time, especially if you were a Catholic.

Round and up came her eyes to his, amazed, outraged, furious; even now, even now! Time suspended, she stared at him so, and he was forced to see, breath caught astounded, the grown woman in those glass-clear eyes. Meggie's eyes. Oh, God, Meggie's eyes!

He had meant what he said to Anne Mueller; he just wanted to see her, nothing more. Though he loved her, he hadn't come to be her lover. Only to see her, talk to her, be her friend, sleep on the living room couch while he tried once more to unearth the taproot of that eternal fascination she possessed for him, thinking that if only he could see it fully exposed, he might gain the spiritual means to eradicate it.

It had been hard to adjust to a Meggie with breasts, a waist, hips; but he had done it because when he looked into her eyes, there like the pool of light in a sanctuary lamp shone his Meggie. A mind and a spirit whose pulls he had never been free from since first meeting her, still unchanged inside that distressingly changed body; but while he could see proof of their continued existence in her eyes, he could accept the altered body, discipline his attraction to it.

And, visiting his own wishes and dreams upon her, he had never doubted she wanted to do the same until she had turned on him like a goaded cat, at Justine's birth. Even then, after the anger and hurt died in him, he had attributed her behavior to the pain she had gone through, spiritual more than physical. Now, seeing her at last as she was, he could pinpoint to a second the moment when she had shed the lenses of childhood, donned the lenses of a woman: that interlude in the Drogheda cemetery after Mary Carson's birthday party. When he had explained to her why he couldn't show her any special attention, because people might deem him interested in her as a man. She had looked at him with something in her eyes he had not understood, then looked away, and when she turned back the expression was gone. From that time, he saw now, she had thought of him in a different light, she hadn't kissed him in a passing weakness when she had kissed him, then gone back to thinking of him in the old way, as he had her. He had perpetuated his illusions, nurtured them, tucked them into his unchanging way of life as best he could, worn them like a hair shirt. While all the time she had furnished her love for him with woman's objects.

Admit it, he had physically wanted her from the time of their first kiss, but the want had never plagued him the way his love for her had; seeing them as separate and distinct, not facets of the same thing. She, poor misunderstood creature, had never succumbed to this particular folly.

At that moment, had there been any way he could have got off Matlock Island, he would have fled from her like Orestes from the Eumenides. But he couldn't quit the island, and he did have the courage to remain in her presence rather than senselessly walk the night. What can I do, how can I possibly make reparation? I *do* love her! And if I love her, it has to be because of the way she is now, not because of a juvenile way station along her road. It's womanly things I've always loved in her; the bearing of the burden. So, Ralph de Bricassart, take off your blinkers, see her as she really is, not as she was long ago. Sixteen years ago, sixteen long incredible years . . . I am forty-four and she is twenty-six; neither of us is a child, but I am by far the more immature.

You took it for granted the minute I stepped out of Rob's car, isn't that so, Meggie? You assumed I had given in at last. And before you even had time to get your breath back I had to show you how wrong you were. I ripped the fabric of your delusion apart as if it had been a dirty old rag. Oh, Meggie! What have I done to you? How could I have been so blind, so utterly self-centered? I've accomplished nothing in coming to see you, unless it is to cut you into little pieces. All these years we've been loving at cross-purposes.

Still she was looking into his eyes, her own filling with shame, humiliation, but as the expressions flew across his face to the final one of despairing pity she seemed to realize the magnitude of her mistake, the horror of it. And more than that: the fact that he knew her mistake.

Go, run! Run, Meggie, get out of here with the scrap of pride he's left you! The instant she thought it she acted on it, she was up out of her chair and fleeing.

Before she could reach the veranda he caught her, the impetus of her flight spinning her round against him so hard he staggered. It didn't matter, any of it, the grueling battle to retain his soul's integrity, the long pressing down of will upon desire; in moments he had gone lifetimes. All that power held dormant, sleeping, only needing the detonation of a touch to trigger a chaos in which mind was subservient to passion, mind's will extinguished in body's will.

Up slid her arms around his neck, his across her back, spasmed; he bent his head, groped with his mouth for hers, found it. Her mouth, no longer an unwanted, unwelcome memory but real, her arms about him as if she couldn't bear to let him go; the way she seemed to lose even the feel of her bones; how dark she was like the night, tangled memory and desire, unwanted memory and unwelcome desire. The years he must have longed for this, longed for her and denied her power, kept himself even from the thought of her a woman!

Did he carry her to the bed, or did they walk? He thought he must have carried her, but he could not be sure; only that she was there upon it, he was there upon it, her skin under his hands, his skin under hers. Oh, God! My Meggie, my Meggie! How could they rear me from infancy to think you profanation?

Time ceased to tick and began to flow, washed over him until it had no meaning, only a depth of dimension more real than real time. He could feel her yet he did not feel her, not as a separate entity; wanting to make her finally and forever a part of himself, a graft which was himself, not a symbiosis which acknowledged her as distinct. Never again would he not know the upthrusts of breasts and belly and buttocks, the folds and crevices in between. Truly she was made for him, for he had made her; for sixteen years he had shaped and molded her without knowing that he did, let alone why he did. And he forgot that he had ever given her away, that another man had shown her the end of what he had begun for himself, had always intended for himself, for she was his downfall, his rose; his creation. It was a dream from which he would never again awaken, not as long as he was a man, with a man's body. *Oh, dear God! I know, I know!* I know why I kept her as an idea and a child within me for so long after she had grown beyond both, but why does it have to be learned like this?

Because at last he understood that what he had aimed to be was *not* a man. Not a man, never a man; something far greater, something beyond the fate of a mere man. Yet after all his fate was here under his hands, struck quivering and alight with him, her man. *A man, forever a man.* Dear Lord, couldst Thou not have kept this from me? I am a man, I can never be God; it was a delusion, that life in search of godhead. Are we all the same, we priests, yearning to be God? We abjure the one act which irrefutably proves us men.

He wrapped his arms about her and looked down with eyes full of tears at the still, faintly lit face, watched its rosebud mouth drop open, gasp, become a helpless O of astonished pleasure. Her arms and legs were round him, living ropes which bound him to her, silkily, sleekly tormented him; he put his chin into her shoulder and his cheek against the softness of hers, gave himself over to the maddening, exasperating drive of a man grappling with fate. His mind reeled, slipped, became utterly dark and blindingly bright; for one moment he was within the sun, then the brilliance faded, grew grey, and went out. This was being a man. He could be no more. But that was not the source of the pain. The pain was in the final moment, the finite moment, the empty, desolate realization:

ecstasy is fleeting. He couldn't bear to let her go, not now that he had her; he had made her for himself. So he clung to her like a drowning man to a spar in a lonely sea and soon, buoyant, rising again on a tide grown quickly familiar, he succumbed to the inscrutable fate which is a man's.

———————

From *The Thorn Birds* by Colleen McCullough, 1977

She Does It With Both of Them

Big, brash, racy, vulgar and full of appetites; irresistible. Also the first book many of us read about the downsides (and what downsides) of celebrity.

*M*aria . . . Maria had been the most beautiful girl in school, and Jennifer, along with the other polyglot first-termers, had idolized the glacial Spanish beauty. Maria was a senior, and she spoke to no one. And if she was aware of the hero worship she inspired in the other students, it failed to touch her; she made no friends. This hauteur only added to her glamour with the younger girls, and to the speculation and envy among her contemporaries. It looked as if Maria would graduate and leave Switzerland without allowing anyone to penetrate the imperial barrier. Until that day in the library . . .

Jennifer was in tears, reading a letter from her mother. The money had run out; she was to return home at the end of the term. Had she made any valuable contacts? Cleveland was still feeling the depression, although the war in Europe was opening new factories. Harry had married Harriet Irons and still worked in a gas station. It was the part about Harry that had brought on the tears . . .

'Come, nothing can be that bad.'

Jennifer looked up. It was Maria. The majestic Maria, talking to her! Maria sat down, Maria was sympathetic. She listened while Jennifer talked.

'I don't know what my mother expected,' Jennifer finished wearily. 'Maybe she thought the English teacher would be a lord with a manor . . .'

Maria laughed. 'Parents . . .' Her English was stilted but excellent. 'I am twenty-two. I will be expected to make a marriage with a man of my father's choice. It will be a matter of his land adjoining ours, or other mutual family interests. Since our civil war our country is devastated. It is the duty of the few remaining families in power to unite. I agree with these decisions but unfortunately, as a woman, I am expected to sleep with this pig . . .'

'I was in love with Harry,' Jennifer said sadly. 'But he didn't suit my mother.'

'How old are you, Jeannette?' Jennifer had been Jeannette then.

'Nineteen.'

'Have you ever had a man?'

Jennifer blushed and stared at the floor. 'No, but Harry and I . . . we went pretty far. I mean – I let him touch me . . . and once I touched his . . .'

'I have gone to bed with a man,' Maria stated.

'All the way?'

'But of course. Last summer. I vacationed with an aunt in Sweden. I met a beautiful man. He had been in the Olympics. He was working as a swimming instructor. I knew the men my father was considering. It would be a fat German who escaped with all the art treasures, or one of the Carrillo family. None of the Carrillo boys have chins. So I decided to at least try it for the first time with a beautiful man.'

'I wish I had done it with Harry. Now he's married to another girl.'

'Be glad you didn't! It was awful! The man . . . he mouths your breasts . . . he pushes into you. It hurts. Then he perspires and breathes heavily like an animal. I bled – and I got pregnant.'

Jennifer couldn't believe this was happening. Maria, the unapproachable school goddess, confiding in her!

'Oren!' Maria spat out the name. 'He took care of things. A doctor . . . more pain . . . and good-bye pregnancy. Then I got the fever and was very sick. I was taken to the hospital . . . the operation . . . I can never have children.'

'Oh, Maria, I'm so sorry.'

Maria smiled slyly. 'No, it is good! I will let my father make all the arrangements he wishes. Then I will tell the man. No man wants to marry a woman who cannot have children. I will never have to marry,' she said triumphantly.

'But what will your father say?'

'Oh, my aunt has taken care of the answer. She had to learn the truth. But I was her responsibility, so she must stand behind me. I shall say I was ill, that I had a tumor in my uterus and it had to be removed.'

'Was it?'

Maria nodded. 'Yes, my uterus was removed – peritonitis had set in. But it is wonderful. I am no longer bothered with the monthly period.'

Jennifer wanted to say she was sorry, but she couldn't offer sympathy to a girl who regarded the incident as a stroke of marvelous luck. 'Well, at least you've got everything settled,' she said. 'But I still have to return to Cleveland.'

'You do not have to return,' Maria said emphatically. 'You are too beautiful to spend your life waiting to be mauled by the first available man.'

'But what can I do?'

'In two weeks the term is ended. You come back to Spain with me for the summer. We will think of something.'

'Maria!' It was too wonderful. 'But I have no money – just a return ticket home.'

'You will be my guest – I have more money than I can use.'

The last two weeks in school had been a personal triumph for Jennifer. The news raced through school – Little Jeannette Johnson had been befriended by Maria. The girls stared in envy. Maria continued to keep her imperial distance, even with Jennifer, except to stop and chat briefly whenever they passed in the hall.

The moment they left school, Maria's attitude changed. She became warm and friendly. It began when they took the cab to Lausanne. 'We can't leave for Spain right away. My father's cable . . .' She handed it to Jennifer. It advised Maria to spend the summer in Switzerland. Spain was still feeling the devastation of the war. With one million dead and several hundred thousand injured, it was impossible to staff the house at present, so they had closed it and were staying at a hotel. But things would soon return to normal. Meanwhile she was to enjoy herself abroad. He had cabled the number of a Swiss bank account.

'We have plenty of money,' Maria said. 'Enough to travel around the world and back. But the war is on in Europe, so France is out. So are Germany and England.'

'Let's go to America,' Jennifer suggested. 'We could go to New York. I've never been to New York.'

'How? I am not a citizen. Travel is impossible with Europe at war. You might make it on a Red Cross boat — as an American citizen you would have priority — but there would still be the mines and submarines. Anyway, I have no desire to go to New York. We shall stay here for the summer. Hitler will win any day and the whole thing will be over.'

They were to remain in Switzerland three years.

They became lovers the first night. Although Jennifer had been startled at the proposal, she felt no revulsion; in fact, she was even a little curious. Maria was still the exalted school-girl heroine. And Maria's logical explanation removed any taint of abnormality. 'We like one another. I want to make you know about sex, to feel thrilling climaxes — not let you learn about it by being mauled by some brutal man. We are doing nothing wrong. We are not Lesbians like those awful freaks who cut their hair and wear mannish clothes. We are two women who adore one another and who know about being gentle and affectionate.'

That night Maria undressed and stood before Jennifer proudly. She had a lovely body, but Jennifer felt a secret delight in the knowledge that her own was superior. She dropped her clothes to the floor shyly. She heard Maria's startled gasp as she exposed her breasts.

'You are more lovely than I dreamed,' Maria said softly. Her hands stroked Jennifer's breasts lightly and endearingly. She leaned over and rested her cheek against them. 'You see, I love your beauty and respect it. A man would be tearing into it now.' She ran her fingers gently over Jennifer's body. To her amazement, Jennifer began to feel a sensation of excitement . . . her body began to vibrate . . .

'Come.' Maria took her hand. 'Let us lie down. We will have a cigarette.'

'No, Maria. Keep touching me,' Jennifer pleaded.

'Later, I will touch you and hold you to your heart's content. But I want you to feel comfortable with me. I will be gentle . . .'

Maria had been gentle, and very patient – taking more liberties each night, slowly teaching Jennifer to respond, erasing any embarrassment. 'You cannot just be loved, you must love back,' Maria would insist. 'Make me thrill as I thrill you.' Each night Maria urged her on, until at last Jennifer found herself responding with equal ardor and reaching peaks of exaltation she never dreamed existed.

She enjoyed a dual relationship with Maria. At night she was eager for Maria, demanding and ecstatic. But during the; day she regarded Maria as a friend. She felt no other personal attachment. When they shopped together or explored strange little towns, Maria was just another girl. She felt no involvement. Often they met attractive men – ski instructors, students – and Jennifer found these encounters quite difficult. Maria remained aloof to their advances, but Jennifer found some of the young men quite appealing. Many times as they danced, she felt her body thrilling to the touch of the strong masculine one that held her close. When a boy whispered an endearment, she found herself longing to respond.

Once she had slipped out for a brief walk with a particularly handsome Panamanian boy. He was a medical student, and he was going to New York after the war for further studies. He wanted her. They kissed, and she found herself clinging to him, responding to his kisses with equal passion. It was wonderful to hold the strong shoulders of a man, to feel a man's chest against her own . . . the strength of a man's hand after Maria's soft, tender one . . . the firmness of a man's lips. She wanted this boy desperately, but she tore away from him and returned to the café. Maria had noticed her absence; there was a slight scene that night when they were alone. Jennifer swore it had been a headache, that she had just wanted some air. At last, in bed, Maria relented . . .

But most of the time it was wonderful. Maria was wildly extravagant. She bought Jennifer beautiful clothes. Jennifer learned to ski. Her French grew fluent and effortless. When they grew bored with Lausanne they moved to Geneva.

After three years in Switzerland Maria's father wanted her to return, but she refused. Then, in 1944, he stopped her checks. She had no choice.

'You will come with me,' she told Jennifer. 'But we will have to cash in your return ticket to America. I have not enough money without it.'

Jennifer knew she was handing in her ticket to freedom. For the past year she had grown increasingly weary with Maria's demands on her body, yet Cleveland and her mother were even less appealing. But Spain! She might find some handsome Spanish man of good family. She was twenty-three, technically a virgin . . . why not?

Jennifer remained in Spain over a year. She met many eligible men. A few were passable, but Maria kept a hawklike watch on all her activities. They were always chaperoned by one of Maria's aunts. Maria repelled all advances and saw to it that Jennifer made no progress. Jennifer grew desperate. Maria's possessiveness was stifling. For the first time she understood her mother's fear of poverty. Money bought freedom; without it one could never be free. In Spain she could live luxuriously and wear beautiful clothes, but she belonged to Maria. If she returned to Cleveland she faced a different kind of imprisonment – marriage to some third-rate man who would also demand the use of her body. Whichever way you looked at it, without money you were someone's captive. But there had to be a way out!

She began lying awake nights. She suffered through Maria's lovemaking, returning an ardor she did not feel, feigning sleep until Maria's even breathing assured her of safety. Then she would slide out of bed and sit by the window, smoking endlessly, staring at the stars, thinking . . .

Money. She had to have money. The answer was in her body — it would work for her. It had carried her this far. She would go to New York, take a different name, lie about her age . . . maybe she could model. Somehow she'd get money. She'd never be trapped again.

*

Sure, Tony thought she was twenty. But once he saw a girl who was really nineteen or twenty she might look a little beat. Miriam had been staring at her lately — asking funny questions, trying to trip her with dates about school. Thank God Tony wasn't too bright. She stopped suddenly. It was true — Tony wasn't too bright. Or was it just that Miriam took over so much he never had the chance? He certainly was bright about performing. He knew if the music was off even a fraction. No, it was just that Miriam never gave him a chance to think. Miriam! She rubbed more oil under her eyes. She *had* to sleep. She returned to the bedroom. Anne was almost asleep. She got into bed and turned off the light.

An hour later she was still wide awake. This was going to be another of those nights. She got out of bed quietly and went into the living room. She *could* sleep — if she had the nerve. She went to her bag and took out the small bottle. She stared at the tiny, bullet-shaped red capsules. Irma had given them to her last night. ('Just take one and you'll sleep for hours.')

Seconals. Irma had given her four. ('They're like gold to me. I can't give you any more.') Irma had replaced Neely in the show. She claimed the little red 'dolls' had saved her life. ('I'd give you more, Jennifer, but you need a doctor's prescription. I can only get ten a week.')

Should she try one? It was a frightening idea, that a little red capsule as tiny as this could put you to sleep. She walked to the small pantry and poured a glass of water. She held the pill for a second, feeling her heart pound. This was dope — but that was ridiculous! Irma took one every night, and she was fine. Irma had been nervous going into the show and she was still nervous seven months later. ('I feel everyone is comparing me with Neely when I sing. She has such a big following with her albums now.')

Well, one pill couldn't hurt. She swallowed it, replaced the bottle in her bag and rushed into bed.

How long would it take? She still felt wide awake. She could hear Anne's even breathing, the clock on the night table ticking, the traffic sounds outside – in fact, everything seemed intensified . . .

Then she felt it! Oh, God! It was glorious! Her whole body felt weightless . . . her head was heavy, yet light as air. She was going to sleep . . . sleep . . . oh, the beautiful little red doll . . .

The following day she visited Henry's doctor. He turned her down cold. She was in excellent condition. What was this nonsense! No, he would not give her a prescription for Seconals. Stop drinking all that coffee. Cut down on cigarettes. She'd sleep. If she didn't, then her body didn't need it.

'That isn't the way to do it,' Irma explained a few days later. 'You can't go to a good doctor and just come out and ask for them. It's best to find a little doctor – one whose ethics are a little shady.'

'But where? Irma, I slept four nights in a row with those blessed red dolls, and it was heavenly. I haven't slept in two nights without them.'

'Look for one of those third-rate hotels on the West Side. You'll see a doctor's sign on a dirty window,' Irma explained. 'But don't just walk in and ask for pills. You have to play the game. Walk in and say you're from out of town – California is always good. Don't wear the mink, or the rates will go up. Tell him you can't sleep. He'll make a stab at listening to your heart, and you keep saying all you need is a few nights' sleep. Then he'll charge you ten bucks and give you a prescription for a week's supply, knowing you'll be back. And he knows he's good for ten bucks a week. But believe me, it's worth it. You may have to try a few doctors before you hit the right one – two turned me down – but you'll find one. Don't go to the Mackley Hotel – that's mine. He might get suspicious.'

Jennifer found her doctor on West Forty-eighth Street. She knew he was the right one when he disinterestedly dragged out a dusty stethoscope and made a half-hearted attempt to feel her pulse. Sure enough, he pulled out his prescription blank. 'Nembutals or Seconals?' he asked.

'The red ones,' Jennifer mumbled.

'Here's a week's supply of Seconals.' He handed her the prescription. 'This should straighten you out. If not, come by again.'

Anne was delighted at the change in Jennifer. She knew nothing about the pills, but she was pleased to see Jennifer sleeping through the night. She wondered if Tony had dropped any encouraging hints.

Then, a few days before Christmas, as Anne was packing a bag for her usual weekend at Lyon's, Jennifer made her big decision.

'This is *it*,' she announced. 'I'm going to get Tony to drive to Elkton tonight, or never see him again. I figured it out last night. If it doesn't work, at least I'll have six weeks going for me. Six weeks that he's in town, where I can show up places looking divine with some other guy and drive him crazy. Crazy enough to relent and marry me. If I wait till he goes to the Coast I'm dead.'

'Where's Miriam tonight?'

'Where she always is. With us! There's a new show opening at La Bombra. I've told Tony I'm going home from the theatre to change and to pick me up here. Miriam will be waiting at La Bombra with his group. I'll have him alone and take him by surprise. And if I play it right . . .'

She was in a robe when Tony arrived.

'Hey . . . hurry and get dressed. The show goes on at twelve-thirty.'

She came to him. 'Hold me first,' she said softly.

When he broke the embrace, he gasped. 'Baby, let me come up for air. Jesus! I need a blood transfusion just being near you.' His hands stroked her breasts. His fingers fumbled with the buttons on her satin robe. 'Jesus . . . why do you wear robes with buttons?' He pulled the robe off her shoulders, down to her waist. He stood back, his breath coming faster.

'Jen, no one should have boobs like that.' He touched them lightly.

She smiled. 'They're yours, Tony.'

He buried his face in them, sinking to his knees. 'Oh, God. I just can't believe it. Every time I touch them, I can't believe it.' His mouth was greedy. She held his head gently. 'I never want to move,' he mumbled.

'Tony, let's get married.'

'Sure, baby, sure . . .' He was fumbling at the rest of the buttons on her robe. It fell to the floor. She backed away. He crawled on his knees after her. She backed away again. 'Tony, all of this' – she stroked her body – 'is *not* yours . . . it's *mine!*'

He came after her. She eluded him again. She stroked her thighs, her fingers touching between her legs. 'That's mine, too,' she said softly. 'But *we* want you, Tony,' she whispered hoarsely. 'Take your clothes off.'

He tore at his shirt. The buttons ripped and fell to the floor. He stood before her naked.

'Your body is nice,' she said with a slow smile. Then she backed away. 'But mine is nicer.' She stroked her breasts deliberately, almost as if she thrilled to the touch. He stood watching, his breath coming in quick gasps. He rushed to her but she backed away.

'You can look,' she said softly. 'But you can't touch. Not until it's yours . . .'

'But it is mine – you're mine!' His voice was almost a growl.

'Only on loan.' She smiled sweetly. 'And I'm taking it back. Unless you really want it.' She stroked her breasts again. 'Want it for keeps.'

He followed her, trembling. 'I do. Just come to me . . . now!'

'Not now. Not until you marry me.'

'Sure,' he said hoarsely. 'I'll marry you.' He kept following her, but she eluded him, smiling all the while and stroking her own body, letting her hands play with her breasts, sliding them to her legs and touching herself. Her eyes were riveted to him.

'When will you marry me, Tony?'

'We'll talk about it later – right after . . .' He kept after her, hypnotized by this new game she was playing. She let him reach her . . . he grabbed at her breasts . . . his mouth sucked at them hungrily . . . his hands reached between her legs. Then she pulled away.

'Jen!' he gasped. 'Stop it. What are you trying to do – kill me?'

'Marry me, or that was the last time you touch me – ever!'

'I will, I will . . .'

'Now. Tonight.'

'How can we get married tonight? We have to take blood tests . . . we need a license. We'll start that jazz first thing tomorrow. I promise.'

'No. By then Miriam will talk you out of it.'

Mentioning Miriam was a wrong move. It snapped him back to reality. His passion began to dissolve. Quickly, she moved across the room, undulating her body, caressing her breasts. 'We'll miss you, Tony,' she whispered.

He crossed the room quickly and grabbed her.

'Marry us tonight, Tony. We *want* to belong to you . . .' She rubbed against him.

'How can I?' he whined.

'Get your car. We could drive to Elkton, Maryland.'

He stared at her. 'You mean they'd marry us – just like that?'

'Just like that!' She snapped her fingers.

'But Miriam—'

'I'll tell Miriam,' she said. 'We'll call after we're married. I'll tell her. Let her yell at me. You'll be in my arms. All of me will belong to you . . . forever.' She moved her body against him. 'Touch me, Tony – it will all belong to you. You'll be able to do anything you want to me, Tony. Anything – even the things I wouldn't let you do.' She broke away and stood, swaying, her hips moving rhythmically. 'And I'll do all the things you've begged me to do . . . after we're married.'

'Now,' he begged. 'Now, please – then we'll go to Elkton.'

'No. After Elkton.'

'I can't stand it. I can't wait until then!'

She came close. 'Yes you can. Because tonight, after we're married' – she let her fingers caress his body, nibbled at his ear – 'then we'll have a ball.'

His lips were dry. 'Okay, you win. Only for Christ's sake, let's get going.'

She threw her arms around him. 'You won't regret it . . . I'll make you wild.'

There was a sharp knock on the door. Jennifer broke the embrace. 'I'm not expecting a soul. Tony, did you tell anyone you'd be here?'

He shook his head. She pulled on her robe. It was an apologetic bellboy with a telegram.

'It's for Anne. I'd better phone her at Lyon's. It might be important.'

She sat on the bed and called Anne. Tony came into the bedroom. Oh, God, this was a stupid thing to do! She stood up, clutching her robe around her. Where was Anne? Why didn't they answer?

'Hello.' It was Lyon. Yes, he'd get Anne. Tony was fumbling at her robe. She pushed him away.

'Hello, Anne? A telegram just came for you. Sure, one second. She ripped it open. Tony gently but firmly pushed her on the bed. She held the telegram and the phone and silently tried to push him off. She clamped her hand over the phone. 'No, Tony! Not now. No!' He was on top of her. She looked at the wire. Tony's mouth found her breasts. Oh, God . . . 'Anne . . . yes, I'm here . . . Anne . . . Good Lord, your mother is dead!' She felt Tony enter her, roughly, pounding into her. She clenched her teeth and kept her voice even. 'Yes, Anne. That's all it says. I'm terribly sorry.' She hung up. Tony had fallen across her, panting in satisfied exhaustion.

'Tony, that wasn't fair. That was taking advantage of me.'

He smiled lazily. 'Baby, you were born with the advantages – a pair of them.' He flicked her breast lightly.

'We'd better get dressed. Anne is coming back here.'

He pulled on his shirt. 'Christ, I was hot for you, wasn't I? No buttons left on this shirt. I'll run back to the hotel and grab a new shirt.'

'Pack a bag, Tony.'

'What for?'

'We're going to Maryland – remember?'

He smiled. 'Not now, baby. If we hurry we can still catch part of the show at La Bombra. Now be dressed when I come back – in about twenty minutes.'

'Tony; if we don't elope tonight, I'll never see you again.'

He walked over and chucked her playfully under the chin. 'You'll see me, baby. I'm the greatest. Who could replace me?' He walked to the door. 'Wear something gorgeous – the newspapermen will be there.'

From *Valley of the Dolls* by Jacqueline Susann, 1966

The Ripped Bodice

Amber knows she's awful, with her greed and her ambition and determination to stop at nothing to get what she wants, but she does it all anyway, and ends up, *inter alia*, mistress to Charles II. She was described as 'amoral' when the book was first published. I disagree: throughout the novel's vast time-span, Amber loves only one man, with heart-breaking consequences. She is magnificent.

'That Amber St Clare!' muttered the eldest girl with a furious toss of her long blonde hair. 'If ever there's a man about, you may be sure *she'll* come along! I think she can smell 'em out!'

'She should've been married and bedded a year ago – that's what my mother says!'

The third girl smiled slyly and said in a knowing sing-song: 'Well, maybe she ain't married yet, but she's already been—'

'Hush!' interrupted the first, nodding toward the younger children.

'Just the same,' she insisted, though she had lowered her voice to a hiss, 'my brother says Bob Starling told him he had his way with her on Mothering Sunday!'

But Lisbeth, who had started the conversation, gave a contemptuous snap of her fingers. 'Uds Lud, Gartrude! Jack Clarke said the same thing six months ago – and she's no bigger now than she was then.'

Gartrude had an answer. 'And d'ye want to know why, Lisbeth

Morton? B'cause she can spit three times in a frog's mouth, that's why. Maggie Littlejohn seen her do it!'

'Pooh! My mother says *nobody* can spit three times in a frog's mouth!'

But the argument was cut short. For suddenly a sound of galloping hoofs echoed through the quiet little valley and a body of men on horseback rounded the turn of the road above St Catherine's and came rushing headlong up the narrow street toward them. One of the six-year-olds gave a scream of terror and ran to hide behind Lisbeth's skirts.

'It's Old Noll! Come back from the Devil to get us!' Even dead, Oliver Cromwell had not lost his salutary effect on disobedient youngsters.

The men reined in their horses, bringing them to a prancing nervous halt not more than ten yards from where the girls stood in a close group, their earlier fright and apprehension giving way now to frank admiring interest. There were perhaps fourteen men in all but more than half of them were either serving-men or guides, for they wore plain clothes and kept at a discreet distance from the others. The half-dozen in the lead were obviously gentlemen.

They wore their hair in the shoulder-length cut of the Cavaliers, and their dress was magnificent. Their suits were black velvet, dark red velvet, green satin, with broad white linen collars and white linen shirts. On their heads were wide-brimmed hats with swirling plumes, and long riding capes hung from their shoulders. Their high leather boots were silver-spurred and each man wore a sword at his hip. They had evidently been riding hard for some considerable distance for their clothes were dusty and their faces streaked with dirt and sweat, but in the girls' eyes they had an almost terrifying grandeur.

Now one of the men took off his hat and spoke to Lisbeth, presumably because she was the prettiest. 'My services, madame,' he said, his voice and eyes lazily good-humoured, and as he looked her over slowly from head to foot Lisbeth blushed crimson and found it difficult to breathe. 'We're looking for a place to eat. Have you a good tavern in these parts?'

Lisbeth stared at him, temporarily speechless, while he continued to smile down at her, his hands resting easily on the saddle before him. His suit was black velvet with a short doublet and wide knee-length breeches, finished with golden braid. He had dark hair and green-grey eyes and a narrow black mustache lined his upper lip. His good looks were spectacular — but they were not the most important thing about him. For his face had an uncompromising ruthlessness and strength which marked him, in spite of his obvious aristocracy, as an adventurer and gambler, a man free from bonds and ties.

Lisbeth swallowed and made a little curtsy. 'Ye mun like the Three Cups in Heathstone, m'lord.' She was afraid to recommend her own poor little village to these splendid strangers.

'Where's Heathstone from here?'

'Heathstone be damned!' protested one of the men. 'What's wrong with your own ordinary? I'll fall off this jade if I go another mile without food!' He was a handsome blonde red-faced young man and in spite of his scowl he was obviously happy and good-natured. As he spoke the others laughed and one of them leaned over to clap him on the shoulder.

'By God, we're a set of rascals! Almsbury hasn't had a mouthful since he ate that side of mutton this morning!'

They laughed again at this for apparently Almsbury's appetite was a well-established joke among them. The girls giggled too, more at ease now, and the six-year-old who had mistaken them for Puritan ghosts came out boldly from behind Lisbeth's skirts and edged a step or two nearer. At that instant something happened to create an abrupt change in the relationship between the men and girls.

'There's nothing wrong with our inn, your Lordship!' cried a low-pitched feminine voice, and the girl who had been talking to the two young farmers came running across the green toward them. The girls had stiffened like wary cats but the men looked about with surprise and sudden interest. 'The hostess there brews the finest ale in Essex!'

She made a quick little curtsy to Almsbury and then her eyes turned to meet those of the man who had spoken first and who was now watching her with a new expression on his face, speculative, admiring, alert. While the others watched, it seemed that time stopped for a moment and then, reluctantly, went on again.

Amber St Clare raised her arm and pointed back down the street to the great sign with its weather-beaten gilt lion shimmering faintly as the falling sun struck it. 'Next the blacksmith's shop, m'lord.'

Her honey-coloured hair fell in heavy waves below her shoulders and as she stared up at him her eyes, clear, speckled amber, seemed to tilt at the corners; her brows were black and swept up in arcs, and she had thick black lashes. There was about her a kind of warm luxuriance, something immediately suggestive to the men of pleasurable fulfillment — something for which she was not responsible but of which she was acutely conscious. It was that, more than her beauty, which the other girls resented.

She was dressed, very much as they were, in a rust wool skirt tucked up over a green petticoat, a white blouse and yellow apron and tight-laced black stomacher; her ankles were bare and she wore a pair of neat black shoes. And yet she was no more like them than a field flower is like a cultivated one or a sparrow is like a golden pheasant.

Almsbury leaned forward, crossing his arms on his saddle bow. 'What in the name of Jesus,' he said slowly, 'are *you* doing out here in God's forgotten country?'

The girl looked at him, dragging her eyes away from the other man, and now she smiled, showing teeth that were white and even and beautifully shaped. 'I live here, m'lord.'

'The deuce you do! Then how the devil did you get here? What are you? Some nobleman's bastard put out to suck with a cottager's wife and forgotten these fifteen years?' It was no uncommon occurrence, but she looked suddenly angry, her brows drawing in an indignant scowl.

'I am *not*, sir! I'm as much my father's child as you are — or more!'

The men, including Almsbury, laughed heartily at this and he gave her a grin. 'No offense, sweetheart. Lord, I only meant you haven't the look of a farmer's daughter.'

She smiled at him quickly then, as though in apology for her show of temper, but her eyes went back immediately to the other man. He was still watching her with a look that warmed all her body and brought a swift-rising sense of excitement. The men were wheeling their horses around and as his turned, its forelegs lifted high, he smiled and nodded his head. Almsbury thanked her and lifted his hat and then they rode off, clattering back up the street to the inn. For a moment longer the girls stood silently, watching them dismount and go through the doorway while the inn-keeper's young sons came to take care of their horses.

When they were out of sight Lisbeth suddenly stuck out her tongue and gave Amber a shove. 'There!' she cried triumphantly, and made a sound like a bleating female goat. 'Much good it did you, Mrs Minx!'

Swiftly Amber returned the shove, almost knocking the girl off balance, crying, 'Mind your knitting, chatterbox!'

For a moment they stood and glared at each other, but finally Lisbeth turned and went off across the green, where the other girls were rounding up their charges, running and shouting, racing with one another, eager to get home to their evening suppers. The sun had set, leaving the sky bright red along the horizon but turning to delicate blue above. Here and there a star had come out; the air was full of the magic of twilight.

Her heart still beating heavily, Amber crossed back to where she had left her basket lying in the grass. The two young farmers had gone, and now she picked it up again and continued on her way, walking toward the inn.

She had never seen anyone like him before in her life. The clothes he wore, the sound of his voice, the expression in his eyes, all made her feel that she had had a momentary glimpse into another world – and she longed passionately to see it again, if only for a brief while. Everything else, her own world of Marygreen and Uncle Matt's farm, all the young men she knew, now seemed to her intolerably dull, even contemptible.

From her conversations with the village cobbler she knew that they must be noblemen, but what they were doing here, in Marygreen she could not imagine. For the Cavaliers these past several years had retired into what obscurity they could find or had gone abroad in the wake of the King's son, now Charles II, who lived in exile.

The cobbler, who had fought in the Civil Wars on his Majesty's side, had told her a great many tales of things he had seen and stories he had heard. He had told her of seeing Charles I at Oxford, of being almost close enough to have touched him, of the gay and beautiful Royalist ladies, the gallant men — it was a life full of colour and spirit and high romance. But she had seen nothing of it, for it disappeared while she was yet a child, disappeared forever the morning his Majesty was beheaded in the yard of his own Palace. It was something of that atmosphere which the dark-haired stranger had brought with him — not the others, for she had scarcely noticed them — but it was something more as well, something intensely personal. It seemed as though, all at once, she was fully and completely alive.

Arriving at the inn she did not go in by the front entrance but, instead, walked around to the back where a little boy sat in the doorway, playing with his fox-eared puppy, and she patted him on the head as she went by. In the kitchen Mrs Poterell was rushing about in a frenzy of preparation, excited and distraught. On the chopping-block lay a piece of raw beef into which one of the daughters was stuffing a moist mixture of bread-crumbs and onions and herbs. A little girl was cranking up water from the well that stood far in one corner of the kitchen. And the turnspit-dog in his cage above the fireplace gave an angry yowl as another boy applied a hot coal to his hind feet to make him move faster and turn the roasting-joint so it would brown evenly on all sides.

Amber managed to catch the attention of Mrs Poterell, who was careening from one side of the room to the other, her apron full of eggs. 'Here's a Dutch gingerbread Aunt Sarah sent you, Mrs Poterell!' It was not true, for Sarah had sent the delicacy to the blacksmith's wife, but Amber thought this the better cause.

'Oh, thank God, sweetheart! Oh, I never was in such a taking! Six gentlemen in my house at once! Oh, Lord! What shall I do!' But even as she talked she had begun breaking the eggs into a great bowl.

At that moment fifteen-year-old Meg emerged from the trap-door which led down into the cellar, her arms full of dusty green bottles, and Amber rushed to her.

'Here, Meg! Let me help you!'

She took five of them from her and started for the other room, pushing the door open with her knee, but she kept her eyes down as she entered, and concentrated all her attention on the bottles. The men were standing about the room, cloaks off though they still wore their hats, and as she appeared Almsbury caught sight of her and came forward, smiling.

'Here — sweetheart. Let me help you with those. So they play that old game out here too?'

'What old game, m'lord?'

He took three of the bottles from her and she set the other two on the table, looking up then to smile at him. But instantly her eyes sought out the other man where he stood next the windows with two companions, throwing dice on a table-top. His back was half turned and he did not glance around but tossed down a coin as one of the others snapped his fingers at a lucky throw. Surprised and disappointed, for she had expected him to see her immediately — even to be looking for her — she turned again to Almsbury.

'Why, it's the oldest game in the world,' he was saying. 'Keeping a pretty bar-maid to lure in the customers till they've spent their last shilling — I'll warrant you've lured many a farmer's son to his ruin.' He was grinning at her and now he picked up a bottle, jerked out the cork and put it to his lips. Amber gave him another smile, arch and flirtatious, wishing that the other man would look over and see her.

'Oh, I'm not the bar-maid here, sir. I brought Mrs Poterell a cake and helped Meg to carry in the bottles.'

Almsbury had taken several swallows, draining half the bottle at once. 'Ah, by God!' he declared appreciatively. 'Well, then who are you? What's your name?'

'Amber St Clare, sir.'

'Amber! No farmer's wife ever thought of a name like that.'

She laughed, her eyes stealing swiftly across the room and back again, but he was still intent on the dice. 'That's what my Uncle Matt says. He says my name should be Mary or Anne or Elizabeth.'

Almsbury took several more deep swallows and wiped his mouth with the back of his hand. 'Your uncle's a man of no imagination.' And then, as she glanced toward the table again, he threw back his head and laughed. 'So that's what you want, is it? Well, come along——' And taking hold of her wrist he started across the room.

'Carlton,' he said, when they had come up to the group, 'here's a wench who has a mind to lay with you.'

He turned then, gave Almsbury a glance that suggested some joke between them, and smiled at Amber. She was staring up at him with her eyes big and shining, and had not even heard the remark. She was no more than five-feet three, a height convenient for making even a moderate-sized man feel impressive, but he towered over her by at least a foot.

She caught only a part of Almsbury's introduction. '——a man for whom I have the highest regard even though the bastard does steal every pretty wench I set my eyes on – Bruce, Lord Carlton.' She managed a curtsy and he bowed to her, sweeping off his hat with as much gallantry as though she were a princess royal. 'We're all of us,' he continued, 'come back with the King.'

'With the King! Is the King come back!'

'He's coming – very soon,' said Carlton.

At this astonishing news Amber forgot her nervous embarrassment. For though the Goodegroomes had once been Parliamentarian in sympathy, they had gradually, as had most of the country, begun to long for monarchy and the old ways of life. Since the King's murder his people had grown to love him as they had never done during his lifetime, and that love had been transferred to his heir.

'Gemini!' she breathed. For it was too great an event to realize all at once – and under such distracting conditions.

Lord Carlton took up one of the bottles which Meg had set on the table, wiped the dust from its neck with the palm of his hand, and pulling out the cork began to drink. Amber continued to stare at him, her self-consciousness now almost drowned in awe and admiration.

'We're on our way to London,' he told her. 'But one of our horses needs shoeing. What about your inn? Is it a good place to stay the night? The landlord won't rob us – there aren't any bed-bugs or lice?' He watched her face as he talked, and for some reason she did not understand there was a look of amusement in his eyes.

'Rob you?' she cried indignantly. 'Mr Poterell never robbed any-body! This is a mighty fine inn,' she declared with stanch loyalty. 'The one in Heathstone is *nothing* to it!'

Both men were grinning now. 'Well,' said Almsbury, 'let the landlord steal our shoes and the lice be thick as March crows in a fallow field, still it's an English inn and by God a good one!' With that he made her a solemn bow, 'Your servant, madame,' and went off to find another bottle of sack, leaving them alone.

Amber felt her bones and muscles turn to water. She stood and looked at him, cursing herself for her tongue-tied stupor. Why was it that she – who usually had a pert remark on her tongue for any man no matter what his age or condition – could think of nothing at all to say now? Now, when she longed with frantic desperation to impress him, to make him feel the same violent excitement and admiration that she did. At last she said the only thing she could think of:

'Tomorrow's the Heathstone May Fair.'

'It is?'

His eyes went down to her breasts which were full and pointed, upward tilting; she was one of those women who reach complete physical maturity at an early age, and there had long since ceased to be anything of adolescence about her.

Amber felt the blood begin to rise in her neck and face. 'It's the finest fair in all Essex,' she assured him quickly. 'The farmers go ten and twenty miles to it.'

His eyes came back to meet hers and he smiled, lifting one

eyebrow in apparent wonder at this gigantic local festival, then drank down the rest of his wine. She could smell the faint pungent odour of it as he breathed and she could smell too the heavy masculine sweat on his clothes and the scent of leather from his boots. The combination gave her a sense of dizziness, almost of intoxication, and a powerful longing swept through her. Almsbury's impertinent remark had been no very great exaggeration.

Now he glanced out the window. 'It's growing dark. You should be getting home,' and he walked to the door, opening it for her.

The evening had settled swiftly and many stars had come out; the high-pitched moon was thin and transparent. A cool little breeze had sprung up. Out there they stood alone, surrounded by the talking and laughter from the inn, the quiet country sounds of crickets and a distant frog, the whir of tiny gnats. She turned and looked up at him, her face white and glistening as a moonflower.

'Can't *you* come to the Fair, my lord?' She was afraid that she would never see him again, and the idea was intolerable to her.

'Perhaps,' he said. 'If there's time.'

'Oh, please! It's on the main road — you'll pass that way! You *will* stop, won't you?' Her voice and eyes pleaded with him, wistful, compelling.

'How fair you are,' he said softly, and now for the first time his expression was wholly serious.

For a moment they stood looking at each other, and then Amber swayed involuntarily toward him, her eyes shut. His hands closed about her waist, drawing her to him, and she felt the powerful muscles in his legs. Her head fell back. Her mouth parted to receive his kiss. It was several moments before he released her, but when he did it seemed too soon — she felt almost cheated. Opening her eyes again she saw him looking at her with faint surprise, though whether at himself or her she did not know. The world seemed to have exploded. She was as stunned as though she had been given a heavy blow, and all the strength had gone out of her.

'You must go now, my dear,' he said finally. 'Your family will be troubled to have you out so late.'

Quick impulsive words sprang to her lips. I don't care if they are! I don't care if I never go home again! I don't care about anything but you— Oh, let me stay here and go away with you tomorrow—

But something kept her from saying them. Perhaps the image – somewhere not too far back in her mind – of Aunt Sarah's troubled, cautioning frown, Uncle Matt's stern, lean, reproving face. It would never do to be so bold, for he would only hate her then. Aunt Sarah had often said men did not like a pert woman.

'I don't live far,' she said. 'Just down this road and over the fields a quarter mile or so.' She was hoping that he would offer to walk the distance with her but he did not, and though she waited a few seconds, at last she dropped him a curtsy. 'I'll look for you tomorrow, m'lord.'

'I may come. Good-night.'

He made her a bow, sweeping off his hat again, and then with a smile and a glance that took her in from head to foot he turned and went inside. Amber stood there a moment like a bewildered child; then suddenly she whirled about and started off at a run and though she stopped once to look back he was gone.

She ran on then – up the narrow road and past the church, quickening her pace as she went by the graveyard where her mother lay buried, and soon she turned right down a tree-lined lane leading over the fields toward the Goodegroome farm. Ordinarily she would have been a little scared to be out alone when it was almost dark, but ghosts and witches and goblins held no terror for her now. Her mind was too full of other things.

She had never seen anyone like him before and had not realized that such a man could exist. He was every handsome, gallant gentleman the cobbler had ever described, and he was what her dreams had embroidered upon those descriptions. Bob Starling and Jack Clarke! A pair of dolts!

She wondered if he was thinking of her now, and felt sure that he must be. No man could kiss a woman like *that* and forget her the next moment! The kiss, if nothing else, she thought, would bring him to the Fair tomorrow – draw him there perhaps in spite of himself. She complimented herself that she understood men and their natures very well.

*

Amber waited impatiently for the months to pass and wrote one letter after another to Almsbury at Barberry Hill, asking if he had heard from Lord Carlton or if he knew exactly when he would arrive. The Earl answered each one the same. He had heard nothing more – they expected to reach England sometime in August or September. How was it possible to be more explicit when the passage was so variable?

But Amber could not think or care about anything else. Once more the old passionate and painful longing, which ebbed when she knew she could not even hope to see him, had revived. Now she remembered with aching clarity all the small separate things about him: The odd green-grey colour of his eyes, the wave in his dark hair and the slight point where it grew off his forehead, the smooth texture of his sun-burnt skin, the warm timbre of his voice which gave her a real sense of physical pleasure. She remembered the lusty masculine smell of sweat on his clothes, the feeling of his hands touching her breasts, the taste of his mouth when they kissed. She remembered everything.

But still she was tormented, for those piecemeal memories could not make a whole. Somehow, he eluded her. Did he really exist, somewhere in that vastness of space outside England or was he only a being she had imagined, built out of her dreams and hopes? She would throw her arms about Susanna in a passion of despair and yearning – but she could not reassure herself that way.

Yet in spite of her violent desire to see him again she had stoutly made up her mind that this time she would conduct herself with dignity and decorum. She must be a little aloof, let him make the first advances, let him come first to see her. Every woman knew that was the way to prick up a man's interest. I've always made myself his servant, she chided, but this time it's going to be different. After all, I'm a person of honour now, a duchess – and he's but a baron. Anyway – why *shouldn't* he come to me first!

She knew that his wife would be along but she did not trouble herself too much about that. For certainly Lord Carlton was not the man to be uxorious. That was well enough for the citizens, who had no better breeding, but a gentleman would no more fawn upon his wife than he would appear in public without his sword or wearing a gnarled periwig.

*

'Almsbury,' she said slowly, and all of a sudden her throat felt dry and tight. 'Almsbury — what did you come out here for?'

He strolled up to stand very close beside her, and his eyes looked down into hers. 'I came, sweetheart, to tell you that they're here. They got in last night.'

She felt as though she had just been struck across the face very hard, and for a paralyzed moment she stood staring at him. She was aware that one of his hands reached out and took hold of her upper arm, as if to steady her. Then she looked beyond him, over his shoulder, out to where his crested coach stood waiting.

'Where is he?' Her lips formed the words, but she heard no sound.

'He's home. At my house. His wife is here too, you know.'

Swiftly Amber's eyes came back to his. The dazed almost dreamy look was gone from her face and she looked alert and challenging.

'What does she look like?'

Almsbury answered gently, as if afraid of hurting her. 'She's very beautiful.'

'She can't be!'

Amber stood staring down at the wood-shavings, the scraps and piled bricks that lay all about them. Her sweeping black brows had drawn together and her face had an expression of almost tragic anxiety.

'She can't be!' she repeated. Then suddenly she looked back up at him again, almost ashamed of herself. She had never been afraid of any woman on earth. No matter what kind of beauty this Corinna was she had no reason to fear her.

*

Back at the Palace she immediately wrote him a letter, imploring him to come to her, but she got no reply until the next morning and then it was merely a hasty scratched note: 'Business makes it impossible for me to wait on you. If you're at Arlington House

Thursday, may I claim the favour of a dance? Carlton.' Amber tore it into bits and flung herself onto the bed to cry.

But in spite of herself she was forced to take certain practicalities into consideration.

For if it was true that Lady Carlton was a beauty then she must somehow contrive to look more dazzling Thursday night than ever before in her life. They were used to her at Court now and it had been a long while since her appearance at any great or small function had aroused the excitement and envy she had been able to stir up three and a half years ago. If Lady Carlton was even moderately pretty she would be the object of every stare, the subject of every comment, whether it were made in praise or derogation. Unless – unless I can wear something or do something they won't be able to ignore, no matter how they try.

She spent several hours in a frenzy of worry and indecision and then at last she sent for Madame Rouvière. The only possible solution was a new gown, but a gown different from anything she had ever seen, a gown no one had ever dared to wear.

'I've got to have something they can't *help* staring at,' Amber told her. 'If I have to go in stark naked with my hair on fire.'

Madame Rouvière laughed. 'That would be well enough for an entrance – but after a while they would grow tired and begin to look at the ladies with more on. It must be something *indiscret* – and yet covering enough to make them try to see more. Black would be the colour – black tiffany, perhaps – but there must be something to glitter too—' She went on, talking aloud, sketching out the dress with her hands while Amber listened in rapt attention and with glowing eyes.

Lady Carlton! Poor creature – what chance would she have?

For the next two days Amber did not leave her rooms. From early morning until late at night they were filled with Madame Rouvière and her little sempstresses, all of them chattering French and giggling while scissors snipped, deft fingers stitched and Madame wrung her hands and shrieked hysterically if she discovered a seam taken in a bit too far or a hem-line uneven by so much as a quarter of an inch. Amber stood patiently hour after hour while the dress was fitted, and they literally made it on her. No one was allowed to come in or to see it and to her great delight all this secrecy set up a froth of rumours.

The Duchess was going to come as Venus rising from the sea, dressed in a single sea-shell. She was going to drive a gilt chariot and four full-grown horses up the front stairs and into the drawing-room. Her gown was to be made of real pearls which would fall off, a few at a time, until she had on nothing at all. At least they did not doubt her audacity and their ingenuity gave considerable credit to hers.

Thursday they were still at work.

Amber's hair was washed and dried and polished with silk before the hair-dresser went to work on it. Pumice-stone removed every trace of fuzz from her arms and legs. She slathered her face and neck a dozen times with French cold-creams and brushed her teeth until her arm ached. She bathed in milk and poured jasmine perfume into the palms of her hands to rub on her legs and arms and body. She spent almost an hour painting her face.

At six o'clock the gown was done and Madame Rouvière proudly held it up at full length for all of them to see. Susanna, who had spent the entire day in the room, jumped and clapped her hands together and ran to kiss the hem. Madame let out such a screech of horror at this sacrilege that Susanna almost fell over backward in alarm.

Amber threw off her dressing-gown and – wearing nothing but black silk stockings held up by diamond-buckled garters and a pair of high-heeled black shoes – she lifted her arms over her head so that they could slide it on. The bodice was a wide-open lace-work of heavy cord sewn with black bugle beads, and it cut down to a deep point. There was a long narrow sheath-like skirt, completely covered with beads, that looked like something black and wet and shiny pouring over her hips and legs and trailing away in back. Sheer black tiffany made great puffed sleeves and an over-skirt which draped up at the sides and floated down over the train like a black mist.

While the others stood staring, babbling, ecstatically 'oh-ing,'

Amber looked at herself in the mirrored walls with a thrill of triumph. She lifted her ribs and tightened her chest muscles so that her breasts stood out like full pointed globes.

He'll *die* when he sees me! she told herself in a delirium of confidence. Corinna could not scare her now.

Madame Rouvière came to adjust her head-dress which was a great arch of black ostrich-feathers sweeping up over her head from a tight little helmet. Someone handed her her gloves and she pulled them on, long black ones clear to her elbows. Against the nakedness of her body, they seemed almost immodest. She carried a black fan and over her shoulders they laid a black velvet cloak, the lining edged in black fox. The stark black against her rich cream-and-honey colouring, something in the expression of her eyes and the curve of her mouth, gave her the look of a diabolical angel — at once pure, beautiful corrupt and sinister.

Amber turned now from the mirror to face Madame, and their eyes met with the gleaming look of successful conspirators. Madame put her thumb and fingers together and made the gesture of kissing them. She came up to Amber and said with a hiss in her ear: 'They'll never see her at all — that other one!'

Amber gave her a quick grateful hug and a grin. Then she bent to kiss Susanna, who approached her mother very carefully, almost afraid to touch her. And with her heart beating fast, her stomach churning maddeningly, Amber walked out of the room, put her mask to her face and went along a narrow little corridor leading out to where her coach waited. She had not felt so excited at the prospect of a party, so apprehensive and frightened, since the night she had first been presented at Court.

*

At seven o'clock, the night being still young and most of the guests sober as well as curious, they were gathered in the main drawing-room and keeping one eye at least on the new arrivals. They were waiting for two women who had not yet come: the Duchess of Ravenspur, and Lady Carlton. Her Ladyship — whom almost no one had seen — was rumoured to be the greatest beauty ever to appear in England, though opinions on this score were already strong and divided. Many of the women, at least, were prepared to decide the moment she arrived that she was by no means as beautiful as had been reported. And the Duchess of Ravenspur, no doubt from fear that her Ladyship would outshine her, was expected to do something spectacular in order to save herself.

'How I pity her Grace,' said one languid young lady. 'It runs through the galleries she lives in terror now of losing what she has. Gad, but it must be a bothersome thing to be great.'

Her companion smiled with lips pressed together. 'Is that why *you* never climbed the ladder? – for fear of falling off?'

'I don't care a fig for Lady Carlton or what she looks like,' commented a thin young fop who kept his hands busy with manipulating a woman's fan, 'but I'll be her slave if she can put the Duchess's nose out of joint. That damned woman has grown intolerable since his Majesty gave her a duchy. I used to lace her busk for her when she was only a scurvy player – but now every time we're presented she makes a show of never having seen me before.'

'It's her vulgar breeding, Jack. What else can you expect?'

A voice like a trumpet interrupted them. 'Her Grace, the Duchess of Ravenspur!'

Every eye in the room swept toward the door – but only the usher stood there alone beside it. They waited for an impatient moment or two and then, with her head held high and a kind of fierce challenging pride on her face, the Duchess came into view and slowly walked through the doorway toward them. A wave of shock and amazement swept along before her. Heads spun, eyes popped and even King Charles turned on his heel where he was talking to Mrs Wells and stared.

Amber came on imperturbably, though it seemed all her insides were quaking. She heard some of the older women gasp and saw them set their mouths sternly, square their shoulders and fix upon her their hard reproving glares. She heard low whistles from the men, saw their eyebrows go up, their elbows reach out to nudge one another. She saw the young women looking at her with anger and indignation, furious that she had dared to take such an advantage of them.

Suddenly she relaxed, convinced that she was a success. She was hoping that Bruce and Corinna were there somewhere to have seen her triumph.

Then, almost at once, she became aware that Almsbury was just at her side. She looked at him, a faint smile touching the corners of her mouth, but something she saw in his eyes made her expression freeze suddenly. What was it? Disapproval? Pity? Something of both? But that was ridiculous! She looked stunning and she knew it.

'Holy Christ, Amber,' he murmured, and his eyes went swiftly down over her body.

'Don't you like it?' Her eyes hardened a little as she looked up at him and even in her own ears her voice took on a confident brassy sound that was part bravado.

'Yes, of course. You look gorgeous—'

'But aren't you cold?' interrupted a feminine voice, and turning swiftly Amber found Mrs Boynton beside her, looking her over with feline insolence.

Another voice, a man's this time, came from her other side. 'Ods-fish, madame. But this is the greatest display that ever I've seen in public since I was weaned.' It was the King, lazy, smiling, obviously amused.

Amber felt suddenly as if she had been hurt inside.

She turned sick with a feeling of horror and self-disgust. What have I done! she thought. Oh, my God! what am I doing out here half undressed?

Her eyes swept round the room and every face she saw was secretly smiling, covertly sneering at her. All at once she felt like the person in a dream who sets out confidently to go up-town stark naked, gets halfway there and then realizes his mistake And, like the dreamer, she wished passionately that she were back home where no one could see her – but to her wild dismay she realized that this time she was caught in her own trap. She could not wake up from *this* bad dream.

Oh, what am I going to do? she thought desperately. How am I going to get out of here? In her anguish and self-consciousness she had all but forgotten Lord Carlton and his wife.

And then, so unexpectedly that she almost started, she heard their names called out, loud and clear: 'My Lord Carlton! My Lady Carlton!'

Without even realizing that she had done so she grabbed Almsbury by the hand and her eyes turned toward the door. The colour drained out of her face and neck as she watched them walk in; she did not even see the quick glance Almsbury gave her but she felt the warm reassuring pressure of his hand.

Bruce looked very much as he had when he had left London two years before. He vas thirty-eight years old and perhaps a little heavier than when last she had seen him, but still handsome, hard-skinned and vigorous-bodied, a man who changed little with the years. Amber only glanced at him – and then shifted her attention to his wife who walked beside him, her fingers resting upon his arm.

She was rather tall, though slender and graceful, with clear blue eyes, dark hair, and a skin pale as moonlight. Her features were delicate, her expression serene. To look at her brought up some elusive emotion – the same feeling evoked by an exquisitely painted porcelain. The gown she wore was cloth-of-silver covered with black lace and a black-lace mantilla lay upon her head; about her neck was the diamond and sapphire necklace which had belonged to Bruce's mother and which Amber had always hoped might one day be her own.

The King, ignoring ceremony, went forward with Lord and Lady Arlington to greet them – and as he did so all the room set up a noisy buzzing.

'My God! But she's a glorious creature!'

'I know that gown was made in Paris, my dear, it must have been, it couldn't have—'

'Can they really have women like that in Jamaica?'

'Poise and breeding – than which I admire nothing more in a woman.'

Amber was actually sick at her stomach now. Her hands and arm-pits were wet, all her muscles seemed to ache. I've got to get out of here before they see me! she thought wildly. But just as she made an involuntary movement to escape. Almsbury's grip on her hand tightened and he gave her a little jerk. She looked up at him, surprised, but then quickly composed herself again.

Charles, with no respect for etiquette, was asking Lady Carlton to dance with him, and now as the music started for a pavane he led her onto the floor. Others followed and it was soon crowded with slow-moving figures, pacing to the rhythmic cadence of spinets, flutes and a low-beating drum. Amber scarcely heard Almsbury asking her to dance. He repeated his request louder this time.

She glanced at him. 'I don't want to dance,' she muttered, distracted. 'I'm not going to stay here. I — I've got the vapours — I'm going home.'

This time she picked up her skirts and took a step, but the Earl caught her wrist and gave her so vigorous a jerk that her breasts shook and her curls bounced. 'Stop acting like a damned fool or I'll slap you! Smile at me, now — everyone's watching you.'

With a quick shifting of her eyeballs beneath half-lowered lashes, Amber glanced round the room. She wanted to turn and scream or pick up something to throw at them, something that would destroy them all where they stood and wipe out of her sight forever those pleased smirking faces. Instead she looked up at Almsbury and smiled, pulling the corners of her mouth as tight as possible to keep the muscles from quivering. She put her hand on his extended arm and they moved toward the floor.

'I've got to get out of here,' she told him, under cover of the music 'I *can't* stay!'

His expression did not change. 'You won't leave if I have to tie you up. If you had the courage to wear that thing in the first place, by God you'll have the courage to stay till the end!' Amber clenched her teeth, hating him, and as her feet kept moving in time to the music she began to plan how she would escape — slip away through some side-door the first time he let her out of his sight. Damn him! she thought. He acts like my grandmother! What's it to him if I stay or don't! I'll go if I—

And then, all unexpectedly, she saw Lady Carlton not more than ten feet away. Corinna was smiling at Almsbury, but she gave a little gasp of surprise as she caught sight of his partner. Amber's eyes blazed in fury and Corinna looked swiftly away, obviously embarrassed.

Oh, that woman! thought Amber. I hate her, I hate her, I hate her! Look how she minces and smiles and sets her foot so! Hoitytoity! How mightily prim and proper! I wish I was stark naked! That *would* make her eyes pop out! I'll pay her back for that! I'll make her sorry she ever clapt eyes on me! Just wait—

But suddenly her energy was consumed. She felt weak, lost, helpless.

I'm going to die, she thought wretchedly. I'll never live through this. My life won't be worth tuppence to me now— Oh, God, let me die right here, right now – I can't take another step. For the moment it seemed that Almsbury's arm was all that kept her from collapsing. Then the music stopped and the crowd began to move about, gathering into groups. Amber, with Almsbury still at her side, pretended to see no one as she made her way among them.

I'm going now, she told herself. And that damned blockhead isn't going to stop me!

But as she started toward a door he took hold of her arm. 'Come over here and meet Lady Carlton.'

Amber jerked away. 'What do I want to know her for?'

'Amber, for the love of God!' His voice, scarcely more than a whisper, was pleading with her. 'Look about you. Can't you see what they're thinking?'

Amber's eyes again flickered hastily around in time to catch a dozen pairs of eyes which had been fixed upon her glance aside, eyes that glittered, set above mouths that curled with amusement and contempt. Some of them did not even trouble to look away but met her with bold scornful smiles; they were watching, and waiting—

She took a deep breath, linked her arm with Almsbury's and together they walked toward where Lord and Lady Carlton stood in a group made up of the King, Buckingham, Lady Shrewsbury, Lady Falmouth, Buckhurst, Sedley and Rochester. As they approached, the small gathering seemed to grow quieter – as if expecting something to happen from the mere fact of her presence. Almsbury presented Lady Carlton to the Duchess of Ravenspur and both women, smiling politely, made faint curtsies. Lady Carlton was friendly and gracious and obviously altogether unaware that her husband might know this gorgeous half-naked woman. While the men, including his Majesty, all turned their heads to look at her, their eyes admiring her figure.

But Amber was conscious of no one but Bruce.

For an instant Lord Carlton's expression might have betrayed him — but no one was looking — and then immediately it changed, he bowed to her as though they were the merest acquaintances. Amber, as their eyes met, felt the world rock and tremble beneath her. The conversation began again and had been going on for several seconds before she was able to follow it: King Charles and Bruce were discussing America, the tobacco plantations, the colonists' resentment of the Navigation Laws, men the King knew who had gone to make their homes in the New World. Corinna said little, but whenever she did speak Charles turned to her with interest and unconcealed admiration. Her voice was light and soft, completely feminine, and the brief glances she gave Bruce revealed that here was that unheard-of phenomenon in London society: a woman deeply in love with her husband.

Amber wanted to reach out and rake her long nails across that tranquil lovely face.

When the music began again she curtsied, very cool and aloof and with some delicate suggestion of insult, to Corinna, nodded vaguely at Bruce and left them. After that she defiantly began to pretend that she was enjoying herself and was not at all embarrassed by her own nudity. She ate her supper attended by half-a-score of gallants, drank too much champagne, danced every dance. But the evening dragged with interminable slowness and she thought wearily that it would never end.

*

Amber found Bruce at the raffling-table — for he never remained long in a ball-room when the cards were being dealt or the dice were running — and so absorbed in the play that he did not see her until she had been standing across from him for several moments.

Self-consciously she had put on her most becoming expression, lower lip softly pouting, brows slightly raised to tilt the corners of her eyes.

The instant he looked at her she knew it and glanced over swiftly, a half-smile on her mouth. But his mouth did not answer and his green eyes looked at her seriously for a moment, then lightened and slid down her body with a kind of lazy insolence. Slowly they returned to her face and one eyebrow lifted almost imperceptibly. At that instant she felt like the commonest kind of drab, displaying herself for any man to see and appraise and — worst of all — to reject.

Ready to cry with rage and humiliation she turned swiftly and walked away.

*

Amber alternated between fury and despondent misery.

How *can* he have forgotten me? she frantically asked herself. He acts as if he's never seen me before. No, he doesn't, either! No man who'd never seen me before would look the way he does! If his wife had any wit at all she'd begin to suspect he knows me only too well— But she won't of course! Amber thought petulantly. I swear she's the greatest dunce in nature!

But despite his seeming indifference she could not believe it possible that he had been able to forget all they had meant to each other, for happiness and sorrow, over the nine years past. He could not have forgotten the things she remembered so well. That first day in Marygreen, those early happy weeks in London, the terrible morning when Rex Morgan had died, the days of the Plague— He could not have forgotten that she had borne him two children. He could not have forgotten the pleasures they had shared, the laughter and quarrels, all the agony and ecstasy of being violently in love. Those were the things that could never fade — nothing could ever erase them. No other woman could ever be to him exactly what she had been.

Oh, he can't forget! she cried to herself, lonely and despairing. He can't! He can't! He'll come to me as soon as he can, I know he will. He'll come tonight. But he did not.

*

Amber lay on a low cushioned day-bed, her eyes closed, her face serenely peaceful and content. Her hair had come down and fell in tawny masses about her shoulders. Bruce sat on the floor beside her, arms resting on his knees, head bent forward to lean on his wrists. He had taken off his periwig, coat and sword, and his wet white-linen shirt clung to his back and arms.

For a long while they continued silent.

Finally Amber, not opening her eyes, reached out and put one hand on his, her fingers tender and warm. He raised his head to look at her. His face was moist and flushed. Slowly he smiled, bent his head again and laid his lips on the back of her hand where the blue veins swelled.

'My darling——' Her voice lingered over the word, caressing it. Then slowly she lifted her lids and looked at him; they smiled, a smile born of recent memories and long acquaintance. 'At last you're back again. Oh, Bruce I've missed you so! Have you missed me too — just a little?'

'Of course,' he said. It was an automatic reply, made as if he thought the question a foolish or unnecessary one.

'How long will you be here? Are you going to live here now?' She could have been almost grateful for Corinna if she had insisted that they live in England.

'We'll be here a couple of months, I think. Then we're going to France to buy some furniture and visit my sister. After that we'll go back to Virginia.'

'We.' Amber did not like the sound of it. It reminded her again that his life, all his plans, included a woman now — a woman who was not herself. And it hurt her pride that he was taking Corinna to visit his sister for she had asked Almsbury once what kind of woman Mary Carlton was; he had told her that she was very beautiful, proud and haughty — and that she and Amber would not like each other.

'How d'you like being married?' she challenged him. 'You must find it mighty dull — after the gay life you've lived!'

He smiled again, but now she knew that with every word she said he drew farther away from her. She was scared, but she did not know what she could do. She felt, as always, helpless to contend against him and hold her own. 'I don't find it dull at all. In Virginia we have a better opinion of marriage than you do here.'

She rolled her eyes at that and sat up, straightening her bodice around and beginning to fasten it again. 'Hey day! How mightily proper you've grown! I vow and swear, Lord Carlton, you're not the same man who left here two years ago!'

He grinned at her. 'I'm not?'

She looked down at him sharply, then suddenly she was on her knees beside him, held close in his arms. 'Oh, my darling, darling — I love you so! I can't stand to know you're married to another woman! I hate her, I despise her, I—'

'Amber — don't talk that way!' He tried to make a joke of it. 'After all, you've been married four times and I've never hated any of your husbands—'

'Why should you? I didn't love any of them!'

'Nor the King, either, I suppose?'

She dropped her eyes at that, momentarily abashed. Then she faced him again. 'Not the way I do you— Anyway, he's the King. But you know as well as I do, Bruce, that if you'd let me I'd leave him and the Court and everything I have on earth to follow you anywhere!'

'What?' he asked her mockingly. 'You'd leave all this?'

As he spoke she realized all of a sudden that he did not consider her position, the luxury and pomp in which she lived, to be of any real worth at all. It was the sharpest disillusionment she had had. For she had expected to brag about it, to impress him with her title, her power, her money, her gorgeous rooms. Instead, he had made her feel that all she had got from life — these things for which she had been willing to make any compromise — were unimportant. Worse, were trash.

'Yes,' she said softly. 'Of course I'd leave it.' She had an inexplicable feeling of humility and almost of shame.

'Well, my dear, I wouldn't dream of asking such a sacrifice of you. You've worked hard for what you have and you deserve to keep it. What's more, you're exactly where you belong. You and Whitehall are as well suited as a bawd and brandy.'

'What do you mean by that!' she cried.

He shrugged, glanced at the clock and got to his feet. 'It's growing late. I've got to go.'

*

In Hyde Park there was a pretty half-timbered cottage set beside a tiny lake, where all the fashionable world liked to stop for a syllabub or, if the weather was cold, a mug of lambs'-wool or hot mulled wine. It was almost Christmas now and too late in the year to ride, but there were several crested gilt coaches waiting in the cold grey-and-scarlet sunset outside the Lodge. The drivers and footmen smoked their pipes, sometimes stamped their feet to keep warm as they stood about in groups, laughing and talking together — exchanging the newest back-stairs gossip on the lords and ladies who had gone inside.

A sea-coal fire was burning high in the oak-panelled great room. There was a cluster of periwigged and beribboned young fops about the long bar, drinking their ale or brandy, throwing dice and matching coins. Several ladies were seated at tables with their gallants. Waiters with balanced trays moved about among them and three or four fiddles were playing.

Amber — wearing an ermine-lined hooded cloak of scarlet velvet and holding a syllabub glass in one hand and her muff of dripping ermine tails in the other — stood near the fireplace talking to Colonel Hamilton, the Earl of Arran and George Etherege.

She chattered fluently and there was an ever-shifting, vivacious play of expression over her face. She seemed to be engrossed in the three of them. But all the while her eyes watched the door — it never opened that she did not know who came in or went out. And then, at last, the languid golden Mrs Middleton sauntered in with Lord Almsbury at her elbow. Amber did not hesitate an instant. Excusing herself from the three men she wove her way across the room to where the newcomers were standing, Jane still pausing just within the doorway to give the crowd time to discover her.

Amber gave Middleton only a vague nod as she came up. 'Almsbury, I've got to talk to you! I've been looking for you everywhere!'

The Earl bowed to Mrs Middleton. 'Will you excuse me for a moment, madame?'

Jane looked bored. 'Oh, lord, sir, *you* must excuse *me*! There's Colonel Hamilton beckoning me now — I just recalled he asked me this morning to meet him here and I'd all but forgot, let me die.' With an airy wave of one small gloved hand she drifted off, not even glancing at Amber who seemed unaware she had ever been there.

'Come over here — I don't want a dozen big ears listening to us.' They crossed the room to a quiet little corner near the windows. 'Tell me what's happened!' she cried without an instant's hesitation. 'I haven't seen him alone for fourteen days! I write to him and he doesn't answer! I talk to him in the Drawing-Room and he looks at me as if I'm a stranger! I ask him to visit me and he doesn't come! Tell me what's happened, Almsbury! I'm going stark staring mad!'

Almsbury gave a sigh. 'My Lady Castlemaine showed his wife the satire that Rochester wrote about you—'

'Oh, I know *that*!' cried Amber scornfully, cutting him off. 'But what's happened to make him treat me like this!'

'That's what's happened.'

She stared at him. 'I don't believe you.' Both of them were silent, looking at each other, for a long moment and then Amber said: 'But that can't be the only reason. Just because his wife found out. It must be more than that.'

'It isn't.'

'Do you mean to tell me, John Randolph, that he's been using me like this because his *wife* told him to!'

'She didn't tell him to. He decided it for himself. I may as well tell you the truth, Amber — he doesn't intend to see you alone any more.'

'Did he tell you that?' Her voice spoke to him, just above a whisper.

'Yes. And he meant it.'

Amber stood helplessly. She put her drink down on the broad sill of the casemented window and stood staring out at the bare-branched trees. Then she looked up at him again. 'Do you know where he is now?'

'No.'

Her eyes narrowed. 'You're lying. You do know! And you've got to tell me! Oh, Almsbury — *please* tell me! You know how much I love him! If only I can see him again and talk to him I can make him see how foolish this is! Please, Almsbury — please, *please*! He's going away soon and then I might never see him again! I've *got* to see him while he's here!'

For a long moment he hesitated, looking at her shrewdly, and then finally he gave a jerk of his head. 'Come along.'

As they passed Jane Middleton he stopped to speak to her but she tossed her curls and turned him a haughty shoulder. Almsbury shrugged.

The afternoon was cold and the mud hard and slippery with a thin layer of ice. Together they got into Amber's enormous crested gilt coach which was drawn by eight tawny horses, their manes and streaming tails braided with gold and green ribbons. The coachman and eight running footmen wore her emerald-velvet livery and there was another dressed all in white and carrying a white wand with an orange fastened to one end for his refreshment, who ran ahead to proclaim her coming. Some of the footmen hung onto the sides, while others jogged along in back or went ahead to order the rabble out of the way. Inside, the coach was upholstered with emerald velvet, deep-tufted on seat and sides and roof, festooned with gold swags and tassels.

Almsbury gave the coachman his directions and then climbed in beside Amber. 'He's at his stationer's in Ave Maria Lane, I think, buying some books.' He looked around him, whistling softly. 'Jesus Christ! When did you get this?'

'Last year. You've seen it before.'

She answered him abruptly and without paying much attention for she was absorbed in her own thoughts, trying to plan what she would say to Bruce, how she would convince him that he was wrong. It was several minutes before Almsbury spoke again.

Then he said: 'You've never been sorry, have you?'

'Sorry for what?'

'Sorry that you left the country and came to London.'

'Why should I be sorry? Look where I am!'

'And look how you got here. "All rising to great places is by a winding stair." Have you ever heard that?'

'No.'

'You've come by a winding stair, haven't you?'

'What if I have! I've done some things I hated, but that's over now and I'm where I want to be. I'm *somebody*, Almsbury! If I'd stayed in Marygreen and married some lout of a farmer and bred his brats and cooked his food and spun his linen — what would I be? Just another farmer's wife and nobody would ever know I'd been alive. But now look at me — I'm rich and a duchess and one day my son will be a duke — Sorry!' she finished with scornful positiveness. 'My God, Almsbury!'

He grinned. 'Amber, my darling, I love you — but you're an unprincipled calculating adventuress.'

'Well,' retorted Amber, 'I didn't have anything to start with—'

'But beauty and desirability.'

'There are other women aplenty who had that — but they aren't all duchesses today, I'll warrant you.'

'No, sweetheart, they aren't. The difference is that you were willing to make use of both to get what you wanted — and didn't care too much what happened to you on your way.'

'Lord!' she cried impatiently. 'You're in a scurvy humour today!' Abruptly she leaned forward and rapped on the front wall, shouting at her coachman: 'Drive faster!'

Ave Maria Lane was one of the tiny streets which formed a maze about the great burned pile of old St Paul's. When at last they arrived, Almsbury took her to the entrance of a new-built brick courtyard and pointed to one of the signs. He should be in there — the "Three Bibles and Three Bottles of Ink."' Too excited even to thank him, she picked up her skirts and ran into the court; he watched her go and, when she had disappeared into the building, turned about and left.

It was now dark outside and the shop was dim-lit; there was a thick dusty smell of ink, paper, leather and frying tallow. The walls were lined with book-shelves, all of them crowded, and piles of brown- or green- or red-bound volumes were stacked on the floor. In one corner, reading by a flickering light in the wall-sconce stood a short plump young man. He had a pair of thick green spectacles on his nose, a hat on his head, and though it was close and too-warm in there he wore his cloak. No one else was in the room.

Amber looked about and was on the point of going through the door beyond when an old man came out, smiling, and inquired if he might help her. She crossed to him and asked, very softly so that if Bruce were there he would not hear her: 'Is my Lord Carlton in there?'

'He is, madame.'

She put a cautioning finger to her lips. 'He's expecting me.' Reaching into her muff she took out a guinea and pressed it into his palm. 'We don't want to be disturbed.'

The man bowed, glancing surreptitiously at the coin in his hand, still smiling. 'Certainly, madame. Certainly.' He grinned, pleased to be party to a rendezvous between his Lordship and this fine woman.

She went to the door, opened it, stepped inside and softly closed it. Bruce, wearing his cloak and plumed hat, stood several feet away examining a manuscript; his back was to her. Amber paused, leaning against the door, for her heart was pounding and she felt suddenly weak and breathless. She was almost afraid of what he might do or say when he saw her.

After a moment Bruce, without glancing around, said, 'This manuscript of Carew — how did you get hold of it?' And then when he got no answer he turned and saw her.

Timidly Amber smiled and made him a little curtsy. 'Good even, my lord.'

'Well—' Bruce tossed the manuscript onto a table just behind him. 'I would never have taken you for a book-collector.' His eyes narrowed. 'How the devil did you get here?'

She ran toward him. 'I *had* to see you, Bruce! Please don't be angry with me! Tell me what's happened! Why have you been avoiding me?'

He frowned slightly, but did not look away. 'I didn't know any other way to do it — without a quarrel.'

'Without a quarrel! I've heard you say that a hundred times! You, who made your living fighting!'

He smiled. 'Not with women.'

'Oh, I promise you, Bruce, I didn't come to quarrel! But you've got to tell me what happened! One day you came to see me and we were happy together — and the next you'd scarce speak! *Why?*' She spread her hands in a gesture of pleading.

'You must know, Amber. Why pretend you don't?'

'Almsbury told me, but I wouldn't believe him. I still can't believe it. You, of all men, being led by the nose by your wife!'

He sat down on the top of the table near which they were standing and braced one foot on a chair. 'Corinna isn't the kind of woman who leads a man by the nose. I decided myself — for a reason I don't think I can explain to you.'

'Why not?' she demanded, half insulted at that. 'My understanding's as good as another's, I'll warrant you! Oh, but you must tell me, Bruce. I've got to know! I have a *right* to know!'

He took a deep breath. 'Well — I suppose you heard that Castlemaine showed Corinna the lampoon — but she said she'd known we were lovers long before that. She's gone through a kind of agony these last weeks we don't know anything about. Adultery may seem no serious matter to us, but it is to her. She's innocent and what's more, she loves me — I don't want to hurt her any more than I have.'

'But what about me?' she cried. 'I love you as much as she does! My God, I think I know a thing or two about agony myself! Or doesn't it mean anything to you if *I'm* hurt?'

'Of course it does, Amber, but there's a difference.'

'What!'

'Corinna's my wife and we'll live together the rest of our lives. In a few months I'll be leaving England and I won't come back again —

I'm done travelling. Your life is here and mine is in America — after I go this time we'll never see each other again.'

'Never — see each other again?' Her speckled tawny eyes stared at him, her lips half-parted over the words. 'Never—' She had said that to Almsbury only an hour before, but it sounded different to her now, coming from him. Suddenly she seemed to realize exactly what it would mean. '*Never*, Bruce! Oh, darling, you can't do this to me! I need you as much as she does — I love you as much as she does! If all the rest of your life belongs to her you can give me a little of it now— She'd never even know, and if she didn't know she couldn't be hurt! You can't be here in London all these next six months and never see me — I'd die if you did that to me! Oh, Bruce, you can't do it! You can't!'

She threw herself against him, pounding her fists softly on his chest, sobbing with quiet, desperate, mournful little sobs. For a long while he sat, his arms hanging at his sides, not touching her; and then at last he drew her close against him between his legs, his mouth crushing down on hers with a kind of angry hunger. 'Oh, you little bitch,' he muttered. 'Someday I'll forget you — someday I'll—'

———

From *Forever Amber* by Kathleen Winsor, 1944

Molly Bloom's Soliloquy

Molly Bloom, in the last and most truly wonderful section of Joyce's *Ulysses* – often called the 'Penelope' chapter, after Molly's counterpart in Homer's *Odyssey* – lies in bed and summons the spirit of love and longing she feels for the book's central character, Leopold. Every atom and cadence of her soliloquy is steeped in the pure sound of Dublin, and the womanliness and sensuality of her voice stands in powerful contrast to the intellectualism of the other characters. Reading it, you can feel the salt-spray off the coast at Howth, you can smell the flowers at the Moorish wall, and begin to understand that Leopold Bloom must get a great deal of his famous humanity from this woman, who is so passionately alive.

Also, it's really sexy.

I saw him driving down to the Kingsbridge station with his father and mother I was in mourning thats 11 years ago now yes hed be 11 though what was the good in going into mourning for what was neither one thing nor the other of course he insisted hed go into mourning for the cat I suppose hes a man now by this time he was an innocent boy then and a darling little fellow in his lord Fauntleroy suit and curly hair like a prince on the stage when I saw him at Mat Dillons he liked me too I remember they all do wait by God yes wait yes hold on he was on the cards this morning when I laid out the deck union with a young stranger neither dark nor fair you met before I thought it meant him but hes no chicken nor a stranger either besides my face was turned the other way what was the 7th card after that the 10 of spades for a Journey by land then there was a letter on its way and scandals too the 3 queens and the 8 of diamonds for a rise in society yes wait it all came out and 2 red 8s for new garments look at that and didnt I dream something too yes there was something about poetry in it I hope he hasnt long greasy hair hanging into his eyes or standing up like a red Indian what do they go about like that for only getting themselves and their poetry laughed at I always liked poetry when I was a girl first I thought he was a poet like Byron and not an ounce of it in his composition I thought he was quite different I wonder is he too young hes about wait 88 I was married 88 Milly is 15 yesterday 89 what age was he then at Dillons 5 or 6 about 88 I suppose hes 20 or more Im not too old for him if hes 23 or 24 I hope hes not that stuck up university student sort no otherwise he wouldnt go sitting down in the old kitchen with him taking Eppss cocoa and taking of course he pretended to understand it all probably he told him he was out of Trinity college hes very young to be a professor I hope hes not a professor like Goodwin was he was a patent professor of John Jameson they all write about some woman in their poetry well I suppose he wont find many like me where softly sighs of love the light guitar where poetry is in the air the blue sea and the moon shining so beautifully coming back on the nightboat from Tarifa the lighthouse at Europa point the guitar that fellow played was so expressive will I never go back there again all new faces two glancing eyes a lattice hid Ill sing that for him theyre my eyes if hes anything of a poet two eyes as darkly bright as loves own star arent those beautiful words as loves young star itll be a change the Lord knows to have an intelligent person to talk to about yourself not always listening to him and Billy Prescotts ad and Keyess ad and Tom the Devils ad then if anything goes wrong in their business we have to suffer Im sure hes very distinguished Id like to meet a man like that God not those other ruck besides hes young those fine young men I could see down in Margate strand bathing place from the side of the rock standing up in the sun naked like a God or something and then plunging into the sea with them why arent all men like that thered be some consolation for a woman like that lovely little statue he bought I could look at him all day long curly head and his shoulders his finger up for you to listen theres real beauty and poetry for you I often felt I wanted to kiss him all over also his lovely young cock there so simple I wouldnt mind taking him in my mouth if nobody was looking as if it was asking you to suck it so clean and white he looked with his boyish face I would too in 1/2 a minute even if some of it went down what its only like gruel or the dew theres no danger besides hed be so clean compared with those pigs of men I suppose never dream of washing it from 1 years end to the other the most of them only thats what gives the women the moustaches Im sure itll be grand if I can only get in with a handsome young poet at my age Ill throw them the 1st thing in the morning till I see if the wishcard come out or Ill try pairing the lady herself and see if he comes out Ill read and study all I can find or learn a bit off by heart if I knew who he likes so he wont think me stupid if he thinks all women are the same and I can teach him the other part Ill make him feel all over him till he half faints under me then hell write about me lover and mistress publicly too with our 2 photographs in all the papers when he becomes famous O but then what am I going to do about him though

no thats no way for him has he no manners nor no refinement nor no nothing in his nature slapping us behind like that on my bottom because I didn't call him Hugh the ignoramus that doesnt know poetry from a cabbage thats what you get for not keeping them in their proper place pulling off his shoes and trousers there on the chair before me so barefaced without even asking permission and standing out that vulgar way in the half of a shirt they wear to be admired like a priest or a butcher or those old hypocrites in the time of Julius Caesar of course hes right enough in his way to pass the time as a joke sure you might as well be in bed with what with a lion God Im sure hed have something better to say for himself an old Lion would O well I suppose its because they were so plump and tempting in my short petticoat he couldnt resist they excite myself sometimes its well for men all the amount of pleasure they get off a womans body were so round and white for them always I wished I was one myself for a change just to try with that thing they have swelling upon you so hard and at the same time so soft when you touch it my uncle John has a thing long I heard those cornerboys saying passing the corner of Marrowbone lane my aunt Mary has a thing hairy because it was dark and they knew a girl was passing it didnt make me blush why should it either its only nature and he puts his thing long into my aunt Marys hairy etcetera and turns out to be you put the handle in a sweepingbrush men again all over they can pick and choose what they please a married woman or a fast widow or a girl for their different tastes like those houses round behind Irish street no but were to be always chained up theyre not going to be chaining me up no damn fear once I start I tell you

———————

From *Ulysses* by James Joyce, 1922

Sweetness

The only book here to have been written specifically for teenagers. Sweet, touching and true.

'How'd it go with Artie?' I asked Erica on Monday. We were in zoology, classifying molluscs.

'I'll tell you how it went,' Erica said, '. . . it didn't!'

'He never showed up?'

'Oh, he showed up all right.'

'So?'

'Still nothing . . . not even a kiss.'

'Weird.'

'And I'm sure he likes me. He asked me to his school play . . . he's got the lead.'

'I heard. I'm going with Michael.'

'I know . . . Artie said he'll arrange for you two to bring me.'

'Fine.'

'If he doesn't try anything after the play I'm going to do something about it. I can't sit around waiting forever.'

Mr Kolodny looked up from his desk. 'Will you girls in the back stop talking and get to work.'

I pulled out a sheet of notebook paper, wrote *Like what?* and shoved it at Erica.

She wrote back, *Something drastic!*

On the night of the play Michael, Erica and I sat together in the fourth row of the auditorium at Summit High. The play was

Butterflies Are Free and Artie played the blind boy trying to make it on his own. Michael was right – Artie really surprised me. He was as good as a professional. Somehow, he seemed different on stage – more sure of himself. He made me forget he was Artie Lewin, game freak.

Sybil played his mother and Elizabeth played his girlfriend but they couldn't compare to Artie. It didn't help that Sybil looked fatter than ever and kept fidgeting with her grey wig. Elizabeth's costume consisted of the world's skimpiest bikini and when she first came on stage Erica nudged me with an elbow. For some stupid reason I felt I had to say something to Michael – something to show I'm not the jealous type. So I leaned over and whispered, 'She's very pretty.' How did I ever think up such a clever remark?

'Uh huh,' Michael said.

When the play ended Artie got a standing ovation.

'I had no idea . . .' Erica said over and over. 'I just can't believe it.'

'Me neither.'

'I told you,' Michael said. 'It's the most important thing in his life.'

As I watched Artie take another bow I could see that Michael was right again.

We tried to go backstage but there were two teachers in charge of keeping everyone out since the custodians were anxious to lock up the school for the night. Erica said she'd wait for Artie and that we should go on to the party.

I wasn't looking forward to going to Elizabeth's house and facing her close up. But there was nothing I could do about it without being obvious. Besides, how would Artie feel if his best friend didn't show?

Elizabeth's house was on a street a lot like mine. Her mother answered the door.

'Michael . . .' Mrs Hailey said, 'it's so nice to see you again.'

'Mrs Hailey . . . this is Katherine Danziger,' Michael told her.

'Hello,' I said.

'Come in . . . come in . . .' Mrs Hailey said, looking me over. 'Everyone's downstairs . . . Michael, you know the way.'

Could she have said that for my benefit, just to let me know that Michael had been there before?

It was a big party – maybe thirty or forty kids – and as soon as the cast arrived everyone surrounded them, offering congratulations. Michael gave Artie a couple of friendly punches, then bent down and whispered something to him, and Artie smiled, nodded and said, 'Thanks, buddy.'

Elizabeth's father took movies of us for the next half hour. Artie really hammed it up. Michael kissed Elizabeth on the side of her face and said, 'The part was made for you . . . you were great.' And Elizabeth answered, 'I'm glad you thought so.'

I walked away with a sinking feeling in my stomach. Sybil was standing in the corner talking to some boy. I went over to her and said, 'I enjoyed the play a lot . . . you were good.'

Sybil laughed. 'Thanks, but I know better . . .' She introduced me to the boy who turned out to be Elizabeth's younger brother. I wondered if he would make her list.

Erica took me aside, looked in Artie's direction, and said, 'He's flying very high . . . I wouldn't be surprised if tonight's the night . . .'

'Good luck,' I said, without enthusiasm.

'Oh, here you are.' Michael stood next to me and reached for my hand.

'Have we met?' I asked, pulling away.

'What's that supposed to mean?'

'Nothing,' I said. 'Just forget it.' I made my way over to Artie, who was sitting on the couch surrounded by fans. When I got a chance I said, 'I know you've heard this all night but you were really sensational.'

'Thanks, Kath.' He moved over, making room for me beside him.

'How'd you do it? You actually convinced me you were blind.'

'I don't know . . . it just comes naturally.'

'Seriously, Artie . . .'

'I'm serious. I don't know how I do it. I've always wanted to act . . . ever since I can remember.'

'You mean for real . . . professionally?'

'Yeah . . . it's tough to get started but I'm going to give it a try.'

'I think you're going to make it.'

'I hope you're right . . . where's my buddy?'

'Over there . . . talking to Erica . . .'

'Hey . . .' Artie called, motioning for Michael and Erica to join us. This time Michael didn't reach for my hand.

I watched and waited all night for some secret look to pass between Elizabeth and Michael but as far as I could tell nothing happened and when we finally got around to talking she was just plain friendly and even said that she remembered me from New Year's Eve, which only made me feel worse.

The party was still going strong when Michael said, 'Let's get out of here.'

'Why . . . aren't you having a good time?' I asked.

'Not especially . . . are you?'

I didn't answer. I went upstairs to get my coat and sulked all the way home. Michael didn't say a word. He didn't even look my way.

When we got to my house I unlocked the front door. 'Are you coming in?' I asked him.

'Do you want me to?'

'If you want,' I said, like it really didn't matter.

'It's up to you,' he answered.

'Don't do me any favours.' As if I hadn't been waiting all night to be alone with him, I stepped into the foyer.

Michael followed me. We took off our coats. 'Did I do something . . . is that it?' he finally asked.

'No.'

'Then what?'

'Oh, I don't know . . . just everything . . . thinking about you and Elizabeth . . .'

'You're jealous?' he asked

'Maybe that's it . . . I'm not sure.'

'That's why you've been such a bitch all night?'

'I guess.'

He started to laugh. 'I didn't know you were the jealous type.'

'I'm not!' But as soon as I said it I realized how dumb it sounded and I laughed too.

'Hey . . . I dreamed about you last night,' Michael said.

'What was I like?'

'Very sexy . . .'

I took his hand and we went into the den. 'I'm sorry I was such an ass tonight.'

'Forget it,' he said. 'It's nice to know you care. Just promise me one thing . . .'

'What?'

'From now on we're honest with each other. If something's bothering you, say it, and I'll do the same . . . agreed?'

'Agreed.'

'Good.'

We lay down on our rug and after a while, when Michael reached under my skirt I didn't stop him, not then and not when his hand was inside my underpants.

'I want you so much,' he said.

'I want you too,' I told him, 'but I can't . . . I'm not ready, Michael . . .'

'Yes, you are . . . you are . . . I can feel how ready you are.'

'No . . .' I pushed his hand away and sat up. 'I'm talking about mentally ready.'

'Mentally ready,' Michael repeated.

'Yes.'

'How does a person get mentally ready?' he asked.

'A person has to think . . . a person has to be sure . . .'

'But your body says you want to . . .'

'I have to control my body with my mind.'

'Oh, shit . . .' Michael said.

'It's not easy for me either.'

'I know . . . I know . . .' He put his arm around me. 'Look . . . we can satisfy each other without the whole thing . . .'

'We will . . . soon . . .'

'If I didn't know better I'd think you were a tease.'

'I'd never tease you.'

'Yeah . . . I know that too.'

'You want me to be honest, right?'

'Uh huh.'

'Well . . . the thing is . . . I don't know exactly how to do it . . . satisfy you, I mean.'

'It's the easiest thing in the world,' Michael said, loosening his belt.

Not now . . .' I told him.

'When?'

'Soon, but not tonight.'

'Promises . . . promises . . .'

After Michael went home and I was in bed, trying to fall asleep, I thought about making love with him – the whole thing, like he said. Would I make noises like my mother? I can always tell when my parents are making love because they shut their bedroom door after they think Jamie and I are asleep. It's hard not to listen. My room is right next to theirs. Sometimes I'll hear them laughing softly and other times my mother will let out these little moans or call *Roger . . . Roger . . .* Even though I know it's natural and I'm glad my parents love each other I can't help feeling embarrassed. What would it be like to be in bed with Michael? Sometimes I want to so much – but other times I'm afraid.

*

After dinner we sat around the fire and talked for a while, then Michael got up and went to the window. 'The stars are out,' he said. 'You want to take a walk?' My insides still turn over when he looks at me that certain way.

I got my boots and jacket.

'Don't get frostbitten,' Sharon called after us.

As soon as we were outside and away from the house we kissed. 'I had to get out of there,' Michael told me. 'All I could think about was being alone with you.'

'I know,' I said, '. . . same here.'

We held hands as we walked. 'I've never seen so many stars,' I said.

'That's because it's so dark and clear . . . no city lights, no traffic, no pollution . . .'

'I love to look at stars.'

'I love to look at you.'

'Oh, Michael . . . come on . . .' I gave him a friendly punch.

When we got back to the house Sharon and Ike were stretched out in front of the fire smoking grass. 'Hi,' Sharon said. 'Did you freeze your tails off?'

'Almost,' I told her. I was really surprised to see Sharon smoking. I thought she was so straight, especially after that business about Michael being vulnerable and getting hurt.

'Your cheeks are bright red,' Ike told me.

'They always get that way.'

'I like them,' Michael said, putting his hand against my face.

Ike held the joint to his lips and took a long drag. Then he offered it to Michael.

'You want to?' Michael asked me.

'I don't think so,' I said.

'We'll skip it,' Michael told Ike, taking my hand. 'Katherine's very tired.'

'Goodnight,' I said, as Michael and I headed upstairs.

'Get a good night's sleep,' Sharon called.

'We will.'

Michael lay down on the bed in my room.

'I thought you don't smoke,' I said.

'I don't, anymore . . . except with them, sometimes . . .'

'Oh.' I walked over to the window and opened it a little. I like plenty of fresh air in my bedroom. 'I've only tried once . . . and nothing good happened . . . I felt sick to my stomach.'

'It can be like that the first time.'

'Besides,' I said, going to the dresser and picking up my hairbrush, 'I don't like to lose control of myself.' I was thinking about later, wondering if he would get into bed with me again. Last night was so nice.

'I know it,' Michael said.

'Would I . . . if I smoked again?'

'I don't know . . . probably not.'

I started brushing my hair. Michael was watching me. I wanted to ask him *what next?* Did he have plans? Did he already know? I wished I had a script to follow so I wouldn't make any mistakes. *Don't forget about my period, Michael*, I felt like saying. 'There are kids at school who are high all the time.'

'That's different,' he said.

'I suppose . . .' I put my brush down. 'I'm surprised that Sharon and Ike smoke at all . . . I mean, Ike being a doctor and all.' I opened the dresser drawer and pulled out my nightgown. I should wear it, shouldn't I? Yes, but leave it unbuttoned this time.

'They're not exactly addicts,' Michael said.

'I know that . . . should I use the bathroom first?'

'Sure.'

I put on my nightgown and bikini underpants and after I'd washed and brushed my teeth I said, 'You can use the bathroom now.'

I got into bed and waited. In a few minutes Michael opened my door. He was wearing his same blue pajamas. He kind of waved at me and said, 'Hi.'

'Hi,' I answered.

He put his glasses on the night table, turned out the light and climbed into bed beside me. After we'd kissed for awhile he took off his pajama top, then said, 'Let's take yours off too . . . it's in the way.'

I slipped my nightgown over my head and dropped it to the floor. Then there were just my bikini pants and Michael's pajama bottoms between us. We kissed again. Feeling him against me that way made me so excited I couldn't lie still. He rolled over on top of me and we moved together again and again and it felt so good I didn't ever want to stop – until I came.

After a minute I reached for Michael's hand. 'Show me what to do,' I said.

'Do whatever you want.'

'Help me, Michael . . . I feel so stupid.'

'Don't,' he said, wiggling out of his pajama bottoms. He led my hand to his penis. 'Katherine . . . I'd like you to meet Ralph . . . Ralph, this is Katherine. She's a very good friend of mine.'

'Does every penis have a name?'

'I can only speak for my own.'

In books penises are always described as hot and throbbing but Ralph felt like ordinary skin. Just his shape was different – that and the fact that he wasn't smooth, exactly – as if there was a lot going on under the skin. I don't know why I'd been so nervous about touching Michael. Once I got over being scared I let my hands go everywhere. I wanted to feel every part of him.

While I was experimenting, I asked, 'Is this right?'

And Michael whispered, 'Everything's right.'

When I kissed his face it was all sweaty and his eyes were half-closed. He took my hand and led it back to Ralph, showing me how to hold him, moving my hand up and down according to his rhythm. Soon Michael moaned and I felt him come – a pulsating feeling, a throbbing, like the books said – then wetness. Some of it got on my hand but I didn't let go of Ralph.

We were both quiet for a while, then Michael reached for the tissue box by the side of the bed. He passed it to me. 'Here . . . I didn't mean to get you.'

'That's all right . . . I don't mind . . .' I pulled out some tissues.

He took the box back. 'I'm glad,' he said, wiping up his stomach.

I kissed the mole on the side of his face. 'Did I do okay . . . considering my lack of experience?'

He laughed, then put his arms around me. 'You did just fine . . . Ralph liked it a lot.'

I settled next to Michael with my head on his chest.

'Kath . . .'

'Hmmmm?'

'Remember last night when I said I loved you?'

'Yes.'

'Well . . . I really meant it . . . it's not just the sex thing . . . that's part of it . . . but it's more than that . . . you know?'

'I know . . . because I love you too,' I whispered into his chest.

Saying it the first time was the hardest. There's something so final about it. The second time I sat up and said it right to him. 'I love you, Michael Wagner.'

'Forever?' he asked.

'Forever,' I said.

*

Sharon and Ike live in a garden apartment in Springfield. All the outside doors are painted green. 'I hope nobody thinks we're trying to break in,' I said, as Michael put the key in the lock, 'because there's an old lady watching us.' I pointed to a window.

'Don't worry about her.' Michael pushed the door open. 'That's Mrs Cornick . . . she lives downstairs . . . she's always in the window.' He waved at her and she dropped her shade. 'Come on . . . their place is upstairs.'

The stairs led into the living room. 'It's nice,' I said, looking around. There wasn't much furniture but they had a fantastic Persian rug and three posters of chimpanzees riding bicycles. I walked over to a plant and held up a leaf. 'Too much water . . . that's why all the edges are turning brown.'

'I'll tell Sharon you said so.'

'No, don't . . . then she'll know I've been here.'

'So?'

'So, I just don't want her to know . . . okay?'

'I don't see why . . . but okay. You want something to eat?'

'Maybe . . .' We went to the kitchen which was small and narrow with no outside window.

Michael opened the refrigerator. 'How about an apple . . . or a grapefruit? That's about all I see.'

'I'll have an apple.'

He polished it off on his shirt, then tossed it to me. 'I'll show you around the place,' he said.

Since I'd already seen the living room and the kitchen we started with the bathroom. 'Notice the indoor plumbing.' Michael demonstrated how to flush the toilet.

'Very interesting,' I told him.

'And hot and cold running water.' He turned on both taps.

'Luxurious.'

'Also, a genuine bathtub.' He stepped into it and I pulled the curtain around him. While he was in there I wrapped the apple core in some toilet paper and hid it in my handbag. Michael jumped out of the tub, grabbed my hand and said, 'Onward . . .'

We both knew there was just one room left to see. 'Presenting . . .' Michael said, and he bowed, 'the bedroom.'

There was a brass bed, covered with a patchwork quilt and a LOVE poster hanging on the wall, above it. There were also two small chests, piled high with books.

Michael jumped up and down on the bed while I watched from the doorway. 'Good mattress . . .' he said, 'nice and firm . . . in case you're interested.'

'For jumping, you mean?'

'For whatever . . .' He lay down and looked at the ceiling. 'Kath . . .'

'Hmmmm . . .'

'Come here . . .'

'I thought we were just going to talk.'

'We are . . . but you're so far away . . . I don't want to shout.'

'I can hear you fine.'

'Cut it out . . . will you?'

I went to the bed and sat on the edge. 'There's one thing I'd really like to know . . .'

'What's that?'

'Have you brought any other girls up here?'

'Your jealous streak is showing.'

'I admit it . . . but I still want to know.'

'Never,' he said. 'I've never brought a girl up here.

'Good.'

'Because I just got my own key.'

'You rat!' I yelled, grabbing a pillow and swatting him with it.

'Hey . . .' He knocked the pillow out of my hands and pinned me down on the bed. Then he kissed me.

'Let me go, Michael . . . please.'

'I can't . . . you're too dangerous.'

'I'll be good . . . I promise.'

He let go of my arms and I wrapped them around him and we kissed again.

'You're beautiful,' he said, looking down at me.

'Don't say things like that . . .'

'Why, do they embarrass you?'

'Yes.'

'Okay . . . you're ugly! You're so ugly you make me want to puke.' He turned away and leaned over the side of the bed making this terrible retching noise.

'Michael . . . you're crazy . . . stop it . . . I can't stand that!

'Okay.'

We lay next to each other kissing, and soon Michael unbuttoned my sweater and I sat up and unhooked my bra for him. While I slipped out of both, Michael pulled his sweater over his head. Then he held me. 'You feel so good,' he said, kissing me everywhere. 'I love to feel you next to me. You're as soft as Tasha.'

I started to laugh.

'What?' Michael asked.

'Nothing . . .'

'I love you, Kath.'

'And I love you,' I said, 'even though you're an *outsy*.'

'What's an *outsy*?'

'Your belly button sticks out,' I said, tracing it with my fingers.

'That's not the only thing that sticks out.'

'Michael . . . we're talking about belly buttons.'

'You are . . .'

'I was explaining that you're an *outsy* and I'm an *insy* . . . you see how mine goes in?'

'Umm . . . he said, kissing it.

'Do belly buttons have a taste?' I asked.

'Yours does . . . it's delicious . . . like the rest of you.' He unbuckled my jeans, then his own.

'Michael . . . I'm not sure . . . please . . .'

'Shush . . . don't say anything.'

'But Michael . . .'

'Like always, Kath . . . that's all . . .'

We both left on our underpants but after a minute Michael was easing mine down and then his fingers began exploring me. I let my hands wander across his stomach and down his legs and finally I began to stroke Ralph.

'Oh, yes . . . yes . . .' I said, as Michael made me come. And he came too.

We covered up with the patchwork quilt and rested. Michael fell asleep for a while and I watched him, thinking the better you know a person the more you can love him. Do two people ever reach the point where they know absolutely everything there is to know about each other? I leaned over and touched his hair. He didn't move.

The next night Michael picked me up at 7:30 and we headed straight for the apartment. I knew we would. Neither one of us could wait to be alone together. And when we were naked, in each other's arms, I wanted to do everything – I wanted to feel him inside me. I don't know if he sensed that or not but when he whispered, 'Please, Kath . . . please let's keep going . . .' I told him, 'Yes, Michael . . . yes . . . but not here . . . not on the bed.'

'Yes . . . here . . .' he said, moving over me.

'No, we can't . . . I might bleed.'

He rolled away from me. 'You're right . . . I forgot about that . . . I'll get something.'

He came back with a beach towel. 'Down here,' I called, because he couldn't find me in the dark.

'On the floor?' he asked.

'Yes.'

'The floor's too hard.'

'I don't mind . . . and we won't have to worry about stains.'

'This is crazy.'

'Please, Michael . . . just give me the towel . . . I hope it's not a good one.'

He lay down next to me. 'It's freezing down here,' he said.

'I know . . .'

He jumped up and grabbed the quilt off the bed. We snuggled under it. 'That's better.' He put his arms around me.

'Look,' I said, 'you might as well know . . . I'm scared out of my mind.

'Me too.'

'But you've at least had some experience.'

'Not with anyone I love.'

'Thank you,' I said, kissing the side of his face.

He ran his hands up and down my body but nothing happened. I guess I was too nervous. 'Michael . . . do you have something?' I asked.

'What for?' he said, nibbling my neck.

'You know . . .'

'Didn't you just finish your period?'

'Last week . . . but I'm not taking any chances.'

'If you're thinking about VD I promise I'm fine.'

'I'm thinking about getting pregnant. Every woman has a different cycle.'

'Okay . . . okay . . .' He stood up. 'I've got a sheath in my wallet . . . if I can just find it.' He looked around for his pants, found them on the floor next to the bed, then he had to put on the light to find the sheath. When he did he held it up. 'Satisfied?' he asked, turning the light off again.

'I will be when you put it on.'

He kneeled beside me and rolled it on. 'Anything else?'

'Don't be funny now . . . please . . .'

'I won't . . . I won't . . .' he said and we kissed.

Then he was on top of me and I felt Ralph hard, against my thigh. Just when I thought, Oh God . . . we're really and truly going to do it, Michael groaned and said, 'Oh no . . . no . . . I'm sorry . . . I'm so sorry . . .'

'What's wrong?'

'I came . . . I don't know what to say. I came before I even got it in. I ruined it . . . I ruined everything.'

'It's all right,' I told him. 'It's okay . . . really.'

'No, it's not.'

'It doesn't matter.'

'Maybe not to you . . .'

'It could have been all that talking. We shouldn't have talked so much.'

'Next time it'll be better,' Michael said. 'I promise . . . Ralph won't fail me twice.'

'Okay.' I took his hand and kissed it.

'Let's just sleep for a while, then we can try again.'

'I'm not tired,' I said, 'but I'm very hungry.'

'There's nothing to eat here.'

'We could go out.'

'Get dressed and go out?'

'Why not?'

'Yeah . . . I suppose we could,' he said.

We went to Stanley's for hamburgers and on the way back to the apartment we stopped at a drugstore so Michael could buy some more sheaths. I stayed in the car.

'Let's try the living room,' Michael said when we got back.

'I couldn't . . . not on that beautiful rug.'

'Oh hell . . . it's got so many colours nothing would show on it anyway . . . and it's softer than the wood floor.'

'I don't know . . .' I said, looking at the rug.

'I'll double up the towel.' He spread it out. 'There . . . that should take care of it.'

This time I tried to relax and think of nothing – nothing but how my body felt – and then Ralph was pushing against me and I whispered, 'Are you in . . . are we doing it?'

'Not yet,' Michael said, pushing harder. 'I don't want to hurt you.'

'Don't worry . . . just do it!'

'I'm trying, Kath . . . but it's very tight in there.'

'What should I do?'

'Can you spread your legs some more . . . and maybe raise them a little?'

'Like this?'

'That's better . . . much better.'

I could feel him halfway inside me and then Michael whispered, 'Kath . . .'

'What?'

'I think I'm going to come again.'

I felt a big thrust, followed by a quick sharp pain that made me suck in my breath. 'Oh . . . oh,' Michael cried, but I didn't come. I wasn't even close. 'I'm sorry,' he said, 'I couldn't hold off.' He stopped moving. 'It wasn't any good for you, was it?'

'Everybody says the first time is no good for a virgin. I'm not disappointed.' But I was. I'd wanted it to be perfect.

'Maybe it was the sheath,' Michael said. 'I should have bought the more expensive kind.' He kissed my cheek and took my hand. 'I love you, Kath. I wanted it to be good for you too.'

'I know.'

'Next time it'll be better . . . we've got to work on it. Did you bleed?'

'I don't feel anything.' I wrapped the beach towel around my middle and went to the bathroom. When I wiped myself with tissues I saw a few spots of blood, but nothing like what I'd expected.

On the way home I thought, I am no longer a virgin. I'll never have to go through the first-time business again and I'm glad – I'm so glad it's over! Still, I can't help feeling let down. Everybody makes such a big thing out of actually doing it. But Michael is probably right – this takes practice. I can't imagine what the first time would be like with someone you didn't love.

––––––––––

From *Forever* by Judy Blume, 1975

Biographical Notes

Lisa Alther (1944—) was born in Tennessee. She worked for Atheneum Publishers in New York before moving to Vermont where she raised her daughter. Lisa Alther's first novel, *Kinflicks* (1976), is the story of a young woman's sexual, emotional and political coming of age during the turbulent 1950s, '60s, and early '70s. Alther went on to write four other novels, *Original Sins* (1981), *Other Women* (1984), *Bedrock* (1990) and *Five Minutes in Heaven* (1995). Both *Kinflicks* and *Original Sins* are published by Virago.

Judy Blume (1938—) grew up in Elizabeth, New Jersey, and has written many popular novels for children and young adults. She has tackled issues such as teenage sexuality, menstruation and divorce in books including *Are You There, God? It's Me, Margaret*; *Superfudge*; *Blubber*; *Just As Long As We're Together*; and *Forever*. Her allegedly ambiguous treatment of moral issues made her at one time a regular target of school library censors and the religious right and she is recognised as one of the most banned children's authors in the United States. She moved into adult fiction with *Wifey*, *Smart Women*, and her latest, *Summer Sisters*. Judy lives on islands up and down the East Coast with her husband George Cooper.

Geoffrey Chaucer (*c.*1340–1400) was born in London to vintner John Chaucer sometime between 1340 and 1344. Chaucer held a variety of posts at King Edward's court, culminating in his appointment as clerk of the king's works (1389–91). Around 1387 Chaucer began his master work, *The Canterbury Tales*. He died on 25 October 1400, and was buried at Westminster Abbey.

John Cleland (1709–1789) was an English novelist, most famous and infamous as the author of *Fanny Hill: or, Memoirs of a Woman of Pleasure*. The novel's notoriety led to a number of official efforts to ban it.

Jilly Cooper (1937—) was born in Hornchurch, Essex, and started her career as a journalist. She wrote her first book *How To Stay Married* in 1969 and since then has written or helped to compile thirty-nine other books. Her most popular titles include *Riders* (1985), *Rivals* (1988), *Polo* (1991), all of which were No. 1. bestsellers. She lives in the Cotswolds.

Rosalind Erskine is a pseudonym of Roger Longrigg (1929–2000). Roger Longrigg was born in Edinburgh, Scotland, and wrote under a total of eight pseudonyms, including 'Laura Black', 'Ivor Drummond', 'Frank Parrish', and 'Domini Taylor'. Longrigg was eventually exposed as the author of *The Passion-Flower Hotel* (1962) by the gossip columnist Richard Berens in the *Daily Express*.

Georgette Heyer (1902–1974) was born in Wimbledon, London. Her first published work, *The Black Moth*, was inspired by Baroness Orczy and written when Heyer was just seventeen. In all, she published fifty-six works, the most popular of which were set during the English Regency. The last, *My Lord John*, was published posthumously. As well as her Regency romances, Heyer also wrote several detective novels, four contemporary novels and a number of short stories.

Erica Jong (1942—) is the author of eight novels including *Fear of Flying; Fanny, Being the True History of the Adventures of Fanny Hackabout-Jones; Shylock's Daughter; Inventing Memory*; and *Sappho's Leap*. She has also written several works of non-fiction and six volumes of poetry. In 1998, Erica Jong was honoured with the United Nations Award for Excellence in Literature. She lives in New York City and Weston, Connecticut.

James Joyce (1882–1941) was born in Dublin and entered the Royal University (now University College, Dublin) in 1898. During his time living in Trieste with his wife, Joyce wrote the poems that became *Chamber Music* (1907), *Dubliners* (1914), and *A Portrait of the Artist as a Young*

Man (1916). By the time he and his family moved to Zurich in July 1915, Joyce had also begun *Ulysses*, which was eventually published in 1922. His next project occupied him for sixteen years and was published in 1939 as *Finnegans Wake*. When Germany invaded France the Joyces left Paris, first for Vichy then on to Zurich, where Joyce died on 13 January 1941.

John Keats (1795–1821) was one of the principal poets of the English Romantic movement. During his short life, his work was the subject of constant critical attacks, and it was not until much later that the significance of the cultural change which his work both presaged and helped to form was fully appreciated. Keats produced his most original and most memorable poems towards the end of his life.

Judith Krantz (1928—) is an American novelist, who writes in the romance genre. She graduated from Wellesley College in 1948. Her works include *Princess Daisy* (1980) and *Till We Meet Again* (1986).

D.H. Lawrence (1885–1930) was born into a miner's family in Nottinghamshire. His first novel, *The White Peacock*, was published in 1911 and *Sons and Lovers* was published in 1913. However *The Rainbow*, completed in 1915, was suppressed, and for three years he could not find a publisher for *Women in Love*, completed in 1917. His last novel, *Lady Chatterley's Lover*, was published in 1928, but was banned in England and America. In 1930 he died in Vence, in the south of France, at the age of forty-four.

Colleen McCullough (1937—) was born in Australia. A neurophysiologist, she established the department of neurophysiology at the Royal North Shore Hospital in Sydney, then worked as a researcher and teacher at Yale Medical School for ten years. Her writing career began with *Tim* (1974), followed by *The Thorn Birds* (1977), which became an international bestseller. The author of nine other novels, McCullough has also written lyrics for musical theatre. She lives on Norfolk Island in the South Pacific with her husband, Ric Robinson.

Grace Metalious (1924–1964) was born in a French-Canadian ghetto in New Hampshire. She married in 1942 and had three children. Her other novels include *Return to Peyton Place* (1959), *The Tight White Collar* (1960), and *No Adam in Eden* (1963). She died of cirrhosis of the liver at age thirty-nine.

Anaïs Nin (1903–1977) was a writer and diarist. Born in Paris to a Catalan father and a Danish mother, she spent many of her early years with Cuban relatives. Later a naturalised American citizen, she lived and worked in Paris, New York and Los Angeles. Author of avant-garde novels in the French surrealist style, she is best known for her life and times in *The Diaries of Anaïs Nin, Vols. I–VII* and *The Early Diaries of Anaïs Nin, Vols. I–IV*.

Pauline Réage was a pseudonym of Anne Desclos (1907–1998). Anne Desclos was born in France and studied at the Sorbonne. Her lover and employer at Gallimard Publishers, Jean Paulhan, remarked to her that no female was capable of writing an erotic novel, and to prove him wrong she wrote a graphic sadomasochistic novel that was published under the pseudonym 'Pauline Réage' in 1954. Titled *Histoire d'O* (*Story of O*), it was an enormous, though controversial, commercial success. Finally, forty years after the book was published, in an interview with *The New Yorker* magazine, Anne Desclos finally admitted for the first time publicly that she was the author of *Story of O*. She died in Corbeil-Essonnes, Île-de-France.

William Shakespeare (1564–1616) was born in April 1564 in Stratford-upon-Avon, Warwickshire. The legendary poet and playwright published his first poem, 'Venus and Adonis', in 1593 and went on to write 154 poems and 37 plays.

Jacqueline Susann (1918–1974) was born in 1918, the daughter of a portrait painter. An indifferent student, she was nevertheless praised for her writing at school. She left her hometown of Philadelphia in her teens and moved to New York, where she acted extensively and won the Best Dressed Woman in Television award no fewer than four times. She wrote three blockbuster novels – *Valley of the Dolls*, *The Love Machine* and *Once Is Not Enough* – and was the only writer ever to have three novels in a row hit no. 1 on the *New York Times* bestseller list. Jacqueline Susann was married to producer Irving Mansfield, had one son, and died in 1974.

John Updike (1932—). John Updike's first novel, *The Poorhouse Fair*, was published in 1959 and was followed by *Rabbit, Run* (1960), the first volume of what have become known as the Rabbit books. *Rabbit is Rich* (1981) and *Rabbit at Rest* (1990) were awarded the Pulitzer Prize for Fiction. Other novels by John Updike include *Marry Me*, *The Witches of Eastwick*, *Memories of the Ford Administration*, *Brazil*, *The Beauties of the Lilies*, *Toward the End of Time* and *Gertrude and Claudius*. He has written several volumes of short stories as well as poetry, criticism and essays.

'Walter' No one knows the true identity of 'Walter', but there has been some speculation that it could be the pen name of Henry Spencer Ashbee.

Kathleen Winsor (1919–2003) became fascinated with Charles II and his court while her first husband was writing his college thesis on the same subject. Six years and much research later *Forever Amber* (1944), her most famous novel – though she went on to have a long and successful writing career – was published.

Acknowledgements

We are grateful for permission to use the following copyright material in this book:

Lisa Alther: from *Kinflicks* (Chatto & Windus, 1976), copyright © Lisa Alther 1976, reprinted by permission of the author.

Judy Blume: from *Forever* (Penguin Books, 1997), copyright © Judy Blume 1975, reprinted by permission of the publishers, Penguin Books Ltd and Atheneum Books for Young Readers, an imprint of Simon & Schuster Children's Publishing Division.

Geoffrey Chaucer: from 'The Wife of Bath's Prologue' in *The Canterbury Tales* translated into modern English by Nevill Coghill (Penguin Classics, 1951, 4th revised edition 1977), copyright © Nevill Coghill 1951, copyright © the Estate of Nevill Coghill 1958, 1960, 1975, 1977, reprinted by permission of Penguin Books Ltd; from 'The Wife of Bath's Prologue' in *The Wife of Bath's Prologue and Tale* from *The Canterbury Tales* edited by James Winny (revised edition Cambridge University Press, 1994), copyright © Cambridge University Press 1965, reprinted by permission of the Estate of James Winny and of Cambridge University Press.

Jilly Cooper: from *Octavia* (Corgi, 1978), copyright © Jilly Cooper 1977, reprinted by permission of Curtis Brown Group Ltd, London, on behalf of the author.

Rosalind Erskine (Roger Erskine Longrigg): from *The Passion-Flower Hotel* (Jonathan Cape, 1962), copyright © Rosalind Erskine 1962, reprinted by permission of Curtis Brown Group Ltd, London, on behalf of the Estate of the author.

Georgette Heyer: from *Regency Buck* (published in the UK by Arrow Books), copyright © Georgette Heyer 1935, reprinted by permission of The Ampersand Agency acting on behalf of the Heyer Estate.

Erica Jong: from *Fear of Flying* (Vintage, 2004), copyright © Erica Jong 1973, reprinted by permission of The Random House Group Ltd, and of the author c/o Rogers, Coleridge & White Ltd, 20 Powis Mews, London W11 1JN.

James Joyce: from *Ulysses* (Oxford World Classics, 1998), copyright © James Joyce, reprinted by permission of the Estate of James Joyce.

Judith Krantz: from *Scruples* (Futura, 1978), copyright © 1977 Steve Krantz Productions, reprinted by permission of the publishers, Time Warner Paperbacks, a division of Little, Brown Book Group, and Crown Publishers, a division of Random House, Inc.

D.H. Lawrence: from *Lady Chatterley's Lover* (Penguin, 2000), copyright © The Estate of Frieda Lawrence Ravagli 1969, 1970, reprinted by permission of Pollinger Ltd and the proprietor.

Colleen McCullough: from *The Thorn Birds* (Time Warner, 1977), copyright © Colleen McCullough 1977, reprinted by permission of the publishers, Time Warner Paperbacks, a division of Little, Brown Book Group, and HarperCollins Publishers, Inc.

Grace Metalious: from *Peyton Place* (Virago, 2002), copyright © Grace Metalious 1956, reprinted by permission of the publishers, Virago, a division of Little, Brown Book Group, and the University Press of New England.

Anaïs Nin: from 'Artist and Model' in *Delta of Venus* translated by Sabine D'Estrée (Penguin Books, 1990), copyright © Anaïs Nin 1969, copyright

legs, and I felt quite modest and accommodating in a button-up shirt and baggy jeans.

When we arrived, I found that the place was more bar than restaurant, and that I was the only female present. Even the waiters were all men. But these details didn't seem important. After all, I had dressed conservatively, and decided to take the precaution—again, recommended by my guidebook—of avoiding direct eye contact with men. What could possibly go wrong?

Since I spoke neither French nor Arabic—and was assiduously avoiding eye contact—it was quite impossible for me to converse with anyone but Alan, who was busy putting his first-year college language skills to dubious use. I was bored. This was a plain-as-bread sort of establishment; there was no big screen TV soccer game, no video arcade, not even a friendly game of cards or a lively bar fight for me to watch. Just a lot of dark men in white robes, sitting in mismatched wooden chairs, speaking softly in a language I could not understand and drinking tiny cups of strong coffee. The bitter, familiar aroma was a meager comfort.

Then the music began; it sounded off-key and was startlingly loud and foreign—a little frightening, even. Next the belly dancers appeared: twelve gorgeous

women, one after another, with long, dark hair, burnished skin, flowing diaphanous skirts in brilliant vermilion and aqua and emerald, gold necklaces, belts, bracelets, anklets. Gold everywhere: tangled cords jangling against long brown necks; fine, weightless strands decorating the swirling fabrics; heavy gold chains slapping in a satisfying way against ample abdominal flesh. They were a remarkable contrast to the stark room and simple furnishings, and I began to realize that things in Tunisia were not entirely as they first appeared.

The music quickened, and the dancers floated across the bar—which had somehow been converted into a stage—and around the room, weaving in and out among tables, lingering occasionally for a long glance at a pleased patron. Soon they were at our table, looking not at Alan but at me, urging me, with their universal body language, to join them.

Did I dare? My stomach clenched momentarily. I knew my dancing would be clumsy and ugly next to theirs, my short-cropped hair and lack of makeup un-attractively boyish, my clothing shapeless and without style or significant color. I wore no jewelry—as the guidebook suggested—just my glasses, which were not particularly flattering.

Of course I am relatively unattractive and clumsy

in this foreign environment, I thought, *but there is no need to be priggish as well.* And the women were by now insistent, actually taking me by both hands and pulling me up to dance with them. Flushed with embarrassment, I did my best to follow their swaying hips and graceful arm movements as we made our way around the room once again. Even with the aid of the two beers, I was not foolish enough to attempt to duplicate their astonishing abdominal undulations.

As soon as I thought these exotic, insistent beauties would allow it, I broke the line and resumed my place—plain, awkward, very white, and completely out of my element—next to Alan. Thereafter, it was excruciatingly embarrassing for me to watch the dancers, and Alan agreed to accompany me back to the hotel. He, too, had had enough excitement for the evening and was ready to retire, so he asked the bartender to call us a cab. A fellow bar patron overheard the conversation and was kind enough to offer us a lift. The man wore Western-style clothing, understood Alan's French, and seemed safe enough; we felt fortunate to have arranged the ride in spite of our limited linguistic abilities and the fact that the night was still young.

But that's when the evening turned ugly. Two well-dressed, middle-aged men left the bar immediately

after we did. We saw them get into a black Mercedes, and we watched in the rear-view mirror as they trailed us, just our car and theirs, bumping along a sandy road in the empty desert. There were no buildings, streetlights or pedestrians, and we saw no other vehicles.

I looked out the window, enjoying the vast, black night sky and trying to ignore my growing sense of anxiety. When we came to an unmarked Y inter-section, our driver, in a bizarrely ineffective attempt at deception, headed steadily towards the road on the right, then veered off at the last second to take the road on the left. Neither Alan nor I could remember which direction we'd come from hours earlier, when it was still light out and we were not under the spell of Tunisian music and belly dancers and beer. The strange feigning and last-second careening alarmed us both.

And it got worse. Immediately after the incident at the intersection, the men in the car behind us revved the engine, chased us down and ran us off the road and into a ditch. They stood in the road, shouting and gesticulating wildly outside our car. My hands went icy in the warm night air. Despite—or perhaps because of—an imposing language barrier, we had the impression that the men who ran our car off the road were attempting to rescue us.

But what, exactly, were they rescuing us from? Was our driver a sociopathic kidnapper bent on selling us into slavery? A rapist? A murderer? And why were our "rescuers," so insistent? Was it out of the goodness of their hearts, or did they, too, have some sinister motive? We had to make a choice. One car would probably take us safely to our hotel; the other might lead to a terrifying fate. But we had no idea which was which.

In this moment of crisis, we clenched hands and Alan looked at me—somewhat desperately, I thought—for a decision. I tried to assess his strength, and wondered whether he was a good fighter. (Probably not—he was a Yale man.) My stomach churned, but I forced myself to concentrate. We had only two options: We could remain in the long black limo, hope it could be extricated from the ditch, and hope our volunteer driver really was the kind and innocuous man he had appeared to be.

Or we could bolt from the car, scramble out of the ditch, and as quickly as possible, put our rescuers and their car between ourselves and the man who had so generously offered us a ride. The two men were still shouting, and began to pound and slap the driver's window. Even so, Alan leaned towards staying. After all, he reasoned, it was only one man, and there were

two of us. Surely we could overpower him and escape if it proved necessary.

I wanted to bolt. Even though there were two men in the "rescue" car, as opposed to only one in our vehicle, I had become certain, in some wholly subjective way, that our man was crazy, and I'd heard that crazy people can be quite strong. Plus, our apparent rescuers, the men who had just run us off the road, warned Alan that we were with *"un homme méchant! mauvais!"*—a wicked man. But the deciding factor was that these two men had actually gone to the trouble of following us out of the bar, chasing us down, running our car off the road and into a dusty ditch, and were now expending a great deal of energy trying to convince us of something.

Surely that constellation of actions bespoke a serious purpose, such as rescuing two foolish young travelers from a lifetime of misery in the North African desert. The two men must be the rescuers; kidnappers were not likely to go to so much trouble, or to risk scratching or even denting their shiny black late-model Mercedes in the process.

Alan was no help; I had to make a decision myself, and quickly. But what about the downside? In the middle of all the commotion—and with Alan sitting next to me looking more than a little uncertain—I realized that we had not yet fully considered the

A Sneak Peek

potential negative consequences of an incorrect choice. If we chose to stay, and it was the wrong choice, the man would undoubtedly drive us to some sort of central kidnapping headquarters—probably an impenetrable, fortress-like stone building with dark, echoing corridors, or perhaps a sweltering, waterless hovel cleverly hidden in remote, sand-swept dunes. In that case, he would have a knife, or a gun, or evil partners—or perhaps all of the above—and the fact that the two of us probably could have overpowered him would be moot. We would be goners.

On the other hand, if we bolted, and that was the wrong choice, we would be double-goners because the two men could also turn out to be the kidnappers or murderers who could easily overpower us. Downsides being equally awful, we decided to go with our gut. Or guts. The problem was that Alan's gut said stay, and mine said bolt.....

I hope you've enjoyed the beginning of "At a Crossroads." To find out whether or not I made it out alive, you can read the entire story—plus twenty-two others—in *Lost, Kidnapped, Eaten Alive! True stories from a curious traveler*, available from your favorite bookseller.

Publication Notes

Many of these essays, or similar versions of them, have previously been published elsewhere:

A version of "At a Crossroads" was first published in *The Kindness of Strangers* (Lonely Planet, 2003), edited by Don George and with a preface by His Holiness the Dalai Lama.

"Cheater's High" was published in *Wandering in Cornwall: Mystery, Mirth and Transformation in the Land of the Ancient Celts* (Wanderland Writers, 2015).

"Chocotherapy" was published in *Wandering in Andalusia: The Soul of Southern Spain* (Wanderland Writers, 2016).

"Finding my Inner Gypsy" was published in *Wandering in Andalusia: The Soul of Southern Spain* (Wanderland Writers, 2016).

A version of "The Ghosts on Angel Island" was published in *Marin* magazine in September, 2016 with the title "Ellis Island of the West."

"Hooked on Hawk Hill" was published in *Marin* magazine in July, 2017.

A version of "Lucky Sama" was published on Medium.com in 2016. The story won the international Planet Earth Gold Award for 2017, for Best Travel Article or Essay for Planet Earth.

"The Mermaid, the Curmudgeon, the Magician, and the Churchyard" was published in *Wandering in Cornwall: Mystery, Mirth and Transformation in the Land of the Ancient Celts* (Wanderland Writers, 2015).

About the Cover Image:

Those of you who are clever about such things will have noticed that the reptile head on the cover is that of an alligator, not a crocodile. I needed a cover image, happened to have an alligator head around the house (it was a gift), and decided it would be an acceptable substitute for the crocodile head I did not have, given that this is not a scientific treatise. The alligator was not killed for this purpose, nor would I have harmed any vertebrate in the service of a cover shot.

About the Ouroboros Image:

In Ancient Greek, ouroboros means *tail-devouring*. I'm captivated by the image—a serpent swallowing its own tail, being created through its own destruction.

The symbol's meaning is nearly as varied as the many cultures that have embraced it over millennia, but there's a beautiful unity in what it represents: regeneration, reincarnation, immortality, the cycle of life and death, the harmony of opposites, the eternal unity of all things, perpetuity and infinity.

The image used here is after a woodcut in a 1760 book titled *Uraltes Chymisches Werck von Abraham Eleazar,* or the Age Old *Chemical Work of Abraham Eleazar.*

Resources

- The Angel Island Immigration Station, where I found out about "The Ghosts on Angel Island—https://www.aiisf.org/

- Din Tai Fung, where I learned the secrets of "The Dumpling Men of Taipei—http://dintaifungusa.com/

- The Fortress of the Bear where I met Chaik, Killisnoo, and the other characters in "Prayer Bear—
  http://www.fortressofthebear.org/

- Golden Gate Raptor Observatory (GGRO) where I learned to band hawks and got "Hooked on Hawk Hill"—
  http://www.parksconservancy.org/programs/ggro/

- The Kunstkamera (or Kunstkammer) where Peter the Great displayed items from "The Cabinet of Curiosities"—
  http://www.kunstkamera.ru/en/

- The Mutual UFO Network (MUFON) that organized the conference described in "They've Seen the Saucers"—
  http://www.mufon.com/

- Nature Seekers, who help educate the public and protect the leatherback turtles in "Leatherback Love"—
  http://www.natureseekers.org/

- Pinawalla Elephant Orphanage, where "Lucky Sama" lives—
  https://lanka.com/about/attractions/pinnawala-elephant-orphanage/

- SkyWalk, where you can test your own "Fear of Not Flying"—http://skywalk.co.nz/

- Sri Dalada Maligawa, where I visited "The Temple of the Tooth"—http://www.sridaladamaligawa.lk/

Acknowledgments

With deep appreciation for Joanna Biggar, who edited several of the stories in this collection, Linda Watanabe McFerrin, who edited almost all the rest, and the members of Linda's Advanced Writers Workshop, whose thoughtful and patient critiques—and inspiring craftmanship—motivated me to finish the book.

And with endless gratitude to Jim Shubin, The Book Alchemist, for editorial help, ongoing encouragement, and a cover I absolutely adore.

About the Author

Laurie McAndish King grew up in rural Iowa, studied philosophy and science at Cornell College, and has traveled to forty countries. She observes with an eye for natural science, and writes with a philosopher's heart and mind.

Laurie's award-winning travel essays and photography have appeared in many publications, including *Smithsonian* magazine, Travel Channel affiliate iExplore.com, Travelers' Tales' *The Best Women's Travel Writing*, and others. Her writing has won a Lowell Thomas gold award and her mobile app about the San Francisco Waterfront earned a 5-star rating on iTunes.

Laurie's first travel memoir, *Lost, Kidnapped, Eaten Alive! True stories from a curious traveler*, was published in 2014 and won four literary awards.

Laurie also wrote *An Erotic Alphabet* (for which she was dubbed "The Shel Silverstein of Erotica") and co-edited two volumes in the *Hot Flashes: Sexy little stories & poems* series. She is an avid photographer—one of her photos was displayed at the Smithsonian—and enjoys gardening, taxidermy, and, on occasion, chasing the cosmic serpent. Her website is www.LaurieMcAndishKing.com.

53448511R00165